ASCENSION

ASCENSION

NICHOLAS BINGE

RIVERHEAD BOOKS NEW YORK 2023

RIVERHEAD BOOKS

An imprint of Penguin Random House LLC
penguinrandomhouse.com

LIBRARY OF CONGRESS CATALOGING-IN-PUBLICATION DATA
Names: Binge, Nicholas, author.
Title: Ascension / Nick Binge.
Description: New York : Riverhead Books, 2023.
Identifiers: LCCN 2022033815 | ISBN 9780593539583 (hardcover) |
ISBN 9780593539606 (ebook)
Subjects: LCGFT: Thrillers (Fiction). | Science fiction. | Novels.
Classification: LCC PR6102.I53 A94 2023 |
DDC 823/.92—dc23/eng/20220812
LC record available at https://lccn.loc.gov/2022033815

Printed in the United States of America
1st Printing

Book design by Daniel Lagin

For Oskar, for teaching me to always keep climbing

I leave Sisyphus at the foot of the mountain! One always finds one's burden again. But Sisyphus teaches the higher fidelity that negates the gods and raises rocks. He too concludes that all is well. This universe henceforth without a master seems to him neither sterile nor futile. . . . The struggle itself toward the heights is enough to fill a man's heart. One must imagine Sisyphus happy.

—ALBERT CAMUS, *THE MYTH OF SISYPHUS*

FOREWORD

My brother disappeared twenty-nine years ago. It didn't happen on a specific day, or even during a specific month. The process was a slow drifting—a realization that grew in me like a poison, a splinter at the stem of my brain.

In 1990, he missed Christmas with the family, sending no message or explanation. He just didn't show up.

I wasn't exactly surprised at the time. He simply was who he was: Harold Tunmore, an esteemed scientist and Renaissance man. There was always some far-flung discovery, some hidden spool of thread he had to pull that would take precedence over other people. I never really understood his devotion to the unknown, but I learned to tolerate it over the years. You simply couldn't count on him. He lived way up in the clouds.

It must be said that he had got better over the previous five or six years, becoming more of an uncle to my daughter, Harriet, in that time. He'd actually show up for birthdays and holidays, bringing with him strange and exotic trinkets from his travels. He'd swing by unannounced, much to my wife's consternation, and take Harriet off on wild trips, exploring Scottish forests and camping by lakes. I'm not sure what had caused this change in him, but it was a welcome one. It was nice to see him more, after so many years of absences and excuses.

Perhaps I shouldn't have been shocked, then, when Harriet refused to come out of her room on Christmas Day until he appeared. She was only fourteen, still young enough to hope for the best in people. As for me, I'd been expecting it. It sounds horrible to say, but I'd been wondering how long it would be before he let us down.

I received his first letter in late February, followed by two more in the spring. They were addressed to Harriet, but after reading them, she passed them to me to take a look. At first, I thought they must have been a joke. The content of them was so bizarre, implausible to the point of absurdity. I see now that was wishful thinking.

They did not lead on chronologically, one letter to the next. There were similar threads in each, but they were dispersed in ways I could not make sense of. I later thought they might be in a code of some kind, a hidden meaning among the fantasy that we were meant to somehow decipher. What he expected Harriet to do with them, I had no idea. It doesn't shame me to say I lacked my brother's intellect. Everybody did. When we showed the letters to my sister, Poppy, she merely shrugged and said, "Leave it, Ben. That's a maze with only dead ends. I stopped trying to work him out years ago."

He never came back. He never contacted me, or anyone, again.

I waited, wishing fervently for some kind of sign, imagining that he was simply out in the world, digging up artifacts and making bold new discoveries. Over time, bit by bit, I found myself actively looking for him. First, I phoned old friends. Then I visited universities he had taught at. All the while the worry grew inside me, bubbling underneath the surface. I told myself that this was just Harold being Harold. This was just the sort of thing that he did.

After two years of searching, I had found nothing. It was an exercise in pure frustration. I spent weeks on the phone with police, with laboratories where he had done research. I spent weekends traveling to see old acquaintances and colleagues, leaning on connections at my legal practice to expedite matters. Urged on by Harriet, I did everything I could to follow the thread of where he might have gone.

But there was no thread.

No hints. Not a single scrap of information. It was as though, in the winter of 1990, he had simply vanished into thin air.

All I had left were those last three letters, now thoroughly dog-eared and coffee-stained. For weeks Harriet and I pored over them, sitting at the kitchen table late at night and right through to morning; they seemed to make less and less sense with each reading.

Years trickled by and my wife watched on as father and daughter lost hope. In the autumn of 1998, Poppy and I had him declared officially dead.

IT'S FUNNY WHICH MEMORIES STICK WITH YOU. EVEN NOW, I CAN STILL see myself sitting in the gardens outside the chapel, tangled in thought. The cool chill of the morning pricked my skin, and I pulled my jacket tighter. It was November. I was due to make a speech at Harold's memorial in two days and I still hadn't written anything.

I've never been much of an emotional writer—drafting depositions and legal summonses is far more my cup of tea—but I wanted to get something down to honor him and the memories he had left us with. And yet, every time I put my pen down, my mind would go blank at the glare of the paper. The longer I waited, the more the pages stared back at me, accusatory.

The truth is I never really knew my brother.

Apart from the last few years before his disappearance, I barely saw him. He spent his twenties training as a doctor, becoming a surgical consultant by the time he was thirty. As such, he was always busy, always sought after. When I did try to get in touch, he'd make excuses and promise he'd visit later. Even when he left medicine, for reasons he never shared with me, he was always elsewhere—investigating rock formations in South America or working on mathematical proofs in India. The life he lived was so far removed from mine, it felt like another world—one that I had never been privy to.

He had been an awkward boy, always quiet and contemplative. His early teachers thought that he was mute. His little round face seemed to be perpetually frowning in concentration, as if everything he looked at confused him. My sister and I were convinced there was something broken in his head. We were all wrong. He simply processed the world in a different way to all of us. Where we accepted assumptions, he saw possibilities. Where we felt clarity, he saw uncertainty. And where we were confused, he made strange connections and improbable links.

Breaking my chain of thought, Poppy settled down next to me, in those gardens. She had a bottle of red and a couple of plastic glasses in her hand. For a while, she didn't say a word. She just sat beside me and stared out at the cemetery where his cenotaph had been placed.

"I don't know if I can do this," I whispered to her.

"There's nobody else, Ben," she replied, putting a hand on my shoulder. "Nobody knew him—not really. There's just us. Maybe we should write down the memories of him we *do* have. The ones we remember clearly. From when he was young and we were growing up."

I shrugged. "He never really talked to me, Pops. Even when he was visiting Harriet, he was always lost in his own little worlds." I swallowed hard. "I think I was too boring for him."

She laughed, putting her arm around me. Despite myself, despite the moment, I felt a smile tugging at my lips.

"My clearest memory of him," she said, "was at the kitchen table in France, when we were on holiday. We must have been, what? Eight or nine? He can't have been more than six."

"In Nice?"

"Yes, yes. It's a small memory—a silly thing. Dad had brought back pastries from the bakery for breakfast, and you and I tore into them, shoving these croissants down our throats, and Harold, he just . . . he just stared at his. And then he started pulling it apart."

"Oh God, yes. I remember now. He didn't eat any of it."

"No, he just tore it into about twenty equal-sized pieces, then started arranging them into different geometric shapes on the table. He did that for an hour and a half. I used to think he was such a weirdo."

I laughed. "He *was* such a weirdo. Mum and I always used to joke that he'd win a Nobel Prize by the time he was thirty. Then when he hit eighteen it stopped being a joke. It felt more like a certainty, you know?" I took a gulp of wine. "The way he *looked* at you."

"Oh dear, that look." She put her hand to her head dramatically. "You remember that look?"

"How could I forget? Like he was trying to work you out. He looked at the entire world that way."

She nodded. "Like there was some kind of instruction manual written on the skin of the universe that only he could read, if he focused hard enough."

We sat for a while, and a nice warmth came over me—the soft heat of kind memories. After a couple of comforting glasses of wine, Poppy worked with me and we wrote a eulogy for him together. I delivered it to a small and somber ceremony. Most of the attendants knew my brother only by name.

I NEVER FORGOT MY BROTHER, BUT I LEARNED TO PUT HIM OUT OF MY mind. It took me about ten years to really accept his death, but I did become absolutely sure of it in the end, if only for my own sanity.

Then, nine months ago, my friend Mikey called me from out of the blue. The conversation can't have lasted more than five minutes, but it is emblazoned in my memory.

"Hi, is that Ben Tunmore?"

"Speaking."

"It's Mike Hart. You know, Mikey. From King's."

"Mikey? Christ—is that really you? It's been bloody ages. A lifetime. How are you, man?"

"Fine. Yes, fine. Listen—I'd love to catch up properly sometime, seriously, but I've got something I need to tell you."

"Sure." I could hear how tense his voice sounded.

"I was just at St. Brigid's Hospital."

"Oh, right." I frowned. "Where's that?"

He faltered a bit. "Surrey. I mean, more like Epsom, really. It's a . . . well, look it's a psychiatric hospital. Mental health facility, you know. Long-term care for crazy people. It's just . . . I go quite often to see my gran."

"Mikey—what is this about?"

"I thought I was mistaken at first. But I remember visiting you up in the Lakes over break one time and, well, he was with us for some of that summer. You don't forget a man like that, even after all these years. He had this look, this way of looking at you like he was trying to figure something out. But then I remembered Toby telling me he'd passed away years back."

My hand squeezed the phone. "What the hell are you talking about?"

"Your brother, Ben. He's here. I'm certain of it. I'd recognize that look anywhere."

THE DRIVE FROM WINDERMERE TO SURREY TOOK ME ABOUT SIX HOURS, though it could just as easily have been a decade. Or an age of history. There were so many questions running through my head; I didn't know where to begin. I couldn't focus on anything except for a single overriding thought: *Don't count on anything until you've seen him. If he was alive, he'd be in his seventies, probably unrecognizable. This is probably a mistake. Mikey hasn't seen Harold since we were kids.*

I said it over and over to myself, like a mantra.

As I approached, St. Brigid's Victorian architecture loomed into view—arched stone windows and rising turrets. Mikey had told me that much of the hospital had fallen into disrepair, and it now housed only two of the original villas, with a total of just fifty-five full-care patients.

I got out of the car and the front face of the building rose ahead, greeting me with frigid wind and biting cold. I wrapped myself up in a coat and hat, but it did little to get the chill out of my bones.

I had to push open the wrought-iron gates, closed, but not

locked. At several meters high, they towered over me. I passed through and the wind picked up, clattering them shut. A metallic shriek rang through the grass courtyard.

I turned to look back at the street behind me. But for my old car, the roads were dead. I put my head down and walked forward, the only sound the crunch of my boots on the gravel path.

When I knocked on the door, a short nurse with an unwelcoming scowl appeared.

"Can I help you?"

"I'm here to see a patient."

She frowned. "I ain't never seen you before. Nobody comes here who ain't come here before. We ain't got no new patients. They've all been here for decades."

I nodded. "I'm aware. I think I may know someone inside, though. Someone I didn't know was here."

"Wha's your name?"

"Benjamin Tunmore."

"And wha's their name?"

"Harold Tunmore."

Her lips tightened into a little circle, and her eyes went down to my feet and back up. "Never heard of him." She began to close the door, but I stepped forward, shoving my foot in the entranceway. The large wooden door clunked against it.

"Listen here now—" the nurse began.

"Please." I put a hand on the door frame. "Please, I've been reliably informed my brother may be in here. I've not seen him for almost thirty years." And, as she seemed to require a final show of emphasis, I added, "*Please.*"

Her lips tightened together and her eyes darted left and right. "Fine. But don't you go mouthing off to any of my patients without my say-so. It's a delicate ecosystem in here. Balanced. All sorts of things can muck with that." She pointed a finger at me. "You look. You don't talk."

I nodded and followed her down a stone hallway. The cold receded quickly, a warmth emanating from the floor beneath. Ornate gold-framed paintings of the home's founders lined the walls, not a single smile among them. There were the crackling sounds of fire and the gentle tinkling of a piano. Pulling off my coat, I followed the nurse into a large sitting room with about twenty people spread across it.

For the most part, they sat or stood silently, staring into space or out the high windows at the fog rolling over the cold fields. An older lady played the piano—slowly but delicately—and there was a shuffling of newspaper as men flicked through pages by the fireplace.

"See?" the nurse said in a voice that almost made me jump. "Delicate ecosystem. Now you wait here. I gotta go talk to the boss."

As my eyes glanced across a number of elderly residents, I noticed that they were all alone. Whether staring out at the windblown trees or sitting quietly on one of the plush Victorian settees, none of them spoke to one another, or even seemed to acknowledge each other's presence. A sharp pang of loss echoed through me. This felt to me like a home for lost souls, for ghosts who had nowhere else to go.

Then I saw him.

An elderly gentleman sat in the corner of the room in a large red armchair, behind a tall mahogany table. He was staring at a chessboard, fully set up but unplayed, with a curious intensity. I took a few steps closer, my heart skipping, and his head rose. His eyes rested on mine.

It was then that I realized Mikey was wrong. Not about my brother—no, that was definitely Harold—but about his distinctive look. It was not the same one I knew. The eyes were different, as though something inside him had been taken away, or replaced.

I rushed over, trying to keep my voice low and quiet. Despite my excitement, a strange trepidation ran through me. A sense that something was not right.

"Harry!" His eyes did not leave me. "Harry, it's me. Harry, you're alive!"

He pursed his lips, as if chewing on a word he did not know how to say. I waited expectantly. When he finally opened his mouth, he said:

"Are the ants alive?"

I blinked. "What?"

"It's a matter of definition, isn't it?" His voice was hoarse and brittle. "A matter of semantics. It doesn't *change the fact*."

"I . . ." I had no idea what he was talking about. "No, I suppose it doesn't."

"Is the sea alive?" He stared up at me, his brown eyes wet.

"I don't know, Harold."

He sighed—a deep, weary, exhausting thing that seemed to empty the essence right out of him.

"Nor do I, Ben." He shook his head. "Nor do I."

My heart surged at the mention of my name. He knew who I was. All I had to do was get him out of the facility. Get him back home, where we could take care of him. Then I noticed his right hand: he'd lost three fingers; only his thumb and forefinger remained.

"Mr. Tunmore." A voice cracked across the room. I turned to find that first, short nurse standing beside a much taller, lankier woman. She held a clipboard almost as rigid as she was. "Can we talk?"

I turned back to Harold, my head swimming. It was hard to leave him, even briefly, after all these years.

"I'll just be over there, okay? I'll just be in the other room, back in a moment."

He ignored me, turning his head back to the chess pieces. The thin lady beckoned me through the door to her office and invited me to sit. The white-walled room was incongruent to the building around it—if not for the tinkling of the piano carrying through, I would have hardly believed I was in the same place.

"My name is Dr. Stranner." She leaned forward, peering down her nose at me. "What brings you here today?"

"That was my brother." I pointed toward the large room we had just left. "Who I was talking to. That's Harold Tunmore. He's been . . . well, he's been missing for almost thirty years. I thought he was dead."

She raised her eyebrows. "Is he really? He's one of our oldest patients, in terms of how long he's been here. Nobody's ever been able to make any headway on his family."

"Well, I'm his family. His brother. I'm here and I can take him home now."

Dr. Stranner's eyebrows came together in a ridge. "Well, I can certainly see the resemblance, but I'm not sure that will be possible, Mr. Tunmore. He requires a *lot* of care. More than you are likely to be able to provide without full-time help."

"What's wrong with him?"

"He displays a wide range of paranoid delusional disorders. He often becomes restless, and at times violent. Sometimes he is completely uncommunicative. Now, if you can return with some kind of documentation to indicate your relationship." Her eyes narrowed in distrust. "Pictures. Old identification, perhaps. Evidence of past association. Then I can go through his file with you. It will take . . . time."

MY BROTHER WAS NOT A WELL MAN. FOR THE DURATION OF HIS STAY AT St. Brigid's, he had experienced schizophrenic episodes and intense psychotic moments, when he was certain that someone or something was watching or controlling him.

I decided to stay down in Epsom for the forthcoming weeks. At seventy-seven, and long retired, I now had that luxury, and a short-stay home wasn't too expensive. I'd called Poppy, but she was away on holiday in the States. We agreed I'd stay close to Harold until she could get here and we could work out what we were going to do.

I visited him every day, and he recognized me without fail but seemed utterly uninterested in answering any of my questions. His fingers had clearly been amputated, and I later learned he had deep scars across the length of his chest. But it didn't matter how many times I asked him about what happened; if he didn't want to answer, he would remain obstinately silent. The only times I could sustain conversations with him, I didn't understand what he was talking about. He mentioned ants a few more times, and octopuses often.

We would play chess, and he would show a keen and fervent enthusiasm in setting up the board. His hands moved deftly, unbothered by his missing fingers, and his eyes gazed greedily as he carefully put each piece in its rightful place. But when it was set up, he stopped. It was as though a light had been switched off. He simply leaned back and stared.

"Shall we play?" I would ask. To which he would shrug, or mutter *fine*. He would then proceed to beat me mercilessly every time, seeming completely and utterly bored while doing so.

"It seems you haven't lost your brains," I joked after he thrashed me one day in about six moves.

"Nothing to do with the matter. Nothing at all. It was all *set up*, you see? All *set up*."

During the second week, I was unfortunate enough to see one of his psychotic episodes. He began shaking violently, as if he were incurably cold, and muttering, "They don't see what it does. That's the problem. That's the *disconnect*. They don't see what it does to the *ants*."

I tried to calm him, but his muttering turned to shouts and the shouts to screams as he rose to his feet.

"They don't see what it does to the ants!"

I watched the nurses restrain him and help retire him down the hall and to his room, assisted by a syringe with a long, thin needle. I followed, hoping to be of some help.

I had not been in his room before. It was sparse, with a single hospital bed and flowers on the windowsill. Not ugly, but frigid— lacking in anything personal. After they had got him to sleep, I stayed with him, sitting by his bed.

There was a single possession in the room: a small leather brief-case in the corner. The nurses told me it had always been with him, since the beginning, and that he got very upset if anyone tried to take it away. After a few hours of sitting, curiosity got the better of me and I cracked it open. The briefcase contained three things: a carving made from a soap block, a copy of *The Tempest*, and a large, loosely tied bundle of papers.

The carving appeared to show the figures of a mother and a

boy, but was roughly made. Not an impressive artistic piece, but rather something hastily hewn without much eye for technique.

The copy of *The Tempest* had clearly been read many times, the pages curled and folded, stained with fingerprints and mud. Inside, the text was largely untouched, but for a single page. At the end of Act 1, Scene 2, when Prospero says to Ariel:

Thou shalt be as free
As mountain winds; but then exactly do
All points of my command.

These three lines were highlighted, then underlined, then circled multiple times. Almost everything else on the page was obscured because of this, but those words stood out, undeniably clear.

When I opened the bundle of papers, I could feel my heart race, thudding against my ribs. The very top page began with *My dearest Harriet*, and I realized, as I flicked through, that they were all letters, all addressed to my daughter. I checked the dates, feeling fortunate that my brother had been a stickler for labeling, and noticed that they were from 1991. They were the follow-up letters to the three my brother had sent all those years ago.

There were hundreds of pages.

I WANTED TO TAKE THE LETTERS HOME, BUT JUST AFTER I HAD PACKED them away in my bag, Harold stirred. I froze, feeling oddly like a thief, as though I was betraying some unspoken confidence by entering his room and opening his briefcase.

"Ben," he whispered. I approached his bed. His eyes were weak, his face gaunt and white. "I couldn't do it. I tried, but I . . . I didn't have the strength."

I leaned in close to him and he took my hand in his—it was cold and clammy. "It's okay, Harry. I'm here." I'd long since stopped trying to figure out what he was telling me. Too many of our conversations had proven futile. I learned that what he wanted, or perhaps what he needed, was merely comfort and reassurance. "It's okay."

"She wanted me to share them. Years ago, but I couldn't. She wanted me . . ." He grimaced, as if in pain. It was clear that he knew I had the letters. Whatever he had become, my brother was not an idiot.

"Don't worry, Harry," I said. "I'll keep them safe."

His face hardened, his features solidifying into stone. "No one can read them." His voice was low, urgent as his hand squeezed mine, knuckles white. "If we should know *what we are* . . . if anyone should . . ." His words were drowned in a fit of coughs and splutters. I stayed close to him, my hand in his, but by the time his coughing ended, he had drifted back off into sleep. Even in his state of unconsciousness, it took some force to extricate my hand from his grip. Although he was now asleep, his brow was still tightened in concentration.

Sighing, I left him, determined to return first thing in the morning.

Under a flickering desk lamp in my rented room, I began to read the letters. They were old and brittle, as if dried after being soaked wet. They resembled the other three that I had obsessed over so many years ago. Some came before, some came after, but together they threaded themselves into a narrative that I could not deny. I felt like I had drifted backward in time, into those dark evenings delving into those words, trying to catch a glimpse into something I had missed. Or that I was not supposed to see.

The next morning, I got a call from St. Brigid's.

When I remember it now, it is not as though I am receiving a call. I don't recall hearing the events explained to me. I can only picture the incident as if I witnessed it myself.

My brother broke out of his room in the night. He made his way into the kitchens with a key that he had procured. None of the nurses knew where it had come from, as theirs were all accounted for; one had a vague memory of the kitchen key going missing some ten years before.

As far as the coroners could tell, he pried open a barrel of oil kept for lighting the old kerosene burners. He poured it all over his clothes and, using a long safety match from the kitchen, he lit himself on fire.

I cried that night, but the tears didn't feel real. They were dulled by time and distanced by shock. The truth was that I was grieving a man I had buried long ago.

I cannot help but blame myself for his death. For almost thirty years before I arrived, he had lived his quiet yet turbulent existence. Poppy tries to convince me that perhaps I had also allowed him a kind of release. Perhaps he, too, had buried himself long before his actual death, and with his letters—his confession—passed on, he was finally allowed to pass.

I have read the letters a hundred times now. The tale he tells is a tall one, and I cannot attest to the authenticity of it. Some of the names check out. Some of the people involved did exist. Of some others, there is no record. I make no comments on the events he relates. I will not summarize them for you—I lack the skill and the science. What happened to him is out of the realm of my understanding, and I can accept that.

I contacted Poppy's husband, Jeremy. He owns a small, independent publishing house just outside of Oxford. It didn't take much convincing—what started as a favor to Poppy and me soon became something more. In a few short months, he helped collate the full contents of the letters, both the original three and those that follow. We all agreed that the general public had a right to know.

Perhaps my brother was simply mad. Perhaps his work had driven him to madness and these letters were nothing more than the final ramblings of a lunatic.

But perhaps there is also truth to them.

Because if what he claims happened in these letters *is* true, if even a fraction of what he tells actually took place, then these might just be the most important letters you will ever read.

Benjamin Tunmore, Windermere
July 2020

TUESDAY, 22nd JANUARY 1991
EVENING
[———]*

My dearest Harriet,

Forgive me, Father, for I have sinned.

Do you remember those words, Hattie? I don't believe Ben would have exposed you to them. He never did take to faith. But when Grandpa used to take us to church when we were kids, every Sunday he'd point out the little box in the corner. "That's where you go to confess," he said. "That's where you find salvation."

Talking to the priest was never easy. Salvation is not an easy thing for children to understand. I don't believe that we're born sinners, any of us. We've yet to discover what "sin" really is. I remember sitting in the dark of that little room, searching my heart for some kind of transgression.

---

* **EDITOR'S NOTE**: Harold's letters are mostly both dated and addressed. However, due to an ongoing legal dispute, some of the locations in Harold's letters have been redacted in this edition.

"I was mean to my sister at school," I would say. "I stole some money from my mum's purse."

None of this ever happened, of course—I never really strayed far from the rules—but I knew enough to know my lines. And though I couldn't see his face to check if I was doing it right, he'd give me my Our Fathers and my Hail Marys and send me on my way. And Dad would smile. I think, perhaps, that was all I was really after. That little approving smile that would appear on his face.

As we grew older, it got more difficult. Puberty made me awkward, self-reflective to the point of nausea. The little white lies didn't come as easily anymore. Real sins bubbled somewhere underneath the surface, nebulous and incomprehensible, and I didn't quite know what to do with them.

Ben stopped going, but I never did.

One day I sat in that cubicle and said nothing. My place in the world had started to weigh on me and I didn't know how to hold it. I had no words to break the holy silence of that little room, until Father Michaels—did you ever meet him, with the red hair?—he said to me,

"You know, son, I can't *make* you speak. You've come here every week since you were a boy and I don't think I've ever heard you say a single thing that's true."

"I . . ." My mind blanked. "I'm sorry."

"Don't be sorry. Everyone has their own relationship with God. The confessional is here to help you, as am I, but I'm just a translator."

"A translator for God?"

He chuckled. "No, my dear boy. None of us are capable of that. A translator for you. Sometimes a man needs help giving his thoughts life, giving his words meaning, so that he can confide that meaning with God. I think, perhaps, your problem is the opposite."

I shifted uncomfortably in my seat.

"If you'll let me give a little advice, I recommend you keep a journal," he said. "Set down your thoughts. Not to me. Not to anyone else but yourself. Just the simple events of your day, in plain form."

"Why?"

"Sometimes what the soul needs isn't to give meaning to hollow words: prayers and confessions that you do not really believe. Instead, we need to let it give words to the unspoken meanings inside of us. To do that, you have to give it a voice. It's not an easy thing, son. Not at first. It's not an obvious task, but . . . write everything down. Don't cross anything out. Don't lie or explain or prevaricate. You have no one to hide anything from but yourself."

I did as I was instructed. I don't think I've ever told you this. It's never seemed appropriate—for all our trips together, my faith has always been a very personal thing, just as your father's pragmatic atheism has always been for him. My journal, for many years, became a form of communication—of speaking to an other. It was Father Michaels who taught me this need not be done on my knees, or in a church.

Pages upon pages of ink spilled out of me then like blood from a thousand cuts. The need to confess has never left me: the curative, cathartic power that comes from sharing oneself with the world and with others. I obsessed over it. But the truth is that in time, it became too much. When everything happened with Santi, and the hospital, I had to step away, wean myself off it, rehabilitate. To look too closely would have driven me mad.

And yet, for the first time in a very long time, events are happening that I do not understand. I feel that I must communicate them with someone, if only to make sense of them myself. That is, after all, my stated purpose, isn't it, Hattie? Making sense of things.

But I find I cannot return to my journal now, not in the way I once did. The words are false. They ring with a cold emptiness.

I write this letter in the hope that you might be my translator, of a sort. I'm sorry to place this burden on you, but you're the only one I have left. You must be what—fourteen now? It was your fourteenth birthday when I took you to paddleboarding, wasn't it? You're old enough, then, perhaps, that you understand what it means to confess. Though in truth, part of me hopes that Ben will hide this away, or burn it. In fact, I expect that it will probably be burned. But there is no one else that I can think of, no one else that I haven't already pushed away.

I no longer believe God is listening.

I watched an old friend die today. I wanted to get that out of the way early, so it didn't come as a shock. I have no wish to scare you, but I am sitting here, staring at camera feeds and desperately clawing at an explanation. I'm not sure I'm allowed to write this; I have no idea how I'll even get it to you. I just needed to share with somebody, with anybody.

* * *

Yesterday, I arrived in New Mexico for work. My own work—not a commission but rather a personal investigation, spurred on by bizarre and contradictory reports of bird migrations coming out of the region. It was as though, all of a sudden, all the swallows that would normally have migrated south for winter were coming back early.

Like they were running from something.

It might seem a strange lead to chase, but you know I like to travel. Living alone in my dusty London flat becomes tiresome and exhausting, as though I can feel my very brain atrophying. And I'd made enough from the Hubble launch in Florida last year—that space telescope I told you about—that I could afford to follow my own interests for a while.

I checked into the Historic Taos Inn, a quaint location set across several adobe houses, thankful that I was here in January. I'd been to New Mexico once before in the summer—you remember that *awful* physics conference?—and I was sweating the moment I stepped off the plane. Winter is appreciably cooler, and for all the desolate and desert landscape, the cold winds remind me a little of London.

As I was led up to my room, I was smiling at the pride the proprietors took in their inn's history. Old pictures and placards littered the walls, consistent blaring reminders that this place was over a hundred years old.

"This main building dates back to the 1800s," the porter told me, chest out. "There's a lot of history here."

He left me just outside my room, key in hand and heavy luggage at the door, and bade me good evening. I stood, still smiling at him, and he at me, for some time. What a fool I must have looked, beaming at him. It took me a good ten seconds to remember that I was supposed to tip in this country. I fumbled in my pockets haphazardly, muttering a poor mixture of apology and an excuse about different cultures. I managed to pull out a crisp ten-dollar note and he disappeared promptly and efficiently.

Sighing, for I was finally to be offered some solitude, I turned the key to my room.

It was not empty.

Two men waited for me. The first was right in front of me: an imposing, straight-backed man with military bearing, tall and wide, his shoulders barely squeezed into the fabric of his suit jacket. He stood, towering over me, the grizzle on his dark face hinting at scars tucked beneath. His leathery brown skin spoke of a life worn by a few too many exotic experiences.

It took me a second to notice the second man behind him. He was sitting at the desk—a pale white man, his face gray and hair fading like an old photograph. The shadow of the curtains fell on his brown polyester suit and almost completely blended him into the dark wooden chair. In front of him, there was a closed briefcase.

"Mr. Tunmore," the first said. "We've been waiting for you."

"Well, I can see that," I replied, squeezing past him and into the room. "Otherwise, this would be an astonishing coincidence."

"Ha!" He let out a deep grunt of a laugh. "People are usually a bit more taken aback. Do you know what happened last time we waited in someone's hotel room? The man fainted—actually damn fainted—I swear, like something out of a movie."

I shuffled forward and took an awkward seat on the bed. "I suppose nowadays I'm always half expecting some sort of corporate or military representative to show up unexpectedly. What can I do for you gentlemen?"

"Oh." His face lit up as if he'd just realized something. "Please, let me get your bags. You relax, maybe have a cup of tea? That's what you English do, isn't it?"

I frowned, trying to reconcile the bullish image of this man with his jovial nature. "I hate to be one to reinforce stereotypes, but yes. I could murder a cup."

The big man laughed, flicked the electric kettle on. As he went to grab my suitcase, I couldn't help but notice there was already water in the kettle. They had been here awhile.

I turned to the man in the chair. "You have me at a disadvantage. You seem to know my name."

The man smiled back at me, wordless.

"Names aren't important right now," the first man called back, lifting my bag like it was filled with feathers. "Just call me the Warden. Everyone calls me the Warden."

"Very well. I suppose I should ask why you're here?"

The Warden ripped open a tea bag and dropped it in a cup, pouring water over it.

The man at the desk reached forward to open his briefcase, and I noted his long, spindly fingers, like the legs of a spider. They deftly clacked at the combination. He pulled out a few pieces of paper, which he tapped on the desk to keep in line before placing them in front of him.

"We've come to find you," the Warden said, looming over me as he handed me my tea. "Because apparently you've got a nose for this sort of thing."

"What sort of thing?"

The Warden frowned, as if a little confused, and looked at his colleague. The man at the desk just smiled.

"You're a physicist, right?" he said. "So . . . physics."

I laughed, and leaned back a little into the bed. There's something about an American using sarcasm that always puts me a little more at ease.

"Physics is a pretty broad umbrella. It encompasses most of the known universe. Could you be more specific?"

"I'd like to tell you, but the problem is . . ." the Warden said, then paused, frowning. "Well, it's difficult."

"Ah," I said. "Top secret, is it?"

"You know the funny thing about that phrase, 'top secret'? It isn't actually the top." The Warden stepped forward, his figure blocking out the light. "It's a common myth. Top secret is just a term people use to convince people with top secret access that they have the highest clearance—to keep them from asking questions about what else might be going on."

I didn't reply.

"You see, there's all sorts of higher clearances than 'top secret.' There's T Access and there's Q Access. Hell, there's accesses that I probably don't even know exist. And trust me—I know a lot. But if we really wanted to tell you anything, anything at all, you know what I'd have to do?"

I shook my head, taking a sip of my tea. "Perhaps you'd have to kill me?"

"I'd have to leave the room," he said, pointing at the door, "and call my superior to ask if you had the specific access required, which you don't. You wouldn't be allowed to be with me, obviously, as then you'd hear the name of the access, and even that would be too much. And if they confirmed that you did—which they won't—I'd have to come back in here and make you leave the room and call your superior, to triple-check that *I* had the clearance required to even be having this conversation."

"Do you?"

He smiled. "I can't tell you that. You don't have the clearance."

I took another sip of tea. "Then why, if you can't tell me anything, are we here?"

"There's a man," he said, glancing at his colleague. "Well, there's a . . ." He pressed his eyebrows together. "Let's call it a . . . phenomenon. The organization I represent would like you to take a look. I am, of course, not at liberty to tell you what it is."

"I'm sort of engaged on a job already. Can you at least tell me *where* it is?"

The Warden shook his head, splaying his hands out as if to apologize.

I sighed. "So, you've got a phenomenon that you can't talk about, in a place you can't tell me, working for people I'm not even allowed to know the names of. It's late and I'm tired—what on earth makes you think that I'll say yes?"

He grinned. "A *more interesting* little bird than you're currently chasing told me you wouldn't be able to resist."

I frowned, thinking about the investigation that had brought me here. Did he know about that? I hadn't told anyone what I'd been looking into.

"I mean—" The Warden shrugged. "I *could* tell you how well you'd be paid, but they said that wouldn't matter. The more obscure the mystery, the more intrigued he'll be, they said."

I sighed again.

The truth is I was tired. I was hungry. All I wanted was to tell these men to leave, that I wasn't interested, and that they could find someone else.

But damn it, Hattie, the man was right. I don't know who he'd been talking to, but this—all the secrecy, the strangeness of their visit, the hint at larger answers? I felt a familiar shiver of excitement run down my spine.

This was a mystery.

* * *

Less than thirty minutes later, we were in a van, my things loaded into the back. The windows were tinted and the curtains drawn. Despite the sudden change, I was overwhelmed with tiredness. I slept, Lord knows how long, and when I woke up and peeked through the curtain, we had arrived at a facility out in the desert.

The morning sun poked over the horizon. Around us was an expanse of cold, flat nothingness. The hot dust kicked up from the van seemed to settle in the air, almost like snow, in a haze that spread out in all directions.

The building was completely nondescript, so out of place that at first I thought I was looking at a mirage or a trick of the light. This flat gray monolith rose out of the yellow sand, all blocky sides and corners. There wasn't a single sign or identifying feature, and even the windows looked so washed out that I could barely distinguish them from the walls. It seemed as though, in the blink of an eye, the desert might swallow it up and there'd be nothing to say that it had ever been there at all.

The van trundled up outside of it, parking beside a couple of black cars that were nestled right against the building wall. I rubbed my blurry eyes from the glare of the desert, then felt a push from the driver behind me. Stepping out of the vehicle, I lifted my shirt in front of my mouth to keep the dust from sticking in my throat. Without so much as a word, the Warden led me inside.

Through the door, the grays transformed to clinical whites. The pristine lemon scent of cleaning products eradicated the dusty smell of desert. The walls were bare, the corridor empty but for several blank closed doors. Only the sound of our reverberating footsteps punctuated the silence. The driver stayed outside by the van and closed the door behind us.

Halfway down the corridor, the Warden opened a door and invited me in. There was a security office, with several chairs and a large desk adorned with four computer monitors. Each one of them showed the feed from a different camera, but all four cameras were looking at the same thing: a small interrogation room, walls blank, with a black-haired man in plain gray clothes sat at a metal table, drumming his fingers against the top. The taps echoed through the speakers and into the sterile air of the office.

Dum-dum-dum-dum. Dum-dum-dum-dum.

His face was unreadable—a halfway point between indifference and serenity. His eyes were glazed, looking outward as if they were not seeing, as if staring ahead at a landscape beyond the cold white walls of his cell. He was not cuffed.

"Who is he?" I asked.

"John McAllister."

I blinked. I knew that name. I looked again, piecing together fragments of recognition. I'd worked with John, about five years ago—an epidemiologist from out of New York. He had led a team containing a smallpox outbreak in Birmingham. I think I told you about this, Hattie? When they brought me in as a consulting physicist to study the impact of wind turbulence on airborne pathogens. Flashes returned to me: John at a whiteboard, scribbling; John smiling, making a joke about seagrass; John buying me coffee. We'd been close for a time—I'd been impressed by his diligence and keen sense of empathy—but it had been so long.

"What's he doing here?"

The Warden shook his head. "Access, Mr. Tunmore. Access. Let's just say he was working on something for us, and . . . things went awry. We're at a bit of a loss as to where to go from here."

"Why is he being held?"

"He isn't," the Warden said. "Well, he's free to leave this room, at least. He just doesn't."

"What do you mean, doesn't?"

"He's been here for four days. Hasn't moved an inch, except to eat and drink what we bring him, and to go to the toilet, but then he goes right back to where he's sitting." He shook his head. "I'll be straight with you. I don't like bringing a civilian into this. But you came to me on recommendation—you're meant to be good at these things. And I'm at my wits' end. There's weird and then there's *weird*. I'll try anything at this point, if we can find out what's happening here. He's been away from the site for too long and the higher-ups are getting antsy."

John's drumming reverberated out of the speakers.

Dum-dum-dum-dum. Dum-dum-dum-dum.

"What site did he come from?"

"You don't have clearance for that question."

"Who recommended me?"

He pulled his lips together. "You don't have clearance."

I sighed. "What do I have clearance for?"

"To talk to him. And to see the test. Then tell us what you make of it."

29

I stood, looking back at him. I was about to tell him that I needed more than obfuscation and mystery if he wanted my help.

John's tapping stopped.

In the quiet of the room, it had become like a metronome; without it, there was only the light hum of electronics and the Warden's stern gaze.

We both shifted to look at the monitor as John's head turned, slowly, deliberately, until he was looking straight at one of the cameras. Though he was in a closed room, his eyes felt as if they were directly on us.

"You can run the test again now, Steve," John said. I shivered at the sound of his voice. It was too cold, too level, as though it were coming from a different body. "I'm sure Harry doesn't want to be kept waiting."

The sound of my name sent a small jolt down my spine.

"You told him I was coming," I whispered.

"No." The Warden gave me a tight smile. "We haven't told him anything. He just . . . well, he just does that."

John's head turned, smoothly as a mechanized doll, back to facing the wall directly ahead of him. His fingers started up again, drumming a steady beat.

* * *

"It's been a long time," I said. I was in a seat opposite John and he was not looking at me. His eyes were on me, but they looked past me. Through me. I fumbled at a pack of playing cards that the Warden had given me. He hadn't told me what they were for. "Can you tell me why I'm here?"

He cocked his head a little to the right. "That's quite a big question, isn't it, Harry? Why are you here? Moving from job to job. Country to country. Too scared to let roots grow. Do you tell yourself there's meaning in that?"

"I haven't seen you in five years," I said, a chill running down my arms. "And you talk about my life like you've studied it. What's happening here, John?"

"I was shown truth," he said. His face smiled, but it didn't touch his eyes. "It turns out truth isn't all it's cracked up to be."

His voice was still emotionless: a man reading a script for the first time, not understanding the inflections of the lines.

This was not the John I had known. His features were the same—the facial structure, the hair, the shape of his body—and, though aged, they individually seemed to belong to the same man that I had worked with all those years ago. If I had seen a picture of him, I would not have noticed anything wrong. But in front of me, they didn't quite seem to come together. It was as though each bit of him had been gradually taken away and replaced. They combined to form an accurate simulacrum of John McAllister, but the cohesive whole, the essence of the man, was gone.

He leaned forward. "Open the cards."

I blinked, taken aback by the flat monotone of his demand. Obliging, I flicked open the pack and pulled them out. John's fingers kept drumming.

Dum-dum-dum-dum.

"Shuffle them."

I did as I was told, under the table. "What is this?" I asked. "A magic trick?"

He cocked his head slightly to the left. "You tell me. Three of spades."

"Excuse me?"

"Nine of hearts. Jack of spades. Four of clubs."

I looked down at the pack in my hand and at the card lying face-up, away from John: the three of spades. As he spoke, I peeled one card back and then another, then another. The nine; the jack; the four. He kept reeling them off—perfectly and completely accurate.

The hollowness of his voice echoed around the room as card after card fluttered past, his distant eyes staring out and beyond. With each prediction, I felt a tightening in the room. A claustrophobia pressing itself into me.

"Stop."

He fell silent.

"I don't know why you're doing this." I leaned in. "I'm impressed, I am. Deeply intrigued, and I would love to know how, but . . ." I glanced up at the camera. "Look, I don't know why I'm here, but something isn't right. I can see that. I want to help you."

He laughed and my whole body shuddered. Hattie, do you remember that old amusement park I took you to? I think you must have been ten—and that mechanical rabbit that laughed when you shook its ears? You were so *scared* of it, because you told me "It was a laugh with no laughter in it." That's what John sounded like. Empty.

"Don't be a fool, Harry. No one can help me now." He leaned across the table toward me, close enough that I could hear him whisper. "But I'm glad you came. I knew you would. I've been waiting for you. For this moment. I didn't know why it would be you, but I do now. I've seen it through a glass, darkly."

My ears perked up at the Bible verse, as though he was trying to send me a coded message. I lowered my voice, matching his whisper. "What is it, John? What have you seen?"

"Everything, Harry. It's all been set up. Listen to me now: in a moment, two guards will come in here because I'm whispering too quietly for them to hear it on the cameras. One of them will be armed. After what I'm about to tell you, you'll shout a warning at them, but it won't help. It'll only confuse and panic one of them, and he'll take out his weapon. In the ensuing struggle, I'm going to take his pistol and shoot myself in the head."

"What?"

He grabbed my hand. "Why does Sisyphus keep pushing the rock up the hill, Harry, if he knows it'll just fall down again? Why does he keep *pushing*?"

The door swung open.

I've replayed the moment again and again in my head, asking myself a hundred questions. Would I have blurted out a warning if he hadn't told me I would? Would John still be alive? I have no answers at the moment—only the series of recurring images: the stumbling guard, surprised by my scream; the grabbing of the pistol; the splatter of blood on those pristine white walls.

I'll spare you the details; I'm not sure I could write them anyway. I'm fine, at least physically. I know how you worry. But they've had me sitting in an office surrounded by screens, reviewing footage of the last day.

I'm watching John sit there, barely moving. I'm watching as they shout at him; they cajole him; they interrogate him. Most of the sound has been redacted—information I do not have clearance for.

His face barely changes throughout his last minutes. His posture never shifts. His damn fingers never stop drumming. It's as though his consciousness has left him; he's just a puppet, an automaton reciting lines that have been programmed into him.

They're expecting some kind of explanation from me, but I don't have any. There are guesses, the starts of ideas that have popped into my mind, but each time they do they're clouded by the image of his head exploding all over the room.

How did he know about the cards? How did he know about the gun? Why did he mention Sisyphus? Those final words were not just any old words, Hattie. I could tell they were meant for me. And the more I think about them, the more I think about Santi. I don't want to; I can't help it. I heard John's words and I was back in that hospital, shouting at nurses. I was back in the confessional, screaming at my own impotence.

Oh God—there's still blood on my hands as I write this. I haven't even been given time or space to properly clean it off. Every time I close my eyes, the drumming of his fingers runs through my head.

Dearest Harriet,

I must tell you what I've just seen. You won't believe me, I'm sure of it, but we are together at least in that. I still do not believe my own eyes.

Let me take a step back. My arms are shaking with excitement. I need to reflect, to contextualize how I came to be here. I'm on a plane. Not a large one—not a commercial airliner like you might imagine, with its rowed seating and cabin crew. No, I am in a single military cabin, a long corridor with gear and equipment chained to the hull walls. There is one window and out of it I can see nothing but blue. We

---

* **EDITOR'S NOTE:** It is important to point out that despite their chronological appearance, forensic examination after the fact does not indicate that all the letters were written sequentially. The type of paper is different for some of them, and the level of weathering varies dramatically from letter to letter. For reasons that will become clearer in the text, it is perhaps impossible to date them accurately. As such, in an attempt to present a clear narrative, the editors have chosen to present the letters by the dates on their headings.

are miles above what I am guessing is the Pacific Ocean. We have been traveling for several hours.

Things have become a little complicated.

I'm sorry for how I ended my last letter. I was overwhelmed and I let my emotions get the better of me. I haven't felt that way in many years—and deliberately so. You see, it became clear to me over the years that emotion had no place in my work. I learned to embrace the raw logic of the problem, the physics of the case at hand, untempered by the capricious waxing and waning of my feelings.

Sometimes, Hattie, when these feelings stumble into my path and I find myself blinded, I imagine a box. I have never told you this before, but I think you are old enough now. I think perhaps it is time that I told somebody. It is a hard box, made of tungsten—the hardest of metals. There is a single slot with a tight lid that is never opened. The inside is lightless, soundless, without shape or size. If I close my eyes, and I focus, I can put these emotions in the box and keep them there, out of sight and out of mind, until the problem at hand is solved.

This is what I must do with John.

It is the only way to survive.

I will pick up from where I left you last. I slept a fitful night in a cold and metallic dormitory. There were very few people there, and those that I did see didn't talk to me. They appeared in rooms with clipboards and files to give to the Warden and then disappeared, wordlessly.

When I woke, they moved me to a room very similar to the one John had been kept in, and I was joined by both the Warden and his silent friend. The former remained standing, his bulging frame taking up most of the room. The latter sat down, took out a notebook, and began writing.

"Do you know the first time I saw someone get shot?" the Warden said, pacing calmly. "I don't. Not that that's a good thing, of course, but it just sort of blends into time. I remember how I felt, and I can remember what I thought—isn't that weird? That I can remember clearly what was running through my own head at the time, but I can't remember the event itself?"

"What was running through your head?"

"That I would never forget this moment. That it would stick with me forever. But time passed and the moment drifted into obscurity like all moments eventually do. I know. It feels like this will haunt you forever. But it won't. Things never do."

I tried to smile, but it felt weak.

"So, about John . . ." he said. "Any thoughts?"

I sighed. "Yes."

The silent man stopped writing. He looked up at me expectantly.

"No conclusions, certainly. But thoughts? I have many of those. I had some time to think about the events of yesterday pragmatically and, if we're going to do this, I'd like to begin with a clear reckoning of facts, if I may? Then you can correct me if I get anything wrong."

The Warden nodded for me to continue.

"John McAllister had been working on a site somewhere else and he was brought here because he started exhibiting strange behaviors. This originally included having a preternatural understanding of events that he could not have seen or otherwise been aware of."

I waited for confirmation or denial, but got neither. Both men watched me.

"We must ask ourselves, then: Is there any way he could have come across this information beforehand, through some other means?"

"Is there?"

I gave him a little shrug. "On the surface, no. The cards were the perfect example of this and John must have known it. A deck has fifty-two cards. The number of ways they can be ordered is the factorial of fifty-two. This is a number so big that if you shuffled a deck of cards every second since the start of the universe, you wouldn't even come close to repeating the same variation twice. Therefore, if you shuffle a deck thoroughly, you'll most probably end up with a configuration that has never been seen in the history of shuffling. Assuming it was a normal pack of cards, untampered with . . ."

"It was."

"Then logic tells us that he could not possibly have known. But, whatever your precautions, this was not, in my mind, something that couldn't have been pulled off by a well-trained magician. In my experience, there is usually a trick of some kind. A gimmick. I just can't see what it is yet. This is problem number one."

The Warden leaned forward. "What is problem number two?"

"I have no doubt in my mind now that I am here because John wanted me to be here. But how did he orchestrate it? In order to know that, I need to know who recommended me."

"You know I can't tell you that."

"Then I must move on to problem number three. Before he shot himself, John told me exactly what was going to happen."

The Warden raised his eyebrows.

I nodded. "In specific detail, he predicted the future."

"He predicted the future?"

"I was skeptical, of course. The mere possibility that such a thing would be within his capability raises a huge number of complex existential questions about free will and determinism, not to mention the general reach of human ability. If I'm honest, it was something I had actively intended to disprove."

He raised his eyebrows. "You say you *were* skeptical."

"It was an interesting challenge, but I feel I have come to a conclusion."

The two men waited, staring at me. I said nothing.

The Warden's hands squeezed tightly. *"Well?"*

"Well," I said. "It depends."

"Depends on what?"

"On whether you're going to properly tell me what happened here or not."

The Warden frowned and I leaned into him.

"I understand that this is confidential, secretive, whatever you want to call it. Trust me, I've worked with people like you before. That's why you brought me here. But this was someone I knew. A *good person*." I swallowed, taking a deep breath. "And now he is dead. I want to know what he was doing, where he was, and what happened to him. I suppose what I'm saying is: you have the opportunity to find out whether or not a human being somehow became capable of seeing into the future. For the price of that, I don't think I'm asking much."

The Warden looked over at his colleague, who raised his eyebrows suggestively, and then he looked back at me. "I'll need to talk to some people, of course."

"Of course."

I spent the next four hours alone in the dormitory, lying on the bed, waiting for the Warden. There was little for me to do but wait. I started writing another letter, but my thoughts were too murky, clouded in consternation and guilt. In time, the room began to feel like a prison: the blank walls, the metal gleam from the bedframe, they started to press in on me. Despite the Warden's assurances that this too shall pass, the sight of John's suicide still plagued my thoughts, if indeed it was a suicide at all.

Why *does* Sisyphus keep pushing the rock up the hill? Why do any of us? If you had asked me a decade ago, the answer would have come quickly to my lips: faith. A belief in something greater than ourselves. It came so easily to me once, but I stumble at those old words now, like a child, or a man blinded.

Nothing comes to me easily anymore.

The door pushed open and the Warden poked his head in. "I think you'd better follow me."

He led me down the hall to an office surrounded by computer screens, on each one the image of the face and torso of a man. Some were in suits, some in military uniforms. I thought apprehensively about the fact that the United States had just embarked on a war in the Gulf last week, and what on earth the military were doing here. A couple smiled appreciatively at me. Most scowled. It took me a moment to realize that these were not recordings, but two-way conduits, like a phone call. I've never seen technology like it before in my life.

The Warden invited me to sit, but did not take a seat himself. He stood perfectly straight—a stiff board before these nameless faces. Any hints of his earlier jovial nature were long gone. "You are to explain what you have learned, in brief and precise clarity. Dependent on the quality of that information, your potential for clearance will be reassessed."

"Those weren't my terms."

He looked at me, his eyes hard. "No. They weren't."

"In which case, I have nothing to share."

The Warden's eyes flashed impatiently. Some of the men on the screens shifted uncomfortably. "This isn't a game, Harold."

I sighed. "Everything's a game. We're just trying to establish what the rules are. Look, you're at a loss. I can see that. You've come to me. All I'm asking is that you work *with me*." I got up and took a step toward the door. "If you can't do that, then I'm done here."

"Harold. Wait."

The Warden looked to the screens, expectant. Seconds passed. More. Eventually, one of the men gave him a single nod. He turned back to me.

"I have the authority to tell you one thing, and one thing only. Once you've heard that, you will share everything you can. Then we'll assess where we stand."

"And why would I agree to that? That's still not what I asked for."

"John was on an expedition to discover something. He was part of a team of ten people. Ten brilliant minds, all specialists in their fields. Of those ten, only two came back alive. Alive, but . . . different. And, given John's situation, that means that only one person is left. I think when I tell you who it is, you'll want to tell us everything that you have deduced."

I raised my eyebrows, smiling at him. "Oh, really? And what makes you say that?"

"It was Dr. Naoko Tanaka."

* * *

That name might not mean anything to you, Hattie, and that is my own failing. You know I've always been a private man. There's a lot to do with my life that I have not been entirely truthful about—not to you or Ben or Aunt Poppy—or to anyone, really. Anyone but Naoko. I suppose that's why I asked her to marry me.

Given you've never heard of her, I probably have some explaining to do.

I met Dr. Tanaka when I was a junior doctor in the NHS in London. It was 1973, almost twenty years ago. I was twenty-eight, a specialist registrar coming toward the end of my surgery training, and she was my supervising consultant, just a couple of years older than me. Our relationship was professional, but she quickly became a kind of mentor to me. She'd never admit it, but she was by far the most talented doctor in the entire hospital, with a skill set that often eluded me.

You have to understand: as a student I'd never struggled with medicine. Not with the technical aspects of it—the workings of the human body, diagnosis, prescriptions, prognosis. Often to my discomfort, these things came to me quite naturally. People would always tell me I was gifted, that I could do anything I wanted. This might seem an odd thing to be uneasy with, but it drew attention to me, at first. I've never desired the spotlight, Hattie. The cocksure certainty that many of my colleagues exuded repulsed me. *Humble yourselves, therefore, under God's mighty hand*, St. Peter writes, *that he may lift you up in due time*.

I was not there to impress, but to learn. The human body is like a huge and deeply complex jigsaw puzzle, and each piece fit neatly among the others if you could just step far enough back to see the whole picture. This is what drew me to medicine initially, I think, just as my fascination with physics has never left me. It's the puzzle. The mystery of it all. The detachment suited me: life had taught me it was easier to keep to yourself.

Working as a junior doctor—particularly when I was a registrar—was an entirely different experience. The relentless hours, the sleep deprivation, the mountains of paperwork. It is not a job that previous life can really prepare you for. It shames me to say so, but I began to think of patients as little more than clipboards and prescriptions.

The first time Naoko and I spoke outside the usual bounds of professional duties, we were working with the same patient. She had brought me in to give the patient a rundown of his options for surgery.

She had kind eyes. That was the first thing people really noticed about her.

When I entered the room, the patient was apprehensive, as they often are of new faces—especially surgeons—but one look from her seemed to calm him, reassure him that we were here to help.

I didn't think this at the time. All I could think about were the three other patients I had to get through in the next twenty minutes, the last two surgeries I still had to write up, and my lunch getting cold in the staff room. So I told him, clinically and robotically, what was going to happen. The anesthesia, the cuts, the recovery. His face whitened, his eyes stricken.

"Are you a good surgeon?" he asked. "Are you the best surgeon they have here?"

I shrugged, annoyed at the question. "That's not something I can answer." And I left him.

She found me some hours later, eating my cold lunch.

She stood opposite me, across the table. "You didn't have to do that, you know."

"Do what?"

"Treat him like he was a problem that needed to be solved."

I stared at her. "I didn't see how his question had any bearing on the matter. I told him the facts. That's what he needed to hear."

"No, it wasn't," she said, sitting down opposite me. "You were telling him what *you* would have wanted to hear. That's not the same thing."

I frowned, unsure what to say. She rested her eyes on mine, and I couldn't help marveling at how brown they were. It's a memory that will always stick with me.

"People like to think empathy means being able to imagine how you'd feel in a certain situation," she said, head tilted, holding my gaze. "But it really doesn't. It means being able to imagine how *they'd* feel, and how it might be completely different from you. That man—he didn't need the specifics of the procedure. He needed to hear that you're an amazing doctor. The best that's ever walked planet Earth. Is it so difficult to tell him that?"

I waved off the idea. "We're all amazing doctors. Everyone here is as good as I am."

She snorted. "That's not true and you know it. I've seen you work cases—difficult cases. I've been watching you for some time. There's something inside you, Harold, when you're confronted with a challenge. I've never seen anything else like it. You . . . you *ignite*."

I shifted uncomfortably. She reached across and put a hand on mine.

"It's a gift," she continued, "a beautiful one, but what gets me is that you walk around like you're oblivious of it. Almost avoiding it. You push people away. You're trying your best to be humble, Harry, but it's making you callous."

Something about her words that day clung to me, got stuck inside of me. Nobody had ever spoken to me quite so honestly before. She had that way about her. She would never hide what she thought of you.

From that day on, I strived to work with her on any case I could, to learn from her. The hospital had made me hard-hearted, but she was kind, and she taught me kindness. Pure, unadulterated kindness.

I wish there was a word for things that you do not because you want to do them but because you want to be the sort of person that wants to do them. Naoko was that sort of person for me, unimpeachable. And so I wanted—no, I *needed* to be close to her. To understand her.

What started as mentorship soon developed into more. We would work late nights on cases together, sometimes at her flat, sometimes at mine. For all that she was brilliant, she would agonize over every medical decision. She never saw the patients just as problems, but as whole people—with lives and hopes and dreams. For every treatment, she would second-guess the impact, the long-term consequences, the resulting quality of life. We'd break down each treatment together, discuss the solutions, the possibilities. When we pored over diagnostics, she used to say I was making her a better doctor, but she had it the wrong way round. She was forcing me to see people in a way I never had before.

She was making me a better human.

The second I moved out from under her supervision and into a new residency, we started dating. I'm not sure I can even tell you how it started, Hattie. It felt natural—like slipping over an edge, or getting caught in a current.

She propositioned me, of course, even as I was becoming obsessed with her. To be honest, I was so shy back then that if she'd waited for me, we'd still be waiting here now. After about four months, we moved in together. A nice two-bedroom flat in north London, so we'd both have space to work.

At first, I was loath to move out of my small one-bedroom place. I was scared of losing my privacy, my quiet space, but it never actually became an issue. In some ways, the opposite was true. It was Naoko who would get lost in these bouts of deep focus—these small, intensely private hobbies—and barely speak a word to me. On weekends, she'd spend hours cooking, washing and rinsing rice, tossing and boiling. She'd sit in the spare room carving small sculptures—Japanese netsuke—and then she'd go out for long runs and come back and spend the afternoon quietly humming to herself in our living room.

I loved it. Sometimes I would just sit and watch her work, her hair tied back and her face scrunched in concentration. And as I did, it occurred to me that I would never know quite what was going on inside her head. She would exist, for a time, in a world utterly separate to mine, with no expectation that I should enter it. I realized that her mind, unlike anything else I had ever encountered, was a mystery I would never be able to solve. It might sound strange, Hattie, but that mystery brought me peace. For the first time, my life felt simple. There was a completeness to it that I can only compare to a kind of divinity.

I even found time for church again, nestled in my busy schedule. Never during Mass, but this didn't bother me. I preferred churches in the evenings, or late at night when they were empty. It is a space you can fill yourself.

We got married about a year after that, on the fifth of March, 1975. I was thirty years old and I felt like my whole life had just started.

A year later, Santi entered our world. Naoko had taken annual leave and gone to visit her family in Osaka. I'd met them once at the wedding, but the whole event had been a source of deep awkwardness for me. I'd wanted a small ceremony, and hadn't even invited your dad or Aunt Poppy, out of a strange sense of embarrassment, but Naoko had insisted her father had to be there. Neither of my parents were still alive. The truth was I still found interacting with others difficult—the whispers and undercurrents of social expectations often eluded me. Only with Naoko did I feel entirely at ease. She understood this better than anyone, and she never expected me to come with her.

While she was away, I'd been called in as a surgical consult for a possible appendectomy. He was just a small boy, the only one on the ward—only about six or seven years old, I guessed.

He'd been brought into the hospital, this skinny little thing with brown eyes and a mop of black hair. He was weak and drowsy with a heavy fever, and no one could really account for his family or background. I asked every attending, but there wasn't much information anyone could give me. Someone had found him in the cold, called an ambulance, and that was that.

He'd been sleeping on the streets: starving, freezing, ignored by the grand machinery of society. He had no papers, no documents, and he did not speak, in English or any other language. We did what we could—called social services and treated the fever—but knew that as soon as he was well enough, he'd be swallowed up by the system. Perhaps foster care, if he was lucky, or more likely a social care institution. At his age, we all knew, he was an unlikely candidate for adoption, but what options did we have?

We were there to treat people and make them better. Beyond that, there was little we could do.

But each day I walked past, I saw the fear on his little face. The unblinking stare he would give the social workers who came to speak to him, the nurses who changed his clothes. He had no idea where he was. He was so utterly alone, and I couldn't help but empathize with that. I knew what it felt like to be completely out of place.

I felt uncharacteristically compelled to dig deeper for information. I contacted charities and homeless shelters to see if I could find anyone that recognized him. I stayed up late on the phone at home, being passed from person to person, until someone—a manager of the soup kitchen at a local church—realized who I was talking about.

Some months back, the boy and a number of others had come off a ship from Santiago filled with Chilean exiles fleeing the Pinochet regime. When he arrived, he'd been alone—no family, no friends. In all likelihood his parents, like thousands of others, had disappeared into concentration camps and detainment centers.

Without anyone to look after him coming off the boat, he ended up on his own. There are supposed to be systems in place, of course, for the arrival of refugees—homes and shelters—but it's a big machine with a lot of cogs. People fall through the gaps, especially if nobody really knows they exist.

When Naoko got back, I couldn't help but talk about him. She listened quietly, and when I was done, she immediately asked me a single question:

"What's the right thing to do here?"

"I'd like to help him," I said.

"How?"

I shrugged. "I don't know. There's not much we *can* do. In the long run, the best thing that anybody could do for him is to take him in and give him a loving family to grow up in, I guess."

She gave me a long, hard look. "So, why aren't we doing that?"

And that was that.

We signed up as foster parents and took him into our home.

It didn't take long—as a young married couple with steady income, we were the perfect candidates.

In the absence of a name, we called him Santi, after Santiago, the city he had left behind. It was Naoko's decision: even though he was being taken in by a white British man and a Japanese woman, she never wanted him to forget where he had come from.

It's funny; when Naoko worked, she was always so uncertain. She was never sure if she was making the right medical decision or financial choice or career move. But when it came to matters of the heart, she was a colossus.

I truly loved her. I still love her.

That's why it was so difficult to leave.

* * *

I was settled back in a chair, in front of these men, as if in an interview. The Warden still stood stiff beside me. My old arguments had completely left me.

I didn't know if Naoko would ever want to see me again, but knowing that she had survived whatever clandestine thing sent John mad brought with it an unshakable certainty.

Whatever this expedition the Warden mentioned, I knew I must go to this site and find the solution to this problem, so I could fix this, and tuck it away, and move on. I feared that if I didn't, the box would break open, Hattie, and spill its ugly guts across the life that I have curated for myself. There was no walking away from this now.

I cleared my throat, steeling myself. "In the mid-eighties I worked with the researcher William Condon," I said. The men on the screens straightened in their seats. "You know him? A fascinating man and a top-rate neuroscientist. We'd been contracted to look at a bizarre set of murders taking place across the Balkans—local police were confounded and Interpol were at a dead end. They'd brought me in because the locations of the murders seemed to make uncanny geometric patterns on the map, like the murderer was leaving a code. They wanted a physicist to unpack the implications, and I was recommended. But the murders had gone public, you see, and they ended up with about forty people confessing, dead to rights, that they were guilty. Thirty-nine of them were lying, of course, or even all forty. It was clear from the forensic evidence that there was only one perpetrator. But how to get to the bottom of this?"

A few of the men leaned forward. One scribbled something on a piece of paper.

"As I told you yesterday, John's case is a difficult one, particularly in the way he predicted his own death. While unlikely, the most logical explanation remains that he took a gamble, hoping that the events would fall just the way that they did. Why he would do so remains a mystery to us all. However, there was another distinctly less plausible explanation that I needed to disprove first."

A couple of the men nodded, encouraging me to continue.

"What Condon taught me in the Balkans was the value of looking at microexpressions. These are innate, involuntary tics that trigger in the amygdala. The phenomenon was discovered by Haggard and Isaacs some years before, but they'd never been used in criminal investigations. The research shows that, despite people's ability to lie and fabricate, if you record their faces and slow down the footage to an extreme degree, you can catch little flickers of human emotion. They last but a fraction of a second and are usually unnoticeable by the human eye, but the conscious brain has absolutely no control over them. It doesn't matter if you intend to lie, to act, or to otherwise cover up your thoughts. There is always a flicker that betrays you."

I smiled and continued. "Cicero once wrote that the face is the picture of the mind. I wonder if he knew quite how accurate he was. I studied John's microexpressions from the video footage you took. They were there, though I almost expected them not to be. A canvas hidden under the cold demeanor. Despite his robotic nature, his face flickered, just for an instant, at all the right emotional notes. Disgust when you were shouting at him; contempt; sadness. Even . . ." I shook my head. "Even happiness when I walked in the room.

"But the key is this: his microexpressions didn't appear in a response to an event. They appeared just *before*. Believe me—I played them back again and again. The pack of cards, the interrogation, and his own murder. He was not fabricating or lying. He knew every movement before it was made, as if he had seen it played out a thousand times. As unlikely as it sounds, I can say with some confidence that John was able to see the future. It was written all over his face."

For a while, nobody spoke. The men on the screen appeared to be talking to one another, but their voices were muted. It made me wonder where the Warden's quiet partner was. After what felt like an age, another man gave the Warden a definitive nod. He straightened up and went over to the screens, turning them off. With just the two of us alone in the room, he turned to me.

"You have been granted permission to come to the site, to see if you can pursue this line of inquiry further."

"Where is the—"

He shook his head. "That's all the information I'm allowed to give. Don't ask any more about it, Harold—you're pushing your luck. You will find out when you get there."

He bade me rise and follow him out the door. As soon as it closed behind him, his stony face dropped. He chuckled to himself, shaking his head. "God, you're an obstinate bastard, aren't you? I was told you'd be difficult, but Jesus! Get your stuff together, man. A plane leaves in ninety minutes."

* * *

There are three people on the plane: me, the Warden, and his silent associate. The Warden is telling outlandish war stories and humorous anecdotes, but I've stopped listening. I'd even stopped looking out the plane window for some time. All there had been for a few hours was blue—stretches and stretches of watery desert as far as the eye could see. It was tiring to watch. Instead, I started to collect my thoughts together, to begin to write this letter.

Despite their desire for secrecy, I have told the Warden that these letters constitute a sort of scientific journal: a necessity if I am to offer my skills on this case. I must have notes to refer back to. I must make observations and links. I do not know how I will get these letters to you, Hattie. But perhaps knowing that I intend to will suffice, for now.

About an hour ago, we saw it. At first, the other two got up, moving toward the small portholes so they could each get a better look. When I followed, it took me a moment to work out what I was really looking at.

A massive ink blot in the distance. A scar on the horizon.

To call it just a mountain would be a disservice. It has the form and shape of a mountain, rising dominant above the sea and soaring up into cloudless blue sky. It appears to be made of rock, formed by the same geological pushes and pulls that create all the mountains on our planet.

But the size of it. Oh God, Hattie, the size!

I write this now as we approach, though they say it will still take a good hour. I hadn't wanted to lose my initial thoughts, but as we get closer I can barely find the words.

I traveled to Bhutan and India in the eighties, and have seen the Himalayas, with their mighty Everest. I was duly awestruck then, but *this*—this is something else. Something utterly sublime.

We are flying at a cruising altitude of some 30,000 feet and still the peak twists up high above us, as if trying to claw its way out of the world and into the heavens above.

I pressed my face against the window, looking upward as if I might find the gods of Olympus frolicking ahead of me. "How *tall* is this thing?"

The Warden walked over to me. "Initial estimates are anywhere between thirty-eight and forty-two thousand feet."

"That's impossible." My heart pounded at the immensity before me. "There's no mountain range around it. How could it have formed? We're in the middle of the damned . . . That's just not possible. How does nobody know this is here? How did *I* not know this was here?"

"Ah, well, that's just the thing, Harold." The Warden grinned wolfishly back at me. "Until a couple of months ago, it wasn't."

Dear Harriet,

I'm beginning to think that I should not have come to this place. The past day has been exhausting, a medley of introductions, briefings, and conferences. I have met new faces and heard about others, some I already knew by reputation. Everyone is treating this like it is a scientific expedition—an attempt to empirically explain a new and bizarre phenomenon. And perhaps that's exactly what it is. I must admit that the pull of this mountain is strong: the draw of the inexplicable, the desire to discover something completely and utterly new.

But perhaps this is all a tactic to avoid something else, something unspoken. I've spent most of my time with people who have arrived recently, brought from outside like me. There are others, though. Those

---

* **EDITOR'S NOTE**: This is first of the three letters that were posted to Harriet after Harold's disappearance. The preceding letters were found in his briefcase in St. Brigid's.

that have been here longer. I have seen the looks that they suppress when we walk past. I have heard whispers in the dark.

Not everything here is as it seems.

Our plane descended onto a landing strip that had been carved out of the rock. The bottom of this mountain doesn't really flatten out before reaching sea level, but rather continues to plunge downwards, making any kind of seaport impossible. Instead, a small plateau was found in the cliff and leveled out to create a short runway. There was little else there: a hut and a few unoccupied tents.

Without much explanation, we were bustled from the plane into a helicopter, the only vehicle able to land on the inclines further up. The Warden's silent associate stayed behind, waiting in the plane to return to whatever facility we had just left.

As we rose, I couldn't help but marvel at how, after all these years, nature is still able to surprise me.

The Japanese have a word, yūgen, for when one becomes aware of the immensity of the universe. It is, in part, a feeling of total insignificance and abject humility. A realization of how tiny one really is. But only in part, for it also intersects with a sensation of perfect peace and pure balance, a sudden understanding of one's place in the harmony of the cosmos.

Have you ever stayed up at night staring at the stars? If so, you may have felt the deep black of the universe washing over you gradually, creeping through the mind like water.

That is not what happened here.

The helicopter rose against the sheer wall of mountain, so tall and so wide that I could not see its horizon. All the windows were filled with the sight of rock. This feeling, this yūgen, did not settle over me gradually, but immediately drowned me in its boundlessness. I leaned backward, my mind blanking. Never before have I felt so inconsequential, Hattie. Never before have I felt so small.

At 15,000 feet, we arrived at Base Camp and I was thankful that I was able to put my shortness of breath down to the altitude and the thinning air. The others did not seem to be so affected.

"The helicopter can't go much higher in these winds," the Warden told me as I stepped out onto the rock. I had to hold on to the door not to be blown over by a giant gust of freezing wind. "We need to stay here for a while, to acclimatize. It's crazy—the human body—an amazing thing. Give it enough time and it'll suit itself to anything. But if you climbed any higher now your brain would swell up so big your head wouldn't be able to contain it. Then . . ." He pointed a finger to his head, grinning. "Pop!"

I raised my eyebrows, and he simply shrugged before he turned away. It seemed this mountain had multiple ways to remind me of my own mortality.

Base Camp was bigger than the arrival runway, a construction of about forty large portacabins tied down onto a rocky plateau. Tents were dotted between them and people bustled in and out, wrapped in gloves and coats. The ground crawled with military personnel, saluting as they passed one another, though they had no national insignia on their uniforms. As I watched them, it occurred to me that this operation was much larger than I had first thought. I must admit: it only served to heighten my curiosity.

I shivered in the wind, having brought little more than the clothes I left Taos with. Despite my eagerness to find out what was going on, a tiredness enveloped me—a deep exhaustion—and my stomach felt a little queasy. The altitude was already beginning to take its toll.

"Come on," the Warden shouted over the roar of the wind and the whirr of the generators. "Let's get you inside and warm."

He led me into a portacabin. It was small—about five meters by ten—and decorated with a military sparseness: two tables, surrounded by chairs. The walls were blank and gray, with nothing but a door leading to an adjoining office. A few people darted in and out, while a guard stood in the corner, motionless, his gun held tight against his body.

I turned to the Warden. "Where's Naoko?"

He put his hand up. "All will come in time," he said. "Just take a seat while I find out where everyone is, then we'll do a formal briefing."

I nodded, still very cold, and moved to an empty chair away from the door. Before long, a tall man sat beside me. His face was creased under a fringe of black hair, wrinkles blossoming around soft eyes. I guessed he was somewhere in his fifties. He handed me a blanket and a mug of something warm.

"I'm not going to call it coffee." He smiled, though I didn't miss his furtive glance at the guard by the door. "But on a spectrum with coffee at one end and mud at the other, it's just close enough to coffee that we accept the moniker."

"Thank you." I wrapped the blanket around me, looking down at my short-sleeved polo and pale, shivering arms. "I don't think I packed for the right weather."

"Difficult when they don't tell you where you're going. I saw you come in with the Warden—I figured you were another recruit. Nice to hear a British voice here, anyway. Almost makes me feel at home." He stuck out his hand. "Thomas. Thomas Fung."

I took it in mine. "Harold Tunmore."

He blinked, not letting go of my hand.

"Really?"

"Er . . . yes."

"The Harold Tunmore who cracked Shroffman's Dilemma? Who discovered the Eastern Ridge?"

I shook my head, a little uncomfortable. "Really, the Shroffman thing was a team effort. I was barely—"

"Wow. It really is an honor." He looked down. "Sorry, I'll stop shaking your hand now. It's just . . . well, it's nice to put a face to a name, you know?"

"How long have you been here?"

"A few days." He looked cautiously about him. "They don't tell us much. It seems like all of us have arrived just . . ."

He trailed off as the door opened and the Warden re-entered. "There will be a briefing at eighteen hundred hours. You have a little bit of time to rest." Looking at my watch, I realized that I had no idea what time zone we were in. "I see you've already met our geologist, Dr. Fung," he continued. "Perhaps he can show you around."

"How many of us are there?"

"Most of the team is up at Camp One," he said. "A good few thousand feet up. This is just a holding ground for new arrivals: you, Dr. Fung, and Mr. Towles, the young chemist who arrived yesterday. There are a number of other maintenance and supply roles that keep this camp running in a smooth manner, but you won't need to be dealing with them on a daily basis, just this smaller team."

"Then why . . ." I frowned. This was already a very complicated setup for what had supposedly been a recent discovery. "How many expeditions have there been?"

"All your questions will be answered soon, Harold," he replied. "For now, grab some food, get a tent, and unpack. We'll be staying at Base Camp for a night to acclimatize before we move upward."

I felt myself wanting to object, to demand answers, to ask about Naoko again, but as the Warden turned away from me, I knew it would be pointless.

Thomas leaned inward, his voice gentle. "I should show you where you can requisition clothes. And you'll probably want some food."

* * *

I decided to hold on to my questions, at the very least, until the briefing. Thomas was a courteous guide, but I was wary of trusting anyone too quickly. There was too much being withheld. I still hadn't seen Naoko. Despite all that had happened, the need to see her face, to make sure she was all right, was overwhelming. I could hardly focus on the immense mystery of the phenomenon beneath my feet. But one thing was clear—for all the authority with which this operation seemed to be taking place, not everything was as it seemed. We stood on an impossibly large mountain that had appeared out of thin air like magic. Why was the Warden acting like this was normal? Why was anyone?

We ate a quick meal—a spartan porridge dish with a tiny dash of honey—and Thomas showed me how to set up a tent to sleep near the others.

I, of course, could not rest.

There was still an hour before the briefing, so, once alone, I thought I would stick my nose where it didn't belong. Couldn't help it, really. Never could abide this much mystery.

Pulling on my new boots, just a couple of sizes too big, and a thick coat, I ventured out into the wind. I was surprised how quickly I was out of breath. While I hardly count myself an athlete, I've always prided myself on maintaining a healthy physicality, and yet in this altitude a short walk had me feeling like I'd just run a marathon.

Figures bustled in and out of the tents and portacabins, heads lowered and hoods up, carrying boxes to and fro. I hurried to catch up with one of them, my chest heaving, and walked alongside him.

"Hello," I managed. It was swallowed by the wind.

The man scurried on, not replying, and I fell back. Not to be deterred, I put myself directly in the path of another, who stopped short as I approached.

"Hi," I tried again.

"What?" It came out like an accusation. His eyes were sunken, his face lined with wrinkles so deep they seemed like cuts. There was blood leaking out of his nose. I shuddered, unable to help thinking of John, and, inevitably, his grisly suicide.

"I was hoping I could ask you some questions."

"Well, you can't," he replied, and pushed past me, disappearing into a portacabin and closing the door behind him.

I was about to walk away when I noticed the door creak open a little, like an invitation. I hurried over and moved to push it fully open, but it didn't budge. The man's wrinkled face appeared in the gap, his hand gripping the door like iron.

"Leave it alone."

"Leave what alone?" I asked.

His eyes narrowed, but he said nothing.

"What's happening here?"

His face disappeared, leaving only a black line between door and frame. I tried once again to push it further open, but it wouldn't budge. A moment later, his face reappeared. Except the lines on the man's brow and eyes were almost gone, the skin firm and pinking in the cold, as if he were suddenly ten years younger. I blinked, trying to resolve this trick of the light. He leaned forward.

"This is not for you."

The door slammed shut.

* * *

I arrived at the briefing room early. The little tent I had been assigned was small and, truthfully, I found being alone in it to be claustrophobic.

The room was another small portacabin, with seats laid out in a circle. Two more guards stood, gargoyle-like, at the corners. The only other person there was a very young-looking man with pasty skin and a head of naturally flaming red hair. As I entered, he looked up at me, half smiling, as though he instinctively wanted to say hello, but the harsh silence of the room seemed to quell his greeting almost immediately. One of the guards shifted. The young man looked back down to the floor.

I took a seat at the far side of the room. Before long, Thomas joined us. He sat next to me, but we did not speak. At one point, he opened his mouth, but then it fell shut before he let a word escape. Both men seemed racked by the same fear and anticipation I had felt the moment I saw this mountain, silenced in awe of its immensity. Thomas rubbed the finger on his left hand, and I noticed an imprint where a ring had once been. In our collective stillness, we waited.

I got up and poured myself another cup of coffee from the kettle in the corner. Every sound—every splash of water or clink of spoon—seemed to echo through the silence of the room like a trumpet. Sitting back down, I tried to catch Thomas's eyes, but they were closed, his head tilted slightly upward.

After what felt like an age, the door opened. A stocky brown-haired woman strode in purposefully, skin reddened by the cold. We turned to face her. Her expression was hard, the lines of her face tightened forward like a knot. Her hair was tied back into a taut bun and she was decked in a full military uniform, rigid and unmoving.

The Warden came in quickly behind her. She moved to the front of the room, and he went to stand at the back.

"Welcome to the site," she said, her accent American. "I am Colonel Palmer, and I am in charge of this expedition. You have already met Major Bautista."

She must have noticed our confused faces, because her mouth twisted in annoyance. "The major may have introduced himself to you as 'the Warden.'"

I turned in my seat to see the Warden, standing uncharacteristically quiet. My limited understanding of military hierarchy told me that, as a colonel to his major, Palmer was his superior. But in response to her jab, he glowered at the woman—it was an expression I had not seen on his face before. Palmer opened her mouth as if to say something further, but no words came out. Clearing her throat, she paused, looking across the room.

"I take it you three may have met each other informally, but for protocol's sake, I'm going to cover the basics. You are here as part of an expeditionary science team. You have been picked for your particular field of specialty—chemistry, geology, physics. The remainder of your team—our biologist and anthropologist—await us at Camp One."

I looked at the others for signs of surprise, but saw nothing. A biologist made sense, but why on earth did we need an anthropologist? Were there *people* living here?

"For now," Palmer continued, "I'd like each of you to give a brief introduction. Mr. Towles?"

The redheaded young man stood, giving the room an awkward wave.

"Hi, everyone. I'm Jet. I'm from New Jersey. I'm your chemist, I guess. I work mostly in private research these days, but I've got a standing contract with MIT for a bunch of stuff." He looked at Colonel Palmer, then back at us. "Is that enough? Should I . . . give an interesting fact? Say what my favorite food is? It's pizza, by the way. It's totally pizza."

I laughed, despite myself. It was a welcome feeling. A human feeling.

Palmer frowned. "That will do, Mr. Towles. You may sit. Let's continue."

I looked at Thomas and gave him a shrug, feeling a little strange about the forced formality. He smiled.

"My name is Thomas Fung. I'm a professor of climate sciences and meteorology at Cambridge University, and it seems I'm also your resident geologist. I'd like to say it's an exciting job, but mostly, well . . . it just gives me a lot of time to read. I must say this mountain is a marvel. It's an honor to be here with you all."

He sat down and the eyes of the room collectively landed on me.

"Ah, yes. Harold Tunmore. Physicist. I've always liked the term 'consulting physicist,' but somehow it's never caught on. Erm . . . I was a doctor once." I attempted a brief smile, but my lips faltered. "Anyway, just found out about all this yesterday. Nice to meet you all."

The Warden snorted from the corner. "Well, that's everyone except Roger. Looks like we'll have to wait a bit. Not that it should come as a surprise."

"Roger will be joining us soon," Palmer replied. "He assures me he will not miss it. However, I will not stand on ceremony."

She turned on a small projector and plugged in a laptop, a diagram of the mountain appearing before her.

"We are here to establish why this mountain is here and what it means. A range of anomalies were reported by the last expedition, which we believe you are best placed to investigate. The nature of these anomalies will be explained soon—this an expedition briefing, not a science briefing. The science is not my area. There will be a full scientific briefing at Camp One when we meet the rest of the team, Dr. Amai and Dr. Volikova."

I choked on my coffee, spluttering. "Excuse me?"

Colonel Palmer gave me a stern look, annoyed at the interruption. "What?"

"Did you say Volikova? Your biologist is *Polya* Volikova?"

"I did," she replied. "She is here on loan from the University of Moscow."

Blinking, I realized that I must have been giving her the same look that poor Thomas had given me earlier. Starstruck. Let me tell you, Hattie, that the Warden had been right in saying that Naoko was enough to draw me here, but if I'm honest, the opportunity to collaborate with Polya Volikova would have been almost as compelling. Her work on DNA sequencing and mapping the human genome is second to none in the entire world.

Palmer's voice interrupted my thoughts. "We are currently at fifteen thousand feet. Some of you will have noticed the change in altitude already. In time, your body will acclimatize to this and we will be able to move upward. Initial conservative estimates put the—"

The door flew open and a tall blond man in white-and-gray camouflage print strode into the room. Despite Palmer being mid-sentence, he walked directly across her path without giving her a second thought. At the small table, he proceeded to fill up a paper cup with water.

She closed her eyes for a half second, then she continued.

"Estimates put the mountain at thirty-eight to forty-two thousand feet, some ten thousand feet above the summit of Mount Everest. Current temperature is around zero degrees Celsius, and this will only decrease as we move higher up."

The man huffed, his back to us. He banged around with things on the table at the far wall, as though he barely noticed anyone else in the room was there, let alone receiving an important briefing.

"It's important to note," Palmer continued, barely betraying her frustration, "that the further up we go, the more pronounced some of the impacts of altitude become. There will be—"

The man downed his water in two or three extremely loud gulps. He turned around, crossing his arms and leaning back against the table. His face was handsome, with a square, clean-shaven jaw, his brows furrowed above bright blue eyes. Palmer glared back at him. He waved his hand toward us as if to say, *Well, get on with it.*

Palmer sighed. "Everyone, allow me to introduce Sir Roger Bettan."

He didn't move. "Nice to meet you," he sneered. "This playdate is just an absolutely fantastic use of my time. Look—I'm in charge of getting you up the mountain in one piece. Questions?"

No one spoke.

He glanced at Palmer and shook his head. Straightening up, he moved over to her computer and started tapping on the keys.

"You're a . . . mountaineer?" I asked.

"I'm a soldier." He didn't even glance upward. "Australian Special Forces, First Commando Regiment. And yes, I've climbed more mountains than you've even seen. Everest, K2, Annapurna. All of the Seven Summits."

"What do you mean, 'getting us up the mountain'?"

Palmer took a step forward. "The last expedition lacked mission experience. That's why Bettan is here—to ensure things don't go the same way."

I glanced over at Thomas, who shook his head in confusion. Bettan tapped Palmer's computer again and a detailed schedule appeared on the projector.

"This is our ascent calendar," Bettan said. "To fully prep you for acclimatization and the effects of altitude sickness. It's adapted to take into account the fact that you are novices in this arena, but we're still going to have to move more quickly than will be comfortable. We'll spend a night here before climbing to Camp One, a few thousand feet up, where we stay the next four nights. The helicopter can't get us much above this altitude—the air density is too low for the blades to work—so this will have to be done old-school. We rise to—"

He stopped short. Jet was holding up his hand.

"*What?*"

"I'm sorry," Jet said, "but I've climbed a couple mountains before; some were even big ones. That ascent schedule is ludicrously fast. There's no way we'll be fully prepped for the altitude sickness."

Bettan's eyes flared. "Oh, you've climbed a couple of mountains, have you? Well, my deepest apologies. Would you like to come up and take over?"

"No," he muttered. "I just—"

"So you just butt your head into something you know absolutely nothing about? Great. Good to know I'm working with idiots. If you'd kept your mouth shut and listened, you'd realize we don't have the time for anything else. This mountain is in the South Pacific, just below the equator, which means monsoon season runs until about late March. Do you know what that means?"

Jet stared back at him, floundering under his aggressive tirade.

"It's the only time you can climb a mountain this big," Thomas cut in. "The monsoon calms the winds. Without it, you're looking at over one-hundred-mile-an-hour gusts that'll throw you right off the cliff side. It would be impossible."

"*And* with a mountain this size, that window is tightened," Bettan continued, jabbing a finger at his ascent calendar. "We've got until end of February at the *latest*, or this thing closes off for good. The first team went early, but they failed. This is our one window and it's closing."

"Roger's done this sort of thing with a lot of teams," Palmer said. "If he says the ascent timing is possible, I believe him. This can be done."

Jet sat back in his seat, not looking convinced.

I raised my hand. Bettan glowered at me.

"What?"

"Excuse me if I'm being dim," I said, "but it seems to me we can do a lot from down here. Is it really worth climbing further up if it's so dangerous? Why do it?"

Bettan laughed. It was a strange, ugly sound. "*Why?* Because until about a month ago, I thought I had climbed the tallest peaks on planet Earth. Now I find out that something has gone and plonked an even greater one right in the middle of the ocean. Because this thing just got here and if we wait until the next monsoon, we don't know that this mountain will even be here anymore. There's only one thing we can do. There's only one thing possible to do if you've got an ounce of adventure in you. We're gonna climb to the top."

* * *

When Bettan finished, he walked out of the room. He did not wait for comments. Palmer quietly waited as the door swung shut behind him. I couldn't help but think of the fusillade of questions that were not being answered: What were we really here for? What was going on with the other camp staff? What actually happened with the last expedition? And, perhaps most importantly, *where on earth was Naoko?*

Now in front again, Palmer spoke, but this time her voice was quieter.

"As Roger said, the last expedition failed. Ten went up and only two—Mr. McAllister and Dr. Tanaka—made it back. We discovered them at Camp Two, trying to get down. The rest are presumed dead, frozen at the top of the mountain. That is what those who returned told us. We have not found their bodies." She paused, looking around the room for a moment before continuing. "While Mr. Tunmore is right, and there is plenty to study down here and at Camp One, the last team made the decision to climb. Our final communications with them were muddled, but it is clear that they found something important, something groundbreaking, something that we have *not* found yet down here. Our two survivors have not been able to properly communicate to us what happened. We intend to follow in their footsteps, but better prepared."

She looked across at our faces and must have been able to sense the trepidation.

"I will not lie to you and pretend that this is not dangerous. Climbing a mountain half this size is treacherous enough, and, yes, as I said, there have been some . . . anomalies. This is your opportunity to get out. If you do not wish to continue, there is a way back. The helicopter can take you down, and we'll radio in the plane. However, this time *will* be different. We have Dr. Tanaka with us, who has ascended the mountain before and experienced its challenges. We have one of the most seasoned mountaineers on the planet. Roger can be difficult, but he knows what he's doing. He has saved lives and guided dangerous expeditions safely countless times. This time, we will be ready."

She paused for a moment for questions, and while I had many, I wasn't entirely sure that they would be answered truthfully. The fact is this mountain *is* a challenge—not just a physical one, but a challenge of the mind. How is such a thing here? How did it come to be? The answers to these questions could fundamentally change how we see the universe. In the face of that, any concerns I had felt trivial.

"Get a good night's rest," Palmer said. "We meet here at first light tomorrow morning."

As we filtered out of the room, I watched her turn her back and pop what looked like a piece of nicotine gum into her mouth.

* * *

Back in my tent, I found myself unable to sleep. Several hours had passed and it was well past 11 p.m., but my feet were ice blocks. No matter how I shifted, the cold seemed to trickle its way into me. I thought, briefly, about getting up and making my way to the requisition tent to get more layers, but the sound of the howling wind kept me where I was.

Snow fell. The patter of heavy flakes drummed against the fabric of my tent, and as I stared upward, they merged together into dark shapes—shadows of figures against the moonlight. Now and then, one would become too large and slide onto the ground with a thump, making me jump.

A light flickered outside. I strained my ears, my body tightening. There were footsteps approaching. My pulse quickened. Who would be up at this time of night? And why?

The door of my tent unzipped and I jerked upward.

A mass of red hair shoved itself through the hole.

"Hi! I'm Jet. Harold right?"

"I . . . uh. Yes."

"I knew you'd be up. No one sleeps the first night here. I brought you some more socks." The door unzipped further, and a hand produced a plastic water bottle full of sloshing amber liquid. "You want a drink?"

I rubbed my eyes. "God, yes."

We sat in my little tent, wrapped in blankets that Jet brought. I don't know if it was the extra body, the extra layers, or the rum that we were working our way through, but for the first time since I arrived, I started to feel warm.

"How did you get this?" I asked. "They searched my bags."

He grinned. "Had to smuggle it in. Old college trick—you put the booze in shower gel and shampoo bottles. Nobody ever thinks to actually open those and check inside. When they came and recruited me, I figured this would definitely be a place where I would need some rum. Turns out I was right, but there's no point in drinking without someone to drink with, you know? So, sorry for breaking in like this. I can be a bit forward."

Smiling, I took a swig of the rum. "That's nothing to apologize for."

"You're Harold Tunmore, right? Like, *the* Harold Tunmore?"

I nodded. "I'm not sure I'm *the* anything, but yes. That's my name."

"You know what? When I found out who you were, it was a relief. You're a real man of science. I was worried you were another religious nut. You aren't, are you?"

I blinked, taken aback by the question. "No. Once, perhaps, but . . . no."

Jet grinned at me. "Thought so. Finally seen the light, huh? Well, at least you're not into that nonsense anymore."

I frowned. "You said *another* religious nut?"

"Oh." He rolled his eyes. "Thomas is nice enough, but honestly I've never really understood how people can be scientists and believe in God, you know? The whole knowledge framework is just completely incompatible. My parents were always on about it, forcing me to go to church when I was a kid, to chant hymns like I'm in a cult, and I always remember thinking, *You're such intelligent people! How can you not see the hypocrisy here?* Seriously, and this is going to sound awful, but as soon as someone starts going 'God this' and 'God that,' I honestly think they're an idiot."

I fell silent next to him, unsure how to reply. He looked shyly at his feet for a moment, as if he'd just realized he'd gone on a bit of a rant. I was about to open my mouth to fill the awkwardness, but he spoke first.

"How *weird* is all of this? Am I right?"

I laughed. "'Weird' is certainly one way of putting it. And confusing. U.S. military personnel, Australian Special Forces, scientists from Moscow—who's running this show?"

Jet shrugged. "No idea. And, I mean, I know I should be worried and concerned, but really, I'm just super excited. Think about it!" He waved his gangly arms in the air. "The implications of a mountain like this, well . . . that's if we aren't all experiencing some kind of mass hallucination, of course."

I passed him back the bottle. "You think such a thing is possible?"

"Highly improbable, but you know what Sherlock Holmes says about the improbable."

"'When you have eliminated the impossible, whatever remains, however improbable, must be the truth.'"

"Bingo!" He grinned again.

"But that's the rub, isn't it?" I said. The rum was working its way into me and I warmed to the conversation. "Figuring out what's impossible and what isn't? We are here, after all. This place exists. If nothing else, it tells us there are gaps in our understanding of the world."

"Well, that's why I'm glad it's not just me. Working out the mysteries of this place will be *fun*. And for us to be here, for *us* to be the ones to make these discoveries, to be the first to reach the summit. It's terrifying and thrilling all at once."

"You know," I said, taking the bottle back, "I think you and I might end up being friends."

"Christ, I hope so. Nothing worse than working with people who aren't your friends."

He leaned forward then, as if someone might overhear him. For the first time in the dim light, I could see his freckles, and the flicker of red in his eyelashes. He looked so young. "You want to know something weird?"

"Go on."

"I've started taking some samples of the mountain already, since I arrived. They told me most of the lab equipment is up at Camp One, but I brought some portable stuff myself. Couldn't wait to have a look at the chemical makeup of the mountain, the snow, the rock, things like that."

"And?"

"So—" His voice dropped as he looked left and right conspiratorially. "There's trace samples of magnesium, sodium, and even ammonium in the ice. I mean, that's not completely unexpected. Snow crystals have a way of scavenging chemicals from the atmosphere as they freeze. But once unfrozen, some elements—magnesium, for instance—are going to start to degrade or corrode."

"Sure."

"Okay—so I'd expect the amount of magnesium I uncovered and thawed to degrade gradually, in anywhere from a few weeks to a couple of months. Rough estimate. You know how long it took? *Five hours.*"

I rubbed my eyes, leaning back in toward him, both of us now talking in hushed voices. "How . . . Why do you think that is?"

"No idea. Maybe there's something in the atmosphere on this mountain contributing to it, but I can't identify anything." He shook his head. "It's like someone's taken a remote control and pressed the fast-forward button on the degeneration. It doesn't make any sense, but there's definitely things they're not telling us. There's something else, too. I spoke to some of the workers down here that helped build this camp. They seemed to think that—"

A thump came from outside. We both jumped.

"What was that?" Jet whispered urgently.

"It might have been snow. It's been—"

The tent door unzipped.

The Warden peered inside at us. "I see you're up."

I glanced at Jet, clinging to his rum bottle like a naughty schoolchild, and suppressed an urge to laugh. "What is it?"

"I need to talk to you outside, Harold." He glanced at Jet. "Alone."

Jet shrugged and gave us both a nod. If anything, he seemed relieved not to be in trouble. I pulled my gloves back on and trudged out into the snow.

"What's going on?"

"I figured you'd want to check in on her," he said. "Given why you came."

"Naoko?" My heart rate accelerated. "She's *here*? But I thought Palmer said everyone was at Camp One?"

"No—she had to be brought lower to reacclimatize. She was unwell. Altitude sickness, maybe. She's being kept in a cabin just over the way. I can take you to her."

"Being kept?" I echoed, incredulous. "What happened to her?"

"Just . . ." He put up his hand. "Just come with me."

I followed him out across the camp. Guards stood at the entrances to the portacabins, everyone else confined to their tents. At night, the area was mainly lit by dim electronic lights, flickering over the snow. A pale moon hung in the sky, clouds drifting across it. Shadows danced across the rock.

The Warden trudged forward and I hurried to catch up, finding my breathing once again heavy in the thin air.

"Why was she even on the first expedition?" I panted as I caught up to him.

The Warden frowned. "She's one of the most talented field medics in the world. Her work for the Red Cross in Ethiopia in the mid-eighties is the stuff of legend. You don't know this?"

I didn't reply. It had clearly been a busy ten years for the both of us. I hadn't realized that she'd also left hospital medicine, but I can't say I was wholly surprised. After what happened, nothing could have stayed the same.

"I didn't climb the mountain with her on the first expedition," he continued. "I was just in charge of vetting and recruiting the team, along with Colonel Palmer."

"But you're going up this time."

He nodded. "We all are. I feel it is . . . necessary." He was moving so urgently, so quickly, that I found myself falling behind. Icy breath caught in my throat.

"Please," I said, grabbing his arm. "Before we see Naoko. Tell me what happened to her."

"Don't worry. She's fine, physically," he said. "That's better than most. But she didn't come back quite . . . right."

"What do you mean?"

"It's difficult to say. I'm no psychiatrist. Paranoia. Psychosis. The symptoms were broad. I mean, you saw McAllister yourself. When we found them, huddled at Camp Two, he barely said a word. He just had that bizarre, serene look on his face. But there was nothing serene about Tanaka."

He trailed off, shaking his head, and pushed forward. I followed, my mind plagued with images—of Naoko, of John, of that room where he shot himself and the blood on my hands. We arrived at a small metal cabin at the perimeter of the camp. We were not far from the edge of the mountain, but it was too dark to see down. If I could, I think the vertigo would have been too much. The cabin had a single metal door, padlocked, for which the Warden produced a key.

"She's in here," he said. "For safety."

"Safety from what?"

"After McAllister? Herself, mostly." His hands stopped at the door. "Let me be clear: Your friend John was not normal, but he was coherent. He spoke clearly, logically, even if what he was saying was crazy. That was why they shipped him off to get a second opinion. But Tanaka . . . she's confused. Obsessive. She doesn't stop talking about the time. She demands to know the time every few hours. We gave her a watch, but she doesn't trust it. She records manically. After her first day back down at Base Camp, she asked for us to provide her with chalk and a blackboard, so she could mark up every day she stayed here. So that she could keep time. She said it had to be done. But she doesn't make a lot of sense. Not to me, not to anyone."

I put my hand on his shoulder, stopping him. "Why didn't we do this earlier? Why did you come to me in the middle of the night?"

The Warden lowered his voice. "Colonel Palmer didn't think this was a good idea, but I'm hoping a familiar face might help her. Are you sure you want to see her?"

I swallowed, careful to keep my voice steady, to keep the lid on the tungsten box.

"Absolutely."

"Good. Let me go in first," he said. "Stand just behind for now."

He pushed open the door. With no light illuminating it, the cabin was pitch-black. Only the cold moonlight shining in showed me a little of the inside. The Warden reached for a lever by the door and pulled it. A bulb hanging from the ceiling flickered on, flooding the room in yellow light.

My stomach tied into a knot. From just outside the door, I could see someone was there, asleep under a blanket. She stirred a little at the light. By her bed was a chalkboard covered in scraped, sharp marks. But that wasn't all. Chalk marks were scratched onto every wall, some in thick clumps, others standing alone. There were *hundreds*.

"How long has she been here?" I whispered.

"Twelve days."

I fought the urge to rush over to her, to wake her and hold her.

The Warden shuffled forward. She rolled over in her bed, sitting up and looking at him. Her expression was stern, her whole figure sedate. My mind grappled with the dissonance. My mental image of her was from years past, and her features had not only aged, but hardened. Where she had once been open, she looked aloof. Distant. As if she was in some other dimension and I was seeing only a fragment of her. And yet, here she was. I opened my mouth, but nothing came out. What does one say to the Ghost of Christmas Past? Especially when that ghost seems to have aged more than you.

"Dr. Tanaka?" the Warden said. "There's someone here to see you. Someone you might know."

At his prompt, I took a deep breath and stepped into the light.

She looked at me for a long, hard second.

And then she screamed.

* * *

I'm back in my tent. Jet had gone by the time I returned. I'm trying to sleep, but I can't. I'm still so damn cold—my feet, my fingers, my whole body. I can't seem to get them warm. All I can see is her face—the round O of her mouth and the piercing wail that came out of it. It wasn't fear, I don't think. It didn't sound like fear. It was sadness.

It's all flooding back to me, the choices I made, the memories I've had to bury. I can't do this. My hand is shaking from the cold. From the worry. I can write no more. Not tonight.

I wanted to talk to her, Hattie. I wanted to ease her pain and her sorrow, whatever it was, but I couldn't.

I just couldn't.

She wouldn't stop screaming until I left the room.

My dearest Harriet,

We began the climb to Camp 1 at sunrise, taking advantage of the warmth of the day. Daylight is all one can rely on up here, and Bettan said we would need every hour of it.

Our team was ten strong as it stood, with the two more up at Camp 1 waiting to join us. Thomas, Jet, and I had basic packs—water, flashlights, essential climbing and medical gear. Bettan, Palmer, and the Warden each had much larger packs than ours, with extra food and water and more climbing gear for the treacherous parts. With us were three other men, one I recognized to have been one of the guards from the day before.

They were briefly introduced to us as Privates Parker, Sanderson, and Miller. They did not speak to us. Covered as they were in thick gear and balaclavas, it was difficult to tell them apart. On their backs they carried larger oxygen tanks, and they reminded me of scuba divers preparing to submerge themselves in an unwelcome deep.

By all of their sides, I saw both a rifle and a shotgun. It sent a bristle of cold down my spine. The questions about bringing along an anthropologist rose into my mind again.

Who are we expecting to encounter? What are we expecting to find?

Naoko was at the front, just behind Bettan. She hadn't screamed at me when they'd brought her from her shack—but she hadn't looked at me, either. I'd kept my distance as we prepared this morning, in the dark. I couldn't tell if she remembered the previous night. Colonel Palmer was just behind her. She was the one who insisted Naoko join us, as the only surviving member of the last expedition. Naoko had seen things, of that much Palmer was certain, but whatever had happened, she seemed incapable of either remembering or expressing it. Palmer hopes it will come back to her as we climb. I'm not sure if I agree.

The rest of us followed in a line, tied to one another with climbing rope. It had been Palmer's decision to keep Naoko front and center, as the frailest among us. I was grateful to Palmer for that, if uncomfortable that Naoko should be climbing at all after what I had seen. But looking ahead at her, I couldn't help but think she was not frail at all—she walked with her small back straight and focused, as if the altitude and the climb meant nothing to her. She didn't wear a balaclava, like the rest of us. I suppose she'd been up here much longer than the rest of us.

Unlike Naoko, I was already exhausted. The lack of sleep in the night and the thinning air made my whole body feel a hundred years old. Wind pummeled my face and my eyes immediately began to water. I shut them against the ferocity, cursing myself for not wearing goggles, and the water froze my eyelids shut. Painfully, I pried them apart, the ice pulling against my skin.

I tried to put my head down, focusing on my steps. But I couldn't keep my eyes off Naoko ahead, pushing up the mountain. All I could think about was how I would approach her again soon, and what I would say.

My foot caught on a rock and I stumbled. The rope ahead of me tugged as I slipped, keeping me upright, but lurching everyone sideways. The combined inertia was enough to keep them on track, but they still jostled.

"Christ!" Bettan's voice called back. "You lot are about as coordinated as a drunk on ice skates. *Watch your feet.*"

"Sorry," I muttered, only loud enough that Thomas, behind me, and Jet, just ahead, could hear. The Warden brought up the rear.

Jet looked back and through his balaclava it looked like he was trying to give me an empathetic smile.

"Don't worry about that guy," Thomas said. "You're doing fine."

The terrain was difficult—an incline of about twenty degrees up shifting layers of rock, scree, ice, and snow. The thick boots we had on clung to snow well enough, but when the ice subsided, we were faced with the deeper issue of scree—tiny rocks and chips of stone scattered across the ascent. Every step became treacherous, the surface ready to either skid away, taking your foot with it, or send a tiny avalanche of rocks tumbling into the climber below.

While Bettan claimed the weather was ideal, the freezing wind found its way into all of my clothes, regardless of the number of layers. I thought I'd started to acclimatize, but the altitude still wore on me like increased gravity—my body felt heavier, each step like lifting a giant rock. Liquid dripped from my nose, the thick trails freezing to my face.

"You'll need to suck it up," Bettan said to us at an early break in the climb. "We've barely left Base Camp, and you already look like a bunch of sweaty cadavers. Focus. If you're flagging now, you'll never make it past the first ridge."

I bit back my reply. I would not match his insults with my own. From the moment he appeared, he had been unnecessarily crass and uncaring. I would not let him imagine we were all the same. Not for a second.

In time, the patches of rock gave way to more and more snow, until all that lay beneath us was a white nothingness that seemed to stretch onward without limit. We had been walking for what felt like hours. Days, even. And I knew we were nowhere near the next camp, let alone the summit. The sun was still low in the sky. This trek would take us all day and it was barely close to noon.

We trudged onward.

Time seemed to stretch and I wondered for a moment how long we'd been climbing.

I was staring at the ground. My whole face felt heavy, my forehead pushing downwards as if I were being forced asleep. I touched my balaclava and my glove came away with dense ice that had been building on my face. But for its weight, I had not felt it there. My skin was too numb.

When I looked up, Naoko was in front of me.

Right in front of me—like an apparition—obscuring everything else from view.

I almost jumped backward from the shock. There was a deep purple bruise on her face that hadn't been there this morning, running from her right eye and all the way down her cheek. It throbbed in the cold wind.

"I'm sorry," she whispered. "I got confused."

"Naoko," I said, reaching forward. "Are you okay? Are you—"

"Harry?" Thomas said from behind me. I turned to see his concerned face. "You okay? You stopped."

"I—" I looked back in front of me.

There was no one there.

Just the ascent, and Naoko still near the front of the group, marching forward.

The exhaustion and the altitude were making me hallucinate— that's what it was. A vision, a mirage, no more.

Focus on the climb, I told myself. *Focus on the steps.*

I shook my head and took another step forward.

"Sorry. Just having a moment."

"I get it," Thomas replied, his breath heavy. "Never thought I'd climb a mountain. Never really been that outdoorsy."

"I hiked an alpine crossing in New Zealand," I replied, wheezing a little, trying to clear my head of that strange apparition. "But, dear God, nothing like this. We barely felt the altitude there."

"I don't think there *is* anything else like this. It's magnificent," he said. "It's like glimpsing heaven."

I groaned. The cold seeped under my skin and into my very bones. If this was heaven, I was in no rush to get there.

At the top of the next ridge, Bettan signaled for us to stop and rest. I grunted, pushing through the last few steps so I could just sit down and catch my breath. I had not expected the climb to be this demanding already.

But when I arrived at the ridge myself, all of that was forgotten. Looking down from that high vantage point, we could see the entire path we had climbed—a sea of white that dipped down and spread out into a shining canvas of blue. Where the mountain met the ocean, the perfectly blue sky melded with sea, stretching outward to infinity.

The sun beamed down on my face, ripples of welcome warmth melting the ice and massaging their way across my skin. It glinted off the ice and water, making the entire vista glitter. There was a smoothness to the snow that streamlined and clarified the view. Looking down at them, jagged spires became rolling white hills; rock and scree flattened. The whole landscape unified.

Almost as one, like an exhalation of breath, we turned away from the sea and looked at the towering behemoth that loomed ahead of us.

Nobody spoke. Words felt insufficient, out of place. In the face of its magnitude, simile and metaphor felt ridiculous.

This mountain—it rejects language. It renders it impotent. All that exists in its place is an utter disbelief, and an almost religious awe.

* * *

I've thought about God a lot over the past few days, Hattie. Dreamed about Him. It's strange what old faces will do to you. I've not wanted to think about Him for many years now. The whole time you've known me, I've done whatever I could to avoid the thought of Him. I'm ashamed to say that it brings me too much pain.

I am not a believer.

I was, once. And wasn't, before that. My relationship with Him, as with most things, has had its ups and downs.

When I was a boy, things were quite the opposite. I didn't believe He existed, Hattie, but I missed Him. I had a nostalgia for faith, even though it was something that I had never really experienced. This is, perhaps, the most toxic kind of nostalgia—egged on by envy of those who I could see believed, *truly believed*, in divine purpose. My parents and their community of churchgoers were so assured of their place in the universe, of what they meant to it.

Oh, I went to Mass, and to Sunday school, and I studied my Bible. I wanted to believe so much that I thought I could make myself do it. If I bashed myself over the head with God enough, He would eventually find a way in.

But He didn't. Not then. All that I was left with was a deep sensation of something missing. Something that had maybe been there once before, but was long gone.

That all changed with Naoko.

This might seem strange to you, but when I first moved in with Naoko, I felt a little like a fraud. You see, Hattie, my whole life I had never felt at ease with others, never quite understood the complex boundaries of white lies and withheld truths that define acceptable social interaction. Math and science and numbers and angles made sense to me. People did not. I'd survived by imitation, for the most part, even if that imitation never quite worked.

I had never been in a romantic relationship before, and all I had gleaned of what they were *meant* to look like had come from observation of others, of media, of the world. And so I tried my best to emulate that, to make her happy, but much like my belief in God there was something about it that rang false.

I remember cooking her dinner one night, a month or so after we got our new flat. I wanted to make it a special occasion, something nice that I could do for her, to demonstrate that I could be nurturing, too. Now, you know how terrible of a cook I am, Hattie, and it was no different in those days. In fact, I was probably worse.

At first, she was irritable. The kitchen had always been her domain and she was possessive over it.

But I *tried*. I followed the recipe precisely: chopped onions so finely they disappeared and grilled the chicken for twice the time recommended, just to be sure.

The whole procedure was extremely stressful.

When I'd finished—and to be honest, I can't even remember exactly what it was that I had attempted to cook—she took a bite, looked at me straight in the face, and burst out laughing.

"Harry, this is terrible."

I sighed. "I know. I'm sorry."

She wiped tears from her eyes. "Did you enjoy doing it?"

I hung my head. "Not particularly."

"Well, why did you do it?"

"Because . . ." I said, getting a little frustrated. "That's what people do, isn't it? That's what normal couples do. Cook dinner for each other."

She shook her head, smile still creasing her lips. "Not if you're awful at it, it's not."

The part I remember most clearly, more than anything else, was that she took my face in her hand and said, "I don't need you to pretend to be like other people, Harry. That's not why I'm with you. I'm with you because you're *not* like other people. Because seeing the world through your eyes, I see it differently. And also"—she gestured at the food with a small giggle—"because you're frequently ridiculous and it's very funny to watch."

I leaned into her embrace, laughing with her now at the mess I'd made, but I couldn't stop thinking about why I had done it. It was then that it occurred to me that she never, for a second, stopped to think about whether what she was doing was normal, or how it would be perceived by others. She lived for herself. She did what she believed was right.

I hoped that maybe I could learn from that.

When we took Santi in, he was still recovering physically. He had contracted pneumonia from sleeping out in the snow, and had lost two toes to frostbite. The hospital had to amputate them. But we had taken him home, and, with Naoko's care, he was getting better. The same, unfortunately, could not be said for his emotional state.

Naoko took a leave of absence from work. While she'd had days off before, she'd not taken her full complement of annual leave in the last five years. As such, the hospital allowed her an entire month, during which she stayed home and cared for him, nurturing him back to health.

There was a determination born in her like I had never seen before. A fire. She worked tirelessly—during the day when he needed hot soup, blankets, and a warm presence in the room to read to him; at night, when he would wake in terror and needed to be held as he shook, rocked by the storms inside his head.

After the month passed, we agreed we'd be able to survive on one salary. From the look in her eyes, I knew there was no real choice to be made. She quit her job, and I left them each morning to fight off the onslaught of the day ahead.

We never quite found out what happened to him, not the specifics. The Pinochet regime was still in power and there was never any news of his parents. The past was determined to remain the past, refusing to be dredged up except for in his nightmares.

I don't know how old he was then, but our guess was between seven and eight. Too young. Far too young. And because of his trauma, he acted like he was a lot younger.

Despite the connection I'd felt with him in the hospital, I can't say I had a relationship with him in those days. He still wasn't speaking and would barely even look at me. I never saw him during the day, and the hospital made me work most weekends. When I would come home, he would hide from me, like I was some sort of bogeyman or a kidnapper out to get him. When I turned the key to the front door, I'd hear the scurry of feet as he scrambled to get out of the living room and hide somewhere—a cupboard, his room, the bath.

That didn't upset me. Not really. What upset me was that he felt that he had to hide, and whatever had happened to him to make him this way. But I didn't feel spurned. It was never about me.

I did miss Naoko, though. She would spend most of her time with him, because he needed it. It was hard not to feel like I was missing out, too. Not so long before, we would put our feet up together at the end of a long day, with glasses of red wine and a quiet candle whispering away in the corner. We would put on the TV and talk all the way through it—about life, about medicine, about the world.

Now she was too busy bathing him and putting him to bed to take much notice. And by the time she had finished, she was so tired that all she wanted was to sleep herself. We sometimes made a point of staying up and watching TV like we used to, but it wasn't the same. We didn't talk through it. We didn't say a single word.

It was difficult not to resent that. I told myself that it wasn't Santi that I resented, but the situation. But that wasn't true.

And with that resentment came an overwhelming guilt that I didn't know what to do with. It sat on me all day, like a beast on my shoulders. It whispered in my ear, reminding me that, for all the images I had of myself being a good person who did good things, it was a narrative to cover up my own self-centered desires.

I did the only thing I knew how—I worked harder. When I was home, I took over every chore that I was capable of doing—laundry, shopping, cleaning the flat. I washed up all the dishes, even when I had to eat my dinner in the other room. I took care of everything I could and left nothing for myself. I was exhausted, upset, almost broken.

But the guilt lifted, if only a little.

Eventually, Santi wouldn't hide as much when I came home. I'd see his little face poke out from around the corner as I walked through the door: wary, but curious. He'd dash over and come to see what was in my shopping bags. He loved bread, any kind of bread, really, but bagels were his favorite. If there were any there, he'd grab them and run away.

He still wasn't speaking yet, after almost eleven months. We didn't know if he ever would.

But Naoko's love for him was immeasurable, and it was abundantly clear that would never change. When she suggested we file adoption papers, there never felt like any question in the matter. It had become inevitable—this boy was a part of our lives now, and he always would be.

As time passed, I would come home and Santi would be waiting for me by the door. Not always, not every day, but enough. Naoko would be crouched down beside him, smiling and cuddling him, and when the door opened a huge smile would break out onto his face. He would coo, a low "*oooh*" of happiness that warmed up the entire room, and run to me, hugging my legs.

In those moments, I felt no guilt at all. Because I felt no resentment, or sadness, or exhaustion. Only love, deep and strong as a river, rushing through me.

One evening, when I was bathing him, he reached up to me. He was holding a little boat that we used to play with in the bath and waved it at me, cooing. It was covered in bubbles.

"What is it, Santi?" I asked. "What's up with the boat?"

He giggled at me, waving it.

"Too many bubbles?"

He nodded his head, then said, "Bubbles."

I can still remember that word—his first word to me—to this day. The clarity of it. The certainty.

"Bubbles?" I repeated.

"Bubbles."

I leaned forward and placed my forehead against his. He dropped the boat, and his hands came up to either side of my face. He held me there, our foreheads touching, and cooed a little. And suddenly there were more than just two of us in that room. There were three: in that little space between Santi's face and mine, there was God. I felt Him, stronger than I have ever felt anything in my entire life.

Without thinking, I spoke. "I love you, Santi, you know that, right?"

He smiled, gave a definitive nod, and said, "Bubbles."

It was at that moment, in that little bathroom in our flat in London, that I believed.

* * *

I don't know why those memories came back to me on that ascent. Perhaps the freezing snow reminded me of him out in the cold. Perhaps seeing Naoko pried open the box I have worked hard to keep closed, if only for a moment before I could shut it again. It has been many years since I have thought about them. I had locked them away, with so many others, and I must be careful that they don't get in the way now. There is a clear task ahead of me: I must find out what caused this mountain to appear, what made Naoko the way she is, and I must help her overcome it.

* * *

It must have been about one o'clock when Naoko started screaming. I felt it first—a tug on the rope, being pulled forward. We stumbled as one, pressing our boots into the snow for traction. Then I heard her over the wind—wailing and shouting at the people in front. My eyes flicked up: she was struggling with the rope, trying to unclip herself and pull her body free of our train.

Palmer darted forward, grabbing her before she tumbled to the side.

"Let me go!" she screamed, pushing back. "Leave me alone! It *watches*. You should *not* be here, all of you . . ."

Bettan swung round and placed his hands on her shoulders, shoving her to the ground. I tried to dash to her, but I hadn't unclipped my rope and it lurched Thomas forward. Naoko was still shouting.

Falling to my knees, I looked up in time to see Bettan lift his hand and smack her hard in the face. Her head twisted and she shuddered, falling back into the snow and going silent.

"What the fuck?" I shouted, unclipping my harness and storming up the rise.

Bettan twisted round to me. "Get back in the line."

"Get away from her!" I pulled her up beside me, looking at her face. She stared down at the snow, her eyes locked on the ground, her cheek red.

"Naoko, are you okay?"

She didn't reply. She didn't look at me.

"What the hell are you thinking?" I said, glaring at Bettan.

"Cut the sentimental bullshit," he replied. "She's a loose cannon—if she's going to behave that way, she deserves the consequences. If she's coming up with us, she needs to stay in line."

Palmer came up to stand beside him. Two of the guards appeared behind her, but she put up her hand and they stayed back.

"Is that how you get people to follow your lead?" I spat. "By beating them?"

Bettan took an angry step toward me.

"Let's all calm down," Palmer said, pulling him back.

Bettan scowled at me. "Don't expect any sympathy from me just because you and Crazy here used to be lovebirds."

My breath caught in my throat. My eyes flicked to Palmer. "You told him? Did you tell everyone?"

Bettan laughed. "I'm fucking your mother and she talks in her sleep, that's who told me. Get over yourself and *get back in line*. We've got hours to go yet and I don't have time for this."

I stepped toward him, my fists clenched, until a hand fell on my shoulder. I twisted round to find the Warden leaning over me.

"Come on, Harold. Let's go. It's not worth it—not here."

I took a deep breath, turning back to Naoko.

She looked up at me. A bruise was developing, just below her eye, running the length of her cheek.

I had seen that bruise before, on the climb.

This had already happened.

"I . . ." I muttered. Images of John's bloody suicide flickered through my head. Of a face suddenly becoming younger. What the hell was going on?

"I'm sorry," Naoko muttered. "I got confused. Let's go."

"But—"

She turned her back to me and took a step forward. *"Let's go."*

There was nothing I could do. This wasn't the right time. I threw Bettan one last dirty look before trudging back toward Jet and Thomas.

"Alrighty!" I heard him shout behind me. "Let's get this shit show back on the road, shall we?"

* * *

About an hour later, the encounter was still on my mind. We were pushing up an icy rock face when Palmer announced that we would be taking a short break to eat some of our snacks and rest for ten minutes. Everyone spread out. The Warden went to talk to the soldiers, and I watched Palmer deliberately place herself as far from him as possible. She sat down and popped another piece of nicotine gum in her mouth.

Thomas sat beside me, his face wrapped in thick layers and goggles. We didn't speak much at first, each individually trying to recover our breath, hoping that the food would settle our nauseated stomachs and fight back our altitude headaches. The wind howled around our ears.

While we were eating, Jet came to sit next to us, too, flickers of his bright red hair peeking out from his balaclava.

"Hey, man. What the hell happened up there earlier? I just caught the end of it, but that all seemed . . . pretty intense."

I waved my hand, unable to explain, not sure how to express what I'd seen. "Tensions are high. It's a dangerous situation. I'm just . . ." I shook my head, glancing over the rocks to where Palmer was now talking to Bettan. He was a simpler topic; one I understood well enough. "I'm not sure how much longer I'm going to be able to last being led by that man—I don't think I've ever seen such a self-centered narcissist in my entire life."

Jet glanced over at him, and then, for a split second, at Naoko. I could see what he was thinking, even if he didn't say it: *Bettan's not the liability on this expedition. She is.*

"Sure, he's a dick," Jet said. "But if he's competent, does it matter? I mean, I get it, that was totally uncool. But if he can get us all through safely, isn't that the most important thing?"

"Pride like that never leads to anything good," Thomas muttered from beside me, lifting his goggles to take us both in.

Jet frowned. "There's nothing wrong with a bit of pride. It's good to be proud of things. This isn't about *sin* or something, is it?"

"I didn't mention sin," Thomas replied, his wrinkled eyes soft. "You did."

Jet raised his eyebrows at me and shook his head, but left it at that.

Palmer gestured for us all to come together, and we stood in a circle, coats and hats tight around us to keep out the wind.

"Eyes up," Bettan said. "We're coming up to an icefall. It's a section of constantly moving and melting ice that's hard to predict. It moves at about the rate of three meters a day, which doesn't seem much, but if it's anything like Khumbu Icefall on Everest, expect sudden shifts, falling ice, and unexpected crevasses. The ground is treacherous here. Don't fuck around."

He gazed purposefully at all of us, as if he were giving a challenge.

Nodding at the soldiers, he said, "The boys and I went ahead a few days ago to set up ropes to get you across. Once we cross, we'll be just a short half hour or so from Camp One. We're changing position, so Palmer takes the lead along with Sanderson, Parker, and Miller, and I can keep an eye on you lot. You clip yourself to the ropes, and you go straight. No stopping, no stargazing, no talking to one another. We've dawdled enough already and we'll be out of sunlight if we spend too long. If there's an issue, I'll fix it. I don't lose anyone on my team. Clear?"

We nodded our assent.

"Is that fucking clear?"

"Yes," we said, all together. I resented myself for saying it even as the word came out of my mouth.

One by one, we climbed the ridge ahead, but when I got to the top, I had to stop.

As the ridge crested and dipped down into a small valley, the view before us opened out. I shielded my eyes: shimmering, pearlescent light glittered as the afternoon sun spread across the landscape. On each side of us, the sheer cliffs of the mountain rose, certain and impenetrable. In between them was a river of diamonds. Partially melted ice was broken up into various shapes and sizes that jostled and swirled against one another, refracting the light at a thousand different angles. Blue dominated the palette, a spiraling mixture of light sky and deep sea, but there were other colors, too: glints of fiery red and orange, tiny stars of yellow, and beneath that, the deep, almost magical white of the icefall.

But there was little time to marvel. A tug at my rope told me I was slacking.

We followed in a line, one by one, across a ridge of ice that had been fastened with a rope. It extended like a bridge across the icefall, just barely wide enough for one of us to stand. The ground was pure ice, covered with a thin layer of snow. Our boots crunched against it. Now and then, the snow thinned and our feet would slip a little.

Every step was dangerous. We advanced slowly, excruciatingly slowly. Our packs were tight on our backs, but heavy, changing our center of gravity.

The flow of ice beneath us crackled and moaned as it moved, percussion and vibrations creating an otherworldly music to accompany our crossing. The wind whistled its trebles over the creaking bass and we were all deadly silent, as though sullying this eerie atmosphere with words would be blasphemy.

We had been told the icefall should take about an hour to cross, but the slow, quiet, advance began to feel like an eternity. On the far side, at the end of this ridge, the flow diverted and the ascent path turned back into rock. Our destination: safe, sturdy ground.

Pillars of ice stood on either side of it, like white guardians.

We kept walking.

A deafening crack exploded in my ears.

The whole ridge shuddered, and my foot twisted on the ice. I lurched sideways, my hands grasping at thin air. My feet scrambled for a hold. My left boot landed on a crust of thick snow and I caught myself. Panting, I straightened.

Just in front, Jet slipped and fell sideways. His whole body careened backward as he hit the ice, sliding down the side of the narrow ridge.

"Aaa—" His shout was cut off by a sudden jerk as his line caught and he stopped, suspended in midair. The rope we were attached to pulled taut, keeping him in place. My waist tugged forward, the carabiner cutting into my back, and I bent my knees to hold fast.

He dangled. His hand went to his chest. "Ouch."

Bettan was already with us—though how he had made his way round Naoko I hadn't seen. Reaching down, he grasped Jet's hand and pulled him back up.

"That's why we have safety ropes," he said. "For fuck-ups like that."

"Whew!" Jet shouted. "That felt like an earthquake!"

"You're on an icefall, idiot." Bettan shook his head. "A big pack of moving ice. Guess what? It moves."

I helped pull Jet back onto the ridge and settle him on his feet. Bettan, happy that Jet was properly clipped in, turned away. With a deft little jump, he leaped off the ridge, his line pulling taut against the rope as Jet's had done. But here, he used the momentum to swing himself round Naoko—like a monkey—until he landed perfectly on the icy ridge ahead.

I marveled at his footwork, thinking about how each of us had been taking every step at a snail's pace.

This was not treacherous ground for a man like Bettan.

About three-quarters of the way across, another gunshot-like crack rang through the mountain. Ahead of us, a huge pillar of ice—one that I had thought was mostly rock—fractured at its base. It stood at the end of the icefall, directly above the rocky exit that would be our safe passage.

The top of the pillar slid, letting out a nail-biting screech as ice cut against ice. It began to topple.

"Everybody hold on!" Bettan shouted, and seized the rope. *"Hold!"*

We scrambled to do the same as the obelisk, some ten meters high, fell like a dead weight. It smashed into the pillar on the opposite side and the whole valley shook again, but this time we were ready.

My feet pressed into the ground hard, my arms clinging tight to the secure rope. The ridge cracked underneath us, and felt like it would tear apart, but it held.

We were safe.

Or so I thought.

"Shit!" Bettan shouted. "Right, we're gonna have to move quick now. Really fucking quick."

"What is it?" the Warden shouted from the back.

Bettan pointed up at the pillar. It hadn't quite hit the ground, but instead lay half-fallen, suspended against the other pillar it had collapsed into. It still creaked and moaned, gravity and ice fighting with each other to take control.

"That thing isn't going to hold very long. It's gonna fall soon, and when it does . . ."

He didn't need to say the rest. Directly underneath the pillar was the narrow rocky path out of the valley. The outcrop where our secure rope line was attached.

Our one exit.

"We go fast and we go now!" he shouted back to us. "Watch your feet, hold the rope, no slackers. Palmer sets the pace."

And with that, Colonel Palmer pushed forward.

It wasn't quite a jog—it couldn't be. The ice was still too treacherous and the path too narrow. Even clinging to the rope, we couldn't get much speed. But we tried. Throwing caution to the wind, we walked as fast as the route would allow.

I was light-headed from both the adrenaline and the altitude. I tried to take deep breaths, but it felt like there was nothing there.

One foot in front of the other.

My chest tightened in pain.

If we made it, I could rest. I could stop. I could breathe.

I tried to keep my eyes on my feet, not on the ridge below. As we got closer to the end, the crevasse on each side deepened—the drop was now five, then ten, then forty or fifty meters. My stomach twisted with nausea as I was pulled forward by Palmer's pace.

One foot in front of the other.

The pillar let out a loud creak. My eyes snapped up to see how far we were, and I saw Naoko slip.

Her left foot slid down the ice and she tumbled.

I gasped, sickness rising into my throat.

In a single move, Bettan swung round and grabbed her line with his glove, tugging her upward.

Back on the ridge, stable, she straightened up and Bettan pushed her to keep moving.

Another almighty crack shot its way across us. The ground shuddered. A fracture cut halfway up the fallen pillar, twisting across its surface like a lightning bolt.

"Go, *now!*" Bettan shouted.

Palmer doubled the pace—we weren't jogging. We were *running*.

Running on a thin strip of slippery ice, above a sea of diamond shards and death, secured by one measly rope.

My legs were burning. My lungs were aflame.

One foot.

In front of the other.

The exit was just twenty meters ahead.

We were going to make it.

We were going to make it.

I felt the pillar fall before I saw it. I was too focused on my feet. On my balance.

When the ground convulsed, I clung for dear life, twisting my body into the rope for security. But it was no use. The falling pillar tumbled into the mountain right where the rope was secured and the line snapped.

The safety rope fell slack.

Still leaning into the rope, a half second too late, I fell, tumbling onto the ridge. My chest slammed into the ice, pain shooting up through my ribs. I scrambled, slipping over the edge, down into the crevasse.

A fruitless battle against my own weight, against gravity.

I tore at the ice, trying to get a handhold, but there was nothing.

Just screams.

All around me.

Screams.

A hand yanked my jacket collar and jerked upward. Twisting, I saw Thomas—panting with exertion. With one hand, he clung to a pick lodged into the ice. The other pulled me back onto the ridge.

"Thank you," I panted, lying flat on the ridge. "Oh God, thank you."

My eyes darted over the scene: the pillar had fallen, smashing against the exit, but not covering it completely. There was still a narrow passage through the wreckage. Still a way out. Palmer was already there, some fifteen meters ahead, helping people through. Nobody had fallen. Everyone was still with us, some on the ground, some clinging on with their picks. Bettan stood tall, somehow still maintaining perfect balance. He was shouting something at us, but I couldn't hear it over the wind.

Then I saw it: the ridge itself was cracking.

The ground we were standing on.

The impact had sent a fissure down it—it was tearing apart.

"Let's go!" Thomas urged, his hands under my arms, trying to drag me to my feet. Ahead, I saw Naoko cross onto the safe rock, then Jet.

I stumbled forward, electrified by panic, adrenaline running through me.

The ice cracked again and we scrambled, holding on to each other.

The ridge still held.

When we were just a few feet away, Thomas jumped, dragging me with him, and we tumbled onto the rock, the Warden close behind us.

Safe.

A wave of relief washed through me.

I stood up, my body aching. I looked back at the treacherous passage we'd just crossed, panting, trying to recover my breath. But there was something odd out there: two black lines on the other side of the icefall. I frowned, trying to make out what they were.

"Can you . . ." I tried to say, but it came out as a wheeze. No one was listening. Everyone was in recovery. Now on safe ground, we'd all unclipped ourselves from the tether, taking a moment to rest.

I strained my eyes. They weren't lines.

They were people.

Two figures on the ice—faces covered by balaclavas. Somehow, they were down on the icefall itself, looking up. They were pointing at us. One of them was tied to a rope, being pulled halfway up a cliff.

"There's someone down there." I turned to the others. "Can you see them?"

Naoko appeared next to me, her voice soft and distant.

"I . . . know them."

"What?"

She didn't reply; instead, she took a few steps forward, off the rock and back onto the icy ridge we had just escaped.

"Naoko, wait!" I reached to grab her arm, but she slipped away, like a ghost.

She didn't stop—she kept walking forward, reaching out, transfixed by this vision. Five steps, then ten. Not looking where she was going.

When her foot hit the crack in the ice, it split. The ridge tore open with a violent tug, as if in slow motion, and she tumbled.

I was frozen in place.

There wasn't time for her to grab anything.

There wasn't time for her to run.

The hungry earth opened up beneath her.

In between heartbeats, a figure dashed past me.

I stumbled backward in surprise, falling to the rocky ground. I recognized the figure as, without breaking stride, he slammed a heavy pick into the ice, a rope attached to his body.

With an almighty leap, Roger Bettan threw himself off the cliff, down into the dark beneath us.

He met Naoko in midair.

His arms wrapped around her falling body as he hit her, tugging her inward. The rope pulled taut as they both swung back to the rocky cliff face. He twisted as he hit the wall, his shoulder and arm protecting Naoko from harm.

They dangled there for a moment before I got over my shock. The rest of the crew were in motion all around me, pulling at the rope. We joined in together, tugging Naoko and Bettan up, up, up, until they were back on the safe ground.

When Bettan stood up, he stood tall. The icy winds blew the tassels of his coat upward and pushed through his hair, and, for a bleary second, I felt as though I was looking upon some kind of mountain god—not a man, but a force of nature. He looked like he had barely broken a sweat.

He leaned down and offered Naoko a hand, pulling her up.

"I told you," he said. "I don't lose anyone on my team."

I stepped forward clumsily, putting a heavy hand on his shoulder. "Thank you," I said. "Thank you for saving her."

He looked at me in disdain and rolled his eyes.

"Fuck off."

* * *

We arrived safely at Camp 1 just before dusk—some tents and cabins haphazardly built into the rock face. It was smaller than Base Camp, but there were still all the signs of a larger operation: tents for each of us, portacabins, tables and chairs. I wondered how many people had crossed that treacherous pass before us, and how many had not survived.

There is to be a science briefing in the morning. We are all too tired to talk tonight. I ate a quick meal and retired to my assigned tent, wrapping up as warm as I possibly could.

I tried to thank Bettan again, but despite his heroics, he seems just as much of a bastard as he ever was. I'm trying not to hate him, I am, but I'm not sure it's working.

I don't know how you're going to get these letters. There's obviously no way to post them from here. I've decided to keep writing them, though, and collect them together. Maybe when I see you again, it'll make for a good story. Maybe we can read them together, you and me, by a roaring fire. Maybe, if I'm still alive.

I must rest. I have not spoken to anyone about the people that Naoko and I saw. I have not talked about the man with the shifting face, or the vision I had from the future. I am still not sure who to trust. There is something about this place—the altitude, the cold, the sheer colossal size of it—that oppresses the mind. I do not want the team to think me crazy.

I will speak to Naoko tomorrow, about what she saw. I will find out the truth.

I have to.

We are not alone.

My dearest Harriet,

I dreamed of falling last night. There was no slip or tumble. No false footing that dropped me from a ledge, no jump off a cliff.

Just falling, through black and void.

I could see nothing but darkness. Nothing to tell me I was falling but the wind against my face, the cold on my skin.

There was no bottom. No end. No sense of time. Just an eternal fall.

And despite the lack of sense—no touch or smell or sight or sound— I felt someone falling with me, through the dark. There was someone else there, just too far away to reach. My fingers stretched out, grasping for them, but found only air.

I woke up cold. Sweating. Panting.

I don't think we should have come here, Hattie. This is not for us.

* * *

The scientific briefing had been scheduled for first thing in the morning. The night, for all my strange dreams, was a restless one—a mixture of tiredness, fear, intrigue, and what I assumed must be jet lag. There has been so much confusion over the past few days that my circadian rhythm seems to be completely out the window. I slept fitfully, in short segments. An hour here, a couple of hours there. The biting cold didn't help, and while I wrapped myself heavily in layers of clothes inside my sleeping bag, my feet remained freezing the whole night through. I pray that you never feel this cold, Hattie, not even in your coldest of winters. It is not something any human being should be subjected to.

Living in the modern world has caused a strange forgetfulness in me. My brain doesn't expect to find a cold that cannot be fixed with a turn of a dial, a darkness that cannot be cast away with the flick of a switch. I have forgotten what the wild is really like: inflexible, heartless, uncompromising.

When the sun rose, it was a relief. A new day ahead, and hopefully some answers to the many questions I had.

My head felt a little less clouded than it did yesterday. The Warden was right, my body was already beginning to acclimatize to the altitude. I started to question some of the things I had seen—were they really visions of the future, or just imaginings of my oxygen-starved mind?

As I stared out at the horizon, it occurred to me: this mountain is a desert. There is just snow and ice and the purity of the high-altitude sunlight. Nothing living exists, no animal or plant. Man's very nature tends toward places rich in life—cities built near rivers and coasts, on edges of streams. And yet here we were, trudging upward. This should not be. We do not belong.

Turning, I looked up at the peak, still so high above us. Its gargantuan immensity loomed over me, forcing me to contend with the uselessness of our expedition, the utter pointlessness of it all. The absurdity brought with it a sharpened sense of our mortality. I found myself thinking of Naoko, wondering if she was okay. The image of her falling returned again and again to my mind. This was no longer some scientific fancy, some curious expedition. Yesterday's events brought that into clear focus: decisions up here are life and death.

Was it worth it?

I needed to get to the briefing. Regardless of my fears, there were too many mysteries up here to leave behind. I was determined to speak to Naoko individually, but first I hoped that she might share with us what she had experienced. On the way to the portacabins, I couldn't help but notice that here, too, the three soldiers we had brought took shifts patrolling. They spread across the camp silently, like parts of the landscape, never digressing, never deviating from their prescribed paths.

I walked up to one of them and held out my hand. "Harold Tunmore. I can't believe I didn't catch your name."

"Private Parker." His voice was gruff and curt, the ends of the syllables clipped off. He gave my hand a brief, firm shake. Perhaps one of these men could give me some of the answers that I'd been looking for.

"And how did *you* get roped into this?"

He shrugged. "Not my place to ask questions. Got given my orders and they shipped me out."

"Ah yes, of course. And which facility were you stationed at?" I probed.

He smiled and raised his eyebrows a little. "I may be just a soldier, but I'm not an idiot."

I laughed. "No, obviously not. Well, it's cold out here. If there's anything I can get you, just let me know. You're doing a fine job. Can't believe you're out here on your own. Has it been all night?"

"Thank you, Harold. It's my watch. I took over from Sanderson at midnight, and Miller got a night off to have a beer in his tent. He gets grumpy if he doesn't get some alone time with a beer at least once a week."

"Well, I can empathize with that. Just to be clear, what *are* you keeping watch for again?"

Parker's smile grew a little wider—and for all his gruffness, it was surprisingly kind. "I'm just trying to keep you alive. Good-bye, Harold."

With that, he turned around and walked away.

I briefly entertained the notion of following him, but the commotion from the briefing cabin ahead caught my attention.

"What I'm saying is we should be *told*." Jet's voice came carrying just over the wind, thin and loud enough to pierce through the walls. Muffled voices responded behind the closed door. I climbed the metal steps and opened it.

Jet and Colonel Palmer stood facing each other.

"We don't even know what we're doing here," he insisted. "Not really."

"You've been told everything we know so far," Palmer said. She was standing opposite him, her arms crossed, her face tight. Thomas sat quietly beside them. "We've not lied to you at any point."

"A lie by omission is still a lie," I said, entering the cabin. She turned to look at me. "Let's be honest here: we don't know who you work for, so, by extension, who *we're* working for. We don't know much about this camp or how long it's been here. We know almost nothing about the last expedition. You talk about how you've assembled some of the best minds in the world, and yet you expect us to believe naively when you say you've told us everything. Given the circumstances, that seems stupid."

"It is not our policy to disseminate information before it's confirmed. Speculation doesn't help anyone."

"Oh, come on," Jet replied. "Isn't it exactly our job to speculate? Isn't that precisely why we're here? If we're going to risk our lives up here, if we're going to *die* up here . . ."

The door slammed behind me. I turned to see the Warden looming.

"It seems to me that we have a scientific briefing scheduled," he said calmly. "Designed to answer your questions about the anomalies on this mountain. And yet, you are delaying the start of this briefing by complaining that questions are not being answered. That seems a little counterproductive."

Palmer's lips drew together in a thin line. "Thank you, Major. I was just getting to that."

He smiled graciously, and she turned away from him.

"If you'd please take a seat," Palmer continued. "We have a couple more introductions to make."

We settled, but there was an underlying current of tension that bubbled through the room. Dissatisfaction. Distrust. In many ways, our leaders shouldn't have been surprised. They had hired investigators; were they really to believe we would investigate only where they pointed us?

Things were being hidden—that much was clear—but the promise of some answers to this mystery mountain was enough to get us to be quiet.

The Warden took a seat with us, facing Palmer with a smirk on his face. And though he had just come to her aid, I couldn't help but feel that he was aligning himself with us. That battle lines were being drawn.

I looked around the room. Thomas was sitting in the corner, sifting through notes. Naoko was not there. Nor was Bettan.

Palmer gestured through a door to another section of the cabin and two people came out. The first was an older lady—a pale face full of wrinkles and character—dressed in surprisingly spartan clothing for the current cold: just trousers, a blouse, and a thin gray cardigan. She carried a thick briefcase.

Behind her, a tall man, a good way over six foot, entered. By contrast, he seemed to be wrapped up too much. Gloves, hat, scarf, the full mountaineering works, even though we were protected from the bitter wind. His gait was a little off, as though he had a limp, or was stumbling. He sat in the corner and crossed his legs.

The woman stood at the front of the room and opened her briefcase.

"This is Dr. Polya Volikova," Palmer said. "Our biologist and scientific team leader. And this is Dr. Neil Amai, our anthropologist. They arrived about two weeks ago."

Polya pulled out a laptop from her briefcase and placed it on the table. I stared at her, both wanting to speak and unsure of what to say. It is a strange thing to meet one's idols: When you see them in the actual flesh it is as though something is missing. Something doesn't quite fit. I shouldn't be sitting here, I thought, opposite a scientist of Polya Volikova's caliber, just as I shouldn't be sharing a table with Da Vinci or breaking bread with Galileo.

It was clear that she would be leading this briefing.

"This is Camp One," she said. Her Russian accent was thick, her voice hard and wintry. "It is important we establish a baseline for our anomalies before we climb further. Who is the geologist?"

Thomas put up his hand.

"Good," she said. "You begin."

"Hm?"

"Your observations so far." She gestured at the front of the room, and then sat down. She pulled out a small journal and a pen, looking at him expectantly.

"Oh." He stood up tentatively. "Yes, well. Okay, then." Walking to the front of the room, he frowned, taking a moment to compose himself.

"Well . . . we're definitely on a mountain." I laughed, though nobody else did. Thomas gave me a grateful smile. "And the thing about mountains," he continued, "is they're contingencies of geography and of time. It may have only appeared a few months ago, but all mountains come from the earth—the rock tells us stories."

He leaned back on the desk, falling into a steady rhythm of speech.

"When mountains are formed, they are forced up by deep geographical forces over millennia—the top is ages older than the bottom. Ascending, in many ways, is less like moving upward through space than it is like moving backward in time. Victorian geologists used to call mountains 'the great stone books'—they are the archives of our planet. With the right tools, we can read this one."

"And what have you read?" I asked.

"A very strange tale indeed. When we first arrived, I noted that the base was formed primarily of batholithic rock, my guess is Mesozoic from the makeup, which makes sense for this part of the world and this area. It's undoubtedly complete madness that a mountain of this size doesn't have a mountain range accompanying it, but I'm just going to have to shelve that query for later. As we have moved up, however, that rock shifts to a mixture of Cenozoic-era sedimentary rock and what seems to be Precambrian metamorphic rock, which is geographically completely different. Now we're at Camp One and I'm starting to see more batholiths and granite under the ice, *on top of that.* It's almost as though someone has chopped up three different mountains and put them on top of each other."

"What could have caused this?" Polya asked.

Thomas shrugged. "No idea. If it were possible, I'd have said it looked like this mountain's been traveling."

Jet looked up. "Traveling?"

"Like it's spent some time being pushed out of the ground in Asia, then a bit of time in the Americas, then somewhere else. The rock is . . . well, it's from *everywhere*. And that's . . . well, that's really all I have."

Polya nodded, taking a note in her journal. "Good. Chemist?"

Jet looked at his hands and then up around the room. He glanced at me first, then over at Palmer in the corner. "I don't have anything to share right now. I . . . I need more time with the equipment up here."

"Noted," Polya replied, barely pausing. "Physicist?"

I walked to the front of the room, all the while wondering what I should share and what I should keep to myself. Was Jet doing the right thing here? We were not being trusted with all the information by those above us, so how much should we trust them in return?

And where was Naoko? She had seen more than any of us—why was she not a part of this?

"I don't have any concrete evidence," I said, clearing my throat. "But we've got some extremely clever people in this room and so I'd like us to consider a thought or two together. I've been brought here to consider physical anomalies, presumably as to how a mountain of this size can appear out of thin air, but the main thing that has been on my mind since we arrived has been time."

Polya raised her eyebrows, but said nothing.

"There are now twelve of us up here at Camp One. At Base Camp, there were many more. Did any of you talk to them?"

Palmer shifted uncomfortably at the back of the room. The Warden cast a glance over at her, but she ignored him. Nobody spoke. The wind rattled the portacabin walls like an intruder trying to break in.

Thomas put up his hand. "I asked one of them how long the camp had been here. He didn't want to tell me. But I pressed him, and he said *official establishment of the camp was six weeks ago.*" He shook his head. "It's an odd thing to say, but I can't help but feel like he sounded bitter when he said it, or even mocking."

"They think they've been there for years," Jet said quietly. "Decades, even. I tried to tell you down at . . . But honestly, they weren't being very clear."

The Warden's mouth opened just a fraction of an inch, and he glanced at Palmer again. She gave him an almost imperceptible shake of the head and his mouth fell shut. Another small interaction—but it confirmed a suspicion I had been harboring for some time. They both knew this already.

How much are they hiding from us?

The Warden sighed. "Well, it's clear whichever member of camp staff you spoke to isn't making any sense."

"And yet," Thomas said, slowly treading back into the murky waters of the conversation, "I couldn't help but feel, when I was talking to them, like I was the one not making any sense."

"Okay," I said. I didn't want to antagonize Palmer and the Warden more than was completely necessary. "And the survivors of the last expedition. If we're talking about temporal anomalies. Naoko was . . ." I paused, looking around the room. It felt strange talking about her when she was not there. "She was recording time. She seemed to think she'd been here longer than she actually had as well. And then there was John—who I met after he was taken off this mountain."

"He claimed he could see the future," Palmer muttered. I raised my eyebrows, surprised at her joining in.

"Not claimed," I said. "Whatever it was he could do, there was no fakery about it. He possessed some kind of insight into events that had not yet come to pass. So, here's my thought experiment—if we take this to be true, what *could* cause such things to happen?

"Things slow down as you approach the speed of light. Relativity, right?" Jet piped up, his earlier frustration overshadowed by the problem at hand. "Now, I know we're not zooming through space here or anything. But isn't that a similar phenomenon? Time moves more slowly for people who are on spaceships traveling that fast than it does for the people back home."

I nodded. "Or gravity. Einstein posited that if you approached a black hole, time would slow down, or even stop, due to the immense gravity. In fact, the closer you are to a body that emanates high levels of gravity, the more time slows. It happens on an infinitesimal level, but technically time moves slower for people on the ground than it does for someone at, say, the top of a skyscraper, because they're further away from the planet."

"Man, I remember the first time someone told me that." Jet turned to me, a childlike wonder in his eyes. "And it always still gets me. The universe is just so damn cool."

I couldn't help but smile at his optimism, despite the circumstances—his joy at the strange workings of the world. He reminded me, for a half moment, of Santi and the pleasure he took in learning small new things. But as that memory came to me, so did a blackness, weighing down heavy on my mind.

Silence filled the room. The door banged in its frame, the wind violent.

"So," Thomas added, filling the gap. "Either we're moving close to the speed of light, or we're next to a black hole. Interesting. And for seeing the future?"

"I'm not sure," I said, trying to regain focus. "It's too early to make conclusions." I thought of the vision I'd had of Naoko, and the people we saw on the ice, but no longer wanted to mention them. Palmer and the Warden's behavior were making me uneasy. I wanted to have those conversations with Naoko alone first.

Polya Volikova got up out of her seat and opened the laptop on the table. She plugged it into a projector, which flashed with light and then failed to connect. She muttered something frustrated in Russian and banged the computer with an open palm. The projector screen flickered to life.

It occurs to me only now, Hattie, as I try to write and remember all of this, that Neil—the anthropologist—didn't say a single word.

Polya gave a crooked smile.

"Microbes are very important. I've been studying the ones on this mountain closely," she said. "People forget about microbes. They are small and so people think they are irrelevant. This is arrogance. It is the bacteria and the microscopic life forms that make environments what they are, that make species look how they look, that guide evolution and set the playing field for complex life. If we want answers to anything, we must always look at them."

She clicked a button on her computer, and photographs of the landscape outside appeared.

"The first thing I did was to take a sample of microbes from the snow, the rocks, and the air present here. There are no obvious types of flora or fauna at this altitude from which I could garner them. There had to be some care to make sure that the microbes were not ones that had been brought to the mountain by us, but ones that were indigenous here. This involved traveling further than anyone at camp had been and bringing them back. I did this. The microbes showed me something very interesting."

Polya tapped the computer again and another slide appeared on the projector screen.

"This is taken from a microbe that resembles common protozoa. They are free-living eukaryotes. Alive and not obviously parasitic."

It took me a moment to realize what I was seeing, and to confirm in my head what she was showing us. Others in the room—those without a background in biology—frowned, turning their heads this way and that.

"Is that DNA?" Thomas asked, squinting at the spindly figure against the black.

Polya shook her head. "Not quite. This is the sample under an electron microscope. I had to send the sample down to Base Camp and then get the image sent back up."

I leaned forward, looking closely. "Except . . . something's odd about it."

Polya smiled at me. "It is ribonucleic acid arranged in a double helix structure," she explained. "It is the primary storer of genetic information for the living microbes on this mountain. That is all we can say for now. More study is needed." She shrugged and sat down.

Breath caught in my throat. My chest was ice.

Jet, sitting next to me, shook his head. "That's impossible."

Looking around the room, I could see we were split into two camps—amazement and confusion. Those of us who understood the implications of what had just been said, and those who did not. Thomas was the first to speak up.

"Look, I'm just the geologist here—can someone explain this to me?"

"You know what DNA is, yeah?" Jet asked.

Thomas frowned. "Of course I know what DNA is."

"If Polya is right. If . . . if *that* is right—" He pointed at the picture. "Then the eukaryotes on this mountain appear to be built not on DNA, but on RNA. It's a single-stranded molecule. It doesn't have a double helix structure. It doesn't form the base of living things. It . . . it just can't!"

"No, I get that," Thomas replied, scratching his head. "Fine. That's weird. But given everything else that's happened here, why does everyone look like they've seen a ghost?"

"Because all life is based on DNA," Jet said, turning to him. "*All* of it. DNA might as well be the definition for what life is. There's been speculation that ribonucleic acids could carry genetic information in life, but there's no actual examples of it. This . . . this is . . ." He shook his head. "She might as well have just shown us proof of life on Mars.

Alien life. Even then, I would have expected DNA coding. RNA is a catalyst—it pushes on the chemical reactions necessary for life, but it isn't the building blocks. Life isn't built on RNA."

"That's not strictly true," I said. Jet turned to me. "Viruses are. Some viruses have even been shown with double-helical structures."

"Yeah, but viruses aren't alive, though," he pressed, pointing at the screen. "Polya's talking about microbes. About life. *Life*."

"So you've discovered a new species?" Thomas asked.

"No. I mean, yes," Jet said. "But this is more than just discovering another species. New species get discovered all the time. This is discovering an entirely new definition of what life actually is. This is . . ." He took a deep breath, then seemed to sag back in his chair. "This is the most important biological discovery since . . . I don't even have a comparison, it's that big."

Silence dominated the room. There were a mixture of expressions: Polya looked surprisingly unfazed, given the immensity of her revelation. Thomas's brow was pulled tight. Neil looked bemused and both the Warden and Palmer were serious. Jet was gazing down at the floor, muttering to himself.

"What is it?" I asked, leaning toward him. "What are you thinking?"

"It makes sense that they're just microbes," he said. "RNA is far less stable; the radioactive breakdown alone—there's no way it could sustain complex life. Too much energy is needed. There would be too much mutation."

"That's true."

"I'm also thinking about LUCA."

"LUCA?"

"Last universal common ancestor," Polya said. "I, too, have been thinking about this."

"It's pretty commonly assumed that all life originated from one place," Jet explained. "That everything, from bacteria to ostriches to seahorses, all came from a single ancestor. But not these microbes—can't be. But if there are two LUCAs, then . . ."

"Why are the microbes only found here? On this mountain?" I nodded. "Yes. It doesn't make any sense."

Thomas chuckled. "Nothing about this place makes sense."

"Which," added the Warden, stepping forward, "is exactly why we're here. You asked who is in charge of this, and what they want. You asked who hired you, but I don't have clearance to tell you that. What I can tell you is that on this mountain, there are new ways of looking at things. And I can't help but feel this is just the beginning. We are here to find out what we can learn from it, and what we can bring back for the world. Imagine the good we can do with what we discover here—the advancements in science and technology, in human knowledge. That is why we are here."

Jet looked up at me, a harsh urgency in his eyes. "We have to go higher. We have to keep climbing. If this is what we discover by ascending a few thousand feet, imagine what else lies further up, at the summit . . . imagine!"

I frowned, a little surprised at his sudden fervor. But the Warden was right—there was something special here. It would be irresponsible *not* to study it, to discover whatever we could, for the world, in case it disappeared.

As I write this, Hattie, I am reminded of that time we hiked the Grampian Mountains, and the line from Petrarch's sonnets we both saw scrawled into the rock at the peak of Ben Nevis: *"Where another mountain's shadow cannot rise, up to the highest, freest peak of the chain, an intense desire draws me."**

Perhaps we did need to go higher, to ascend.

Perhaps *that* is where we would find our answers.

---

*EDITOR'S NOTE: From Poem 129 of *The Canzoniere*, translated by Stephen Monte.

* * *

When the briefing ended, most left. Colonel Palmer went through the door into the other section of the cabin. She gave the Warden a quick look and he followed her. Thomas leaned over to me.

"You know about those two, right?" he whispered.

I shook my head, pulling in so I could hear him.

"One of the soldiers was telling me about it, before you got here. How he knew, I have no idea. I think the Warden and Palmer go back."

"Telling you about what?"

"Apparently, they used to be married, or so the man said. Years ago, back when they were both in the army."

"Really? And they're working together now?"

Thomas smiled and leaned back in his chair, shrugging.

I sat back, processing this new information. "So, they're not in the army anymore, are they? Whatever this operation is, it's not the U.S. government. I think we've both realized that. So who do they work for?"

Thomas shrugged. "Who knows? But the colonel title is definitely not an official one."

"And 'the Warden,'" I added. "That's not military. And Bettan— how is Australia involved? Is he even acting on behalf of the government, or is he just a free agent?"

"Ah, yes—our illustrious leader."

I shook my head. "How can you stand that man? He's so utterly self-involved."

Thomas laughed, putting a hand on my shoulder. "Oh, trust me, I know what you mean. But you saw him at the icefall. He knows what he's doing."

I sighed. "I know that. I've seen it. I . . . don't know why it rankles me so much."

"I do." Thomas smiled. "Because you're a good person, and there's something about that much pride that's always been synonymous with evil."

"What do you mean?"

"There's a reason that on almost every list, from Evagrius Ponticus through to Cassian and Dante, pride is considered the original and most serious of the deadly sins. It is the perversion of everything that brings us closer to God."

"Ah," I said. "I'm not sure if that's my issue."

Thomas raised his eyebrows. I looked around the room—it was empty but for the two of us. The chill from outside had entered the portacabin and I pulled my coat around me more tightly. The wind had died down a little, but the door still rattled in its frame.

"I can see you're a deeply religious man," I said. "And I respect that. But I . . . let's just say God and I are not on the best of terms."

"Doesn't make a difference." He shrugged. "God doesn't care if you believe in Him or not. Or if you love Him. It doesn't change the fact that when we are at our most holy, when we exhibit dignity and humility, when we are closest to God's image—that is when we feel our most human."

I shivered, lifting my scarf up to cover my chin.

"You're a geologist, right?" I asked.

Thomas nodded.

"And you're clearly very intelligent. You're not discounting things like evolution, or the big bang, are you?"

He laughed. "No, Harry. But geology is humbling. The more I study it, the more I understand the deep time scales that this planet works on. The grand designs that we can barely comprehend. Nothing is really what it seems on the surface. Over a long enough time frame, rocks bubble and liquefy like molten seas. Oceans freeze and stone folds like an ironed sheet. It's breathtaking to think that among these giant movements of the planet, we exist here. As improbable as it is, *we* exist. That's no accident."

A howl of wind screamed outside and the door slammed in its frame. I jerked involuntarily, sitting up. The temperature was dropping and I was cold, so very cold, even in the protection of this porta-cabin. Getting to my feet, I shuffled over to the corner with the terrible instant coffee, hoping that it might do something to warm me up.

"But surely," I pressed as I fumbled at the electric kettle, "you've seen enough to know that Christian dogma is mostly stories invented and adapted by humans over the years. It's a book of tales. It's all fiction."

"Of course it is," he said from behind me. "Fiction is where the soul lives. What I'm talking about isn't new. The first ever dramas to be put onstage, the Greek tragedies, were about men with too much pride, *hubris*—losing their relationship with the heavens. Christianity, like drama, is just a human expression of the soul, of the holiness inside of all of us. Do you know what C. S. Lewis said about pride?"

I shook my head, gesturing for him to go on. The kettle was already bubbling, boiling faster than usual in the altitude.

"'Unchastity, anger, greed, drunkenness, and all that, are mere flea bites in comparison: it was through Pride that the Devil became the Devil. Pride leads to every other vice: it is the complete anti-God state of mind.'"

I turned around, the hot coffee cup prickling my freezing hands. "Are you comparing Bettan to the Devil?"

Thomas laughed. "Of course not. He's a man, just like we all are. But in convincing himself he's better than the rest of us, by refusing to acknowledge his flaws, limits, and wrongs as a human being, he exposes them. He severs himself from his own divinity. You can see this. It is why it bothers you so much."

I fell silent, listening to the howling wind. Though he couldn't have known it, he had touched a deep well of pain. One so deep, Hattie, I had almost tricked myself into thinking it was gone, but at his words it reappeared in me, even for the briefest of moments.

Thomas seemed to take my silence as a cue to leave, and gave me a little pat on the shoulder before disappearing out the door and letting it close behind him.

I'm not sure how long I sat with my thoughts. I didn't want to go outside in that wind, even for the short walk to my tent. I cradled my bitter coffee and waited for the hot liquid to warm me through.

After a while I heard voices rising. They were muffled behind the closed door to the other room, but the tone was clear. An argument next door, where Palmer and the Warden had gone.

I rose to my feet carefully, realizing that they must have thought everyone had left, and inched toward the door. I pressed my ear against it, but it was pointless. The wind outside rattled the metal frame of the portacabin and drowned out the conversation. All I could hear was metal clanging against metal.

Reaching up, I gingerly twisted the handle, pushing the door open just a half inch, then an inch.

". . . acting like you're still in charge here, like rank means anything in this situation." The Warden sounded more exasperated than angry.

"I'm trying to stop another expedition from dying." Palmer's voice shook with a poorly bottled fury.

"And you think I'm not? How does it help them to keep them in the dark? To not share what we know?"

"We don't *know* anything! That's the whole point. If you think I'm going to share baseless rumors that will do nothing but incite panic in the ranks—"

"The ranks? You're not at war anymore, Grace. You left that behind. We both left it behind, and for good reason."

"*You left* . . ." Her accusation cut off, choked by anger. I could hear her breathing to keep herself under control. "I'm not talking about this right now. I'm not bringing up all of the shit from the past."

A beat as long as an age passed. When he spoke again, the Warden was calm and measured.

"If Naoko Tanaka tells the others what she saw out there before they hear it from us, we'll lose any trust that they might have."

Another beat.

"If Tanaka can screw her head on long enough to actually make sense," Palmer replied, "then maybe we'll all learn something about this godforsaken place. Until then, I'm not jeopardizing my expedition based on the fantasies of a madwoman."

"It's not just your expedition," the Warden muttered.

"It is. And you know it. If you want me to radio in to Apollo to double-check that, I'm more than willing to call your bluff. I'm not as scared of them as you are, Steve. Now back off."

Hearing footsteps, I scurried toward the exit and stepped out of the portacabin into the snow.

I write to you now, Hattie, as I warm up before dinner. After dark, when everyone is back in their tents, I will go and find Naoko. I need to make sure she is all right. I need to find out what has been done to her.

I *will* get to the bottom of this.

My dear Hattie,

My thoughts are in a jumble. My mind is circling.

I must begin, I think, by telling you about my confrontation with Naoko.

I call it a confrontation now, in retrospect, but I never planned it to be such. In my head beforehand, it was to be a reunion, a reconciliation, perhaps even—forgive my sentimentality—a homecoming?

None of the above took place.

Once night had fully settled in, I left my tent. My headlamp had proven a little faulty, so I tucked a large flashlight in my jacket pocket just in case.

As I trudged through the snow, my headlamp dimly lighting the

---

depth of night ahead of me, a hand landed on my shoulder and I jerked, spinning around in panic.

"Where are you going?" The guard—Parker—stood over me. In the darkness, he seemed even larger than before, looming over me like a statue.

"I'm just going to check on a friend. I'm allowed to do that, aren't I?" I gave him a little nudge, remembering his friendly smile. "Or am I to be confined to my tower like a princess?"

He frowned, his eyes wincing in the glare of my headlamp. He reached over to it with a large hand and turned it down. "I'm just keeping an eye out, Harold. For your own safety. Just make sure you don't leave the camp."

"Wouldn't dream of it," I said. "Unless you'd care to tell me what you're so diligently keeping an eye out *for* in this barren icy landscape?"

He didn't smile this time.

"I like you, Harold," he said, his voice hardening. "Don't stay out here alone for long."

He turned around and disappeared into the night.

When I got to Naoko's tent, I called out, but she made no reply. There was a shuffling inside and I could see movement from behind the folds, so I knew she wasn't sleeping. Cautiously, I unzipped the door and pushed my way in.

She was in the corner, bent forward over a small table. Her long black hair was draped over her face and shoulders, and in this light she seemed skeletal. A small electric lamp gave the tent a dim orange glow and her thin shadow loomed large on the fabric behind her. She didn't turn to look at me, absolutely focused on the task at hand. And out of nowhere, a wave of old memories hit me hard in the chest.

She was carving a netsuke.

* * *

At the sight of it, I was back in London. I was in our flat, warmed by the fire, the smell of fried gyoza and tonkatsu still wafting out of the kitchen after dinner. Hunched over my writing desk in the living room, I was tucked into the corner because Naoko had cleared the middle of the room for her carving. She was bent forward, intent, with her knife.

Apart from my small desk lamp, the flicker of the flames in the fireplace was the only light in the room. She preferred it that way. It cast wild shadows onto the walls and across the ceiling, light and dark jostling with one another for position.

There was such an intense focus she had when she carved, as there often was when she repeated these little rituals. She was lost in it, consumed by an act that she had repeated time and time again. I could call her name, even shout, and she would not notice. The world would float over her like a stream around a rock, and she would remain steadfast.

In this particular memory, I got up from my desk and sat by the windowsill and I felt, as I often did, a deep sense of isolation. Not from her, but from the world. Have you ever felt such a thing, Hattie? It's a passing feeling, but one that I have had ever since I was a boy. Now and again, I'll feel out of sync with the world, as if it is some giant secret that I'm not allowed into, and I'm completely disconnected from both the past and the present.

When Naoko finished, she placed the little carving up on the shelf with the others. A small ornate sculpture, lost in a sea of netsuke— traditional Japanese ornaments. Some were displayed in the living room, others around the house. Most she had packed away or put in boxes. Each and every one was the same: a small turtle with an ornately decorated brown shell.

"Why do you do it?" I asked her once, after she'd spent an evening ignoring me.

She smiled warmly. "You know, Harry. I've told you the story."

And I nodded, thinking back to the night when the tale had poured out of her. How she used to go scuba diving in Japan with her mother, looking for turtles. Her mother had access to the equipment through her ecology work, and often took Naoko with her. Turtles were the guides of the sea, her mother told her, there to show us a world that was not our own. How they'd swim for hours, chasing the little creatures deep underneath the waves. How her mother's oxygen tank malfunctioned when they were too deep. How she watched her mother drown, unable to help.

"I know, I know. But . . ." I paused, trying to find the right words to express myself. "Why remind yourself? Why send yourself back through that pain and not put it behind you, try to start over fresh?"

She shrugged. "It's not a question of choice. There's no such thing as starting fresh: new beginnings all contain the old ones bundled up inside of them. Starting fresh means not having a history anymore; it means not having an identity. I can't do that to her."

"Okay, I get that. But does that mean you have to constantly relive it?"

She shook her head. "It's not reliving, it's . . . ritual. How can I put it? These days, particularly here, we're always encouraged to try new things. To be innovative, to be inventive. Novelty has inherent value. How I grew up, it was different. In Japan, to be a master craftsman is not to try anything new. It is to pick one thing and perfect it. There are chefs who devote an entire lifetime to making one specific type of sushi. Blacksmiths who make only one knife, over and over and over again, seeking impossible perfection. Everyone here is obsessed with moving on, with the new. They forget about their connection to the past. This . . ." She pointed at the netsuke. "It's like a seed—it carries the past inside of it. Through it, our memories are allowed to grow and flourish. It's how we remember who we are: culturally, individually, spiritually. Through ritual."

I nodded. "So you always carve the same turtle."

"Always," she said, "and forever."

When Santi first started to speak English, it was only ever to Naoko or me. Around anyone else he would remain steadfastly silent. This was one of the reasons that I never told anyone about him—not your dad, or even your aunt Poppy. Our small family unit offered him a safety to grow, and I was scared that pushing on the boundaries might break it.

Looking back now, I wonder if perhaps it was also out of fear. If I never told anyone about my life, about Naoko or Santi, then there would be no one to explain myself to when it fell apart. I didn't quite trust it—this little family of mine—because I still didn't really understand it. For all that I have tried, there are no equations to decode that kind of responsibility. There are no analytics to measure love.

On some of our first trips out, I would take Santi to art galleries. It was 1978 and he'd been with us for two years by then. He looked healthier, a little plumper in the cheeks, but still so small and thin, his limbs sticking out of him like twigs. He liked those trips—how little expectation there was placed on him. He would usually dread social environments. So much pressure is placed on a child to behave a certain way and be a certain thing, and he was never quite capable of knowing what that was. He couldn't respond to an adult's image of what he was meant to be, so he would panic, burrowing deeper and deeper into himself. Sometimes it would take him days to re-emerge.

Naoko was always very insistent that he engage with his heritage. She missed working at the hospital—helping people—that much was clear. But when I suggested she return part-time she rejected it, instead focusing her love and care entirely on Santi. It was crucial, she said, that he retain a link with his past. She would read him books about

Chile, and about Chilean traditions. They would learn Spanish to-gether, short phrases and words. But I always found these lessons seemed to stress him out more than do him good. I think he felt like there was too much expectation there. Too much at stake.

At an art gallery no one looks at you. They are there for the art. For the atmosphere. You can drift through it, unnoticed. The only expecta-tions are that you remain quiet and contemplative, and this suited us both well.

On weekends, I would take him to the Courtauld and show him the Impressionists. He never spoke much, but we had our own little language. Now and again, he'd tug at my sleeve. I'd glance down to see him looking at a painting, not at me, completely rapt. As I watched him, after a moment or two, he would give a single, definitive nod. *I like this one*, it meant. *I like it a lot.*

Each time, I would note down the painting. *Mont Sainte-Victoire* by Cézanne; *Sunset at Ivry* by Guillaumin; *Impression, Sunrise* by Monet. He never liked the ones with people in them, not unless the figures were in the distance or very obscured.

We bought books from the gift shop, coffee table collections of im-pressionist art through the ages, and when we got home we would pore through them together. He devoured them with an obsessive alac-rity, and I couldn't help but laugh. In a few short months, this nine-year-old boy—a selective mute, a social recluse—could tell you more about the history of European impressionism than most museum tour guides.

We went to a modern art gallery once, because there was an exhibi-tion on geometry and art that I was fascinated by. I'd started my part-time doctoral program in theoretical physics at this point, and I'd become obsessed with the relationship between the shapes in our world and the way we perceive things. Santi wasn't sure about all the harsh lines and abstract angles, but there was one particular piece I had brought him there to show him.

He stared up at the sprawling canvas dominating one of the gallery walls. It was a frenzied medley of slanting forms and contours cutting across each other and overlapping with furious geometrical rhythm.

"Dad, what is *that?*"

"It's a tesseract," I said. "It's a representation of what a cube would look like in four dimensions. It's one of my favorite things in the world."

He furrowed his brow in confusion. "There are four dimensions?"

"Oh, yes. And many more than that. There might be an infinite number of dimensions for all we know. We can't see them, but it doesn't mean they aren't there."

"But if you can't see it, how do you know it exists?"

"Well, Santi, I suppose it's a little like love, or God. You can't necessarily see it, or define it, but that doesn't make it any less real. You know it's there because of the way it impacts other things. The way it touches the world. That's not really a tesseract, of course, it's a two-dimensional representation of one, but sometimes the best way to understand these intangible things is to make representations of them, like symbols."

"Like the little turtles Mum makes?"

"Exactly, Santi."

"Why *does* she make them?"

I crouched down to his level, so that we were face-to-face. "Think of it like a seed. Seeds are fascinating things—they have all this genetic information stored up inside them. They're like concentrated little representations of a plant: all of its history, its evolution, its existence. Your mum's netsuke are a bit like that. They're concentrated memories of all the things that brought her here to us—her ancestry, her homeland, her mother. Making them reminds her of all that, reminds her of where she's come from."

He watched the painting warily for a while, then walked back over to me and took my hand, nodding his approval.

Prompted by our talk of sculptures, I bought him a book on Giacometti from the gift shop on the way out. When we got home, he sat on my lap and stared at the strange figures on those pages, baffled.

"What is that supposed to be?"

I smiled. "They're meant to be people. There's galleries of these sculptures around the world. Large ones, small ones, some much bigger than me."

"Why are they so . . ." He lifted his hands, unable to find the words.

"Lanky? They're stretched out like that because the sculptor isn't trying to show what people look like on the outside. It's what they look like on the inside that matters."

He leaned in, his tiny body stretching against mine, and stared intently. "But their heads are so small—it's like they're far away, lost in space somewhere. There are never any together. They're all just so . . ." He flipped through the pages. "Lonely."

I nodded. "Yes, they are, Santi. They're extremely lonely."

He stared at the last page in the book—a long, skeletal figure, like a beanstalk, seemingly massless and weightless as a ghost. It looked like it didn't belong in this world. And I think even without his realizing it, his hand reached over and grabbed my sleeve. His eyes never left the page, but after a few seconds, he gave a hard, definitive nod.

When the Giacometti exhibition came to the Tate Gallery, I took the day off to go with him. He wandered the halls, entranced by sculptures both tiny and huge. As we exited into the courtyard, I found myself taken aback. We came across a large piece—*Grande femme II*—a spindly female figure that rises several feet above a normal human. I'd encourage you to find a photo, Hattie, but it really wouldn't do it justice. It's hard when you aren't confronted with the size, the looming immediacy of the face staring down at yours, to feel the utter sense of solitude that emanates out of it and fills the space.

I could have been in a courtyard of a hundred people and, looking up at that yearning figure, pressing upward into the sky, I would have felt completely and utterly alone.

I felt Santi's hand in mine. Looking down, I saw that there were tears in his eyes. When I blinked, I realized there were tears in mine as well. I knelt down next to him and he pulled his little frame into my arms.

"It's okay, Dad," he said. "I get lonely sometimes, too. But then I remember that I've got you. Does it help to remember that you have me?"

"It does, Santi." I gave him a big, stupid grin. "It really, really does."

When we got back to the flat, Naoko was out shopping. Together, we sat by the fireplace and took out her carving tools. Working softly and slowly, with Santi leading, we carved our own little netsuke. It started as a version of the sculpture we had seen out in the courtyard, but soon it became quite different. Instead of harsh lines and closed body language, he made her open, warm, comforting. Instead of the rough surfaces, Santi etched in small carved circles and wheels.

When Naoko came back, arms laden with bags, she hesitated at the living room door. We had only just finished and her carving tools were still spread around us. I worried, for a moment, that I had transgressed some invisible line.

"What are you doing?" she asked, cautious.

"Santi made you a netsuke," I said, nudging him to hold it out to her. The breath caught in Naoko's throat.

Santi smiled as he handed it over. "Like the turtles you make for Baba, so she doesn't forget you. I made it like those wooden Mapuche sculptures in those books you read me. So you won't forget me."

Her hand closed around it, staring at it, and she blinked. Tears trickled down her cheeks.

I got up, moving toward her.

"I'm okay," she managed, taking my hand and putting an arm round Santi. "I just . . . I love you both so much."

As I held them, I realized that making a netsuke for Naoko was not something that I would have ever thought to do without Santi. It's not a gesture it would have ever occurred to me to make. The word "netsuke," Naoko later taught me, is composed of the characters *ne*, meaning "root," and *tsuke*, meaning "attached." And with my little family in my arms, I felt that palpably—roots that had dug deep and connected me to the world.

* * *

I took a few steps forward, hoping that she might hear me.

"Naoko?" I said, but there was no reply. She was too engrossed in her act. Her hands shifted noiselessly, flitting away at wood. Lamplight flickered across the walls, shadows dancing fervently against the orange glow.

I took another couple of steps and placed my hand on her shoulder.

She jerked backward, scrambling toward the other side of the tent, fear etched across her features.

"It's okay," I said, putting a hand up. "It's okay. It's just me."

She stared at me for a long moment, her brows tightening in fierce confusion, and I was worried she might scream again. Her eyes darted to the floor.

"What are you doing here?" It came out like an accusation.

"I . . ." I shook my head, surprised by her abrasiveness. "Nothing."

"No," she said. Her voice was low and gravelly. "No, that's not right. Something. You're here for something."

I took a deep breath. "You've been through a lot. I just wanted to check that you were all right."

She clicked her tongue distastefully. "Don't bullshit me, Harry. Are you working with them?"

"What?" I paused. "Wait—with who? I don't know what you're talking about."

She barked a laugh at me that sounded more like a cough. "So what? You've just shown up on a mountain to see your ex-wife because you thought it would be nice?"

I took a step back, frowning. "I'm here because you aren't well. Because I want to help you."

She waved her hand dismissively. "Oh, that's rich. Showing up to save the day and be the hero. Don't make this out to be about me, Harry. It's not. It's about you. I was invited on this expedition and I'm in the middle of it."

I furrowed my brow, trying to make sense of the woman in front of me. The anger; the abrasiveness. This was not the Naoko I knew. But was this perhaps, on some level, the Naoko I had created with my actions?

"Fine, look." I shook my head. "I'm sorry."

She sneered. "For what?"

"I—" My words fell short. How can you talk about something you've been running from for years?

"You know what?" Her voice was laced with disappointment. "It doesn't even matter."

"I don't mean to cause you pain—now or . . . before."

"Before? When you left me?"

"It wasn't what I meant to happen, it wasn't about you, it was about—"

She stood up and walked across the tent. "I *waited* for you. For years. I waited for you to come to your senses, to deal with what had happened and come back to me. And you didn't. I can't sit here and watch you pretend the past doesn't exist. I won't!"

"Fine!"

We both fell silent. I stared down at the floor, the humiliation feeling like a ton of weight pressing down on the back of my head. She didn't speak—she just returned to her corner and went back to carving.

* * *

I am sitting alone in my tent once again, and I am forced to question: What am I doing here? I came to find Naoko. After seeing John die, I immediately resolved that I couldn't let anything like that happen to her, but now that I'm here, I can't help but wonder what I expected.

I walked into that tent hoping to offer some kind of support, to provide some comfort, but she wanted none of it. I am stupid to think I am capable of providing it for her. That box—that damned tungsten box of mine—is closed for a reason, and the humiliation of tonight is just a glimpse of what happens why I try to peek inside.

No. What drives me forward is the mountain itself. There are too many mysteries to ignore: the time slippage, the RNA, the men on the ice. I lack too much data. Palmer and the Warden are hiding things from us, and I do not yet know why. Naoko, too, knows more than she shares.

Damn it, Hattie, I'm going to go back there. To her tent. I got sucked in by old sentimentality but I'm more than just her ex-husband—I am a scientist, and I won't make that mistake again. I'm going to get to the bottom of this damned puzzle, whether she likes it or not.

Hattie

There's no time. At camp with cold winds. Deathly winds. We have lost men, I think, how many I don't know, the things have been driven back by something. Gunfire. Blood on the snow. Creatures in the night. I am going to leave my tent to see if I can do anything. Shouts for help are drowned by the wind. Blood on my hands. Creatures in the camp. I am going to leave my tent now. If you ever read this, tell others. Don't come here. Don't come here.

SATURDAY, 26th JANUARY 1991
CAMP 1

Dear Harriet,

I am alive. What that really means up here, I am beginning to call into question. But for the time being, I am safe, I think, from the horrors of this mountain. We were visited last night, in the dark and the cold, by things that we do not yet understand. I wrote you a note in my panic, but I think I shall not send it to you. It was a moment of madness. No more.

This is not new territory for me: confronting the inexplicable; deciphering the key behind the puzzle. And yet the stakes have never felt this high.

Last night, I marched myself back to Naoko's tent. She was still carving, and barely acknowledged me as I unzipped the door and let myself inside, ready to demand answers from her. Her movements were slower, less fevered, and for a moment I simply watched as the knife turned in her hands, deftly whittling a single line across a small piece of wood.

She lifted her head slowly, and all words left me. Though it had

been just an hour or so since our last meeting, her body was more relaxed, her shoulders loose. All confrontation had gone from her eyes—
they were soft, and in the dim light their deep brown drew me in.

"Harry?" she asked.

"It's me."

"I dreamed you were here. With me." Her voice was soft, weak.

I stared at her, unsure. "I was. I just came back to . . . You were so
angry—"

She shook her head like she was trying to clear it. "I don't know
what I said. I can't remember. It's the mountain. I've been here too
long; I'm losing any sense of—I'm not sure. Ever since they brought me
down my thoughts have been fuzzy. My emotions. I was angry at you,
I *am* angry at you, but something on this mountain makes it so much
more intense. And then it goes and . . . I just can't seem to focus. I can't
focus on the *now*."

A beat of silence.

I could only think of one thing to say.

"Why did you scream when you saw me?"

She frowned, tilting her head to one side as though she was trying
to work out where I was. "People tend to scream when they see a
corpse."

A gust of wind shook the tent, and a shiver of ice darted down my
back. I took a deep breath, trying to steady my shaking hands, and
knelt down to her level.

"What are you talking about?"

"This mountain, it . . . it shows you the truth behind certain things."
Her voice fell to a whisper, her eyes urgent. "What things really look
like, under the surface."

The hairs on my skin prickled. I leaned toward her, my gloved
hands on the cold fabric floor.

"What's going on here, Naoko?" I demanded. "With the mountain, and the last expedition? Please, you have to tell me. What did you see up there? What *happened* to you?"

"I can't *remember*. There are pieces—flashes—but they don't come together anymore. You . . ." She shook her head harder, as if trying to shake something out of it. "You have to keep an eye on the time. Tick-tock, tick-tock." Her fingers started drumming a beat against her thigh. "You have to watch the seconds, and the minutes. Because *they're watching you*. You just can't feel it yet. You will soon, if you stay." She frowned, and her whole body shuddered. For the first time, her voice took on that tender quality, the way it sounds in my memories. I could barely hear her over the growing wind. "You shouldn't stay, Harry. You should leave while you still can."

I gritted my teeth, frustrated at the continued vagueness of her answers. Outside Naoko's tent, some shouting came across the ice. Perhaps someone realized that I'd left mine. Palmer. The Warden. Wind howled over the tent, buffeting the fabric around us. The walls shook. It was becoming clear that if I wanted some truth out of her, I wouldn't have much time to get it.

"Yesterday on the ridge," I pressed, taking her hand in mine. "We saw two people in the distance. You said you knew them. How?"

Her eyes lifted up to the ceiling and took on a glazed look, searching for constellations in stars that weren't there. There was another noise out in the camp. "I'd seen one of them before."

"Who was it?"

She gazed curiously at the roof the tent above. "It was you, Harry."

"What?"

My hand squeezed hers. The image of Naoko, bruised before she had been hit, returned to me in a sudden flash. Of John predicting the future. Of faces shifting through time.

What was this place?

More shouts echoed outside, though I couldn't hear the words.

They sounded panicked. Confused. The wind still grew, becoming a steady roar of white noise.

"I was relieved, actually." Her eyes were still glued upward. "At first, I thought it might have been one of them."

I took in a quick breath. "One of who?"

"One of the old team. The last expedition. Before they . . . left."

"What do you mean, 'left'?" I demanded. "Are you saying they're still alive?"

"You've got to watch the seconds, Harry, and the minutes. Otherwise they might change when you're not looking. Tick-tock. Tick-tock." A gunshot fired outside, and her face snapped down to look at me. *"They're here."*

I stumbled back, twisting to find the entrance to her tent. Zipping open the canvas, I stuck my head out to see what was going on.

At first, I saw only white. A snowstorm had begun and the winds tore past me, sheets of white slamming into my face, my eyes. I squinted, pulling down my goggles and tugging the balaclava up from around my neck.

The shriek of the wind surrounded me—deafening, all-encompassing. Beyond the swirling white, there was black. Pure black. Whatever light the camp had to pierce through the night was snuffed out by the snow.

A scream. Or half a scream, severed by a gale of wind. I jerked my head left, thinking it had come from that direction, but there was no way of telling.

My breath was heavy, panting.

I tried to shout back, out into the dark, but my voice was swallowed by the storm. I pushed my head further out of the tent, looking left and right.

"Hello?"

A shadow darted across my vision—a person? No. It was too quick, too spindly—almost like a long rope, or some kind of eel. I jerked back, unsure if I had actually seen anything at all.

Pulling back into the tent, I turned to Naoko.

"We need to get out of here. We need to go to one of the big porta-cabins, not this little tent. We should go now. Something is wrong." As I spoke the words, I realized the weight of them. I could feel the certainty in my very blood. "Something is very, *very* wrong."

"It's too late, Harry," she whispered, returning calmly to her net-suke.

Another scream echoed across the camp. Something was happening and I needed to know what it was, for both of our sakes. In the dim light of the tent, I pulled my clothes tighter around me. I fixed my headlamp and took the heavy-duty flashlight from my jacket.

"*Naoko,*" I pleaded again, to her back. She did not turn. "Jesus Christ, Naoko, if you're not going to come with me, then at least promise you'll stay here. You'll stay in the tent."

She didn't reply. She didn't even glance at me.

I gave her one last look, swore, and stumbled out into the black.

It was a mistake. The winds were rising, the storm worsening. There were no sounds then but white noise, violently loud. My flashlight and headlamp were useless, mere drops in an endless ocean of night and snow. Within a few steps, I realized I had lost my way. I didn't know which way my tent was, or the main camp.

I turned back to Naoko's tent, but the darkness had swallowed that, too, along with any sense of direction.

I stumbled forward, grimacing in pain as the cold pierced into my neck, my face, my fingers—the snow flaying any patch of bare skin like a thousand knives. My hands couldn't move, frozen into tight grips.

There was another gunshot—behind me.

Louder, so much louder than the last.

I spun, unsure whether I should be going toward it or running away from it. But despite the danger, the panic that tightened my throat, it was the only concrete thing in this void.

Tentatively, I edged toward the source and the voices grew. Half shouts made their way to me, escaping the roar of the snowstorm. I followed them, picking up pace. My freezing hands fumbled and my flashlight went skittering across the ice.

I swirled around with my pitiful headlamp and scanned the snow, but it was nowhere to be seen.

I ran through the dark, urging myself ahead—desperate to see someone, to see *anything* that wasn't snow or ice or black.

My foot caught in a ditch and I flew forward, landing hard on the packed ice. My breath exploded out of my lungs. Wheezing, I rolled over, slipping and sliding against sleet and rock. A thick metallic smell filled my nostrils.

Then my headlamp faltered.

Sitting up, I hit it furiously, once, then twice, and it flickered back on.

I stared at my hands, and at the dimly lit ground around me, at the snow where I was sitting. I was confused by what I was looking at, momentarily baffled by this entirely new color.

Red.

I was sitting in a pool of blood.

Another scream reverberated across the mountain.

My headlamp went out, plunging me into the dark.

* * *

Nothingness. No sights to grasp on to, no sounds but the fierce static of wind. Even the cold of the snow had numbed my body so much that I could no longer feel the bitter air. The only concrete sensation was the crunch of icy ground beneath my hands and knees.

I crawled forward, slipping on it. In the absence of light, I imagined that all the mountain was made of blood, and that it had smothered me, that I would drown in it.

I don't know how I was still moving. There was nothing to guide my direction. Nothing to stop me crawling too far and falling head-first into a gorge.

But still, something urged me to move. And it was in that moment that I realized something wonderful. As the initial fumbling panic ran its course and I was left with just my blindness and my fear, the realization came to me like a blow to the chest.

I wanted to live.

The certainty of it jolted through me, a coursing fire that I had not felt in so many years. You must understand: I have never wanted to die. But God! It has been a long time since I've really, *desperately* wanted to be alive.

I would not let this be my end. I would not leave this world with the choices I had made. I would make things right with Naoko, and I would solve the mystery of this damned mountain.

I *would*.

A light flashed behind me from out of the storm, like a beacon in the black. I turned round and lifted my hands to cover my eyes against the sudden brilliance. A hand grabbed me by the collar and I was tugged upward.

"You need to get back to your tent, Harold," Colonel Palmer said, her voice fierce. Light flashed. A bright headlamp shone from the top of her helmet. She held a shotgun tightly in her other hand. One of the soldiers was next to her, holding up a rifle.

"My light went out," I panted, holding up my bloody hands. Red and white streaked across my gloves and onto my wrists. "I got lost."

She nodded, then gestured to the man behind her. "Follow Private Miller back to your tent. Stay close."

"What's going on?" I shouted. "Whose blood was that?" There was no reply. She moved off ahead of me and into the dark. The soldier—Miller—took my arm and pulled me forward. I hurried along beside him, stumbling.

Before long, I saw our tents, their dimly glowing electric lamps finally visible now that I was near enough.

As Miller pulled me forward, we passed the Warden heading in the other direction. He held a thick pistol up in the air, with a flashlight attached to the side. He barely seemed to notice us as he pushed out into the storm.

"Stay here," said Miller, his voice thick. "Get inside and wait. This isn't over yet."

"What isn't—" But it was no use. He was already gone.

Cursing, I stumbled toward the tents. As I reached mine, I heard a low groan.

Jet lay on the ground just outside his own tent. His hand clutched at his leg and his head lolled backward like a doll's, his red hair stark against the snow. I dashed forward and knelt beside him.

"What happened?"

"Something got me," he slurred, lifting his hand. A foot-long gash ran up his leg, oozing blood. "I was trying to get back to the tent and I . . . Ahhh!" His hand shot back down to his leg. "It's so cold. It's so *fucking cold*."

Grabbing his arm, I pulled him up and helped him inside his tent. His arms and face were covered in smaller cuts, but the leg was sliced wide open. Blood gushed from the wound. I laid him down on the floor, grabbing a blanket to use as a tourniquet.

"Just get me warm," he muttered, his speech drowsy. "Just get me warm."

"I need to stop the bleeding," I replied, working quickly. Time was of the essence. Hypothermia impacts the blood's ability to coagulate. He would bleed out for sure if I couldn't isolate the leg from the rest of his body.

He shook his head. "I don't care about that. I don't care. There was a . . . thing. Arms, or . . . long, thin arms, like some kind of . . . *Fuck*, it's freezing!"

His whole body shivered violently. I tied the blanket around his thigh and tightened as hard as I possibly could. He barely seemed to notice.

More gunshots. More shouts, moving closer.

By the time I'd finished checking his open wounds and covering what I could, Jet was asleep, or unconscious. I checked his pulse—it had slowed a little but it was steady. I found any other blankets that I could and covered him with them. He might lose the leg, but he'd survive if he made it through the night.

While I waited for Jet's bleeding to slow, I went to his desk and grabbed pen and paper. In my panic, I scrawled you that quick note, Hattie, in case you should never hear from me again.

But the others were still struggling out there. There was still a battle going on, and they needed all the help they could get.

I fumbled through Jet's things for another flashlight—double-checked it worked—then zipped open the tent door.

Roger Bettan was standing directly in front of me, holding a pistol.

"Where the fuck do you think you're going?"

"I'm trying to help."

"We've got this," he sneered. "Palmer's already had to save you once. Stay in the tent and stay out the way."

I climbed out and stood up. "What's going on? You have to tell me—"

He grabbed the front of my coat, jerking me toward him. "I said, get back in your fucking tent."

"What the hell are you doing?"

"We don't have time for a fucking conference." His face was inches from mine, and I felt the hot steam of his breath. "Go back inside and let the big boys deal with this, *now*."

"Okay, okay!"

I backed into Jet's tent, and Bettan moved to zip it up. The last thing I saw, several meters behind Bettan, was Neil standing motionless in the snow like a statue. He looked at me, and, with his face just barely lit by the tent lamps, I could have sworn he was smiling.

I stayed with Jet for the rest of the night, checking on his pulse regularly and doing what I could to tend to his wounds and keep him warm. His breathing was heavy, and though he ran a little hot, his fever wasn't at dangerous levels.

Perhaps I should have tended to myself better. As I write this now, my hands are red and swollen—they tingle with pain underneath the gloves. My left I have managed to warm, but I can no longer move the fingers on my right. I can't even feel the last three. I think I have sustained frostbite. It is a tiny miracle that I am not right-handed.

I don't know how long the night lasted. I was up for all of it, listening for sounds in the dark. After some time, they abated, and soon the storm ceased as well. In what seemed like an absurdly short amount of time, the sun began to rise and bring light to the campsite.

I stepped outside to find most of our crew standing in a rough semicircle some fifty meters ahead. There was no sign of Jet's blood on the ice. The storm had covered it all up.

I made my way over to them—Palmer, the Warden, Thomas, Polya, and Neil. Bettan was nowhere to be seen. Miller and Sanderson stood at either side, weapons clutched tightly, but I couldn't see Parker.

Just in front of them was a huge creature like nothing else I have ever seen.

The central blue-gray mass was giant, like the headless body of a rhinoceros. There were *four* eyes in the center—lidless and yellow—but no mouth. From the sides of this hulking form sprouted ten tentacles, thick as tree trunks and bristling with ridges, which spread out around it, meters long. A yellow-green substance pooled around the creature and into the snow.

I'm attempting description as best I can, Hattie, because that is all I have to give, but it does this . . . *thing* no justice. Sitting here now, I am still in shock. My hands are shaking, but I can no longer discern why. Fear? Excitement?

Have we just encountered an *alien*?

Polya held a Polaroid camera, and she circled the thing, snapping pictures of it, tucking away the photographs in her jacket pocket as they were produced.

To the left of the beast was a human body that had been only partially covered with a blanket—a makeshift shroud. It was red and crusty, saturated with blood. A head stuck out the top and my breath caught in my throat. Parker.

Palmer saw me stare at him. "He was a good man."

The Warden shook his head. "We still haven't found his left arm."

There was a bizarre calmness about their demeanor—was it military training, or had they seen one of these before? At the very least, Thomas's face told me I was not the only one overwhelmed by this.

I forced myself to look back over at the creature. "*It* killed him?"

Palmer nodded, hefting her shotgun. "Took a fair few hits, that one, but it went down eventually."

"Wait . . . what do you mean, '*that one*'?"

"The others pulled back," she said. "Got away. We don't know how many there were, but at least two more. Maybe now their friend's dead they won't be so quick to return."

An inhuman rattling came bursting out of the creature, and it flailed, its huge weight rolling over on the ice.

Guns flew upward. Everyone jumped back, except for Polya.

She stepped forward and leaned over it.

"I do not think this one is dead."

Dear Hattie,

We have discovered either something very new, or something very old. The longer I spend on this mountain, the more trouble I am having telling the difference. Sometimes the minutes seem to stretch, and what I feel is a lengthy period of writing or study is but a moment when measured by the ticking of my watch. At other moments, when I am not paying attention, hours seem to pass in a flash.

I put this down to my disorientation at first. To the impacts of altitude on the brain. But I can't help but hear Naoko's words echo through my head. *You have to watch the seconds, and the minutes. Because they're watching you.*

The morning after our awful night, the creature that we had felled was hauled into Polya Volikova's makeshift laboratory. The portacabin was the same size as the one we used for briefings, but filled with equipment. What would have looked cluttered under anyone else's care, Polya had formed into organized, clinical perfection: temporary filing cabinets assembled from cardboard lined the back wall, and each tool—microscope, a set of scalpels, notebooks—had a dedicated work surface.

But the lab was not designed for something of this size. It needed six of us and a tarp sledge to get the damned thing across the ice. Inside, the beast took up the entire space, splayed upon a table that creaked under its weight. Its long tentacles spread outward, curling up against the walls when they reached the corners.

Polya was right: it was still alive, though badly injured. It seemed to be unconscious, or in a form of coma state, though I am aware that trying to apply human physiology to something so obviously alien is foolhardy. My medical lexicon does not extend to impossible things.

I don't use the term "impossible" lightly.

It was noon. We crammed into the portacabin, circled around the monster. The morning had been a scrambling for each of us to have some time alone with it—to study it, prod it, figure out what it meant for us. We are a scientific outfit, and despite our differences of background or belief, there is one thing that we all share: curiosity. Each one of us wanted to make a discovery of our own.

Now Polya stood just behind it, almost obscured by the thing's bulging mass. She leaned over a microscope, occasionally jotting down notes on a pad of paper. Around her were Polaroid photos of the creature from different angles, arranged in various orders. The other members of the team were spread into the corners—Palmer and the Warden at opposite ends; Thomas, Neil, and Naoko in a circle, pressed against the walls; Jet in a chair by the door, scowling. Only Bettan had not shown up. God knows where he was.

Miller and Sanderson guarded the outside, weapons at the ready. Despite Parker's death, they remained stoic and unrelenting in their duties.

It had been a struggle to get Jet into the room, but he insisted. I'd spent the morning taking care of him, trying to bandage up his injuries. I'd managed to improvise the supplies to stabilize his blood loss, but the hypovolemic shock had almost certainly impacted some of his internal organs.

His leg wound is extensive: his left tibia sustained multiple fractures and the ankle is utterly shattered. The calf muscles have been, for want of a better term, torn to shreds. I must have found him moments after the injury. It is a miracle that I was able to stop the bleeding when I did—the altitude has thinned his blood significantly.

The rest of his body is scattered with cuts that sliced right through his thick clothes, but, perhaps thanks to layers, they are mostly surface level and will heal with time. This cannot be said of his leg. I have managed to cover the exposed shards of bone with dressing, but without heavy prosthesis I doubt that he will ever walk properly again.

When I told him the news, Hattie, I didn't know what to expect. I had dealt with patients like him before—ones who seemed almost defined by their manic positivity. Most of the time, they take it well; they adapt; they let it fit in with the rest of their outlook on life. That was not what I got from Jet. Instead, I got anger.

"This is fucking ridiculous."

"It's going to be a hard thing to process, sure, but you're a strong man, you—"

"You don't have any idea what I am," he spat back, his brows tightening in anger.

I frowned. Perhaps it was naive of me to expect him to be more optimistic, more resilient in the face of this injury. The Jet I had come to know in the past few days had been defined by a consistent cheerfulness and buoyancy. But this man in front of me looked older, the lines on his face deeper, as though a lifetime of frowning had carved grooves into it. Perhaps the pain medication was affecting his temperament, but it seemed more than that. It was as if someone had come in the night and replaced him with someone else.

"I can carry you into the lab, if you want." I splayed my hands as an offering. "Thomas could help me. We wouldn't want you missing finding out whatever that thing is."

"No." His voice was low, bristling with fury at my suggestion. "I'm going to walk in there like everyone else."

"Your leg is mangled, Jet. You aren't walking anywhere."

His lips curled upward. "So make me a crutch. Or I'll fucking hop. But I'm not being carried in like a dead body."

I put a hand on his shoulder. "Just take it a step at a time, okay? It's common for people who find themselves invalid to—"

"I'm not a fucking invalid!" He bit down, grimacing. "I'm not . . . in*valid*."

"I know that," I said, keeping my voice calm. "But you have to deal with the reality of the situation. If you can bring some of that positive energy that you're so—"

"You think that comes fucking easy? Ever since I've been on this mountain, I've been trying so hard to . . ." He squinted, leaning forward as if he had a headache. "This place isn't *normal*, Harold. And trying to pretend like it is . . . trying to pretend like everything is okay is exhausting. There's nothing real about this situation. Don't tell me to act normal when we haven't seen a fucking normal thing for *weeks*."

I felt my mouth open, dry, as I stared at him. "Jet—we've been here four days."

"What?" He waved his hand, as if he didn't want to hear any more from me. It was probably the stress and the meds talking; maybe the altitude, too. "Just get me something I can use as a crutch. And leave me alone."

He sat in the room now, his face twisted into a scowl, arms crossed, intently watching the creature like it was going to explode.

We all looked at it: the hulking mass at its core, the unmoving yellow eyes, the tentacles that spilled off the table and onto the floor around our feet. The shotgun wounds along its body had scabbed over with yellow-green pus and now its skin seemed to shimmer, as though covered with a thin layer of slime. The tentacles pulsed slightly—almost imperceptibly—reminding us that this thing was still alive. The room smelled faintly of fish.

Palmer shifted, scratching her arm and cricking her neck like she needed a good stretch.

"So, what do we know?" she asked.

"There is no clear delineation between head and body," Polya said, pointing at the center of the beast with a long stick. "They appear to be one central mass, with eyes placed near the middle. Four eyes, as you can see here, spaced in a square. This is excessively rare. There is only one other complex organism on the planet with four eyes—the jawless lamprey."

I kept my right hand tucked in my pocket. I have managed to rewarm it, but already frostbite blisters are beginning to appear. The last three fingers have remained completely numb. I fear that the flesh around them is already dead and will soon display symptoms of necrosis. The thought came as though from far away: when this happens, amputation will be necessary.

Polya circled the central area with her pointer. "There appears to be no mouth, at least not where one might expect it to be. This confused me at first, but then I looked at the tentacles." She took a step back, moving her pointer outward. "These ten tentacles, as I will call them, are long: around four meters each. They are highly muscular and pulsate with fluid—it is possible this works as a form of blood. Each tentacle is lined with what seemed to be teeth, though on closer analysis their composition is closer to hardened collagen—like bones—than to any kind of tooth enamel. They are extremely sharp."

"Don't I fucking know it," Jet muttered from the corner.

"Underneath these serrations are what appear to be hundreds of small pores that I am guessing work in the place of mouths."

Jet winced. "Are you saying this thing tried to *eat* me? Is that what happened to Parker's arm?"

She shook her head. "I am merely hypothesizing. The creature has remained in what appears to be a semi-comatose state; whether this is due to the injuries sustained from shotgun wounds or the heavy sedatives I have applied is unclear. It is still alive. The wounds appear to be healing at a much faster rate than a human wound would."

"Oh," Jet said. "Great. Really fucking great."

"Mr. Towles," Palmer said, her voice firm. "Hold your comments until the end."

"Oh, let the man speak," Thomas said as he leaned back, shaking his head. "He's been through hell. Considering what happened to that other poor man, it's a miracle he's alive."

"Leave your fucking miracles in church where they belong," Jet spat. Thomas shifted, surprised at his vitriol. He looked like he was about to say something, but then his mouth fell shut.

"Initial tests have confirmed my suspicions," Polya said, ignoring the argument entirely. She was focused purely on the mystery at hand, eyes never wavering from the creature. "The genetic makeup of the specimen matches the double-helical RNA structure we discovered in the microbes. The implication of this is clear: whatever this species is, it has not evolved directly from any life form that we currently know or understand on planet Earth."

I kept stealing glances over at Naoko—I couldn't help myself—but she wasn't looking at me. She stared off into the middle distance, consumed by her own thoughts. What I wouldn't have given, in that moment, to know those thoughts.

Thomas leaned forward, rapt. "Then where has it come from? And if it has no common ancestor, why *on earth* does it look like a giant walking squid?!"

"I don't know. There are certain things that are variable and certain things that are constant. We must assume the possible building blocks for life are variable, given that we have clear evidence to support this. Evolution, however, is a constant. It is basic mathematical logic: all living creatures that are born, procreate, and die must go through a process of evolution. I've not been able to specifically identify any genitals or reproductive organs thus far, though parthenogenesis is also a possibility. But the key is this: a specimen as complex as the one we have encountered suggests two possibilities." She raised a single long finger. "One: that it does not originate on Earth. That it is an alien form of life that evolved elsewhere and came to Earth recently, and this is why we have not seen it before." She raised a second finger. "Two: that an entirely separate form of life has existed on our planet for millions of years, alongside us, and we have had absolutely no idea. At this stage, I cannot say which is more plausible."

The Warden raised his hand, brows together in concentration, and Polya nodded at him. "What is the likelihood that these creatures attack us again? How intelligent are they? And, if so, what precautions can we take?"

She shrugged and sat down. "I do not know."

A tense silence filled the room. Cold settled across us, and the smell of fish became tinged with something wilder—fierce and blank as the mountain winds. I must be honest: my whole body was tingling with adrenaline. I felt that we were on a precipice, Hattie. Together, we were on the verge of one of the greatest discoveries of all time, but the individual pieces still eluded me. There were still too many unknowns, and I was beginning to worry that we wouldn't survive long enough to uncover them.

"I have a couple of ideas," a voice said, and I almost jumped. I turned to look at Neil, who sat forward in his chair. He was still wrapped tightly in many layers, just brown eyes and light brown skin peeking out from behind his scarf and hat. It only just occurred to me that I'd never once heard his voice before. It was light and boyish, almost child-like. His accent was difficult to place—vaguely English, but mostly neutral, as if he came from everywhere and nowhere all at once.

"Go ahead, Dr. Amai," Palmer said.

Neil cocked his head at us. "Well, if we're talking about evolution, then we have to talk about intelligence," he said, pulling down his scarf to reveal a wide, smiling mouth. He paused for a moment, looking upward. "There is an a priori assumption that intelligence is an evolutionary trait—something we've evolved to have."

I frowned. "Well, yes. Of course it is. This has been proven. I mean, spend any time with chimpanzees and gorillas and you'll realize how remarkably similar we are."

"Oh, certainly—the emotional lives of humans and other animals have marvelous similarities," he replied in a singsong tone, almost as if he was mocking me. "We see our social structures played out in mon-keys and our emotions reflected in dogs. But come on—think about our *achievements*! In that, humanity stands alone of all species. *Utterly* alone! Alone we try to understand ourselves and the world; alone we build the Taj Mahal and develop machinery and robotics; alone we create complex financial systems and beautiful equations, play symphonies and chess, construct rockets that travel to other planets and observe the shapes of other galaxies! What has any of this got to do with the threat displays of baboons? Of the emotional responses of rats in cages?"

"I'm not sure," Thomas said, leaning in. "That seems like human arrogance. We only think that because humanity imagines itself as the defining model against which every other example is copied. Just be-cause we define intelligence by how closely it apes the human psyche, it doesn't mean that it can't be wildly different."

"*Exactly*," Neil said, standing up, dominating the room. I had forgotten how tall he was. "By placing intelligence on some kind of evolutionary scale we miss the point entirely."

I looked at the tentacles quietly pulsing at my feet. "What point?"

"Nobody has any idea where human intelligence comes from. The human desperation for certainty has forced us to accept the very doubtful framework of evolutionary continuity. We are desperate to imagine that we're just clever apes. But consider the longing that burns in the artist, the ferocity of justice and righteousness that burns in the rebel, the thrill of exultation that impassions the lover. Consider poetry, postmodernism, space flight!" Neil spread his hands wide, almost knocking Thomas in the face. He turned, taking us all in. "How can we compare any of this with the idiot hierarchies of speechless primates? The chasm is *staggering*. Why is there nothing in between? Why no creatures that even begin to use abstract language, or show even hints of true artistic talent? The intellectual pursuits of humanity—religion, science, culture, and history—are unlike anything encountered in the entire universe. It is as if all life evolved up until a certain point and then humanity suddenly spun ninety degrees and erupted in a completely different direction. So *where* did the intelligence come from?"

Thomas laughed. "Someone must have put it there."

"Oh, seriously?" Jet moaned, rolling his eyes. "Not everything that you can't explain is proof that God exists, Thomas."

He shrugged. "And not everything you can explain is proof that He doesn't."

Jet put his hand to his head. I kept glancing over at Naoko, but she just sat wordlessly, watching as though she were at a play. Palmer stepped forward, cutting through the argument. "Look—this is all fascinating, I'm sure. But what does it have to do with the octopus creatures?"

Neil's face broke into another huge grin. "I'm very glad you asked."

He picked up the stick Polya had been using and pointed it at the ridges that rippled up and down the tentacles, following them all the way up to the central mass of body.

"One might easily assume that these marks are biological in nature. Like the stripes on a zebra, perhaps, or the spotting on a leopard. But closer examination reveals them to not be continuous with the biological matter of the animal. Instead, they are quite literally marks, written in tiny font on the tentacles in what appears to be set ink."

I leaned in, looking as closely as I could, covering my nose to avoid the pungent smell. Warmth emanated from the tentacle. He seemed right: a scrawling black script that spread across a wide background. It swirled, like ripples in a pool, before returning to convalesce into twisting shapes, with dips and troughs as it continued.

"Note the way the dips occasionally repeat, at intervals that would suggest a pattern, but not strict enough to imply pure repetition. Instead, it indicates the usage of similar words or grammatical forms."

I stood up, unable to control the electricity sizzling through me, and paced around the creature.

"Language," I said.

Neil nodded. "And not the base calls and responses of flighty birds or the mating calls of playful dolphins. No, *written* language. Complex language, with thought and, while this is speculation, likely the capacity for logic and introspection. Ladies and gentlemen: we may have discovered the only other species in all of our known universe that exists on a similar plane of intelligence to us."

"And you can translate it?" Palmer asked, her voice urgent, also leaning in to look more closely.

"There's no way," I muttered. "Even if this is language, which I think might be a bit of a jump. It would need extensive communication between us and them. We'd need comparative samples. We'd need so much more information."

Jet straightened up. "Then we get more information." His voice was strangled, feverish. "We find where these things have come from and we work out what they want."

"We don't know where they are," I said.

"She does." He pointed at Naoko, who was standing quietly in the corner. Everyone turned to look at her. Most of us were on our feet, bubbling with anticipation, cramped in what felt like an increasingly small lab. "Don't even begin to pretend this wasn't exactly what killed the last expedition. Where did you come across them, huh? Where are they?"

She stared back, a quiet fire in her eyes. The stranger things were becoming, the more lucid she was beginning to seem. Was she acclimatizing? Or were we the ones going mad?

"Higher," she said. "We have to go higher."

Jet nodded in fierce agreement. "Then we go higher. *Yes.*"

"Don't be ridiculous," Palmer said. "You're not going anywhere except back down to Base Camp."

"Are you kidding me? I didn't come this far just to be benched." Fury tightened his face. "I didn't lose my fucking—"

She got up, looming over him. "How are you going to climb a mountain when you can't even walk?"

"Get the all-powerful mountaineer in here! I'm sure he can work it out! He loves a challenge."

"Wait." I raised my hand. "I'm not sure we should be going higher at all. Not right now. We need to wait and regroup. We need to work out what—"

"We don't have time!" Jet pressed, his eyes bright, hands waving. "You heard what Bettan said about the ascent window. It's closing. If we don't keep going now, we'll never make it. The mountain is *waiting for us.*"

"This isn't a democratic decision," Palmer snapped. Then Thomas butted in, and the Warden joined the fray. Before I knew it, the whole group seemed to be shouting at each other.

I took a couple of steps back, suddenly overwhelmed by the madness of it all. The little lab tightened further, as if the walls were getting closer, the light dimming. My hand began to ache—the frostbite eating away at my flesh. Naoko was the only other person not speaking, and as I looked at her, it seemed she was the most in control out of everyone in the room.

Jet was shouting, but his fingers had started tapping on his knee. *Dum-dum-dum-dum. Dum-dum-dum-dum.* A steady rhythm. Neil was almost dancing up and down in fervor. Thomas was rubbing his forehead, his voice getting louder, and I just stared across them, suddenly feeling like I was underwater.

I pictured us pushing further, climbing this mountain higher and higher until we all forgot what it was like on the earth.

Until we all became lost in its impossible spell.

A chill ran down my spine as John's last words echoed through my head, ringing suddenly with new meaning. *Why does Sisyphus keep pushing the rock up the hill, Harry, if he knows it'll just fall down again? Why does he keep pushing?*

"Stop," I muttered, but it came out like bubbles. Like air. I took a deep breath. *"EVERYBODY SHUT UP!"*

They fell silent, turning to me.

I breathed in and out. "Can't you see what's happening? We have to stop. We need to approach this logically. One of us is injured. Another has *died*. If the climb itself wasn't treacherous enough, now there are monsters—actual monsters—trying to kill us. Climbing further up the mountain right now is . . . it's crazy."

Jet shook his head, pushed himself to his good foot. Wincing, he shoved his crutch underneath his shoulder, his face rock hard. "Crazy is a matter of perspective, Harold."

With that, he hobbled out of the room.

For a moment, everyone froze, on edge—Jet's fury lingering among us, at the very top of its crescendo. Polya turned around, muttered something in Russian, and walked out as well.

And like that, the tension broke. With a great sigh, the entire room seemed to fizzle out and, one by one, people got up and left.

Naoko slipped out before I even saw her leave. I wanted to follow her, but I didn't know what I would say. I never know what to say anymore.

Instead, I stood for a while, staring at the scrawling script on the creature without really seeing it. New threads were being tugged together, Hattie, old ideas being brought to the surface. My head was pounding with it all. There was something connecting all this: the creatures, the mountain, the time anomalies, and the men on the ice. A grand unifying theory, close enough to glimpse at its existence but not yet clear enough to see. Something Polya said—*an entirely separate form of life has existed on our planet for millions of years*—and something Neil said, too, but I couldn't quite remember which bit. It was all connected. I was sure of it. The answer was just slightly out of reach.

When I finally looked around me, Thomas and I were the only two left in the lab. It took all I had to avoid looking at the creature, but I needed to tear my eyes away. I couldn't think while it was in front of me.

I sat down next to Thomas. "What's your take on all this?"

"Sometimes I feel," he said, himself staring at the beast, "like science goes in circles. It brings us away from God, then it brings us back. Dangerous or not, I believe we may be some of the first to see one of God's great creations here. That's . . . that's very special for me."

"You actually think we should keep going?"

He shrugged, his focus intent on the thing before him. "This desire to climb higher—I can't explain it. No more than Jet can, I think. But it is there. I can't help but feel someone has put it there. Perhaps the same person who has put this mountain here. Something far greater than all of us. Call it God, or call it whatever you want. Either way, I think I have a duty to find out what that is."

I sighed, perhaps finally realizing what it was that made me uncomfortable about this venture. I shifted in my seat. "Doesn't it bother you to think that, if there is someone out there controlling all of this, we don't have a say in it? That we're being controlled, managed like ants in an ant farm?"

Thomas tore his eyes away from the creature and turned to look at me. "Do we have any say over evolution? Over our desires to procreate, or to eat? Do we have any say over the laws of physics? I'm not sure why we should expect the same from our own minds."

"So what, resign ourselves to the fact that we have no free will? That everything is determined?"

Thomas got up, splaying out his hands. "Free will and determinism aren't opposites, Harold. They coexist. When Achilles was faced with the possibility of joining the Trojan War, his mother, Thetis—a Nereid with the gift of prophecy—told him that his path was set in stone. If he stayed behind, he would live and nobody would ever know his name. If he went to war, he would certainly die, but he would be remembered in glory for all of time. And indeed, he was. He still is. But even though his future was known, he still had a choice."

I nodded, remembering the story. Somehow, in this cabin with this impossible thing, it brought me some comfort. "You're very well read for a geologist."

"Ah," he said. "There are some benefits of marrying a classicist."

"You're married?"

He went to cover his left hand with his right, and I remembered the imprint of the ring I had seen the other day. Thomas said nothing; he just gave me a sad smile.

"I suppose," I said, trying to change the subject, "the very fact that Achilles could see into his future arguably gave him even more of a choice."

"Exactly." He nodded gratefully. He picked up the stick and poked the creature tentatively. "Choice and determinism rely on each other. In order to control someone's destiny, you have to give them choices first. Do you know what Prospero says to Ariel, his slave, in *The Tempest?*"

I shook my head.

"'Thou shalt be free as mountain winds: but then exactly do all points of my command.'"

* * *

Later in the afternoon, Palmer called a final briefing. Jet wasn't there. We'd set up a makeshift cot and sheets, so he wasn't on the hard ground, and I'd left him sleeping, probably knocked out from painkillers in his tent. And though I knew he would likely have wanted to be woken to at least voice his desires, I felt relieved that he wouldn't be. The trauma had not left him sound of mind.

Bettan had deigned to join us this time, and the sight of him riled me. He sat, feet up on a table, drinking from his flask. There was a game smirk plastered on his face. One that seemed to say: *I'm above this.*

I can't get my head around him. Here we are, in the midst of some of the most groundbreaking discoveries in history, and all he cares about is his reputation. His ego. And yet, if I'm being completely honest with myself, perhaps on some level the reason he upsets me so much is because when I look at him—his certainty, his confidence, his arrogance—I see a little too much of myself.

"How's the patient?" Thomas asked, putting a hand on my shoulder.

"Sleeping. He'll be okay, eventually. But I think we need to get him off this mountain."

We sat down next to Neil and Polya. The Warden stood waiting at the back, as usual. Naoko sat on other side of Neil. I still had not brought myself to talk to her since our last encounter, the weight of my embarrassment and shame always turning me away at the last minute. And what would I say? What could I possibly say that would make the past right?

"There have been some discussions about whether or not this mission should continue," Palmer said, taking a deep breath, "given what we have seen and experienced. There is a way out of this. If we return to Base Camp, we can take the helicopter down and call in the plane. We can leave, and the ascent will be over. Nonetheless, I have been in touch with Base Camp on our satellite phone, and we have come to the decision that the climb will continue, led by Roger. We came here to discover why this thing is here, and we haven't done that yet.

"But Mr. Towles *will* be escorted back down the mountain once he is stable enough to travel. We need to send down some samples from this creature to Base Camp anyway. Those of you that wish to go with him may do so. We will not compel you to stay here by force. However, should you wish to climb, you are welcome to join us. I've called this briefing to get a sense of your intentions. Those of us who will be climbing will be going tomorrow morning to take advantage of the weather. Our window is closing. If a storm comes in, we may be stuck here for weeks."

She looked across the room, her eyes resting on our faces one by one, almost like a challenge.

"Who will accompany Jet down the mountain?" I asked.

"I will," the Warden replied from behind me, his voice gruff. "And, if time permits, I will then follow you back up."

Palmer's head jerked to the right. "What? That's absurd."

"I'm not leaving this expedition behind. I'll come back and find you."

"Alone?" A flash of fury flickered on Palmer's face before she could control it. "No, you won't. You absolutely will not."

"I won't abandon this now. These samples are just the starting point. They will want more."

"This isn't Cambodia, Steve! You can't just—" She stopped short, suddenly noticing they had an audience. Her hand rose to her head as if to stop it exploding. She sighed and, for a brief moment, she looked unassailably tired.

She sat down, and I could have sworn I heard her mutter, "I need a fucking cigarette."

"Just to be clear, you all realize this is madness, right?" I said, leaning forward. "I want to find out what's going on up here more than anyone, but . . . maybe that's arrogance. I think perhaps we have discovered enough here for a lifetime. If we all die up here, that is all lost with us. To push further would be foolish. It will get us nothing but more pain and more death."

At that, Bettan stood up. He walked to the front of the room, putting his flask down on the table. He stood straight, taller than I had seen him before. There was an aura about him, a corona of conviction that seemed to ripple from the outline of his body.

"Let me tell you something about pain and death. This is nothing. Parker was doing his job. He knew the risks. And now, we all do. So listen to me: I have been stuck in gorges for three days without food, ready to eat my own arm if it meant survival. I have fought through fiercer battlefields than you have ever conceived of. I have buried more friends and more good men than you have known in your entire life. But through all of this, I have not given up. Fuck arrogance. What we have is *will*. The will to act. It's what makes us human. If we give up when things get tough, then we're just dumb animals scrambling around in the mud. If you can accept that about yourself, go ahead. But tomorrow, I'm gonna climb that mountain."

He took a step forward, and raised his head up into the air as if he was greeting the heavens, or praying. The very room seemed to revolve around him. Clearing his throat, he seemed to look each of us directly in the eye.

"'It matters not how strait the gate,'" he said, "'how charged with punishments the scroll. I am the master of my fate: I am the captain of my soul.'"

Thomas looked at me, eyebrows raised, and then back at Bettan.

"I didn't take you for much of a poetry reader," he said.

"Well," I added, unable to cover my smile. "He knows *one* poem. I'm not sure if that qualifies."

Bettan sneered at us. "Fuck off."

And without waiting for further comment, he walked out of the room.

Polya stood up.

"I'm going up."

Neil nodded, putting his hand up as well.

"So am I," Naoko added, raising her hand.

My heart fell a little, because I realized I had no choice.

Thomas looked over at me and shrugged. "Well, old boy. Looks like that's our decision made for us."

* * *

I returned to my tent to prepare for another day's climb, gritting my teeth as I pushed through the biting wind. Even the short passage from the briefing cabin was a struggle, ducking against gusts that threatened to bowl me over. As I warmed myself in the relative protection of my tent, I couldn't shake the feeling that the answers to all this— whatever all this was—were just at the tip of my tongue. I felt like I had *seen* something or heard something, and if I could just recall what it was, the fog of this damnable mystery would clear and everything would suddenly be plain as day.

Time ticked away, and as the sun began to set, the cold came back with a vengeance. Layers no longer seemed to make any difference. The cold had settled into the bedrock of me and taken root. I was deathly tired, but knowing I wouldn't be able to sleep, I decided to make a pass by the lab and take a look at the sedated creature one last time. Perhaps something about its presence or its physiology would help me pin down the niggling feeling that was bothering me. If nothing else, I might get a chance to take a closer look at the language Neil had pointed out.

The setting sun welled on the horizon like a wound, staining the sky dark purple. I needed a flashlight to see the path clearly enough to walk it. The gusts had calmed, but there was always a steady layer of wind, a permanent baseline that pushed and pulled at me as I moved.

When I reached the door, I already knew something wasn't right. It was open, the cold wind and snow blowing into what should have been a sterile lab. I shoved my head in and my heart dropped down into my stomach, then further, right into the heart of the mountain itself.

The creature was gone.

I stumbled over to the table, confused. This wasn't right. Everything was intact—it hadn't ripped free or torn itself loose. The straps had been untied. The door had been opened by human hands.

I dashed out of the lab and shouted across the camp. Lights flickered on; people poked their heads out of their tents, eyes blinking in the wind. Palmer and the Warden appeared with guns, flashlights tracking the campsite to see what was making the commotion.

My foot hit something heavy and I tumbled, rolling over to find myself face-to-face with a body. No, not a body. *A head*, I thought, with a strange and abstract calm, *severed at the neck*. One of the remaining two soldiers. Not Miller—the other. Sanderson. His frozen eyes stared back at me, as if in accusation.

The others were exiting their tents now.

I blinked against the harsh wind, scrambling backward to get away from the horrific sight. My first thought went to Jet, alone and injured. He was the most vulnerable of us. The least able to fight back. My lungs heaved in my chest and I could feel myself panicking, beginning to hyperventilate. As fast as I could, I stumbled over to the tent where I had left him, tore open the flap, and pushed my way inside.

There was nothing there. His pack, his protective gear, his makeshift crutch—they were all missing. I stared at his empty bed, the sheets fluttering in the wind, so white against the purple sky.

My dearest Hattie,

How hard to believe that when I began writing to you about this journey—a week ago, a year ago, I can't tell—I thought this was merely a tool to process my thoughts. How unimportant that seems now. I don't expect to come back alive, but if these letters survive, by God, Hattie—someone must know. The light is low, and the cold is so deep in my bones it is painful to write. But I am possessed by an unshakable obligation to record these events, as horrific as they are.

This forsaken place is bursting with possibility. Discoveries have been made today—*real discoveries*—and I am beginning to understand how the puzzle fits together. It makes complete sense to me; I don't know how I didn't see it before. There is only one place we can go now.

---

* **EDITOR'S NOTE**: This is the first letter in the collection where the date seems to fall out of sync with the recalling of events. It seems clear that Harold is describing the events of the following day, the 27th, and yet his letter here is dated two full days after that. The day is accurate to the 29th, however, suggesting it is not simply a numerical mistake. He also stops including the year on this and on all future letters.

Higher.

Into the clouds and the snow and the biting wind. To the summit.
I have never been so certain of anything in my life.

* * *

We spent the night searching together for Jet, but he was gone. I didn't
dare to come too close to Naoko after our last confrontation, but I still
couldn't keep my eyes off her. The more time I spend around her, the
more I feel compelled to know where she is. To keep her safe. It's been
so long, but I don't know what I would do if something happened to her.

Tracks led away from the camp, strange tracks that seemed to be a
mixture of a man walking, a crutch, and the slithering wake of a
mighty beast. If it didn't sound so utterly ridiculous, I would say it
looked like Jet and the monster simply walked off together, hand in
hand, into the night.

The body of the soldier—Theo Sanderson—was nowhere to be
found.

It galled me that I had not spoken to him, so lost in my own troubles
that I hadn't even taken a moment to see him as a person, a human
being. Since the climb began, the three soldiers had been quiet and
stoic, keeping to themselves. Only Parker, God rest his soul, had shown
a hint of personality. We, in turn, had all but ignored them, accepting
their silent presence implicitly. But they had fought for us, protected
us, and now two of them were dead.

Miller—the last soldier—had not said a word since Parker's death,
as far as I had seen. I made a conscious decision that night to at least
try to get to know him.

"We have to get Jet back," the Warden said, staring at the marks in
the snow. "Christ, the things plan to pick us off one by one."

"It doesn't look like he put up much of a struggle," Thomas replied.
His hands were tucked into his thick jacket, his face grave.

The Warden shook his head. "We have to . . . *do* something."

"I think the answer is pretty obvious," Bettan said, standing a little way behind us. "Look at the track. That's the path up to Camp Two. They went where we were going anyway. Why do you think that is?"

The Warden twisted around. "That thing's gone to sabotage the camp." Raising his hands to his head, he grimaced. "I knew we should have put tags on you. I knew it. But Palmer said, *Oh, they won't respond well*, and now . . ." He clenched his hands into thick fists. "Nobody goes anywhere until I say. Nobody! Is that clear?"

No one spoke. We were all too stunned by the sudden shift in demeanor; the Warden, always calm, always level, had never snapped at a single one of us.

I was reminded, for a moment, of my confrontation with Naoko in the tent. And then of Jet, earlier that day. Was it just the stress of the climb, of losing a member of the team, or was something *changing* him?

And if it was, was it changing me?

Would I even know?

Grunting, the Warden turned and stormed back off toward the camp. In the morning, Palmer announced that we were all going to climb to Camp 2 together, led by Bettan. The Warden took care to add that if there were any signs of Jet along the way, he'd be the one to pursue them.

No one argued.

* * *

We held a brief funeral for Palmer and Sanderson, or what was left of them. The Warden said a few words that disappeared into the cold wind, and the men were given ice burials. I quickly discovered this just meant being dropped down the nearest crevasse. The terrain was too hard to dig into and the air too thin for a proper fire.

Bettan warned us all to keep an eye out for any signs of altitude sickness. Because of Jet, we would be climbing faster than his initial ascent schedule, and that could be dangerous. But if I'm honest, Hattie, I'm struggling to tell how long we've actually been here. When I came to put a date at the top of this letter, it felt more like guesswork than certainty. Has it been four days? Five?

Why do I not know?

We wrapped up tightly and kept our packs as minimal as possible. Sanderson's supplies were distributed among more experienced climbers: Palmer, the Warden, Bettan, and finally Miller. We needed to carry tents—far smaller than the ones we'd been sleeping in—as there wouldn't be any higher up. As such, some of the food and fuel had to be left behind. Palmer assured us there was a cache of food at Camp 2, and with our numbers dwindling we needed less of it than before. I was glad that I was not the one that had to make those grim calculations. The truth was that the rest of us were too exhausted to carry even another pound. Every step felt like a marathon; each breath inadequately replenished the oxygen I needed to move. I'd barely made it to Camp 1 without collapsing. I had no idea how I would make it further.

I eyed the supplemental oxygen tanks that Miller, and now the Warden, carried with their packs. We were not allowed to use them yet, as they would become crucial higher up. There was also a stash waiting at the next camp, they said. Or at least, there had been at the time of the last expedition. But at around 25,000 feet, Camp 2 would be the last base before the Death Zone: the level of altitude at which the body's cells start to die from lack of oxygen. Above that, there would be no further support. We would need everything we could get.

Miller, in particular, was heavily laden, his pack bulging with tents, food, weapons, medicine, even a fold-up table clipped to the side. And yet he stood tall, as if the death of the other two had granted him a renewed strength and stoic determination.

Paradoxically, despite my exhaustion, I have found myself craving the ascent. The next step. It is as if there is a hunger that has lodged itself inside of me that can only be sated by climbing higher. I recognize it is illogical, that it doesn't make any sense, and yet it is still there, burning a little fire deep inside.

It was a cloudless morning, without much wind. While this might seem like a boon, it meant that it had become impossibly cold. As I stood outside, my clothing stiffened and I had to beat it with my fists to make it bend, like a blacksmith hammering metal. When I looked down, the skin on my neck froze to my jacket, and I had to peel it away slowly so as not to tear it.

Bettan led us up a snowy path and the climb began to steepen. I could already feel the shallow intake of my breath, each inhalation feeling like I had a lifetime of smoking behind me. The sun was blindingly bright, shining down from the sky above as well as up from the reflected white of the mountain. Even with heavy goggles, there was no escaping the glare. I squinted, unable to see much further than twenty meters.

Without the roar of the wind, sound carried differently. The thinness of the air amplified the smallest grind of rock, the tiniest shiver of snow, from as much as a mile away. Despite the brightness of the sun, I felt as though I walked in an old haunted house, groaning and creaking around me with every step.

Those with guns were on high alert. We now knew every shift in the snow could be a monster. Every sound a harbinger of death.

No one spoke. I did not have the energy to talk. All I could do was focus on the climb, on the repetitive trudging steps.

We crossed over a ridge and a loud groan echoed out of the glacier far below. I peered into it. An unfathomable depth: shades of blue upon blue, reflecting and refracting endlessly. I imagined us falling into it. I imagined us falling forever.

Looking forward, I found that I could no longer make out Naoko in the glare. She drifted in and out of sight, like a mirage. All I could see were my own feet and Polya, directly in front of me.

Throughout this expedition, I hadn't heard a breath of complaint from her, or a hint that she might need aid or rest. Her gait was determined, like that of an ancient mammal that belonged in this place as much as the wind and the snow. I guessed she must have been in her late sixties, but she appeared indomitable, much like the mountain itself.

The Warden marched up front with Bettan. Before, he had always taken the back, watching out for the team, ensuring that he could help anyone who might fall. Now he seemed like a man possessed.

I can't say how much time passed—I felt like I was losing myself to the mountain, to the climb. My mind, my whole identity was being reduced to the movement of the steps, to the weight of each boot crunching into the snow. I had the intense sensation that if I climbed much further, I would become part of this mountain, stuck here forever.

I needed to ground myself in something real.

Taking a deep breath, I pushed forward to walk side by side with Polya. Her eyes were fixedly ahead of her, face knotted into a determination that bordered on ferocity. But as she noticed me sidle up beside her, she softened a little.

"Harold Tunmore."

I forced a smile onto my face. "That's me."

"I'd heard of you," she said. "Before this."

"Really? Well, I'm honored. Seriously. I mean, of course I'd heard of you. Who hasn't? But to even be on your radar is really—"

She waved her gloved hand abruptly in the air. "Enough. You blab. This false humility is wasted."

I frowned. The words "false humility" rang in my ears like an accusation. "That's . . . that's not—"

"I have heard of you," she repeated. "I have read your account of solving Shroffman's Dilemma in '86. I have also enjoyed your research on bioluminescence in Sogod Bay. It was very good. I quoted it in one of my lectures at the Lomonosov University. You are a very intelligent man. Why does this embarrass you?"

Under my balaclava, my cheeks went a little red. "It doesn't *embarrass* me. It's just . . . there are many intelligent people out there. People with all sorts of talents. I just happened to have been places. Anyone on the planet has the potential to have done as much as I have."

She snorted. "Even you don't believe that's true."

"So what? Would you have me flaunt my accomplishments at every opportunity? Would you have me be like Bettan?"

"No." She gave a single definitive shake of her head. "That man is an asshole. But you don't have to be ashamed of who you are. That is not humility. That is . . . self-flagellation."

A silence invaded the space between us. We walked on wordlessly.

"We spend so much time categorizing things that we lose the big picture," Polya continued, as if she were talking to herself. "Biology, physics, chemistry. These are all different perspectives on the same thing. Everything that is happening: the RNA microbes, the time, the change in people's personalities—the answers are not individual. The answer lies in the connection between them."

"People's personalities?"

"You must have noticed it. People are becoming more distant: angry; stranger. I do not know if Jet was kidnapped or if he left voluntarily, but it was clear he had begun to change already. He was not his original biological self."

I took in a breath, processing the statement. I thought of Jet, the anger in his eyes, passionate fury in his words, the incessant tapping. If he had changed, did that mean any of us could? "What do you mean, *biological* self?"

"I have been taking blood and gut samples from my own body since I arrived on this mountain. The longer I spend here, the more the new microbes I have discovered are present in my system. It is to be expected if they are part of the landscape: we will be eating them, breathing them, sleeping with them. On a minute level, microbes interact with us constantly. They play a much larger role than they are given credit for—we live with them symbiotically. They define our biology."

She was hiking quite quickly, and I was struggling to keep up. The altitude bore down on me, making me weaker and slower. My pack felt heavy. I was so tired.

"But they're completely different from us biologically," I said, breathing hard. "You think they could cause some actual physiological change?"

She shrugged. "It's too early to say. Any such substantial change would take years, I would think. But it should not be discounted, particularly with how time appears to shift on this mountain."

"God, why are we here?" I shook my head. "I mean, the more we discover, the more stupid this expedition becomes. And now the possibility of microbial infection, I . . . why are you continuing?"

She looked back at me, a little amused. Behind her goggles, I could see her eyebrows rise a little, as if I'd told a funny joke.

"I grew up in the Soviet Union. When I went to university, discovery and science was more than just an interest that people had. It is a part of politics, of ethos. It forms our national identity. It is not quite the same in the West. For us, the function of science and technology is ideologically linked to the path the country is on. It is an expression of Lenin's vision for the future, the Hegelian dialectic as put forward by Karl Marx."

I puffed, keeping up with her. "I'm not sure I understand."

"Discovering new things is more than just a curiosity. It is intimately tied to the destiny of our country. A destiny we all believe in.

Our country was born out of darkness and cold and wasteland, and each year we discovered something new, we did something amazing. I remember seeing Yuri Gagarin become the first man in space. I was thirty-four years old. And I thought—this is not just the destiny of my people, but of all people. To work toward something greater."

"So what's the endgame? Knowing everything?"

She shook her head. "There is no endgame. It continues forever. It is about always being better than we were before, that is all. To keep pushing the rock up the hill. I am here to be a part of that. I am hoping that what we discover in this place will make the world better— scientifically and ideologically."

"But putting yourself at risk? Using your own body as the experiment?"

"In 1924, Bogdanov gave himself experimental transfusions to test the healing properties of blood. Elie Metchnikoff injected himself with cholera in order to pioneer the science of immunology. The lack of safety did not counteract the necessity. Progress is never easy, but it is *necessary*."

"Necessary for who? For the Soviet Union? For humanity?"

She sighed—a deep, melancholy sound—but didn't reply. "I have my reasons. Why are *you* here?"

I didn't answer right away. A flurry of sentences flickered through my mind, none of which I felt comfortable speaking out loud. *I'm trying to keep my ex-wife alive; I'm trying to keep my mind busy; I'm just trying to keep it all together so I don't fall apart again.*

"You know what?" I said with a little chuckle. "I don't really know."

"But you feel it, don't you?" she said, the ferocity returning to her voice. "The pull. The *need* to go higher. You feel it as well?"

"I feel . . . something."

She nodded, as if confirming a theory she had in her head. Quickening her pace, she powered forward and in front of me, signaling our conversation was at a close.

* * *

As I continued to walk a little while in silence, I found I couldn't get something Polya had said out of my head. *You don't have to be ashamed.* Am I ashamed? I suppose I am, perhaps not of the intelligence I possess, but certainly of what I have done with it. That's okay. Sometimes people should be ashamed. Sometimes they deserve to be.

A particular confrontation with Santi kept cropping up in my head. He must have been about ten or eleven that year. In the summer, I'd just transferred to Imperial College, still working in central London. I'd taken up a research position in experimental physics— there was growing excitement about the Higgs mechanism and the underlying properties behind mass and gravity, and I was right at the heart of it.

It took most of my days and a lot of my nights. I saw less and less of Santi and Naoko, but the days when I did, we made the most of it. We took Santi for long walks, sweating in the glorious warmth of the summer. He was getting taller, stronger and more assured in his body than he had been, but he was still so thin. Sometimes he would get tired and I would lift him up onto my shoulders and it would surprise me how little he weighed, like he was made of feathers. Strolling along, we argued over silly things, and loved it. We came home to eat fresh fish marinated in mirin and ginger. Staying close after supper, I would put Santi to bed, and Naoko would listen, shaking her head, as the two of us made up long, stupid stories with thousands of characters—giants and cats and tiny dogs with huge heads.

On long days when I wouldn't get home until late, Santi would stay up, though worn out from the day. He would want a new tale told, a new place to visit in our shared fantasy. And as those evenings passed, I remember feeling that I was being made whole. That what I had been before was just a puzzle piece that had yet to find the place it fit. There was no awkwardness or frustration or self-doubt that Santi didn't unknowingly eclipse with his kind little heart. I don't think he ever really understood quite what he had given me: this sense of belonging.

When autumn arrived, just as the orange on the leaves was deepening and the nights grew a little cooler, I began to feel that I needed to give back to him some of what he had given to me. It became very important to me—very, very important—that he have a good life. The happiest life in the entire world.

I was determined that we should take him out of the city, for him to see some of the beautiful countryside around us. We had been reticent in the past, wanting to keep him where he felt safe, but it was time. A pretty beach with a lovely view of the sea would be perfect.

The drive was pleasant enough. A nice leisurely jaunt up the coastline, with Naoko and me taking turns behind the wheel. Santi was in the back, flipping through books on art, entirely engrossed. This had begun to happen more often. I'd ask him questions and he simply wouldn't reply, not noticing that I was there.

At first, I missed talking to him, sharing that part of me with him. He'd come such a long way in the past few years—engaging so much more with society and the world around him—and I'd have hated to see him backtrack, disappear into himself again. Naoko always told me to leave him alone. He'd grow and develop at his own speed. He was happy, and that was all we could ever ask for. But would he always be happy? Were we giving him the tools to be happy for the rest of his life—financially, academically, but also personally? I didn't know the answer to that, and it bothered me.

It was the first time he had ever been to the beach or seen the sea since we had adopted him. So when we got out of the car and walked down from the car park to see the open ocean spread out before us, I hadn't expected his little squeak of fear. He darted behind Naoko, clinging to her legs.

"No," he said. "I don't want to."

"You don't want to what, Santi?" I knelt down to his level. "What's up?"

"I don't want to go there. It's . . . it's too big."

"Well, okay. I understand you're a bit afraid. But it's important to face our fears sometimes. Maybe you and I could just go down and take a look, huh? We don't have to go in."

"No." He shut his eyes tight.

A small impatience budded in my chest. "Well, we're not going all the way back home just because you're saying no. The only way to build up the courage to do more things is to face your fears, and see that they're not as bad as you think they are."

"Harry," Naoko said flatly.

"No, it's okay. It's important that you try new things." I reached out and took hold of his arm. He curled away from me, inward.

"No, no, no."

He was being silly, I told myself. I pulled his arm again. It was a stupid childish fear that he would get over if he could just—

"*Harry.*"

I saw then just how petrified Santi really looked. Not just of the sea and of the beach we had come to, but of me. He was staring at my hand, grasping his forearm, like I was a threat. A predator come to take him away. I released him immediately.

Standing up, I said, "I'm sorry."

"I think maybe we should just head back," Naoko said pointedly. "Don't you? It'll be a nice drive."

I sighed. "Sure." Before I'd even got the syllable out of my mouth, Santi had dashed back into the car.

We drove home, mostly in silence, which Santi enjoyed, and the next day I had to head into work.

We never really talked about that day afterward. I noticed, more and more often, that when we were at home, Santi would be content with just looking at art and reading about it. Naoko and I had decided to home-school him for now, until he was socially ready for a larger environment, but I couldn't help but feel that he needed to begin to acclimatize to the world if he was going to be happy in it. Life was about moving on, finding new challenges and new mysteries. We wouldn't always be there for him. This became a constant refrain in my mind.

I signed him up for an art class with kids his age: a perfect opportunity for him to explore his passions while pushing himself to improve, to get a little better. But when we went together, he didn't speak. He barely participated, choosing instead to sit sullenly in the corner and not speak to anyone for the entire session.

"Why don't you go use some of the paints, Santi? See what you can do?"

He shook his head at me, not dignifying the question with an answer. I looked around the room and saw all the other children running, laughing, and creating. Each one of them was like a little sapling, pushing and growing upward toward the light, testing each new branch of friendship and achievement before stretching further. Looking back at Santi, I didn't want to compare, but I ended up doing it anyway.

"Why don't you want to get involved?" My voice was probably harder than I wanted it to be.

He shook his head again, this time looking down. I glanced around at the other parents—at the fun they seemed to be having with their children, at the pride they were displaying in their work—and, though it shames me to say it, I felt jealous. I envied them.

I put my hand on his shoulder, trying a different tack.

"It's just . . . it's an opportunity to try new things. To improve. You can't just stay the same forever. Do the same things forever. Life doesn't work that way."

He didn't reply. After ten more minutes of fruitless attempts, I made my apologies to the instructor and we left. Bundled into the back of the car, Santi sat quietly with a book. We drove for a few minutes in silence before he spoke up.

"Are you not happy with me, Dad?"

I didn't pause. "What?" I asked. "No, Santi. I just want to help you grow. Don't you want to . . ." I struggled to find the right words. "To be *better*? To be the best version of yourself?"

"Are you not happy with who I am now?"

"No," I said, gripping the steering wheel. "That's not it. It's just . . . it's difficult to explain."

"It's okay, Dad," he said wistfully, looking out the window. "I'm sorry I disappoint you."

I should have told him that wasn't it at all, that I was proud of him, and I would always be proud of him. But for some reason I can't explain, I just stared at the road straight ahead and didn't say a thing until we were home.

* * *

Bettan had stopped ahead, putting up his hand. When we caught up to him, he looked me up and down in disgust.

"Jesus Christ," he said. "You look like a corpse that died and never stopped sweating."

I sighed, mostly because he was right. I could barely stand up straight without my bones screaming at me. "Why have we stopped?"

He pointed up. A cliff loomed ahead of us: a sheer face of ice and rock that jutted upward. Up close, the immensity of it sat in my throat and sank down to my belly.

How were we supposed to get past *that*?

"I'm gonna call it the Bettan Face," he announced, grinning to himself. "When others come to climb this thing, they're gonna know I was here. That this was my expedition."

While there were jagged edges, its actual rise was mostly flat. Bettan predicted it to be 170 to 180 meters high. *Less than half the Empire State Building*, he quipped jokingly. *Easy.* But as I looked at it now, it seemed utterly insurmountable.

Gathering us at the base, Bettan took center stage. He had rope around his shoulders and a series of metal hooks and rods.

"I'm going to free-climb first. There are still some metal holds from the last expedition, but many will have come off from ice and stormy weather. I will have to replace some and reattach the rope. We're going to make a pulley system so you lazy fuckers don't need to actually do anything. I attach it at the top and throw this end down. We weight it with rocks to counterbalance you as gravity lifts you. The rope gets tied round you and you get pulled up. Just wait here, don't do anything stupid, and keep quiet. Be ready to go in about forty-five minutes."

Before anyone had a chance to argue, he was off. He hit the base of the cliff and, almost without breaking stride, continued up it, affixed to the face like a spider. Before long, he was turning into a glimpse of black against the white—like the shadow of a bird—scrambling slowly toward the sky.

We stood and watched him for a while, and then we began to scatter. The Warden went furthest afield, searching the ground for tracks or signs of the monsters that might have taken Jet. Palmer took up residence right at the base of the cliff, holding her pistol tightly against her. Polya was picking up samples of ice and putting them in test tubes.

For a moment, I didn't know where Neil had gone. He has a tendency to vanish—something about the way he moves, as if he walks with the quietest feet. Sometimes I forget he's even here until he sneaks up behind me, as if he's appeared out of thin air. After a minute, I saw him a little way off, staring out into the sky.

I looked around for Thomas, seeking out the warm comfort that came from talking to him. He was leaning behind a rock, panting.

"You okay?" I said, approaching him. He straightened up quickly, embarrassed.

"Oh, yes. Fine." His face was pale and gaunt, like a faded photograph, or a ghost. "Just . . . having a stretch."

I frowned. "You sure?"

"Give me a moment, will you, Harold?" he snapped, eyes flashing. His normally gentle face was harsh, his hair wet against his forehead.

"Sure," I said, taking a step back. "Sorry."

I turned away, trying to ignore the ache in my hand. The frostbite eating away at my flesh. I knew it was there—the ache had not gone away—but there was far too much else going on. I could deal with it later.

Instead, I walked over to Miller, who stood alone, staring out across the ice.

"I'm sorry for your loss," I said, coming up by his side. "I didn't know Private Sanderson, but Parker . . . he was nice. Friendly."

"Jim." Miller didn't turn to look at me. "Jim Parker and Theo Sanderson."

I nodded. "Thank you. They died keeping us safe. I'll never forget that. Is there anything I can do for you?"

He looked at me, confused for a moment, then chuckled. "I would kill for a beer."

I held out my hands in apology. "I'm pretty sure we're out. Now, if *I* had been the one in charge of supplies . . ." I gave him a knowing wink. He smiled, but it dissipated quickly, and his distant stare returned. "Did you . . . know them well?"

"Always knew it would end badly in our line of work," he said, ignoring my question. "But I thought we'd be able to bury each other. Don't even know where Theo's body is."

"I'm sorry." There was nothing else to say. I looked up toward the towering peak above us. "I hope their deaths are not in vain. We will all have to try to be brave, for them."

Miller grunted—a low echo of a laugh. "Funny to hear you talking about bravery. The only reason you're talking to me is because you're too scared to do what you really want to do."

I frowned. "What do you mean?"

He cocked his head over to his right, where Naoko was sitting on a rock. "You've been avoiding talking to her ever since we left Camp One. You can't keep your eyes off her, but every time you come close to it, you find an excuse to talk to someone else. Is that bravery?"

"You've been watching me?"

"I'm watching everybody," he replied, turning toward me. "It's my job."

I looked over at her and realized he was right. Ever since our encounter in the tent, I'd been dodging her, too worried about what she might say, too afraid of what memories she might dredge up. This was cowardice all over again. No longer.

Looking up at Miller, I took in his gruff stoicism, his blunt honesty. Perhaps I need a little more of that in my life.

"Thank you," I said to him. Taking a deep breath, I traipsed over to where she was sitting.

She turned. She'd taken off her goggles and there was a strange look on her face as she glanced up at me.

"Hi, Harry."

"Naoko," I whispered, her name still sounding strange in my mouth after all these years. "You seem . . . better."

She nodded. "I think . . . I'm not sure. The higher we go, the more myself I feel. When they found us at Camp Two, things were already difficult to remember. I'm not sure how I got there. I think John helped me. But then they brought me down the mountain to recover from altitude sickness, and the lower I went, the more confusing things became. It was like I had left a bit of my mind behind. I couldn't connect thoughts together. Couldn't finish sentences. I can't really remember much—just flashes, nothing useful. But . . . and I know it sounds strange, the higher I go now, the better it is."

"What *did* you see in those flashes? Can you remember anything?"

"I remember those creatures. The tentacles. The anger." She squeezed her eyes shut. "But that's not it. There was something else. The *time* wasn't right. It wasn't . . ." She trailed off, breathing hard.

"What happened to the other team, Naoko?" I asked. "You mentioned them, before the night of the storm."

Her face dropped, stricken. "I'm sorry. I don't know. Whenever I think of them, it gets fuzzy. There was so much anger, when they turned on me, on each other . . ."

"Turned? They killed each other? Is that what you're saying?"

Her eyes grew wet with tears. "I don't know, Harry. I just don't know."

"We need to get you out of this place," I said. "I can't believe they're making you climb. I should take you and we should leave."

"*No.*" Her eyes flashed, anger flaring in them again. "Don't you see? I can't *leave*. It calls me to the top, Harry. And I don't think it's going to let me go. You've felt it, too, haven't you?"

Slowly, I nodded.

She was right.

I think I must put it down plainly, for I can no longer pretend it isn't there: there is a pull upward, Hattie. A hunger inside me to get to the top, and I don't know where it has come from. It is more than curiosity—it is an undeniable need. It scares me.

"Leaving here won't do me any good at all," Naoko said. "You saw what happened to me. No—there's no way off this mountain for me that isn't up."

I fell silent. I stood next to her, looking out at the snow for a while.

"Sorry," she said, glancing up at me. "I can't seem to hold on to my thoughts for very long these days. You came to speak to me the other night, didn't you? What did you want to say?"

I took a deep breath, feeling suddenly caught unawares. "No, I . . . I don't know what to say. It's—I don't know that I have any right to say it. It's been so long. But I just wanted . . . I just want to tell you that I'm sorry."

She frowned, her demeanor shifting. "What do you want, Harry? What are you sorry for?"

"For everything. For leaving you. For . . ." I fought a lump that appeared deep in my throat. "For what I did. For God's sake, Naoko, don't make me say it."

For a moment, she didn't reply. Her gloved fingers traced lines in the dusting of snow beneath her.

"Sit down," she said. I settled awkwardly next to her. "I loved you, Harry. I may be going crazy, but I remember that much. I still love you, I think. Or at least, I love the man that's somewhere deep down inside that shell you've put up all over yourself, if he's still there. I let you run away and hide from our life because I knew that's what you wanted, even if I struggled to forgive you for it at the time. But where did you go?"

"Everywhere," I whispered. "I never settled. I left the university. I . . . I just couldn't stay in one place anymore. I searched for mysteries I could lose myself in. Ten years I traveled the globe, developing a reputation for myself. All to escape." I took a deep breath. "What did you do?"

"I did what I could to make things right," she said, memories of the past seeming to center her, to help her focus. "Specialized in emergency medicine. Fieldwork. It's what brought me here. But I was always waiting. I was always there if you wanted to come back to me." She frowned. "So why now? You're coming to apologize to me like you're expecting me to forgive you."

"I'm not," I said quickly. "I know I don't deserve—"

"You don't need my forgiveness. You need to forgive yourself." She looked up at me, and in those brown eyes, for a moment, I saw the reflection of the man I used to be, the man she used to love. "You had a life once. With me, yes, but also with a past, a present, and a future. Now there's nothing. I see you, Harry. I see you running. You've been running ever since you left, just so you don't have to think about the past or the future, or anything at all. A lot has . . ." She blinked, as if trying to focus. "A lot has happened to me, up here. But it hasn't made me blind. I want to move forward, but I can't move forward with someone who isn't moving, who isn't alive." She put a hand to my face, and though I couldn't feel her skin through the glove, my whole body shivered. "You used to have so much life in you. Now all I see is death."

My breathing was starting to get a little tighter, and as much as I want to blame it on the altitude, I don't think I can. It's very important that I keep the box closed, Hattie. The tungsten box where everything is locked away. Because if I open it, I don't know what I'll do. I don't know what the world will mean anymore.

But I had come here to not be a coward, and I owed Naoko an explanation. She put her hand down and cocked her head sideways, examining me.

"You know that when I was young, I didn't have many friends," I said. "More than that. People thought I was strange. I *was* strange— socially inept. You know I was bullied. I was ignored. Whatever—it didn't bother me. I soon felt I had no need for people. So instead, I sheltered myself in my mind. I kept myself locked away in it, and inside I cultivated my own little home. I protected it furiously. It kept me safe." I spoke softly, trying to keep my voice steady. "Year upon year, I built the walls high. But inside I kept some room open to the heavens: part of me wishing for a small ray of hope, for something more one day. And then, without any way of predicting that it could happen, God came down to me. He came to me in the form of an amazing woman, and an astonishing little boy." I turned away, trembling. "I felt full for the first time, and the beauty of those moments was so pure and so powerful that all my walls were leveled. I had no more need for them, Naoko, don't you see? Love was my protection. God was my protection. And He betrayed me. He offered me salvation, and then He stood by while I tore it all apart. I *destroyed* it all. You tell me to forgive myself. How can I think about forgiveness? How can I even begin to forgive?"

Choking back my last words, I turned away from her. I started to rise, to get up and leave again, to wander off on my own. Her hand reached out and touched my shoulder.

"You don't forgive people because they deserve it, Harry," she said. I turned back—a half turn. A look. "That's not what forgiveness is for. You forgive people because they need it. You need it." She took my hand in hers, her eyes pleading. "Forgive yourself. Please. I'd like to see Harry again someday. The real you, not this puppet you're hiding in."

I looked down at her fingers, clasped over mine. For so many years, I have defined myself by my shame. My regret. It is what I have become, and without it there is nothing left. No—to forgive myself would be tantamount to dying.

"I can't."

Getting up, I walked away from her and back out into the snow.

* * *

When the pulley system was in place, Naoko went up first, then Polya. Attached by ropes around their waists, they were hoisted upward into the sky. The counterweights were just enough to lift them slowly as they walked up the rock face, as if rappelling in reverse.

When my turn came, the rope was fastened around me and I gripped the top tightly. My frostbitten hand was almost useless, howling in pain as I tried to wrap it around the line, but I bit down and put on a brave face. In another life, I would have prayed for safe passage, but that seemed ridiculous now. I was tugged up, a sudden weightlessness in my body like I was walking on the moon, or traveling through space.

The mountain was utterly silent. The wind barely a whisper. Dangling in midair, I looked out at this impossible landscape. Whether it is the thinness of the air or our proximity to the atmosphere, light is different up here. It takes on personality. It assumes shape. Just beyond our position, under the cover of the cliff, there is a gentle light—the calm softness that suggests, for a moment, peace and clarity, the possibility that we will escape this place. Further out, where the sun hits the snow with full force, the light becomes almost godlike. It bathes the landscape in golden richness, elevating it, reminding me of this mountain's awesome eminence. But most commanding is the false light, peeking out from behind a jagged rock ridge or reflecting deep out of the glacial crevasses. I pay most attention to this light, because it reminds me that this mountain is never safe for us, not for a moment. Death lives here, and it does not yield its kingdom easily.

I continued to rise, trying not to look down anymore, not to fall prey to the vertigo.

Now and then, the silence would be broken by an uproar of sound. A cliff would let out an almighty crack, followed by the torrent of a distant avalanche, or a glacier would rip away from the ice with a high-pitched scream. It was impossible not to jump, the rope jerking this way and that as it tugged me up the cliff face. Every nerve was on high alert.

The landscape was not static: all was on the precipice of motion.

At the halfway point, I turned around and looked out.

I gazed across rises and gorges, across vast plains of ice and mountains of rock, and I saw something odd. Off in the distance, I saw *things*. A whole group of flickering, moving black shapes, like ants, clambering over the mountain. They must have been hundreds of meters away. My breath caught in my throat; at first I was certain that they were more of those octopus creatures, but as I squinted I could see that they were people.

I shuddered. There were others on the ice—ten of them. What on earth were they doing up here? How did they get here?

Scanning the scene, I could see them working their way across a thin ridge of rock and ice—the ground beneath them looked to be shifting and cracking. They were moving for the safety of rock at the other end, framed by pillars of ice.

My pulse quickened.

I knew what was going to happen before it did. One of the pillars collapsed and the entire group began scrambling, a panicked dash to get to the end before it collapsed beneath them. I knew it because I had seen it before.

It was us, days ago, crossing the icefall.

Somehow, impossibly, we were *there*, stolen out of time and place. I could see what must have been myself, near the back, and Naoko ahead of me. I could see all of us, just escaping the collapsing ridge. And all I could think—aside from the fact that I was seeing into the past—was that the physics of it made no sense. That icefall was not there—it was thousands of feet below us.

I wanted to shout out, to confirm that the others could also see it, that I was not hallucinating, but as I approached the top of the newly dubbed Bettan Face, the sun started to dip behind the mountain. I could no longer make out that anyone was there.

A hand grabbed my shoulder and lugged me up onto the rock. The Warden looked down at me, his face hard.

"I've just seen . . ." I tried to say. "I've just seen the strangest thing."

"What?"

"It was—" I paused for a moment. Should I tell him? Did I trust him?

"Help!" Naoko's voice cut through. "There's someone here!"

The Warden was running before I could finish my sentence. Scrambling to my feet, I unclipped myself from the pulley and chased after him. Naoko was by the camp—just a few hooks and spaces for tents dotted around on the rock—standing over a body.

Jet.

I swallowed hard after a lump in my throat. But as I arrived, I realized I was wrong. The body was human, certainly, frozen into the ice at the base of a large rock. But it was not Jet. It was not anyone I had ever seen.

The first thing I noticed was that his clothes were strange: an old shirt, formless trousers and waistcoat, and a thick, fussy ruffled jacket that looked like it had been taken out of a costume shop.

I knelt down next to the Warden, who was examining the body. The face was pale and frozen, preserved in ice. The man had clearly been dead a long time.

The Warden riffled through the man's odd clothes, peeling back the frozen layers and pulling out bits of supplies and paper. There were documents in his pockets, frozen hard and brittle. He put them aside as he continued to search the corpse.

Picking them up with my good hand, I glanced over them. Letters, written by hand—something about a crew of mountaineers that had been sent to make a new discovery. I stopped short, sharply drawing a page up close to my face.

"How long did you say this mountain has been here?" I whispered.

The Warden turned to me. "What did you say?"

"How long?"

"A few months. Three or four at the most."

"Are you *sure?*"

His eyebrows knit together. "The intermittent satellite images from before this expedition prove it. It wasn't here, and then it was. Why?"

"Because," I said, licking my cracked lips. "These letters are dated 1754. Whoever this person is, they've been frozen on this mountain for over two hundred years."

I stared at the body—for how long, I don't know—trying to piece together the waves of bafflement and confusion that were running through me. This body, like something stolen out of history. The time dilation. And then the icefall, removed from both time and place, and us still climbing across it, over and over again, eternally.

For some reason, I couldn't stop thinking of Santi, and an art gallery we had once been to together.

Art. Time. Space. Santi.

What was the link? Why are you so hard to put out of my mind?

And like a flash of lightning, it all came together. As though I had been stumbling blindly in a dark room and somebody had flipped on the light.

"Oh," I said, and then started to laugh.

I know exactly what this mountain is.

31st JANUARY (NIGHT)
CAMP 2

My dearest Hattie,

Things are already beginning to shift. New knowledge brings with it questions. Each discovery opens up new realms of inquiry. More and more, I find myself questioning the others—why are they here? What do they want? I cannot deny that I have felt this mountain call to me, reach out to me personally, as though it knows me. Do they all feel it, too, as strongly as I?

I can no longer sleep—the altitude prevents it. At night I lie awake for hours, deathly tired, desperate for some rest. When I do, I hear whispers. Plans being made and secrets kept. People are changing. The Warden is not the same man he was when we arrived. Naoko spoke of her team turning on one another; why not us? Perhaps it happened to Jet already, and he was responsible for Sanderson's death. Would I notice the others before it was too late? I catch glimpses of them sometimes—Palmer, the Warden, Bettan, even Miller now—talking in huddled groups too far away to hear, conversing in closed tents. They are hiding things from us. I do not trust them.

I do not trust anyone.

* * *

Shortly after discovering the body, we stopped at Camp 2 and set up the tents. This camp can hardly be compared with the ones before: it is a rocky outcrop with some small protection from the wind by the ridges rising around it. There are metal poles and stakes that have been drilled into the ground to secure our little tents, but that is it. No sign of those who came before.

Setting up my tent was a difficult task on my own, especially with my frostbitten fingers. Bettan had his up in moments, and casually walked the campsite, not offering the slightest help to anyone. At one point, I asked him if he could throw me one of the lengths of rope that were at his feet as he walked by me, and he merely sneered and kicked it further away.

There are supplies here—locked in a metal box and staked to the ice—but our food is now reduced to nuts, protein bars, and tinned goods: sardines, beans, corned beef. I am beginning to feel like I will soon need supplemental oxygen to make it comfortably through the day. My chest is constantly tight. But we still have a fair climb ahead of us and the oxygen is not to be wasted on comfort.

My own tent is a slightly larger space than one man would need just to sleep, in the expectation that I might use it for work or experimentation. But in truth, the original purpose of our mission feels further and further away with each passing day. It is very cold up here. Our gauges clock the temperature at about −17 degrees Celsius. I cannot take off my many layers of gear, especially at night. Skin freezes immediately on direct exposure to the winds. It is a cold that addles the brain, slows it down to sluggish speeds. Even the most basic thought sometimes slips out of my head.

In the relative warmth of my tent, out of the direct wind, I was able to check on my hand. I could feel nothing. Dimly, I thought: *the fingers are dead now—blackened and rotting.* They need to be amputated or the frostbite will spread. It is only three fingers, down to the third knuckle, but it won't stay that way for long. If I am to have any hope of using my hand again, they must be removed.

Tying a tourniquet around my arm, I took my knife out of my pocket and pressed it against the flesh. It was a small comfort that, at the very least, I couldn't feel the blade. Placing my hand on the table, I lined the knife edge up with the bottoms of my fingers, the edge of the infection, and put a rag in my mouth to bite down.

I took a deep breath, then another.

I couldn't do it.

I put the knife down and slid my glove back on. It wasn't the pain that I was afraid of, no. There's something that runs deeper than that—a biological instinct, perhaps, that won't let you go through with mutilating yourself. I sighed. It must be done soon, I know that. But not right now.

I'd asked the team to stay outside after we had finished eating, so that I could explain my revelation to them. I had run through what I would say a hundred times in my head, and with each rehearsal the explanation seemed more implausible than the last. It was as though the mountain itself was weighing on my brain, preventing me from threading the pieces together in the way that I needed.

More than that, I was unsure how the others would react. The Warden had grown strange of late—quick to anger and deadly serious. Palmer was a closed book. Bettan appeared competent, but his arrogance made him a complete wild card. They purported to be our leaders, guiding us up this forsaken mountain, but the longer I spent with them, the more I worried that they did not have our best interests at heart.

I snuck out while the others were still in their tents to look out at the sky. I walked through our small encampment to the edge of the mountain and stared upward. There is something about the world at this height that is almost impossible to describe: ocean, cloud, and sky blend into a completely encircling canvas, and the solid earth beneath seems to fall away. It is like floating, in a way. Or drowning.

It was in this moment of quiet that I heard a low sound from behind me. Approaching the nearest tent, I recognized Palmer's voice coming out of it.

". . . possibilities for weaponization are likely broad. Further samples have of course been taken consistently. No hint of the other team found, or of the chemist."

I shuffled closer, taking care not to tread too heavily on the crunching snow beneath my boots. There was the crackling of another voice coming out the speaker of her satellite phone, but I couldn't quite make it out.

"Negative," she responded. "There have been no further questions concerning Apollo."

I pressed my ear as close to the tent fabric as I could, trying not to tumble into it. Another crackle of voice, too low to hear.

"Confirmed. The mission will continue as planned. I will make contact at the next opportunity."

There was a beep, and the sound of Palmer getting up. As quickly as I could, I put enough distance between myself and her tent and waited, looking back out at the sky as everyone slowly emerged to hear what I had to say.

There was still daylight left, but it was dimming. As the light darkened, it assumed weight. My vision took on a matte hue and the last few beams from the horizon seemed to dance before me, as if the photons themselves had grown large and visible.

Do you remember when I took you camping in Northumberland, Hattie, when you were ten? We'd spend the evening categorizing light and darkness, coming up with words for each new hue and shade. If only I could show you the sun setting up here. When night falls on this mountain, the darkness is unlike anything that I've encountered.

It is more than just the absence of light.

It lives. It breathes.

We sat around a small fire, fueled by a butane-propane mix that should have been highly flammable, but in this oxygen-rarefied air all it did was smoke and sputter. Enough to give a little heat, but no flames.

All were there except Miller, who was circling the perimeter of the camp, keeping an eye out for monsters.

We ate—some sitting, some standing; crackers and a little bit of cheese that we had left; some beans spooned from a tin. It was only out of the corner of my eye that I saw the Warden rummaging in his pack, expecting to find more and failing to. Supplies were dwindling.

As I nibbled on a cracker, I watched Neil examining a bean on the end of his spoon. He poked at it, turning it around, then put it back in the tin. It didn't seem like he had eaten a single thing.

I looked for Naoko and found her looking right back at me, straight in the eyes. There was a fierceness to her now, a determination that hadn't quite been there before. It was true: the higher she climbed, the stronger she seemed. It felt like the opposite was happening to me.

After eating, the team all looked at me expectantly.

Trying to remember the explanation I had put together, I cleared my throat.

"In 1988, I ran a small research project in Sydney with a man called Ronald Pangborn. Together, we were looking into Van der Waals forces and the Lamb shift. There were interesting implications to be had with Heisenberg's perspective of hydrogen, which . . ." I took a breath, realizing that this information was mostly unnecessary. I was already getting sidetracked. "Basically, we were looking into tiny little quantum particles—electrons and quarks, mainly—that seemed to randomly pop in and out of existence in a vacuum."

"Like the mountain," Palmer said.

I gave her a thin smile, the skin of my lips cracking at the effort. "Yes. I didn't make that connection immediately, though, not until it occurred to me that this mountain hadn't just appeared, but that it seems to have *re*appeared."

Bettan took a step closer, the first time I had seen him genuinely interested in anything other than himself and this climb. "So how does it do it?"

"Look—I've not solved everything, by any means," I began, "because as far as our current understanding of physics goes, the things we've encountered are impossible. And yet, they happened. We have seen them. So we must redefine our assumptions. That was my initial mistake. I imagined that we were still working in a universe that existed along one-dimensional linear time and within three-dimensional space. We're not."

"What are you saying?" Palmer asked.

"The mountain is a tesseract."

She looked at me, dumbfounded. "I don't know what that is."

I thought back to my explanation to Santi all those years ago. "Strictly speaking, a tesseract is a cube in four dimensions, sometimes called a hypercube. I'm using the term a little loosely here—essentially, we are on a structure that exists in four spatial dimensions. A hyper-mountain, if you will."

Palmer screwed up her face, her expression one of disbelief. "How do you know?"

"It's the only explanation that makes sense. Almost all of the phenomena we have witnessed can be explained by the understanding that we are beings with three-dimensional consciousness interacting with a four-dimensional plane, provided that we also accept that we are experiencing two-dimensional time."

Everyone's eyes were intently on me, wide with a mixture of wonder, disbelief, and confusion. Neil loomed tall beside me, rubbing his hands and nodding enthusiastically, smiling like a teacher agreeing with a clever student.

Palmer frowned. "Two-dimensional time? I feel like you're deliberately trying to confuse me."

"Maybe he is," Bettan said quietly. "If the only one that understands this mountain is him, maybe that makes him the one in charge. Maybe that's what he wants."

Palmer shifted uncomfortably, looking from me to Bettan, then back again. I blanched at the accusation, completely baffled as to where it had come from.

When had they stopped trusting me? Why?

"Okay, okay." I took a step back. My throat was dry and scratchy. I glanced over at Naoko for support, and she gave me an encouraging nod. "Let me try to explain better. Imagine a flat surface, like a table. And you want to cover it with pieces of paper, but they can't overlap each other. Eventually you run out of space, right? It's a two-dimensional plane—it has finite space in those dimensions. So, what do you do? You maybe put a filing cabinet or organizer on top of the desk: suddenly you can stack your papers in a new, third dimension, and fit so much more."

"Sure," Thomas said. "That makes sense."

"Now imagine you're an ant and you only really comprehend the desk as a two-dimensional surface. You walk along it, and when you get to the end you have to turn around. For a creature like this, when I lift this paper up onto my organizer, it simply disappears. Gone. It's been taken out of their understanding of existence. It was there for a bit, but then it goes. If I put it back directly on the desk again, it reappears."

Palmer nodded, seeming to catch where I was going. Polya rolled her eyes.

"Now consider my tent: Imagine it is filling up with boxes, and I'm running out of space. Where do I put them? Well, if I had access to a fourth dimension, I could do the same thing. Shift them into there. But for us humans who process things in three dimensions, the boxes would seem to simply disappear. Unless, of course, someone put them back."

"This is what was happening with your quantum particles," Thomas deduced. "So this mountain has definitely been on Earth before?"

"Technically, I think it's always been on Earth. It's just that we can't see most of what Earth actually is. We're blinded by our perception."

"This is crazy," Bettan said, shaking his head. "This is fucking stupid. Four dimensions? And this came to you in what? A flash of inspiration?"

The Warden nodded, turning to me. "I would also like to know the answer to that question."

"I'm just trying to get to the truth!" I insisted, suddenly furious at the three of them—Bettan, Palmer, the Warden. I took a step back from the pathetic fire, surveying them all. After everything they had hidden from us, who were they to start questioning me? "People have *died* and you're giving us *nothing*. You expect us to believe you learned nothing more from the last expedition? Nothing at all? You won't even tell us who's in charge of all this. Who do you answer to? What is Apollo?"

The Warden's face went stone cold. His whole body stiffened.

"That's classified information, Harold," Palmer said, crossing her arms beside him. "That you don't need to know."

"Why not?" I threw my hands up in the air. The whole circle had turned toward me, and I was a few feet back, as if on trial. "If we're to work out what's going on here, we need all the information we can get."

She stared at me. "Because I don't trust you."

"Trust?" I shouted, storming forward until I was right up in Palmer's face. "I don't trust a single damn one of you!"

And I shoved her.

She stumbled backward a half step, boot slipping on the ice. From the corner of my eye, I saw Naoko flinch, as if someone had slapped her. The Warden stepped forward and his hand darted to the pistol at his waist, raising it toward me.

In a split second, Palmer steadied herself, her arm shooting out to grab him. His head snapped round to her, the gun steady between them. I froze, my heart rate doubling, my whole body going hot. The Warden stared at her, his face set, well controlled, but the rigidity in his body screamed: *let me go.*

I didn't move. Everyone else watched, on the precipice of action. All but Naoko, who seemed like she could no longer look at me. A shiver ran across my body—why had I shoved Palmer? I'd barely thought about it. It had just *happened.*

"I think Harold wants to rethink some of his behavior." Palmer's voice was level. Calm. Steam-hot clouds of breath came out of her mouth. Nobody moved an inch. She looked directly at me, and her eyes darted down to the Warden's gun and back up to me. There was a clear implication: get back to the point, and quickly.

"Let's take a step back, all right?" Thomas said, spreading his hands out in a calming motion. "Let's get back to what's important, to this explanation."

Palmer slowly and carefully released the Warden's arm, like she would a snake. He stepped backward, his face still hard, but the light had grown so dim I could no longer see his eyes. I breathed out, but my heart was racing, my body still so tense, so *angry.*

What the hell was going on?

"So has this mountain been *here* before?" Thomas pressed, placing himself between me and the Warden. "In this spot in our three dimensions?" He seemed to find the point crucial.

I shook my head, trying to clear my thoughts. "Maybe. Or maybe somewhere else. If it moves in higher dimensions, it doesn't have to go very far to be in a completely different place. Look." Reaching into my coat, I pulled out a piece of paper that I'd ripped from my journal. "Remember our ant. Now it's starting in the corner of this paper." I pulled two corners of the paper so they were almost touching, but not quite. Letting myself sink into the explanation was helping. "Our two-dimensional ant would have to travel all the way across the piece of paper to get from one corner to another, but an ant who could access three dimensions—well, the corners are barely a centimeter apart. This mountain could have appeared anywhere in the world, or on Mars for all we know, then shifted out into another dimension before reappearing here. It was on Earth in the 1700s, based on the man we found. Before that, who knows how many times?"

"Surely there would be some record of something like that?" Bettan asked, squatting by the pitiful fire.

"Will there be any record of *this* expedition when it's over?" I snapped back.

Bettan replied with a wave, casually ignoring my comment. "I thought *time* was supposed to be the fourth dimension."

"No," I replied, refocusing my mind. "We understand the movement of time in one dimension—a single line. We see it as something that we move forward along, and we can look back behind us at, but that's it. We say that currently, we perceive the world in four dimensions—three being space, and the fourth one being time. What I'm talking about is the existence of a fourth *spatial* dimension."

I let that idea settle for a moment before I moved on. The Warden had taken a few steps back, and Palmer stayed close to him. His figure was silhouetted in the evening light.

"If this mountain exists in higher spatial dimensions, that explains how it can appear in the middle of an ocean. It explains how a man from 1754 can be frozen up here. It does *not*, of course, explain why time appears to dilate in strange ways here."

"So what does?" Thomas asked.

"Let's return to our ant," I insisted, trying to keep everyone focused, trying to keep *myself* focused. Naoko still wasn't looking at me. "Traveling along a single line now. He is a one-dimensional creature. He can go forward and maybe back. That is how he processes all space. Now imagine we aren't talking about space anymore, but time. That ant on the line is how we experience time, forward and back. But if a being lived in two-dimensional or even three-dimensional time, they would see everything just like we can see the whole line from above. Past, present, and future, all existing at once. You could move bits around, connect ends with beginnings, put loops in. It doesn't necessarily explain the sense of time dilation, but it helps explain some of the phenomena we're dealing with—John and his premonitions of the future, for one, and the strange reports of time spent at Base Camp."

And seeing ourselves on the ice days ago, I didn't say. The group was already too on edge for a revelation of that size.

"I think this sounds like bullshit." Bettan snorted.

"Well, I think everything you've hidden from us so far is bullshit!" I fired back. "Are you expecting me to believe you didn't know we'd encounter those things? Then why were you so well armed? What else are you hiding from us?"

"Careful, Harold." The Warden's voice was low, a soft hiss of threat dancing behind it.

"Or what?" I demanded, unable to control a sudden burst of fury. I pushed past Thomas, taking two clear steps toward him. "You'll bury me? Scrub me out of history, just like you did everyone else? Maybe that's what you did to Sanderson? Or *Jet?*"

The Warden's fist hit my face before I registered what was happening. I stumbled, falling into the snow, pain enveloping my cheek. Naoko leaped forward, letting out a small cry as she threw her arms around me in the snow, and my anger subsided as quickly as it had come.

I looked up to see Palmer holding the Warden's arms, pulling him back. From his position by the fire, Bettan was grinning, looking like he wanted to laugh. Thomas threw Polya a worried look, confused, but she didn't seem to register it.

The Warden's eyes were aflame—I'd never seen him so incensed. He struggled against Palmer, but she held him tight.

For a second, I thought he was about to go for his gun again, but instead he sagged and she let him go. He straightened up, threw me a fierce glare, and stormed back off to his tent.

"Okay," Palmer said, straightening up, clearly wanting to move on. "Your big theory is this mountain exists in four spatial dimensions."

"Are we not going to talk about *that?*" I said, pointing after the Warden. Naoko put a hand to my face, and I winced with pain where I'd been hit.

"I'll deal with it." Palmer's voice was laced with steel. "With him. Leave it alone. Four spatial dimensions and two temporal dimensions?"

I sighed, sitting up. Taking my hand, Naoko helped me to my feet. "*At least.*"

"Okay. And it's been put here by some higher-plane beings that are able to understand and perceive these elevated dimensions."

I rubbed the swollen spot where the Warden's blow had landed, sending a jolt of pain up my eye. "I believe so."

She took a deep breath. "*Why?*"

"I have absolutely no idea."

"Great," Bettan added, with mean brightness. "This has all been really useful." Turning around, he walked back toward his tent.

As if that were the cue that this was over, Polya—who had not said a word the entire time—gave a short grunt and left, patting me on the shoulder as she passed behind me.

"If you have any other theories," Palmer said slowly, "or if you *see* any other phenomena, be sure to let us know, will you?"

As she walked away, Naoko turned to me and said, "Let me talk to her. Whatever that was—you pushing her, him hitting you—that wasn't okay. We have to . . . we have to be careful up here. We have to look out for each other."

"Thank you," I said, unable to find any other words. The role reversal was stark, and I didn't understand what had gone wrong. All I'd wanted to do was explain my theory, and somehow it had devolved into shouting, fighting. Why had I been so confrontational? Why had the Warden been so angry? I can't put an answer to those questions, Hattie, and that really scares me.

Thomas walked over to me and gave a sheepish smile. He glanced over his shoulder, at the others trailing off to their tents, disappearing into the night, before saying, "Well, I believe you."

I raised my eyebrows. "Really?"

"Reminds me of an old joke," he said. "There are these two young fish swimming along and they happen to meet an older fish swimming the other way who nods at them and says, 'Morning, boys. How's the water?' And the two young fish swim on for a bit, and then eventually one of them looks over at the other and goes, 'What the hell is water?'"

"Yes. That's *exactly* it," I added, pointing at him, so pleased to just be able to *focus* on the problem at hand. "Our flaw is that we're too accustomed to our environment. Sure, this all seems crazy to us, but if I pulled one of those fish out of the water and had him take a proper look at me, what would he see? If you put him back in the water, what kind of stories would he tell? No one would believe him. He'd be mad, or . . . persecuted."

Thomas gave me a quick grin. "He'd be Jesus."

"What?"

He cocked his eyebrow at me. The fire flickered quietly between us, but the only light was the pale white of the moon, hanging large in the sky. "Oh, come on. Fish comes down from another plane of existence, talks about miraculous things that can't possibly happen. Other fish don't believe him so hard they crucify him. Don't tell me you haven't heard that story before."

I stared at him, and before I could think of anything else to say, he burst into a fit of laughter. In the distance, I saw the Warden pop his head out of his tent, and Palmer beside him. Though it was too dark to see more than shapes, I could feel them eyeing us suspiciously. I could sense the questions running through their minds: *What was he laughing about? What does he know that we don't?*

Thomas's laugh resolved itself into a smile. "I just thought of something."

"What?"

"Just think!" His voice vibrated with excitement and he turned to gesticulate at the landscape around us. "If this mountain—this impossible godlike mountain urging us to its summit—has potentially cropped up again and again throughout time, even if no one believed anyone who told them about it, there would still be tales of it. It would still show up in our stories." His hands were shaking with energy. "*Think about it!* Think about how often the same concept appears across cultures: Moses climbing the Holy Mountain to meet with God and bring down divine law; the Pandava brothers of the *Mahabharata* finding the gateway to heaven at the peak of Mount Kailash; Sisyphus climbing the mountain of Hades again and again through eternal time.

The sacred mountain appears throughout all our religions. Mount Olympus; Hara Berezaiti; Mount Meru." He waved wildly as he talked, and, in his rapture, light almost seemed to beam from his face. "But what if these mountains aren't fictional? What if they just weren't physically accessible anymore?"

"What are you saying?" I asked, as a gust of freezing wind blew past my face. "That we're on Mount Olympus?"

He shook his head, a huge grin painted on his face. "Not just Mount Olympus, but the mountains of *all* gods, throughout *all* time. Harold, if my theory is right, we're standing on the holiest site in the history of the entire human race."

For a second, it looked as though he was about to explode with excitement. Then his eye drooped, his brow coming together in a frown. He tried to form a word, but his mouth fell open uselessly. He staggered forward.

Before I could catch him, he collapsed into a heap on the ground.

* * *

Miller carried Thomas into his tent while Naoko went to fetch the medical supplies. At some point, without discussion, she had become the expedition medic again not just a survivor we were taking care of. Once back, she said she needed space with him. Too many people crowding around wouldn't help. Uneasily, we dispersed, trying as best we could to get a little rest.

Still hungry, I ate a small meal of porridge and tinned sardines. A strange mixture, but I had grown used to strange up on this mountain. Using some snow to clean my plastic bowl and spoon, I tucked them back away in my pack.

After a couple of hours, I poked my head out of my tent. I glanced quickly left and right, not wanting to draw attention. This mountain had never felt safe, even from the first time I stood on it, but now my fellow climbers felt dangerous, too. I couldn't get my mind off the Warden, how he had attacked me, and how quickly his hand had gone to his gun.

I was coldly sure of one thing. Whoever these people worked for, our safety was not their top priority.

It was dark outside, but there were no clouds. The pale moon and a full complement of stars illuminated our campsite like a canopy of lights. The white smear of the Milky Way danced across the sky. I stared upward for a time, marveling at how little of the universe we understood, and wondering if we ever would, or if some things were just not meant for us. Maybe they were out of our reach for a reason.

Moving slowly through the snow so as not to wake anyone, I made my way to Thomas's tent. Unzipping the fabric, I slipped inside.

Naoko had Thomas laid out on his back on the floor. A couple of empty oxygen canisters were beside him. His chest was pulsating quickly, his lungs panting, even while he lay unconscious. Naoko sat by his side with a stethoscope in one hand, taking his blood pressure from the pumped-up cuff on his arm with the other.

"What happened to him?"

She let out a breath and it steamed in front of her. "My best diagnosis is high-altitude cerebral edema." She put her hand on his arm. She was still jittery, subject to occasional shakes and spurts of confusion, but her lucid periods were longer now, and clearer. "The heartbeat is elevated and he has a bit of a fever. He has come round a couple of times, but when he does his speech is slurred, like he's drunk."

I blinked, trying to bring back my medical knowledge. I have not been a practicing doctor in a very long time. "What's the prognosis?"

"His brain is swelling because of the altitude. I've given him supplemental oxygen and acetazolamide, but I don't want him hyperventilating. He must have been hiding the other symptoms."

"Other symptoms?"

"Typically vomiting and headaches in the lead-up to a case like this."

"He never said anything."

"No," she replied, looking down at him with that very same compassion that I fell in love with. "He didn't."

"I can't believe this is happening." I shook my head, sitting down next to her. "What more can we do?"

"We need to get him off this mountain, Harry. If we don't, he'll die."

I gulped, wondering how it would even be possible to get him down at this stage. Could we trust anyone but us? Would he even agree to go down, after the things he said today?

"Stupid man," she muttered. "Men! Stupid, stupid men."

"What do you mean?"

"Hiding that he was sick, when I could have helped him before. But now?" She shook her head.

The weight of her words sank into me and I took a deep breath, feeling a pang of embarrassment. It felt familiar, comical, even. Strangely domestic amidst this strangeness.

"I'm sorry, Naoko," I said, pulling off my right glove. "But I feel really stupid myself."

She looked at my fingers, now utterly black, and put her head in her hands. "How long?"

"A couple of days, I think."

"A *couple of*—" She took in a deep, long breath. "You idiot. Put your hand out."

She reached over and grabbed my wrist, pulling it toward her. Twisting my hand this way and that, she grimaced. Before I knew it, she was reaching for a surgical knife. I jerked back.

"Whoa, hold on a second. Isn't there some kind of—"

"The dead flesh has to go. Now." She held my gaze. "We've got no anesthetic left. The longer this is attached to you, the more it will eat away at you, until you have nothing left."

With her hand resting on mine, the heat of her skin touching my wrist, a sudden intimacy warmed the room, surrounding us. Despite the cold, I felt very hot—a fire that started in my chest and spread outward, to my throat and cheeks. When I spoke, it came out like a gasp.

"What if it's too painful?"

She took my other hand in hers. "It will be. It'll be the most painful thing you've ever experienced. You've got to accept the wound is there, that it is done, and that it can't be undone. Then you've got to cut it off."

The heat rose to my eyes, and I felt them water, tears dripping down my cheek. I looked down at my hand—that blackened stump that had become a symbol of my avoidance and stupidity and self-loathing—and then back up into her impossible, depthless eyes.

I gave her a brief, hard nod.

She let go of my hand, pulling her medical case underneath it. Quickly, she tied a tight tourniquet around my wrist and clicked open a bottle of disinfectant alcohol, rubbing it across the knife to sterilize it. Looking back up at me, she retook my wrist, pushing my hand against the surface of her medical case. Lifting the knife up, she pressed its blade against the base of my three fingers, a little lower than where the frostbite had spread. I shivered at the touch.

"Put that in your mouth," she said, nodding to a rag beside Thomas. His breathing had slowed a little, and he seemed as though he was just fast asleep, peacefully dreaming of places far from this one. I picked it up and put it between my teeth.

"I'm going to count down from three," she said, her voice clinical. She pressed my hand down harder into the case. "I'll try to make it as quick as possible, but I don't have a proper saw. This might be a little messy. But you can do it. I know you can."

I gulped, nodding.

"Three," she said, holding my eyes. Time seemed to stop. A hundred thousand unspoken moments passed between us.

"Two."

I closed my eyes, waiting for the one. It didn't come. Searing pain jolted up my wrist, into my arm. I screamed, my teeth biting down hard on the rag, my eyes clenching shut. My breath came hard and quick, panting for air between each scream.

My mind went, and all I could think about was the pain, the knife slicing through flesh, the warm, wet ooze of blood pooling underneath my hand. All else was obliterated. For a stretched moment, there was just me and my pain.

And then it was over.

Not the pain—not entirely; my hand still burned as though it had been shoved into a fire. But the worst of it was done. I opened my eyes to find Naoko already suturing and bandaging my hand, my blackened fingers, bloody and mangled, off to one side.

I let out a sob, the cloth falling from my mouth. An unstoppable torrent of emotion pushed its way through me—of loss, of grief, of relief. Naoko said nothing—she just took my head in her hands and pulled me toward her, and I fell, like a rag doll, into her lap.

She put her arms around me, stroking my hair. I stayed there, God knows how long, curled up beside her like a child, silently sobbing into the night.

* * *

Hattie—

I must add an addendum to my last letter, in case I never come back. I am scribbling it in my tent right now, pretending to be gathering my things.

It is the middle of the night. I still can't sleep. Moments ago, there was a rustling outside, and thinking it was Palmer, or perhaps the

Warden, sneaking out to conspire against us, I poked my head out into the cold.

It was neither. He stood there, like a figure out of a dream, waiting. Jet.

His leg was no longer broken, though not healed, either. Not entirely—there was something off about it, something strange. It seemed to ripple as though it had a life of its own, and I couldn't help but think about what Polya had said. About the microbes.

"*Jet*," I whispered, coming out of my tent. "Jet, are you okay?"

There was a glint in his eye. His smile reminded me of that mechanical rabbit that had so scared you in the arcade, Hattie. The one with no life in it.

"Oh, yes, Harold. I'm *more* than okay."

"Jet?" Another voice rang behind us. I turned to see Polya pushing out of her tent and into the snow, her face twisted in concern. "What has happened to you?"

"I will show you. I will show you both, but just you. You must come now. Immediately. Do not wake the others. They cannot be trusted."

I hesitated, looking to Polya. I thought about Palmer's phone call, and the sting of the Warden's fist. Polya's face was unreadable.

"Okay," I said. "What are you going to show us?"

"Oh, Harold," he said, with a wolflike grin. "I'm going to show you eternity."

2nd FEBRUARY??
CAMP 2*

Dear Harriet,

By the time I made it out of my tent, Jet was already traipsing off into the dark. The snowy winds were low, and the night was well lit by the blanket of glittering stars above in the cloudless sky. A huge moon hung over us, as though it were ten times closer than it should be, and its beams glimmered as they caught the ice and snow.

But even so, my visibility didn't stretch far. Jet was almost out of sight, and Polya shortly behind him. I took a quick look back at the tents, worried that I was leaving Naoko with the likes of Bettan and the Warden.

Jet passed out of sight, into the black, and Polya's shape grew further

---

* **EDITOR'S NOTE:** There are two curiosities to note about this particular letter. The first is that while Harold's dating previously lost consistency around the 27th of January, this is the first time he consciously recognizes his uncertainty in the dating. Why he becomes unsure of exactly when he is writing is unclear. The second is that an examination of the weathering and decay suggests that this is the oldest of the collection of letters by quite some degree.

away. Cursing, I tugged my pack on tightly, my hand still aching from the makeshift surgery, and chased after them, out into the wilderness.

I caught up to them, breathing heavily. The lack of oxygen burned my lungs as though I'd run a mile. With the pack on her back, Polya was also panting—the first time I'd seen her struggle since we began this journey. She'd taken more with her than I had, I noticed. Her camera was clipped to one side of her pack, and some climbing gear bulged out the top. All I had managed to throw together was my flashlight and some extra clothing. How long did she think we'd be gone? How unprepared was I?

Jet was unfazed. He walked quickly, very quickly, but did not seem to rush. There was no limp in his walk or suggestion that he had been injured. As I approached, I tried to get a look at the leg I had worked on—the one I knew had been shredded beyond belief.

I aimed my headlamp at his feet and tried to keep up with him. The leg flashed in and out of the dark. His trousers were ripped, exposing his skin to the freezing winds, but it didn't seem to matter. The leg gleamed where the light hit it, as though glistening with some kind of fluid. The muscles, thicker than I remembered them, seemed to writhe underneath his skin like tiny snakes.

Just as I was beginning to gather my breath and match his pace, he stopped. It happened so suddenly that Polya and I barreled right past him and had to turn around.

"Where have you been?" I said. "What happened to you?"

He put a hand up to silence me. Polya glanced at me and then back at Jet. Lifting his fingers to his head, he started tapping a rhythm against his skull.

Dum-dum-dum-dum. Dum-dum-dum-dum.

He stretched his other hand far out in front of him, holding his watch in the air.

A few moments passed, and he smiled—that strange, hungry grin again—and said, "Don't worry. We're going in the right direction."

"The right direction for what?"

He didn't answer; he merely picked up his pace again and left us to scramble along behind him.

A loud slithering echoed from underneath the ice. Every muscle in my body tensed. I spun around, too quickly, my headlamp's beam flickering across the ice too fast to be of use. Polya grabbed my coat and pulled me, tugging me after Jet, still walking away.

"What was that?" I whispered to her.

She shook her head, her face red with exhaustion.

"I don't know. But we must not lose him."

There was another crash, and I leaped into the air with a shout. Polya looked at me, her headlamp shining into my eyes. She grabbed my arm and pointed, fixing her lamp on a large rock that had fallen from shifting snow.

"Just a rock," she said, more to herself than me. "It's just a rock."

Then another slither—loud, like a hundred snakes struggling. I winced, unable to contain the gripping fear that built inside me, of the darkness, of our isolation, of the unknown creatures that lurked in the black. I spun, squinting in the dark, seeing nothing but snow and ice.

"That is *not* just a rock. There's something out here with us," I insisted, turning back to Polya. "We should have brought a gun."

Polya gritted her teeth. "I know, Harold. But we didn't. And if we go back now, we lose him. So we must stay calm, and we must stay close to the man who has survived out here. Can you do this?"

I looked ahead. Jet had stopped and was waiting for us.

"Yes," I breathed, unsure if I was telling the truth. "Yes, I can do that."

"Good."

When we caught up to him, he was standing with his back to us, arms raised like he was addressing a congregation. In front of him was a dead end: a rising crag far too tall to climb. A few big rocks were dotted round the front of it, covered in snow. The air was deadly silent.

The wind felt different, too: closer and mustier. I could have sworn that it was a little warmer.

"This is an entrance," he said. "One of many. I can show you the way."

"I can't see anything there, Jet," I said.

He walked round the back of one of the largest rocks, nestled up against the cliff. It rose about fifteen feet into the air. There was a small nook against the crag from where the rock was leaning against it—a little cavity just about big enough to fit a person. With the rock leaning over the top, it was pitch-black, completely blocked from the light of the moon above.

Around the blackness, color shifted a little: blue emanated out of the edges and into everything around it, like a filter. I could feel a tug toward it, like it had its own gravity.

The filter of blue pulsed—inward and outward—and for a moment I thought it looked alive. It looked *hungry*.

Jet ducked into it, and before I could call out in panic, he disappeared.

This was crazy. My body recoiled in horror. Complete madness. But I looked at Polya for a half second, and I knew immediately what she was going to do.

"Polya—"

She stepped into the dark and didn't come back.

For a moment, I stood still. I turned around on the spot, fidgeting, muttering. This had all happened so quickly. My heart was racing so fast, my brain hadn't had time to catch up with it. All I knew was that

I was now alone, completely isolated, and I had no idea how to get back to camp. This was *insane.*

Another gruesome slither echoed off the rocks and I jolted, hand going to my chest.

"*Fuck.*"

Taking a deep breath, I ducked and plunged headlong into the black.

* * *

I felt like I was falling. Not for long—for just a second or two, it felt as though the ground had disappeared underneath me and I was tumbling aimlessly through a void. I landed on hard ground and opened my eyes.

There was rock beneath my feet, and light, but not from the sky. There was no sky. We were underground, in a cave dimly lit by a few flaming torches that had been placed along the rocky walls. Who had put them here? Who was keeping them lit? It occurred to me that trying to light a fire like this at our altitude had been an impossible task, but maybe we weren't *at* our altitude anymore. It was warmer. Not much, but a little. In temperatures like this, a little makes all the difference.

I squinted, seeing Polya standing to my left and Jet just ahead of us. The torches only just flickered, barely providing enough light to shine throughout the tunnel. I couldn't tell where the walls ended and the ceiling began. It felt tight, but for all I knew we could have been in a cavern a mile tall.

"Your eyes will adjust," Jet said, his voice almost musical. "They don't like much light—their eyes aren't used to it. They only come out in the daylight for short moments of time. The torches are more ceremonial than anything."

"By 'they,'" I said, "you mean the . . . creatures?"

Jet gave a little laugh, like I was a child who had told a whimsical joke. "Yes, Harold." He turned round, shaking his head in amusement, a smile on his lips. "The *creatures*."

"Why have you brought us here?"

His smile faded. "So that you can understand what needs to be done." His features hardened, the light from the torches casting shadows across them like tiny black flames. "The others are only here for their own gain, but you two are like me. You came here to discover truth. And the truth is we should not have come here. We must fix our mistakes."

"Is this where they live?"

"This is one of the places," he said. "There are many more. Come, I will show you."

He walked ahead, and I hung back a little to check that Polya was okay. She looked at me, deep lines of concern etched across her face, but she said nothing. With a nod, she gestured for me to follow.

Jet was right: as we walked through the cave, my eyes did adapt. The little light was enough for me to start to see the whole picture. The tunnel was wide, around twenty meters across, but along its walls and ceiling there were more tunnels that led off to other parts of the cave. It appeared to be a giant underground system—constructed, not natural. I wondered how far it spread, and suspected that it was further than I could possibly imagine.

The more attuned my eyes became, the more I noticed that the cave walls were not just textured with natural cuts and divots, but were carved. Complex bas-reliefs of story-like scenes spread across them, seeming to stretch on forever. It was difficult to make out meaning, the style so utterly different to anything I had ever seen—a mixture of ancient hieroglyphics and modern impressionism. And yet, some symbols were clear. The image of a mountain, recurring again and again. Creatures like the one we had encountered were at the bottom, and then, above that, what appeared to be beings composed of rays of light, or of waves. My mind traveled back to confessions made in a dark, small room.

The revelation hit me like a punch to the chest: This was no mere underground cavern. This was a place of worship. A temple.

"Do you hear that?" Polya asked me. I turned to her, frowning.

"Hear what?"

"Listen."

I fell silent, listening for something in between the sound of my breaths. It took a few moments, but I thought I could sense a low hum, more as though it was in my body than my ears, like the deep reverberation of bass.

"What is it?"

"That's them," Jet said. "That's how they communicate. Or, more than that. It's what they are. It's how they share their consciousness between them."

"A hive mind?"

"Of sorts," he replied. He turned a corner into one of the smaller tunnels and we followed. "They are distinct beings, but they are always in concert, always singing together. It's not really a sound. A kind of electrical activity, perhaps. The longer you stay here, the more you begin to pick up on it. I would have loved to have studied the chemistry of it. If I was the man I used to be, of course." He turned back and smiled. "I am more than that now."

The hairs on my arms all stood on end.

"How have you discovered all of this?" I asked, trying to change the conversation. "How did you get here?"

"I began to understand them at the camp, when we hurt one of them, when they touched me. In the night, they made me understand. And the longer I am here, the more I *see*. The more I know. My mind is attuning to their brain waves. It came slowly at first, just flashes of images, of ideas. I have been trying to find a word that describes them best—it is difficult, the intersection between my language and theirs, but one word keeps returning to my mind. *Leviathans*."

The word sent a shiver down my spine. "Like the biblical monsters?"

Jet cocked his head, thoughtful. "Ironic, isn't it? How these stories combine." His eyes focused back on mine. "They helped me. They fixed my leg. Most of all, they showed me truth. They only ask for a little in return."

The question I was too afraid to ask remained on my tongue: *What did they ask in return?*

As we turned out of the last small tunnel, the space before us opened up into a big cavern. I took a sharp breath. The back wall, some fifty meters high, was covered in carvings and a range of colors of paint. Sprawling across the rock, intricate designs twisted up and down like a million stars, large and small, orbiting one another.

It was the most alien thing I have ever seen in my life, and it was beautiful.

"Do you see?" Jet said, waving at the walls. "There is so much to this mountain we do not understand. That we will never understand. This is not for us. We do not deserve to be here. But they will allow you to stay for a time, if you will help them."

Staring at the wall, I staggered slightly, suddenly a little woozy. My head felt light, and slow, as if I were a little drunk. The hum was clear in the background now, more perceptible than before. It wheedled its way inside of my brain. A heaviness pressed into my bones: a deep melancholy.

"They *are* scared, though," Jet said, sadness entering his voice. "The last encounter has worried them. They had not seen guns before; they do not understand them. They need me like a kind of conduit, to understand what we are doing here. I try to explain, but . . ." He touched his head. "I'm still working on the connection. There's only so much I can do, even after all this time."

Tearing myself away from the wall, I looked over at him. "Jet—how long have you been down here?"

He shrugged. "A month and a half? Maybe two? You will come to understand that time is not what you think it is in this place." His tone grew didactic. "I will be back soon. Wait here—I must go attempt to communicate with them that you are here, and that you are friendly, so that they understand that you'll help me to deal with the rest of the expedition."

"Deal with?" I repeated, the persistent hum pushing into the back of my skull. I tried to clear my head by shaking it. "What do you mean? Help you do what?"

"Oh, I thought that was obvious," he said, walking off into another tunnel. As he disappeared into the darkness, his voice carried back to us, echoing a little off the walls. "We need to kill them, of course. We need to kill them all."

* * *

Polya and I stood alone in that room, transfixed by the giant artwork before us. Neither of us spoke for a time, unsure how to broach what had just been said. I twisted my head left and right, trying to make sense of what I was seeing—it looked like a depiction of a galaxy. The longer I looked, the harder it was to tear my eyes away.

"Yesterday, you folded a piece of paper," Polya said. "You said that this fold in a higher dimension would allow your ant to jump, as if by magic, from one location in its plane to another."

"Yes."

"That is how we have come to be here, then. What we stepped through. A fold in space."

I nodded. "That makes sense." I don't know why I hadn't thought of it before. It seemed so obvious, but the incessant humming at the back of my brain made all of my thoughts muddy, as if I were trying to view them through dirty water. My fists were clenched, and I wasn't sure why. Even on my mangled right hand, my remaining fingers strained under the bandaging to press their nails into my palms.

I was aware that both of us were still avoiding what Jet had just told us, whether out of fear that he was still close enough to hear, or merely because it was easier to imagine it hadn't happened. A dampness pervaded the air.

I tried to focus my thoughts, staring at the wall. "That explains the time dilation. Think about it: if these are folds in dimensions, then there could feasibly be much more mass than meets the eye. Just like a folded piece of paper gets thicker, these folds in the mountain could be a hundred, a thousand folds thick. A million even. That much mass would distort time, each one like a little black hole. The light around it was blue-shifted." I turned to Polya. "Hell, I even *felt* a little gravitational pull toward it. Every time we get too close to one, time stretches. That's why Jet has been here for months, and we've only missed him for three days. We just can't see the folds because they aren't happening in our perception."

She nodded at me, approving, and I clapped my hands together in excitement. "That's why Jet was tapping! Measuring against his watch, looking for variations."

You've got to watch the seconds, Naoko had said. *Because they're watching you.*

"If the anomaly is as focused as it appears to be," I explained, trying to ignore the persistent hum in my head, "then the time dilation even between your head and your extended hand would be noticeable. As you approach the anomaly, moving *through* different fields of time, the tapping would fall out of sync with the watch. If you can track where time is distorted, you can find where the folds are."

Polya turned to look at me. "Yes. We are the ants. It makes complete sense."

"What do you mean?" I took a step back. My head was swimming, struggling to see her connection.

"Biologically," she said, "it makes sense. Consider the ants: they have their own worlds, their own societies. They live, they die, they cohabit the planet with us. They live in our houses, in our gardens and our fields. And yet, do you think any individual ant has any idea that humans actually exist, on a conscious level?"

I frowned. "I don't know if they consciously think about *anything* existing."

"No." Polya knelt down, swiped a gloved finger against the rock, and tasted it. "But they have *some* form of consciousness, certainly. It is simply on such a completely different plane to ours that they're not only unable to understand humanity, but likely unable to even recognize that we exist. The threat of a descending boot, perhaps, but it would seem to an ant no different than a river, or a fierce wind."

I stared at her, trying to focus on her words, trying to pick them out from the surrounding hum.

"What's your point?"

She stood up and straightened herself. "I've been thinking about how it has been possible to coexist for millennia on this planet with other complex creatures without knowing they exist. Why would they hide from us? But if we are to them as ants are to us, it makes sense. They haven't been hiding. They've probably been right in front of us since the dawn of the species. We're just too stupid to see them."

"You're talking about these . . . things?"

I couldn't bring myself to say "leviathans." It was too fantastical. Too crazy.

"No," she said, eyeing the map. "I do not think so. I think that they are also ants, though perhaps more advanced than we are, judging by these caves. I am talking about whatever put this mountain here."

Polya reached for her pack, pulled off her Polaroid camera, and started snapping photos of the wall.

The hum rose, as if in response. It was louder now, a buzzing noise emanating from inside my head. I took a couple of deep breaths, trying to focus on something else. Trying to block it out.

"It's a map," Polya said. I looked back up at the swirling constellations on the wall. "It's a map of the mountain. The circles, the ones that look like solar systems? That's where the folds are. Look at the lines of trajectory." She pointed up at carved lines connecting each system with others. "They link together. The creatures here have mapped the entire mountain."

"How do you know?"

"Look at the circles," she said. "The way they connect with the others, but continue on. It forms a circuit—like the track of a train. I do not think these work like doors: you go in one way and get back the same way." She cocked her head, squinting, and in the madness of everything that was happening, I couldn't help but marvel at the fact that I was seeing the great Polya Volikova in action. Working out a problem. Seeing connections and links. "No, look: it is the *entrances* that are appointed. Each entrance takes you somewhere new. And it is the symbols, not their location on the map, that indicate *where* these doorways are on the mountain."

A knocking echoed through the cave walls, like footsteps.

"Jet said he wanted to kill everyone," I blurted out. "And he wants us to help him."

"I know."

"What do we do?" My voice shook.

She turned her head to me and leaned in, whispering. "If he has only been here for two months or so, the RNA microbes have infected his biology faster than I predicted. Look at his leg—that is not human DNA. Our neurobiology is so fragile in so many ways. Perhaps when his leg was cut open, he was more deeply infected than we have been. They may have made him more susceptible to these invasive mental energies. We tell him we will help him, until he can get us out of this cave. Then we run, we warn the others of this danger. It's the only way."

I wanted to discuss further, to explore this idea with her, but each time a thought entered into my mind, it seemed to battle against the rising hum, and before I knew it, it was obliterated. I was so *angry*.

My teeth clenched, my chest tightening—after all, if Jet was susceptible, what if we were, too?

Polya moved swiftly from left to right as she snapped and snapped again, capturing every corner of the grand constellation. She seemed unaffected by whatever was pressing itself into my mind. Each time a Polaroid slide came out, she tucked it into her jacket pocket.

I scrunched my eyes shut, trying to focus on my own thoughts. There was a flash: a vision of the mountain in the dark; howling winds; and that anger, a deep pit that was only just touching the edges of my mind. I gasped—these thoughts were not originating from me, and yet there they were, in my head. And underneath all of that, from what felt like a different source, there was a pull. Not in my mind, but in my body. A hunger. To get to the top of the mountain. To climb.

"We need to get out of here soon," I whispered, my breath quickening. "Do you not feel . . . God, it's in my brain!"

"I feel it, Harold." Her voice was very quiet. She tucked her camera into her pack. "But I am trying very hard not to."

"You're sensing them, aren't you?" Jet's voice came from behind us. I spun round, fists suddenly raised. He put his hand up. "Don't be afraid. This is just the beginning. You're being shown the world that exists beyond humanity, far above it. You're being given a glimpse into eternity. Embrace it, like I did."

He walked toward us slowly, a predatory grin still plastered onto his face.

"How do we help you?" Polya said. "How do we get to the others?"

"They will show you the way, in time. You must be patient. They have said that you can stay here, with me, for a few months. To learn. To understand." He must have seen the stricken look on my face, because he added softly: "Don't be afraid, Harold. Time works differently here. It changes, like the seasons, or the weather. You'll soon learn to stop relying on it."

Jet's eyes narrowed, his focus falling directly on the Polaroids that were sticking out of Polya's jacket pocket.

"What is that?" he demanded, taking a step toward her. She gave him a dismissive wave, turning her back.

"Nothing."

"Don't turn away from me."

His voice turned monstrous as he closed the distance between them in a single breath, like lightning, and tugged the photos from her pocket. She stumbled back. Seething, he flipped through them.

"Why did you do this?" he shouted.

Polya started to back away, holding her hands up in defense. "I was just—"

"You can't do that," Jet screamed, his voice bubbling with fury as he stormed forward. *"IT'S NOT YOURS!"*

"Jet!" I put my hand up to stop him, but he smacked it aside. I stumbled back, surprised by his strength. I saw the knife in Jet's hand too late. A simple utility knife, the type we all had with us for the climb.

"Polya!" I shouted, but it was pointless. She turned to run, but he was faster, *so much faster*. With a sudden thrust, he shoved the knife in her neck, lodging it right into her spine. She stiffened, letting out a tiny

puff of air, then softened into him. Her body arched as he pulled her backward, her spinal cord severed. The knife slid out of her, blood and nerves and spinal fluid sputtering out after it.

"This is not for you," Jet said, suddenly calm, as he lowered her to the ground. Her eyes were wide. Blood coughed out of her mouth. His tone was almost motherly, like he was admonishing a small child. "You must understand. This is not for you."

I stood frozen. As I watched Jet leaning over Polya's dying body, whispering to her, all I wanted to do was run. Run from here as fast as my legs could take me. But I didn't. Where could I go? I just stood, petrified, sweating in my layers, and waited.

Jet stood up and grinned at me. My heart pounded, the hairs on my arms tingling against the inside of my coat. It was suddenly too hot to be wearing a coat, too hot to be doing anything at all.

"It's okay. It'll all be okay now."

The hum had grown into a thick buzz, and with it came an assault of new sensations. More flashes of memories that were not my own—rivers of lava, twisting sandstorms, and climbing, always climbing. They pressed their way into my mind, insinuating themselves into my identity.

I needed a plan. I needed to get out of here before Jet turned on me, or worse, before I started to see the world the same way he did. If I stayed here, I knew it would happen. It was inevitable.

But I couldn't think. Jet walked toward the wall, gazing greedily at it, as though Polya's body were not bleeding out on the floor behind him. There had to be something I could do, but each time I grasped on to the thread of a plan, another thought forced its way into my head. Fierce distaste grew on my tongue, a sickening disgust for these tiny little bipeds that insinuated their way into our mountain, that thought they knew better than us, that spread, and fucked, and vomited them- selves into our—

I shuddered, unsure of where I was.

"Don't worry, Harold," Jet said. His hand was on my shoulder. He was very close to me, staring off into the distance. "It's bad at first, but it will settle. The leviathans were here first, you see? It's theirs, not ours. We do not deserve this. But I will be here to help you through it. To help them."

Pulling away, I stepped backward, further and further, trying to focus on my breathing, my heartbeat—anything that would keep me sane. My ankles knocked into something big and I tumbled backward, falling to the floor.

Polya. Her corpse, face turned to the side, staring at me with her eyes still open.

Good. The thought entered my head unbidden. *She deserves it*.

I recoiled in horror, repulsed by my own mind. Sitting up, I saw them: the Polaroids that she had taken, still slowly developing. Jet had dropped them on the floor. A map, she had said. And maybe, if I could just get away from this maddening place, a way out.

I didn't let myself think about it. I couldn't trust my own thoughts. Lunging over to her body, I gathered them all up and shoved them deep into my jacket.

"There is so much," Jet whispered, staring at the cave walls. He wasn't looking at me. I shuffled backward on the ground, trying to move away slowly, quietly. "Beauty. Artistry. Dignity. And we stole it from them, Harold. We stole it all."

I was some twenty meters away from him now, and he was enraptured by the wall. He seemed to have, for a moment, forgotten I was there.

Taking a deep breath, I pushed myself up to my feet.

I ran.

Stumbling, I tried to dart into the nearest tunnel, running blindly to get away from Jet, to get away from the hum, to escape the very thoughts that were forcing themselves inside of me like parasites.

I ran until my lungs were on fire, until my legs throbbed in torturous pain. Further. Deeper into the cave. Away.

Sounds of slithering and shifting started to emanate out of the cave walls, echoes of movement within the caverns, of a mass shifting of beasts that I was sure were coming to hunt me down. To stop me from leaving.

The buzz was now a racket in my head, a screaming. Memories from my youth dancing across my mind, mad things that had never happened. Scrambling through ice and snow. Worshipping impossible deities. And then memories further back, from before I was born, from before there was humanity or language or time—a great chain of existence, a golden path set out for all life that I was treading and that I would always tread, whether I chose to or not. There was no such thing as free will. I knew that as fact. Only illusions. Only tiny corners of the world we carve out for ourselves.

I stumbled to a halt, gasping. I had no idea where Jet was, but I had to assume he was close. I tried to regain some sense of self. I needed to think about something that was not this mountain, or the cave that I was in. Anything to drown out the buzz.

Naoko.

She was back at the camp. She was waiting for me. I painted an image of her in my head: a perfect untainted vision of her sleeping. I focused on it completely. The curvature of her cheeks; the little freckles beneath her left ear; the way her hair curled into waves at the bottom. And just as I could picture her back in the camp, I saw her throughout all my memory. Every moment we had spent together, lain together, laughed and cried together—I could picture it as perfectly as looking in a mirror.

Squeezing my eyes tightly shut, I let the image of her fill me. I knew what I had to do, and before I could second-guess myself, I'd already done it. I tore open the box inside of me—the box I had only dared myself to peek inside—and let my love for her, a love that I had buried so deep for so long, rage out. And with it came pain, and loathing, and hatred, and a thousand hideous emotions that I never wanted to feel again. But they were *my* emotions. They belonged to *me.*

The buzz lessened to a hum, and the hum to a deep resonant vibration—still there, but not overwhelming. I knew who I was again.

I was Naoko's husband. I was the man that loved her, and I was the man that created a life for her, and also the man who shattered that life into a million pieces. But I would always love her, for all eternity.

That was who I was.

The slithering grew louder and the walls of the tunnel began to shake. My hands fumbling, I tried to look at the pictures Polya had taken, but it was too dark. They were too complex. They would need hours of study, and I barely had minutes.

"*Harold.*" Jet's voice rang through the air, electrified with anger. "*You can't run from me.*"

I started running again, cutting into another tunnel; though there were smaller tunnels that branched off in different directions, I had no idea where any of them led. I took a deep breath, then another, counting them to calm the panic. And as I did, I remembered Jet counting, tapping his head, his arm outstretched.

There were ways out. I just needed to find them.

I stuck out my arm as I ran, thanking the heavens I still had my watch. I tapped against my head, as Jet had done, trying to keep it as regular as possible, trying to stay in sync with the second hand.

I stumbled on a rock, my outstretched arm throwing me off balance, and just barely righted myself. The slithering grew louder.

Taking a deep breath, I started again. *One, two, three* . . . The watch hand fell backward, slowing behind my count. I blinked, reset, and tried again. Once again, the second hand seemed to slow down.

I was nearing a fold.

Then, as I passed a turnoff to a smaller tunnel, the counting stabilized. It felt regular again.

I cut back. The anomaly was down there—I knew it.

The fold.

Returning to that tunnel, I dashed down it, hoping desperately I was right.

The slithers had risen to a rattle, a steady drumming of movement somewhere not far behind me, like the sound of an army marching at my back. Ahead of me was the outline of an archway, built into the rock. Inside it, there was just darkness—no more torches, just a deep pit that disappeared into black—and around it, blue light bleeding into the rock.

The light pulsed around it, changing color as reality itself was dragged inward and consumed.

But there was nothing for it. Taking in a deep breath, I charged forward.

Browns shifted to reds, and then to blues. My body lurched, kicking out as if I'd fallen back off a chair, my legs disappearing from under me.

Time stretched, and I thought I was moving in slow motion, like in a dream.

I was falling, again.

Then snow. And ice. And asphyxiation.

I fell to my knees, hands going to my throat. Wherever I had ended up, there wasn't enough oxygen. I was far too high. Fierce winds slapped against my face, burning my eyes.

Spinning around, I fell to all fours, trying to get a sense of my surroundings. I had exited through an archway, built out of stone and darkness. It stood like a relic of an icy Stonehenge, and inside its curve was an impossible void: a fold into another section of space.

I turned to look behind me, and just up the rise there was a swirling eddy of white and wind. Beyond that—the summit.

I didn't need to see it.

I knew it was there as clearly as I knew my own name.

A deep hunger welled inside of me, to climb to the peak, to be the first. And, somehow, I also knew that if I made it there, I would never come back.

It didn't matter.

Forcing myself to my feet, I took a tentative step toward it, and then another. This was it. This was *right*. There was a niggling sensation in the back of my mind, but I swept it aside.

The summit was waiting for me, and I would be there any moment.

I took another few steps forward, struggling to breathe, but that didn't matter, either.

Nothing mattered but the climb.

Except that wasn't true. I was forgetting something.

Someone.

Someone who needed to be here with me. This wasn't the right moment. Not now, as much as my body wanted it to be.

Summoning all the force of will that I had left, I tore myself away from the peak in the opposite direction. It was like trying to fight gravity. My head was swimming. I needed to breathe oxygen, soon, or I would pass out.

There was no other option.

There was no other way to survive, and I *needed* to survive.

Stumbling forward, I leaped back into the archway and into the fold.

Black.

Then white.

Then a face full of snow.

I took in a deep breath of air and sighed. It filled my lungs, like honey, like cold water in a desert, and soothed me from the inside out.

I pushed myself to my feet and looked around. I wasn't in the cave again. I'd been deposited elsewhere. The realization hit me: Polya was right. The folds aren't two-way doorways. They don't take you back and forth, but onward, to the next stop in the circuit. I could be anywhere on the mountain—alone, without food or water or anything to keep me safe.

I fell to the ground, my head in my hands. This was it. It was over. I was going to die.

Alone, isolated, without ever understanding what had brought us here, what it all meant. Without ever seeing Naoko again.

Then I saw it—about two hundred meters down, and over the next ridge. Relief bubbled up inside me and burst out as a crazed laughter. It was our camp, the tents just beginning to light up in the morning sun.

Dear Harriet,

By the time I made it down to the camp, people were already up. I saw two figures—the Warden and Palmer, by the looks of them—stretching their legs and fetching some tins for breakfast out of their packs. It looked like they hadn't noticed that Polya and I had gone. Thinking about Jet's months to our days, I realized I didn't know how long we were away, or how long it seemed for them.

I was only about halfway down the ridge, climbing gingerly, still physically and mentally recovering from my ordeal. Each rock I clambered over sent pain shuddering up my right hand, the still-fresh stumps of my amputated fingers. Each step I took, I saw Polya's neck sliced open, I saw Jet's mad eyes, and I felt the dreadful pull of the summit.

As soon as they saw me, a figure in the distance, they started pointing and shouting. The others spilled out of their tents with a frantic urgency—any kind of commotion now suggesting danger. I wanted

---

* **EDITOR'S NOTE**: This is the second of the three letters originally sent to Harriet in 1991.

to shout down, to tell them it was just me, that there was nothing to worry about and everything was okay. But even as the thought came into my head, I realized I couldn't say that with any honesty. Not anymore.

It was as I shuffled down the cliff, having to climb down rock and dig my boots into ice, that I realized how utterly bone-tired I was. I had not properly slept in days, only the adrenaline of this crazy journey keeping me going. My body felt like it was on the verge of collapse.

"Where are you coming from?" the Warden demanded as soon as I was within shouting distance. I didn't have the energy to call back, so I just walked. He surveyed me with wary surprise as I approached. "When did you leave the campsite? *Why* did you leave the campsite?" They stood in a line—Palmer, Bettan, the Warden, with Neil hovering just behind. Miller was at the side with his rifle raised, and while it was not pointed at me, he certainly seemed primed to do so. Naoko poked her head out of the tent where she was caring for Thomas, eyeing me cautiously.

"I . . ." The weariness pressed down on me, and as it did, I felt twinges of the strange thoughts that had entered me back in the caves, like flashbacks. I glanced across the four of them and I felt pangs of hatred. Disgust rose up from my stomach and into my throat. I pushed it down.

"As if he'd tell you the truth," Bettan sneered. "Tell us: what experiments are you performing behind our backs? What are you—"

"Stop!" I shouted. "Just *stop!*"

Bettan fell silent, raising his eyebrows. Palmer had yet to say a word, but her eyes were steely, locked on me like the sight of a weapon.

"Can't you see what's happening?" I begged. "This paranoia? This infighting? It's going to get us all *killed.*"

"If you sneak off in the middle of the night," the Warden accused, "then it definitely will—"

"Polya's dead." I took a deep breath, leaning forward to rest my hands on my thighs. I could feel my eyes fluttering, pressing down from sheer exhaustion. "She's dead. Jet stabbed her right in the neck. Jet! And all *you* are doing"—I pointed a finger at the Warden—"is making threats like *I'm* the enemy. But I'm not. None of us are. It's this place! It's doing this to us, and it's more dangerous than you can possibly imagine!"

For a moment, no one spoke. The Warden exchanged a glance with Palmer, then looked back at me. The only sound was the light whistle of the cold mountain wind as it flickered around us.

The Warden took a step forward, put a hand on my shoulder, and said: "Tell me everything."

I looked up at him, pleadingly, desperate to make him understand, and before I knew it my knees crumpled. I was on my back, pressed against the cold ground, and I disappeared into the deep black of sleep.

* * *

When I woke, it was just the Warden and me in my tent. He'd laid me down under a thick sleeping bag, all my layers still on, and waited beside me. He was still as the grave, staring off into the middle distance. There was movement outside, pacing back and forth. Miller, I assumed, and maybe Palmer, keeping guard.

My heart was in my throat. I was scared, still half-drowsy. If I wanted to leave this tent, would I be allowed to? I had visions of him snapping, leaping on me, holding me down and choking me until whatever dark suspicions lingered inside him were spent.

I shuffled, lifting myself up, futilely trying to press away from him. Despite my sleep, my muscles still felt utterly depleted, drained of even the slightest bit of energy. But I was awake. And I could talk. Maybe that would be enough.

"I have . . . noticed a change in my behavior recently," the Warden said slowly. I cocked my head in surprise. He wasn't looking at me. "The higher we climb on this mountain, the more I am realizing that it has affected me. I pride myself on staying calm in the worst of situations, on remaining positive." Looking straight ahead, he gave the brief hint of that jovial smile that I had associated with him before we began our ascent. Then it disappeared, swallowed up inside him. "I'm finding it very hard not to see everyone as a threat. I've been controlling it, but after Jet disappeared . . ." He shook his head. "You're right in what you said, Harold. Something is deeply wrong. All I want to do is protect this expedition. I'm not sure how I do that anymore."

I sat up. I wasn't sure I believed him—if he had succumbed to the same influences that Jet had, that *I* had almost fallen to, then he could not be trusted.

I thought about the worker I had spoken with at Base Camp who seemed to de-age in an instant, to flicker through time. *This is not for you.* Those same words Jet had said after stabbing Polya in the neck. If the leviathans' reach spread as far as Base Camp, how could any of us be safe?

The Warden looked me dead in the eyes. "Tell me what happened."

I took a deep breath. The feel of Polya's Polaroids burned inside my jacket pocket. If I took them out, would he turn on me, would he throw me to the ground, kill me?

My jaw clenched.

I couldn't do this alone anymore. I couldn't hide what I had seen from everyone, or I would be the one that would go insane. It was a risk I was going to have to take.

Pulling the photos, slightly bent now, from where I'd shoved them, I laid them out in front of me. He gazed over them, and I watched for the switch, for a hint of Jet's madness. There was none.

The rest of the story spilled out of me like a flood: Jet and Polya; the leviathans and their tunnels; the folds; the summit. I felt a release, an easing of the tension inside me as I went on. If I could make someone else see what I had seen, have someone else understand, then I would not be alone. That would make all the difference.

He listened intently. He did not question, or argue, or comment. He took it all in, occasionally nodding in encouragement when I struggled to continue.

"I know the distrust you've been feeling," I said to the Warden at the end. It was crucial that he understand. "Those thoughts you are having, they aren't coming from you. You can fight them. If I can, we all can."

He got up.

"I need to consult with the others. I will leave you, for now." Standing over me, he held my gaze. "I have one last question: I have been thinking about abandoning this mission, of going back down. But I also feel that the only way to end all of this is to get to the summit. That the answers are there, and perhaps our only salvation. Are those thoughts mine, Harold? Did I come to that conclusion, or did someone put it there for me?"

I gulped, knowing exactly what the answer was. I thought about Polya's microbes, worming themselves into us. About the hum. And yet, as I opened my mouth, the only words in my mind were Naoko's: *There's no way off this mountain for me that isn't up.*

I thought of the folds, and the way the summit had felt, and for some reason, I said, "I think it's a logical conclusion." The lie tasted bitter on my tongue. "I'd say the same thing myself."

The Warden frowned, eyeing me for a long moment.

"And if we become like Jet?"

"Jet had been down there for months in his time—longer, perhaps. If we can stay out of those caves, if we can get up the mountain as quickly as possible, we should be all right."

He considered me for a time, then nodded. "Our supplies won't keep us up here forever anyway. Already they're dwindling. Food is running low. Can you . . . *use* these folds in the mountain to get us up quicker?"

I took a deep breath, the idea of going back into one of those things sending a shiver through me. "I don't know. They're not as simple as doorways. They shift. I passed through the same fold and traveled between three different places: the caves, the summit, and here. But if Polya was right . . ." I waved my hand at the Polaroids I had scattered before me. "If this is really a map of how they work, then perhaps I can chart us a route, given enough time. She started to figure it out, there in the caves, before . . ."

I trailed off, unable to say the words again. Could I really complete the work that Polya had started? Was I good enough? Was I *sane* enough?

The Warden nodded. "Do that." He unzipped the tent, but just before he stepped out, he turned back. Once again, I caught a glimpse of that friendly face, the one that had recruited me for this mad mission. A smile of genuine warmth. "I'm glad you made it back, Harold."

The smile dropped, he left, and I was once again on my own.

I lay back down, still fatigued from the sleep deprivation and the exertion. Closing my eyes, I tried to sleep. I couldn't. All that flickered through my brain was the image of the knife pressing into Polya's back; the blood sputtering out of her mouth; her glazed eyes, wide open and dead, staring at me.

The tent shook as a gust of wind blew through it, a reminder that we were still at this mountain's mercy.

It wasn't long before Naoko came to find me. As she entered the tent, I felt a warm wave of comfort come in with her. For the first time since I had returned, my muscles relaxed a little. Sitting down beside me, she opened a tin of beans and put them in front of me.

"Eat." She put a spoon in my hand.

My stomach rumbled. "The Warden said we were running low on food."

She placed her hand on my cheek. "That doesn't mean you need to starve. I know what you're like, Harry. You need to eat."

I nodded, slowly spooning the cold beans into my mouth.

"I heard about Polya. It . . ." Naoko said, closing her eyes. "It brings back bad thoughts. My head goes fuzzy again."

I swallowed. "This is what happened to the last expedition, isn't it?"

She paused, looking down and away from me. These were not thoughts she wanted to come back to. "I think so. It's hard for me to say sometimes . . . the memories, they become muddy. I remember it going well, and yes, people started turning on one another. There was the anger, and then . . . those things."

"The leviathans."

"Is that what they're called? I remember them more clearly now, but that wasn't it. There was . . ." She tightened her lips, trying to find the right word. "Something else. Another consciousness. I thought it was the mountain itself. It watched us. It entered into us, became a part of us. I've told you that things make more sense for me the nearer I am to the summit."

I nodded, putting the tin down, realizing I'd already wolfed down the whole thing. I must have been hungrier than I realized.

"But I'm becoming worried that the opposite is true," she continued. "That it's a matter of perspective. I still track the hours, Harry. I have notebooks filled with marks. I can't stop. It's all I can do not to mark down every minute. I . . . I wonder if I only feel sane because you're all going crazy along with me."

My shoulders tightened. She had put words to fears that I had not yet been able to express. Still, I forced a smile, taking her hand in my own. "You've been so much better recently. You seem sane enough to me."

"Maybe that's because we've both gone mad."

"Naoko," I replied, "if I had to go insane, I can't think of anyone else I'd want to do it with."

She laughed, a big smile appearing on her face.

"Hello, Harry," she said. "It's nice to see you again. The real you. I thought I'd lost you."

I sat up, looking into her eyes, and saw a light there that I hadn't seen in more than ten years. A life. Without thinking, I leaned in and kissed her. Her hands went to my neck and she fell into the kiss, a blind and pure moment of exhilarating release.

And with it came memories, still there, regardless of how much I want to purge them. They bubbled up out of the pit of me and invaded the perfect peace of this moment. And I saw him—our little boy. I saw him in every moment we spent together, in every brick that we built our life on.

I broke away, tears welling. My throat was tight, thick as it tried to hold in my sobs. I looked away from her, at the floor.

"I love you," I whispered. "But I can't be with you and not think about him."

"I can't, either, Harry. But I can remember the good. I can't blame myself for things I can't change."

"I can." I fiddled with my hand, a phantom itch where my missing fingers should have been. "It was my *fault*."

She sighed, standing up. "And beating yourself up won't change that. I came in to say that Thomas is up. He wants to see you."

She went to unzip the tent. I wanted to ask her to stay, but I didn't know how.

"How is he?" I asked.

She turned back to me. "Not well. At all. He's being brave, but courage won't keep him alive, I'm afraid." Stepping out of the tent and into the icy wind, she zipped the flap closed behind her.

* * *

I got myself as warm as I possibly could before stepping out into the cold again. I changed back into old layers, drier than the ones I was wearing, though stinking with old sweat. I took a few deep breaths to ready myself and went outside.

I was fortunate that the sun was shining. My boots crunched into snow as I crossed the small campsite. Miller stood outside Thomas's tent, his face stoic. As I approached, he turned toward me.

"You saw Polya die?"

I gave a slow nod. I'd been trying to keep the image out of my mind.

He shifted his rifle. "The things that got her—they were the same things that got to Parker and Sanderson?"

"No." I shook my head. "Jet killed Polya. He's gone mad."

His eyebrows came together in a deep frown. "How?"

I gave a helpless shrug. "It's those creatures, and this mountain, I think. It infects you if you stay too long. It makes you do things. Turn on others. Turn on yourself."

A look of pain flashed across his face. "Do you think that—"

"No," I said. "Not Parker and Sanderson. They died protecting our lives, I'm sure of it."

He nodded. "Thank you, Harold."

Hefting his rifle back up over his shoulder, he walked away, leaving me alone in front of Thomas's tent.

Unzipping the entrance, I stepped inside.

Thomas looked like a cadaver: propped up against a couple of our rucksacks, his body lolled slightly to one side, his skin pale as the cold snow of the mountain outside. His eyes were red and his forehead was sweaty with fever. Neil was sat next to him, cross-legged, and watching him intently, utterly captivated by Thomas's unmoving body. He was still wrapped in all his layers, as if we were mid-climb, but just above his thick scarf I could see a big smile on his face.

"Hello, Harold," he said, his eyes not leaving Thomas. "It sounds like you've had quite an experience."

I gave a halfhearted laugh, trying to shake a deep sense of unease. "You could say that."

His eyes flashed, his eyebrows rising dramatically as he turned to me. I gaped, at a loss for what to say to this man I'd barely spoken to. The truth is, I often find myself forgetting he's even there. And now here he was, face-to-face. Why? The old paranoia rose in me again, ever suspicious, ever questioning this team and everyone on it.

I sat down, trying to push back against it.

"You told the Warden you had seen the summit." He leaned forward until he was quite close to me. "How did it feel?"

I frowned. "It felt . . . I . . . well, I'm not really sure."

"Oh, come now, Harold. That's not true at all, is it? Let's not pretend we are back in the *old world* here. The pull—the desire to climb, to reach the summit. Tell me how it *felt*."

I turned away from him, uncomfortable, feeling a little like he was taking advantage of me somehow, using my isolation to pry into thoughts that I did not want to share.

But I forced myself to think about my conversation with the Warden. If we didn't make a conscious effort to get over our distrust, it could be the end of all of us.

"It's like . . ." I started, trying to find the words. "Being hungry. Really, really hungry. As though I haven't eaten for days, and I know that there's a buffet of the most wonderful food, anything I could eat, and it's right there. My body yearns for it. It's not a mental craving, it's a physical one."

He nodded, as if what I was saying was the most normal thing in the world. The wind picked up outside, whistling through the camp. "And yet you resisted it. You managed to make it back down to us. Fascinating how the mind works." His grin widened. "Truly amazing. It seems so simple, so straightforward, and then you realize there's something you've missed. The world is often like that, isn't it? Sometimes all you need is for someone to turn it on its head, like turning a picture upside down, or spelling a word backward, and suddenly there's a whole new meaning. Something that's been there all along."

I frowned, unable to tell if it was my exhaustion or his words that were making absolutely no sense at all. He stood up, his gangly shape filling the tent, and for a moment I was stung with a sudden fear—as though he was about to attack me, to hold me down and smother me.

"You impress me, Harold." He loomed over me. "That is all I will say for now: I am impressed by you. I hope to continue to be."

Thomas stirred a little, letting out a light sigh. Neil gave me another smile, unzipped the tent, and slipped out. The freezing air swooped into the gap, blowing snow inward, and I scrambled to zip the tent shut again.

Turning back, I saw Thomas was awake. He tried to smile when he saw me, but the muscles seemed to fail him, resulting in a distorted grimace.

I shuffled forward, settling down in front of him and hugging my knees to regain some warmth. He was not an easy sight to look at, but I wouldn't do him the dishonor of looking away.

"Harold," he muttered, his voice only just carrying above his breath. "It's nice to see you. I am not long for this world, I think."

"Don't be ridiculous. We'll get you down the mountain, into lower altitude. The drugs will—"

He put up his hand, weakly, and I fell short. I could see how much of an effort even that was for him.

"No one is going down this mountain any time soon. You know

that as well as I do. I have no need for false hope. Not now. I am not upset. I'm glad I've come here."

I frowned. "Seriously?"

"I am where God wants me to be."

I recoiled at the absurdity of the statement. "What? God wants you to be dying from altitude sickness halfway up a mountain?"

His body leaned fully into the pack that propped him, like a crumbling building on the verge of collapse. His face, oddly peaceful, turned upward to look at the ceiling. "It's necessary. You know—my faith has not always been ironclad. I know why now. Life has been too easy for me. Too obvious. I see now the need for sacrifice, to make my belief in God concrete. To offer God my soul entire."

I put my hand to my head, staring incredulously. "To . . . to die, for no purpose?"

His head was heavy, his neck straining to keep it up, but his smile was infuriatingly calm. "We are called upon to test our faith, Harold, as Abraham was. I must allow the unexpected to happen to me and, in doing so, prove that I trust in God's plan."

"But . . . can't you see how *screwed up* that is?" I demanded. My fists were tight, my hands itching to slap him in the face, despite his frailty. Was this the mountain, working on my brain? This anger inside of me was different, deeper.

I shuffled back, away from him, worried what I might do, but he put a hand out and took my wrist. He was so weak he could barely grip it. "I choose to give myself over to something greater; it makes me happy. And I have always tried to be happy."

"So what?" I snapped back, turning on him. "God wants you to die a painful and horrible death just so he can test your faith?" I was dimly aware that I was shouting. I just needed to breathe, I thought. I just needed to suppress the anger, but I couldn't. No—I didn't want to. He was being ridiculous. My anger felt justified. It felt *right*. "The story of

Abraham is *crazy*. Because it turns out that either God doesn't exist, or He's actively trying to fuck with us. He's a mean kid with a magnifying glass burning an art farm. Because *this*?" I pressed a finger into his chest. "This doesn't look like any love I've ever heard of."

Thomas coughed, a raspy, feeble little splutter that seemed to rock him right down to his core. He gasped for breath. I was standing up. I rocked back and forth, my hands shaking.

"Harold," Thomas whispered, his voice barely louder than the air itself. "Even Jesus thought that God had forsaken Him."

"But it's not *fair*!" I screamed. A decade of pent-up fury rolled out of me. "We're just expected to be playthings? We're just toys for Him to use and discard, however He sees fit?" I knelt down, putting my hands on his shoulders, drawing him close, trying to get him to understand. He *had* to understand. "Damn it, Thomas, it's not good enough. Can't you see that?" I shook him hard. *"Why can't you see that?!"*

As I was shaking him, his eyes fell shut; his breathing became shallow. I stopped, letting go of him.

"Thomas?" I whispered.

His breathing lessened, letting out a little wheeze, then stopped.

"Thomas?"

His head lolled back against the rucksacks. His face, usually so animated, was slack. His eyes closed and his brow smooth. I scrambled, feeling for his pulse, for any kind of rhythm, but there was none. He was dead.

All the anger drained out of me in an instant. I pushed myself backward, staring in horror at what I had done. I don't know how long I sat next to him. I didn't cry, or shout, or scream. None of that felt right. I just sat there, numb, staring at my own broken and mangled hand.

The wind howled outside.

The mountain had done this—*made me do this*.

No. That was a lie. I had embraced the anger. After all these years of burying and avoidance, I had wanted to be angry. I had *liked it*.

And I had killed him.

I held his hand in mine for a few moments and, despite myself, I said a prayer. Rising from the floor where he lay, contemplating the second life I had watched go out in the past day, I stepped out of the tent and into the cold mountain winds to tell the others.

* * *

We held a funeral for Thomas and Polya that evening, just as the sun was beginning to set. It was a tense affair. Forewarned that the creatures preferred the darkness, but also that they seemed to fear our weapons, Miller, Palmer, and the Warden were armed to the teeth. Miller held his rifle tightly. The other two carried shotguns loosely in front of them, as well as pistols at their waists. The Warden had what seemed to be a string of grenades attached to his belt on the opposite side. I'd had no idea they'd been carrying so much firepower with them.

I glanced off into the distance often, thinking that every movement might be Jet. Each gust of wind, each flap of a tent, sent a shiver up my spine.

We were out here, and he knew where we were, and we were vulnerable.

We placed Thomas's body on the ledge of a ridge, right at the mountain's edge. Another ice burial: we agreed that we would say a few words, and then push him over the side. Let his body fall down into the icy wastes below, frozen and lost to the mountain. Oddly, I think that's what he would have wanted.

Part of me felt like we should be holding a funeral for Jet, too. He had also been my friend, and I couldn't help but feel that the man that I had known was just as dead as the people we were remembering. But he remained an unspoken sore. No one was willing to touch it.

I had asked if I could deliver the eulogy. It felt appropriate, but as I had sat down to think about it, I'd struggled to find the words. I spent most of the afternoon wrestling with what I had done.

Naoko told me it wasn't my fault, that he was dying anyway, but I can't help but see his eyes fall shut as I shout at him, and see myself angrily shaking the last bit of life right out of his body.

I also can't stop thinking about his beliefs. There is no doubt in my mind that part of what he said is true: some greater being has put this mountain here, something beyond the realm of our comprehension. I am sure of that now. Whether it is God or not, as I have been taught about Him, I cannot say. Part of me feels that explanation is a little too simplistic, a little too straightforward.

We stood around the body in a little semicircle, somber and reflective. The wind had died down a little, and the cloud cover meant that it wasn't as cold as it had been. I asked for a moment of silence, and we bowed our heads. As we did, I couldn't get Thomas's words out of my head.

And I have always tried to be happy.

Could I say the same? Is happiness something that I've even thought about in the past ten years? Pulling my head up a little, I looked across the others. The figures of Palmer and the Warden stood further out, at the perimeter of the group. They were stone-faced and weary, their eyes glancing from me and then back out to the icy rocks behind me.

Bettan looked different: that easy arrogance was gone. His body was clenched tight, his face cold.

Naoko kept her head solemnly down, and as I watched her—the rise and fall of her breathing, the flutter of a strand of hair in the wind—I felt a warmth grow inside. There had been happiness there for me, once. And maybe, in time, there could be again. But to let myself be happy now feels like an insult to the memories Santi, Naoko, and I shared together. And the memory of Thomas, and everyone else who

I have caused pain. Because if those meant anything, if they still mean anything at all, then surely I deserve to suffer. Don't I, Hattie? Don't I deserve this pain?

I did a double take when my eyes landed on Neil. He was not looking down, but rather staring at me intently with a look of utter fascination, like someone seeing the Grand Canyon for the first time. I held his gaze for a half second before having to look away, averting my eyes back toward the ground.

"We're here today to recognize two of our friends," I said. "They journeyed with us, they faced hardships with us, and they died." My voice was tense, a taut string. "When I was brought onto this expedition, I was not told much. But it began with death. Perhaps I was naive to think it would not continue that way. I hope we can remember Polya and Thomas in their best moments, for their wisdom, and their kindness. If there is a life after this one, I do not know. But I am determined that we all survive this, so that they can live on in our memories as the good people that they were."

"As idiots," Bettan muttered.

I fell short. "What?"

He growled. "If they followed the most basic of instructions, they would still be alive. But instead, they both decided to be fucking idiots."

"Shut up, Roger," Palmer said, from a few meters behind him. "Now is not the time."

"No," I said. "No, go on. I want to know what the hell he's trying to say."

He looked me right in the eyes. "I'm trying to say that Thomas decided that he would hide his growing altitude sickness from everyone else. If I'd known, I could have done something about it. And Polya, the so-called genius, rushed off into the night without protection or weapons, and without telling me. Now she's dead. So much for her."

I shook my head, my whole body recoiling in disgust. "How dare you? They don't deserve this."

"And now the other idiot," he said, addressing the others as he pointed at me, "who is only alive out of dumb luck, is lecturing us. I don't need to listen to this. You're as much to blame for Polya's death as she is."

I staggered, the accusation hitting me like a blow to the face.

"That's not . . ." I clenched my fists. "This isn't what this is about. We're here to honor their memories, not insult them. This is completely inappropriate."

Bettan laughed—an ugly, callous sound. "The only inappropriate thing here is that we're wasting time on two nobodies who probably should have died days ago. For fuck's sake—you've barely known them a week and you're acting like you've lost family. I'm trying to climb the most treacherous peak on planet Earth, and you are here *wasting my time*."

He walked straight past me, to where Thomas lay by the side of the ridge. Without a word, he kicked the body unceremoniously off the cliff.

We stared, speechless, as it tumbled down the mountain. I winced with each crunch of snow as it hit the rocks on the way down, each one sparking fury inside of me.

"There," Bettan said, turning back. "Maybe now we can get on with why we're actually here." He trudged back past me and toward his tent.

I stormed after him, the snow crunching under my feet. Grabbing his shoulder, I twisted him around to face me. "They were people, you self-centered bastard. They were *friends*. You act like you're some kind of hero—"

"But I *am* a hero, Harry," Bettan shot back, voice filled with contempt. "People have devoted their lives to trying to achieve what I have achieved."

I laughed in his face. "You're ridiculous."

He shook his head, his mouth curling into a sneer. "Power isn't about scale. Power is about having the balls to realize that you run your own life. But people, people like *you*." He stabbed a finger into my chest. "They're cowards: shit-scared that they might just be responsible for their own actions, so they invent gods, or disadvantages, or politics, or a whole host of other bullshit to explain away the fact that *they* are in control. You think I'm here because I just happen to be naturally good at climbing fucking mountains? Bullshit, Harold. I'm the master of my fate, because I have the will to be, and because I choose to be. Nothing else matters."

He walked off and left me speechless, shaken from the encounter. I looked over at the others—Palmer and the Warden acted as if they hadn't heard it. Naoko simply shrugged, as if to say, *What did you expect?*

Neil had already disappeared.

* * *

I write this letter now to you in the cold of my tent, surrounded by my work. It is night, and I should be sleeping, but it is far too cold for sleep. Even in the tents, the cold invades inexorably until it is the all that you can think about. Only focus helps drown it out. Only work.

The single fold-up table that Miller has been carrying has been set up inside and Polya's camera work is laid out in front of me. I am beginning to make sense of it. Threads that connect with one another, like orbits around stars. I am seeing pathways. The mountain is opening itself up to me.

But someone has been in my tent since the last time I was here. They have tried very hard to rearrange the Polaroids into the same positions

I had left them, but there are differences. Someone has riffled through my things, checked up on what I'm doing. And here's the worst part, Hattie: I can't say a thing. Not to anybody. Anyone could be compromised. Anyone could have been changed.

I must be wary. I must watch them.

We have all agreed to attempt the summit, but I think our reasons are different. Yes—we all feel the pull, the inexorable hunger that draws us upward. Mine are clear enough: for the longest time, I believed there was nothing left for me in the world. It is a sterile place, and the last ten years have been filled with futile attempts to escape it.

But for the first time in a very long time, I have begun to feel a glimmer of hope. I had been so scared to see Naoko again, but watching her today, having her close, reminded me of a sensation I have not felt since before I left all those years ago.

If only I can save her from this hellish place. If only I can get her away from here alive, before we are all sent mad, or turned upon, or torn apart by primordial creatures.

Any sane man would leave this mountain after what I have seen. Any sane man would be trekking down to Base Camp, getting on that helicopter, and getting out of here.

But up and down no longer mean what they once did—this mountain is like a Möbius strip; it twists upon itself, and what appears to be two sides is only one. For all the dangers ahead, I understand what Naoko meant: leaving is no longer an option. The only way off this mountain is forward, through the pulsing folds and into the anomalies.

I can no longer deny the pull, the hunger.

We must get to the top, together.

That's where the answers are.

Dear Harriet,

By the time morning came, I had put together a plan. The photos were laid out on the tent floor in front of me, carefully placed and just overlapping one another until the closest replica of that wall came into sight.

It was difficult to focus at first, and I found myself unable to separate the photos of that cavern from the experiences I had there—Jet's madness, Polya's death, and the feeling that I was losing my mind. I still worried that the leviathans had affected us more than we knew. I thought of Bettan's behavior at the eulogy. Could he be trusted anymore? Could any of us?

I needed to focus: to see this purely as a puzzle to be put together. An equation to be solved.

Polya had told me that the folds didn't work like two-way portals, but as a circuit, and this had been confirmed to me by my lucky escape. And a strict map that could be painted on a wall indicated that they couldn't be eternally changing, so there *had* to be a consistency to them.

If I imagined that the entrance to each fold led directly to the exit of another, but that second fold's entrance led to a third exit—like a continual circuit of dimensional leaps—then the map started to make sense.

I was able to identify four different repeating graphological patterns which fed in and out of one another. They were distinct, and each individual node was transcribed using a particular pattern. Polya suggested that they indicated location, and I was not in a position to argue with the last thoughts of a woman I admired. Given the propensity for this mountain to change as you move upward, I posited that the four patterns represented different strata on the mountain: the upper reaches, the midsections, the lower sections, and, finally, the caves beneath.

The clearest symbol was the single node at the center, like the middle of a rotating galaxy, around which everything else was connected. I shivered as I looked at it, a cold wind ruffling the walls of my tent. This, I had to assume, was the summit.

Individually, each one of these assumptions was flimsy. I am well aware of that, Hattie. I lacked the data to be able to make more conclusive hypotheses. And yet, when all were brought together in tandem, the shape of the map began to reveal itself to me, almost like intuition.

The mountain creaked outside, as if in response—ice grating on stone, glaciers shifting. I pulled my coat a little tighter around my shoulders.

My final assumption, and perhaps the flimsiest one, was that the nodes that were close to one another on the map were also close in three-dimensional geographical space. I thought this for two reasons: One, because the leviathans appear to inhabit that same space as we do, and it would make logical sense to me to organize it that way. Two, because if they didn't, then I had no idea how we were going to navigate this. My last assumption was one of necessity.

I can only hope it doesn't kill us all.

I had expected Bettan to dislike me taking charge of the navigation. In fact, I had the whole encounter pictured in my mind: him glowering at me like a sullen child, him challenging all of my assumptions and denigrating my work. I'd resolved to not let it get to me like it had done the day before.

To my surprise, he was completely behind the plan.

"This is great work," he said, leaning over the table set up in my tent. The light flickered, casting distorted shadows. The sun was just beginning to rise. He pointed at the copy of the map I had sketched out in my notebook. His tone was all business. "How high do you think these upper sections will be?"

I struggled to look at him, unable to forget the time he hit Naoko, his treatment of Thomas, and the way he had abused my friend's memory. But if we were to get to the top, we would have to work together. There was nothing I could do about that.

"I can't be sure."

The six of us were huddled closely in my tent, packed up and ready to move. Miller stood watch outside. My sleeping bag was rolled up and tied to my pack, with only the small table and the tent itself left to take down and store before we continued our ascent. I glanced across them. Which one of them had been in here yesterday? Who of them could I trust?

Naoko sat in the corner, her legs up and her arms wrapped around her knees.

"I don't need exact altitude," Bettan said. "But I do need to know for our oxygen supplies. As it stands, we're not far from the start of the Death Zone—most of you will be needing oxygen during this next climb."

"I can give you a predictive guideline," I said, "but that's about it. What about you?"

"I can manage a little further. I've done Everest without it. But this is higher. I'll not be taking any more risks than I need to."

Palmer nodded in agreement, her head wrapped in a hat and bala-clava.

We were leaving most of the supplies behind—with so many of our team gone, especially Parker and Sanderson, our ability to carry much more was quickly dwindling. And as the altitude increased, we grew weaker, unable to take any extra weight. We would not take the table with us, and we would leave the tents. We could carry food for three days, Palmer had said. Oxygen for two. But there was no camping out again above this point. This was the final push: either we made it, or we didn't.

We have all stopped talking about how many supplies we'll need to get back down. I'm not sure when this happened.

"What about defense?" Palmer asked. "Will we see leviathans?"

"Difficult to predict," I replied. "I *think* I'm keeping us out of the caves, but we've been attacked on the mountain before."

"We take it slowly, then." She cocked her head at the Warden. "Steve and I go through first each time, to scope out the surroundings. We'll be armed, but lightly so we can move fast. Miller and Bettan stay back with you, just in case."

"The biggest threat isn't the physical one," the Warden said, looking pointedly at the others. "If what Harold told us is true, we could be experiencing a lot of confusion and some heavy mind-fuckery. We need to always look out for one another. If anyone is acting strange, we call it out. If anyone is feeling odd, they make it known."

Everyone nodded in agreement.

"This is it," Palmer said. "Whatever is up there, we find it today."

Everyone took a moment to themselves before the final push. It was still early in the morning, and the sun was just beginning to peek over the horizon. Bettan stood outside, breathing in the rarefied air and holding his hands out to the growing light. Miller checked his guns, cleaning and assembling them. As I took down my tent, I caught a glimpse of Palmer and the Warden sharing a cigarette—the wisp of smoke snaking up into the sky.

Once the tent was stowed, I sat with Naoko, but we didn't speak. She took my left hand, both of us swaddled up in gloves and layers of fabric, and held it close. We looked out at the horizon, each lost in our own little world.

Together, our dwindling expedition team hiked up the rise, planning to use as much daylight as possible. We'd tied oxygen canisters to the sides of our backpacks, and they weighed heavy on our backs. I walked close to Naoko. More and more, I found myself needing her to be near me. The warmth of her presence—I don't know how I'd gone so long without it.

I hadn't slept, of course, except for a couple of half-hour stints here and there, but exhaustion was becoming part of me now. Part of the experience. The blurry eyes. The aching bones.

But as I put the regulator over my mouth, the very first breath of supplemental oxygen sent a rush of relief through my whole body. I had to control myself from not sucking in too much and causing myself to hyperventilate. Why had we not used this before? Each inhalation made my head clearer and my muscles stronger than they had been in a long time.

We kept our eyes peeled for any dangers. At this height, sight was all we had left. Altitude is not forgiving to the other senses—as the air thins, there are no smells; the skin grows too numb to feel; even taste is flattened. The only sounds are the pumping of your own blood in your arteries, the rasp of your lungs reaching for the oxygen. It was like being underwater. If we were to rely on anything, it had to be sight.

When we got to the crest, I let out a sigh of relief. The fold I had come through was still there, a twisting and pulsing black in the crevice of rock. I had assumed they didn't move, otherwise how would there be a physical map? But given everything that had happened, I hadn't been sure.

The deep blackness sucked the color from the air around it. It looked stranger in the daylight, more out of place. Everyone else stared at it, unable to tear their eyes away, perhaps finally believing me fully and completely for the first time.

I looked back at my scribbled map. Even though I knew the entire journey by heart, it didn't stop me obsessively checking whenever I had the opportunity.

"I need to show you all something," I said, taking the oxygen regulator off my face. I dropped my pack and handed a stopwatch to the Warden, holding on to a second one myself. "Here, take this. Stand near that fold. I'm going to stand about thirty feet away. When I raise my hand in the air, start the stopwatch. When it hits thirty, we'll both raise our hands again."

I hiked back a little way, hoping that my test would work. As I raised my hand, I started the stopwatch and the Warden did the same. The seconds ticked by and, finally, my clock hit thirty. I put my hand up.

"Why is your hand up?" the Warden shouted. "It's only at eighteen seconds."

I jogged back over to him, feet crunching in the snow. I showed him my watch. "It was thirty seconds for me. Time moves slower closer to a fold. That's how we find them as we move through the circuit. We work in teams of two and we use the watches."

Everyone nodded, all of us a little awed, I think. Still, it was testament to how strange things had gotten that they accepted such a phenomenon so readily.

"Now, as we step through this one," I said, "we'll be taken upward by a few thousand feet."

Bettan stepped up next to me, serious. "Remember: this will be a massive shock to the body. Gradual altitude shifts can kill, as we know. I have no idea what such a sudden shift will do, but I do know Harold survived it momentarily. You've each got a tank and regulator. I want you breathing steadily before you go through."

"We won't be there long," I added. "We need to all step out of the fold, then step back into the same one. It should then take us to another location, like a circuit. Later on, we will need to switch, to find an entirely separate fold. But here, it's in and out again, and the circuit should take us back down to approximately this altitude, just at a different point on the mountain."

Everyone secured their regulators onto their faces. Palmer stepped forward, hoisting her gun.

"I know we're going in first, but if Harold's right, this door doesn't work both ways. There's no way of sending back a warning, so we just have to hope for the best. Give it a second, then the rest of you follow, with Miller taking the back. As soon as you're all through, we'll follow the same procedure back through the same fold together." She nodded to the burly guard, who acknowledged her with a tilt of his head. "Questions?"

Nobody made any noises, so she affixed the regulator on her face, crouched down a little, and walked into the black. The Warden followed directly behind.

They disappeared.

I took a deep breath, looking out at the others. Stepping up to the fold, I inspected it. Light changed around the edges, the rock pulsing blue as it got close to the black mass at the center. It tugged back at me, as if begging me to step inside. But there was no sign of Palmer and the Warden—I could only hope that wherever they had gone, they were alive. We had no way of knowing. Hope was all we had left.

A few beats passed in silence. Without a word, Miller walked straight over to me and stood right in front of the fold, blocking it.

I frowned at him. "Palmer said for you to go last."

He lifted his rifle and aimed it directly at Bettan.

"What the fuck is going on?" Bettan demanded, and I realized that he was the only one left of us that was armed.

"It's too much," Miller replied, his voice strangely flat, his face stony. His eyes glimmered a little in the sun. "All of this, all the death and the madness. It's . . ." He shook his head. "This is not for you."

Oh, no.

I saw exactly what was going to happen before it did. The finger on the trigger squeezing; Miller firing, successively taking out each one of us: Bettan, me, Neil.

Naoko.

I threw myself at him. As my body crashed into his, the gunshot rang. I didn't get a chance to see if it had hit. We tumbled to the ground, twisting and rolling. Miller's arms jerked up, grabbing my torso and lifting me as if I weighed nothing at all—so much bigger than me, so much stronger.

I grabbed at his rifle and tried to hit him with it, but he caught it. He slammed the butt right in my face.

My head snapped back as I fell into snow. Naoko screamed. Blood welled out of my nose. Someone was bawling, shouting.

Miller rolled on top of me, pinning me down, his face contorted with inexplicable rancor. He lifted the butt of the gun up again, ready to smash it into my skull.

"Remember Jim!" I screamed. "Remember Theo! They died for us! Remember who you are!"

He paused. A flash of confusion.

There were two quick shots. Miller jerked, blood spurting from his chest.

I looked up to see Bettan take aim and fire a third bullet right into his skull.

Miller collapsed on top of me, his face pressed against mine, the warmth of his breath still damp on my skin.

"Oh fuck," I muttered. "Jesus Christ."

The weight rolled off me. Bettan pushed the body to the side. Naoko was on her knees, her head in her hands, shaking, hyperventilating. I scrambled over to her.

"Are you okay?"

"Not again," she whispered between gasping breaths. "No, no, no. Not again. Not again."

"It's okay." I put my arms around her. "He's dead. I'm here and I'm okay. We're all here."

I held her tightly, rocking her in my arms as her breathing calmed. Bettan searched Miller's body and threw his rifle off to one side.

"What the fuck was that?" he demanded.

"The leviathans. The . . ." I shook my head. "Whatever it is. It got to him. Just like Jet."

Naoko moaned.

"But it's over now," I said, holding her, my gloved hand on her hood. "It's over. You're okay."

Except it didn't feel like it was over. It didn't feel like it would ever be over.

Bettan pointed at the fold. "They're still waiting for us."

"Give her a *second*!" I shouted. "Will you? Someone just tried to kill us."

Bettan's shoulders dropped and he lowered the weapon. "Which is why we need to stay together. She can recover on the other side."

I looked down at Naoko. She had stopped shaking and her breathing was more regular. She stood up, slowly, weakly, and gave me a small nod. "He's right. I'm sorry. I'm . . . I can move. We—we need to go through."

"Fine." I gritted my teeth. "Fuck. *Fine.*"

I took one last look at Miller's body on the snow, thinking: *That could be me. Oh God—that could be any of us.*

"Take his rifle," Bettan said. "No point in leaving it behind."

I bent down to pick it up. It was heavy, and I realized I had no idea how to hold it, let alone use such a thing, but Bettan was already by the pulsing black of the fold, gun out, beckoning for us to follow. Neil stood beside him. I affixed my regulator and held Naoko close to me as, one by one, we stepped into the darkness.

When the light came back, my head swam. I stumbled, my stomach lurching as if it had taken a punch. I started panting, sucking oxygen in from the tank frantically, and I had to focus, to calm down and stop myself hyperventilating. Freezing air buffeted me backward and I clung to Naoko for balance, dropping the rifle into the snow. The feel of her against me gave me strength, and we held each other tightly against the wind.

Turning round, I saw Neil and Bettan just ahead. And a little further away, a figure marching toward us.

The Warden, holding Palmer in his arms.

"Where have you been?" the Warden called, pulling his regulator down. His eyes were gaunt and red. "What the fuck were you doing?!"

"Miller went crazy!" Bettan called back. Wind whistled across his voice, muffling it. "Tried to kill us. We were held back!"

"It's been *five hours*," the Warden shouted as he approached. His voice was hoarse as it rattled out of him. Palmer was passed out in his arms, head lolled backward and arms splayed. "We go back through *now*. All together. Go, go, go!"

He stumbled toward us, half running and half falling, and leaped for the fold. Frantically, we scrambled after him, escaping once again into its blackness.

We tumbled out on the other side, all as one. We were on a flat plane of ice and snow—somewhere partway up the mountain, surrounded by ridges and cliffs.

The altitude was lower here. I could feel it in my chest.

The Warden lay Palmer on the ground, breathing hard. He beckoned Bettan over.

"Give me another oxygen canister," he said, checking her pulse, her breathing. "We ran out toward the end—we were sharing from one, trying to preserve air, but . . ." He shook his head. "She lost consciousness. Where *were* you?"

"Miller turned," Bettan growled.

"Turned?"

The mountaineer looked away, his mouth tight. "Like Jet. I had to put him down. The rest of us made it."

I glanced across the group: Naoko was sitting on the ground, staring off into space, still recovering from her panic attack. Neil stood just behind her, breathing hard.

"Shit." The Warden threw his hands in the air. "Shit! Miller was a good man. I *liked* him. And now this? Fuck!"

He paced back and forth, shaking his head, then turned to me. "So what happened with the time? Miller attacked you—that didn't take five hours. Where have you been?"

"I don't know." I held up my hands. "This can't be perfect science. Maybe as you go through, the time dilation is unpredictable. The folds bend time, we know that, but it's almost impossible to tell for how long. I don't know how much of this mountain is superimposed in other dimensions. There's no way I could have predicted that!" I clenched my jaw, trying to convince myself that was true.

Rising, he grabbed me by the cuff of my jacket. "Then why didn't you even say it was a risk?"

"I didn't know!"

"You didn't know?" he accused, reaching up and placing his hands on my neck. I jerked backward, panicking, thinking of Jet, of Miller, but he held me tight. "*You didn't know . . .*"

"Steve . . ." Palmer coughed, reaching up to him.

He ignored her, shaking me violently.

"Steve!" Her voice was weak. "*Think.* Think about why you're angry."

The Warden froze. He was breathing hard, his chest rising and falling. His feral eyes darted from Palmer, to me, then back again. He took a few deep breaths, closed his eyes, then seemed to calm. He took a step back, releasing me.

"I'm sorry. I . . . I just—" He shook his head, turning his back to me.

I backed away. "It's okay. It's fine. I . . . I'm glad you're alive." I turned to Palmer. "Are *you* okay?"

She put her hand to her chest and grimaced. "I think so. I'm breathing. I just need some more oxygen in my body."

"We can't stay here," Bettan said. "Not after what's happened. We need to keep moving." He had his back to us, looking out at the stretch of ice and rock before us. "Will you be ready to go soon?"

She nodded.

The Warden looked down at her, and for a moment I saw a flash of pain in his eyes.

In front of us, the ice stretched downwards in a steep hill. Beyond that was a long plain of flat, snowy rock between two shorter peaks. The sky was clear and the sun warm, glinting off the snow.

"We can't go back through this one," I said. "It takes us the wrong way."

"How far will the next one be?" Bettan asked.

"I'm not sure. Hopefully within a couple of hundred meters, but that's an assumption. You've each got a watch. Spread out, at least a good twenty meters apart. Every so often, stop and let the seconds hand count to thirty. If one of you is off, it means you're getting close."

"I'm staying with Grace," the Warden said. I tried to not show surprise at his using her first name.

I nodded, feeling my legs ache, and holding a searing stitch in my side. "I also need a break. Just for a bit. That last jump was . . ." I sat down on a rock, lowering my head. "It was a lot."

Bettan snorted, turning to Neil. "I'm not waiting any longer than I have to. You coming?"

Neil nodded, walking toward him.

"I'll come, too," Naoko said, and I felt a pull on my heart. "Three pairs of eyes are better than two."

I wanted to tell her to stay with me. To not leave my sight. But I knew I had no right to demand that.

"Don't go too far," I said weakly. "The fold should be close."

She nodded and followed Neil and Bettan, who walked off together down the rise. As I watched them, the contrast couldn't have been clearer: Bettan's secure, controlled footing set against Neil's—gangly and a little off.

I tried to think what I really knew about him: Dr. Neil Amai. Anthropologist. That's how he had been introduced, and despite having climbed, fought, and almost died with him on this mad venture, I honestly couldn't tell you anything more about him than that.

Was he just naturally reclusive, or was I just not interested?

And if not, why not?

I frowned, shaking my head. This mountain does strange things to your thoughts.

Palmer was awake, clearly woozy, fogged up from the lack of oxygen. The Warden laid her back against the snow so she could look up at the sky. He was shaking his head.

"What is it?" I asked.

"I can't believe we're doing this."

"Doing what?"

"All *this*." He waved his hand at the frozen landscape, his voice burning with frustration. "For . . . for nothing. Nothing at all. Two teams, Harold. One dead, the other dying. If any of us make it off here alive it'll be a miracle, and for what? It's a joke. It's all a big joke."

"What are you talking about?"

"When this mountain was first picked up on satellite feeds," he said, looking down at his hands, "it was NASA that passed the information on to the U.S. government. Other countries started clamoring for it, too, of course. Calls from the USSR, China, the UK. It was a scramble, until we stepped in."

"You mean Apollo?"

"The biggest corporation you've never heard of. This is a corporate venture, bought and paid for; that's it."

I frowned. "You mean to tell me a corporation had the power to make the U.S., Soviet, and Chinese governments back off? I thought you told us this was a combined research mission, discoveries for . . . the greater good?"

Even as I said the words, I realized how naive they sounded.

The Warden laughed. "Oh, come on. Line the right pockets and you can do anything. Why do you really think an eminent Russian scientist, ex–army generals, an Australian commando, and *you* are all in the same place? *The greater good?* They bring a geologist in case there's any oil or resources to be mined in this mountain. They bring a biologist in case there are any medical breakthroughs that can be monetized, or any discoveries that can be weaponized. It's all money, Harold. That's all it is. You can hire a private fucking army if you have enough money. You and me? We're disposable."

I stared at him, incredulous. "That's . . . it?"

"What were you expecting? An ancient cult of good and evil? A plan to save the world? There's only one thing that drives progress. The world doesn't give a shit about you or me, or Grace, or any of us. When you realize that, you start to think there are only two options: get paid, or don't. You can't change the way the world is set up, Harold. You've just got to make do."

I don't know why I was surprised. "Why are you telling me this now?"

He stood up. "Because I'm *done*. I'm done watching people around me die. I'm done being responsible for it." His eyes flicked down to Grace, and back up to me. "Maybe it takes some tragedy to realize what's important. We can still leave."

"I . . ." I shook my head. "I don't know if there *is* a way down anymore. I don't know if the mountain will let us. I think the only way out might be up."

He took a few steps toward me. "Can you promise me that, Harold? Because in the logical part of my brain, I'm sure that if we all worked together, and got back to Camp Two, we could slowly make our way back down to Base Camp. But none of us are doing this alone—either we go down together or we go up together. And I can't trust my own thoughts in this place anymore. So if you believe that, if you *really* believe that up is our only way out of this godforsaken hellscape alive, then I'll follow you. Do you?"

I stared at him, thinking, *I don't know. I can't promise you anything. I don't trust my thoughts any more than you do.* But that's not what I said, Hattie. What I said was:

"I do."

There was a call from behind us. I turned to see the other three walking up the rise, big grins on their faces.

"We found it," Naoko shouted. "We found the fold."

* * *

This time, we were all going through together. I had no idea if the time dilation would apply in the same way for each fold, but that was no longer a risk we could take. Fortunately, my assumptions appeared to have been correct, and that meant there were only a couple of journeys left. This fold should take us to another point a little further up the mountain. We would then have to switch once more, finding another nearby fold, and that should take us directly to the summit.

The knowledge of it bubbled inside of me. The image of the archway and the rise leading up to the summit hadn't properly left my mind since I had last turned away from it. It cropped up in my brain last night when I was trying to sleep, huddled in my bag. It slipped its way into my thoughts during conversations, when I was working out the map, when I was climbing. Always, the pull upward.

The hunger.

Soon it would be sated. I didn't know what that meant, but my body was dying to find out. I could tell myself it was because it might be the only way to rescue Naoko. I could tell myself it was out of sheer curiosity. But the truth was more primal than that. I *needed* to be there, and so did everyone else.

The fold that Naoko and Bettan had found was just another hole in a rock, its familiar empty blackness pulsating out at us. So odd, the things you get used to, Hattie. Just days ago, such a thing would have stretched the very limits of my imagination. Now, this space-time anomaly was just a tool to get us where we needed to go.

"Talk us through it, Harold," the Warden said.

"This should take us a little higher, but hopefully not so much that we need supplemental oxygen again." We looked at one another, fidgeting. Each of us had a regulator and canister in case I was wrong. The Warden and Palmer were armed with shotguns, though Palmer looked a little unstable. "Whatever happens, we should *not* go back through this one. I haven't had time to memorize that bit of the map. I have no idea where it leads. We need to do what we did again and find another nearby fold, which should then take us to the summit. We are almost there."

The Warden nodded. Palmer stumbled a little and pressed up against him. He put a supporting arm around her. "I go in first, followed by Grace, Bettan, Harold, Naoko, and then Neil. As quick as you can, with as little space between us. We don't want a repeat of last time."

We nodded.

"One."

I gulped, praying that my assumptions about the map held true.

"Two."

I saw Bettan pull a pistol out of his jacket and ready it in his hand.

"Three."

The Warden darted forward, and we all followed, disappearing into black.

Daylight flickered back.

Soft snow crunched beneath my feet. I took a breath, thankful that I could still feel the oxygen in my lungs. We were in a small valley surrounded by icy peaks on all sides. They rose up around us in ridges, plateauing for a moment before cutting upward again.

I looked up and screamed.

On each plateau there was a giant leviathan. It felt like there were hundreds of them—watching, writhing, waiting—the emptiness of the mountain replaced by a roiling mass of blue-gray monstrosity.

As one, they turned toward us.

"Oh, shit," Palmer said.

I tried to say something to her, but a sudden burst of anger erupted within me. My insides were aflame, about to shoot out and burn everything in my path. My breath caught in my throat. I glanced around me to see our group—our collection of tiny, disgusting little humans. I *hated* them.

I hated everything that they were, and, as I could see clearly in their burning eyes, they hated me, too.

Good. I deserve to be hated.

I am worthless.

I am nothing.

The creatures scuttled down the ridges at an astonishing rate, their tentacles slithering over ice and rock. They were coming to kill us, and I welcomed it. I wanted to die. I wanted everyone to die with me. It was all I was good for.

Getting to my knees, I opened my arms up to welcome them. To welcome death.

I closed my eyes and waited for eternal silence to greet me.

A hand slapped me hard in the face.

I fell to the ground.

Gasping, I looked up. Bettan stood over me.

"Get the fuck up."

I blinked, confused by what I was looking at. A thundering echoed all around me, of madness, and of rage.

"We've got about twenty seconds to get back through that fold." He grabbed the cuff of my jacket and tugged me upward. "I've already dragged the others back through. Now *move.*"

I stumbled to my feet, half pushed, half pulled forward by Bettan.

"But . . ." I said, my mind recovering. "We don't know where it goes—"

"Shut up."

The creatures tore toward us, only moments away.

Gripping one another tightly, Bettan and I dived back into the black, into the unknown.

The first thing I felt was the wind. Only it wasn't just wind: each gust cut at me, slivers of ice and hail whirling through the air like bullets. The roar was deafening. I tried to take a breath, and all I got was ice.

We were in the middle of a snowstorm. Where were we? How high were we? I had no idea.

Where was Naoko?

Bettan still clung to me. I had no sense of time: if we'd delayed too long, the others could have come through hours ago. Days.

Before I knew what was happening, Bettan was dragging me forward. I slipped and tumbled onto the ice. He grabbed me, pulling me back up to my feet. My chest heaved in pain. There wasn't enough air. We were too high. And behind it all, there was still the hum of anger that had nestled itself in my brain—quieter now, but there. Still there.

I fumbled for my regulator and took a deep breath, the sweet taste of air rushing through me. As I did, more coherent thoughts returned to my mind. Images of hundreds of deadly creatures raging toward us.

Would they not follow us through? Would they not be here any moment?

I glanced behind me in fear, but I could no longer see the fold. There was only white.

"There they are," Bettan shouted, tugging me forward.

I blinked against the storm. Ahead, I could just about make out a hole underneath a large rock, a natural cave sheltered from the winds. Inside, there were four shapes: all of the rest of the team. Naoko—alive.

My body flooded with relief. We had all made it. We were going to be okay.

Then I saw something else.

Another figure, at the edge of my vision. It looked like a person, a little more distant, wandering through the storm.

"Did you see that?" I tried to say through my mask, but it came out muffled. Despite the canister, my lungs still ached. My throat burned. Bettan dragged me onward and the figure disappeared.

We made it to the rock, and the rest of the team sheltered under it. Palmer was on the ground, breathing deep from a canister of her own. Bettan let go of me and I collapsed to my knees.

Naoko rushed down next to me, putting her hands round my neck. "Harry, are you okay?"

"No," I muttered. "I mean, yes. I . . . I think so. But I just—"

"What? What is it?"

"There's someone else out there."

"They followed us?" the Warden said, snapping round and pulling his shotgun up into position.

"No. I mean, I don't know. But not that. Some*one*. A person."

The Warden knelt down next to me, his face hard.

"*Jet?*"

I shook my head. "Maybe, I couldn't see. Probably. Who else could it be?"

"I'm going to go out and look."

"Don't be ridiculous," Palmer snapped, straining to keep her head up. "We stay here and shelter until the storm dies down."

The Warden spun around. "If that's Jet out there, we need to know right now. You know what happened. You know about Polya. He wants to kill us all."

"Look," Bettan said. He was standing at the edge of the cave, squinting into the storm. "I think I see someone." We all turned. There was a figure walking past, about thirty meters away. He seemed to move slowly, casually, as if unaffected by the whirling snow around him. My heartbeat quickened in fear, hoping that he would not see us hiding here and bring whatever crazed vengeance was in his head down upon us.

The winds abated slightly, and there was a dip in the blasting snow.

Even though he was still far away, it was enough for us all to get a good look.

Nobody spoke. Nobody had anything that they could possibly say, because we'd all seen the same thing. That wasn't Jet out there in the storm.

It was Thomas.

Dear Harriet,

We've been in our little shelter for some time now. The storm has not dropped—it rages as strong as ever. Only the natural shelter of this cave keeps us safe. The creatures do not seem to have followed us, or if they have, we are hidden from them.

Moments after seeing Thomas out in the storm, the Warden announced he was going after him. Palmer tried to argue, to tell him to stay with us, but it was no use. He was out in the storm before she had finished her first sentence.

He has not yet come back.

I don't know what to think. I keep seeing the vision of my friend, off in the snowy distance, traipsing past us. It doesn't make any sense. What are you doing out there, Thomas? I *saw* you die. I heard you fall down a cliff and hit every rock on the way down. What powers have brought you back?

It is clear my plan has not worked. And though I know I need to return to my map, to understand where on the mountain we have traveled to and how we might be able to get out, I cannot. I am spend-ing all of my time fighting the voices in my head.

They are always there, as strong as they were down in that cave. If I don't focus on something very clearly, they start to take over.

I wrote you the last letter explaining how we came to be in our predicament as a way to keep my mind busy, but I am running out of things to write about, Hattie. When that happens, I fear I will be lost.

* * *

I can tell you what everyone else has been doing. Perhaps that will help. Naoko spent the last hour sorting and organizing the medical supplies in her pack. She must have done it about ten times now: removing every-thing, categorizing and checking labels, and putting it all back. Neil has been watching her, quietly and intently, without saying a word.

After the Warden left, Palmer sat down with her head bowed. She had taken out the satellite phone and was turning it over in her hands. I left her for a while, but after writing the first letter, I began to worry that she might be feeling the same intrusions as me. I hoped that con-versation might help to stem the tide.

"Are you okay?" I said, sitting down beside her.

Her head snapped up, her expression seething, and she looked as though she was about to leap on me. I jerked backward. She took a deep breath, and whispered, "No. I'm trying to get in touch with Base Camp. With Apollo. But every time I call them, I get this."

She pressed a button on the phone; it gave a quick ring, then a muffled voice crackled through.

"Continue with the mission as planned, but ensure . . ." There was a pause where the voice died out. ". . . continued samples are key. The records cannot be lost before they are sent back down."

I frowned. "What does that mean?"

"It's old," she said, her teeth gritted. "Days old. It's a call I had with them back down at Camp One, repeating. Whatever is happening here, we're cut off from them, from help. There's no getting through. And I'm just . . ." She threw the phone to the ground and it clattered against rock. "I'm so angry! I can't even explain why!"

"It's the hive mind, I think," I said gently. "It's how they *think*. You've got to try to focus on something else, on things that are important to you."

"Like what?" All the muscles in her face were strained. The veins on her neck pulsated.

I glanced over at Naoko, remembering what had got me through the last time. It was the only thing I could think of.

"How did you meet the Warden? For the first time?"

She gave me an incredulous look. "Steve? And will you please stop calling him that."

"It's how he introduced himself."

She rolled her eyes. "I know it is. It's how he always introduces himself. He thinks it's romantic, but it's fucking *infuriating*." She spat the last word vehemently, and I couldn't help but wonder if that was part of the anger we were being infected by, or if it was real.

"Romantic?"

She started to chuckle—a low, rueful sound that rocked her shoulders back and forth.

"We met when we were in the U.S. Army," she said. "We were in Cambodia, clearing out Communist sanctuaries of Vietcong that had been using them as bases to raid back into Vietnam. It was a dirty business. But it was the only way we would get our troops safely out of South Vietnam without them being blown to pieces. I was out there as a nurse, technically, though I've forgotten most of that life. Women weren't in combat roles then, supposedly, but it was kill or be killed. Rules didn't come into it. We were young. We were so damn young."

As she talked, the tension in her body seemed to relax a little. Settling into her memories, the anger receded. I eased myself into her words, and the hum in my own mind lessened further.

"And Steve?"

"Steve took us out on a stupid raid—not sanctioned. He thought he knew where the enemy was hiding and figured he could deal with them quickly. That's who he was. He's got a real savior complex. It's an obsession—he can't sit by and watch someone else do something dangerous that he could feasibly do himself. I mean"—she shrugged with a gesture at the mouth of the cave—"he's doing it as we speak.

"There was a firefight in the jungle. Grenades. Five of us were down, and as far as we could see, not a single one of the enemy was hit. I wasn't dead, but I might as well have been. Shrapnel in my gut from the explosion. A couple of gunshot wounds to the leg. I'd bleed out before long."

"But you didn't."

She shrugged. "I barely remember what happened. I passed out, and when I woke up I was in a field hospital. The story they told me—the one that got told all around the camp, and then all around the army for as long as I can remember—is that he stayed out there with me for four days. Steve sent the other guy back to base to get help. He *stayed*. He fed me. He took care of me. And when the Vietcong came back, he killed every last one of them. They found him, bloody and broken, standing in front of my body with his rifle, surrounded by enemy dead. Like a guardian, they said, warding off evil."

"A warden," I said.

She laughed again, and this time it was a little easier. "We got married after the war ended. There's something about a romantic gesture like that . . . you just can't say no."

"Then what happened?"

"Oh." She shrugged. "Life happened. The things that work in wartime never work quite the same way in peace. He's still an arrogant asshole with a hero complex and I'm still a bitch. We avoided each other for years after the divorce. But when we both got assigned on this expedition . . ."

"What?"

"It doesn't matter." She waved her hand. "I . . . No matter how hard you work, you can't escape the past. It doesn't matter how decorated I am, or how commendable my service record, I'll always be the girl who got rescued by Steve Bautista. Sometimes, you've just got to accept who you are."

I left her then, as it seemed like she wanted to be alone. The story had helped, I had no doubt about that, and now she seemed lost in a reverie of her memories, a shield against the thoughts that were trying to invade her brain.

I am stuck once again with my own thoughts. Already I can feel the hum growing as we wait. I am trying to write you this letter now to escape it. Part of me wishes I could disappear into the past like she was able to, and I enjoyed the comfort of her memories for a time.

You've just got to accept who you are.

Perhaps that's why the hum affects me so much. I've buried too much of my own past. I am so out of touch with it. I am thinking about Bettan, and how even in the face of hundreds of those things he seemed unchanged. Untouched. It makes sense: for better or worse, he is a man with complete and utter self-belief. I envy that in him.

My hands are shaking, with cold, with pain, and with the slow-building anger of a thousand ancient beings.

Maybe it is time, if I am going to make it out of here alive, if I'm going to resist being consumed by the darkness, that I tell you what happened. That I crack open the deepest part of that damned box for good and let the contents out into the world. Because for the first time in a life defined by forgetting, I am beginning to feel like remembering is the only thing that will keep me sane.

* * *

It was 1981. I was still deep in physics research for Imperial, but my working time was less rigid. Most of it was theoretical and involved either working from home or traveling abroad to consult or give talks—at CERN in Geneva, in San Francisco, or Berlin. We'd moved out to Surrey then for a bigger house and more space, and Santi had started at the local school. Naoko was working part-time at Royal Surrey County Hospital.

On days off, I'd visit her—bring her lunch or give her a lift home—and in my time spent there I got to know the chief medical officer, a tall, burly man called Paul Idris. He had a reputation for strictness: nurses and doctors would almost stand to attention as he walked down the corridor. But we were friends, Paul and I—we shared a love for puzzles, and for research. I think he secretly wished he had something like my job, in a lot of ways, rather than the administrative role of running a hospital.

In his short breaks, and while I was waiting for Naoko to finish work, we'd get a coffee together, and I'd often marvel that I was able to do such a thing. Before Naoko and Santi, I'd never really had any social encounters. The prospect of getting a drink with a co-worker was as far removed from my experience as walking on the moon. And yet, over the years, as I opened myself up to the two of them, I found it easier and easier to open myself up to others. I remember feeling so grateful for that.

Perhaps that was why I didn't want Santi to have the same experience I'd had when I was young. The truth was I'd still not told your dad or Aunt Poppy about my little family, and I'm not quite sure why. More than anyone, I knew the pitfalls of making yourself an island. Perhaps I still harbored a mad fear that it might all fall apart. Perhaps this life that I had created felt so new, so removed from who I was when I was a boy, that I didn't want those two worlds to merge.

"How's your boy?" Paul asked me one day, as we sipped our terrible hospital café coffees. The staff would try to give them to us for free, because he was the boss, but he'd always insist on paying for the both of us.

"Fine," I lied. "He's doing great. Really settling in well."

In truth, teachers said he wouldn't talk to any of the other students, wouldn't make friends. He was bright, they said, but only on his terms. That didn't play well with a lot of his teachers.

Paul's smile was broad, reaching up to his eyes. "My girl's just got through to the national round of the debating cup. She's an absolute natural, honestly. No idea where she gets it from. She steps up onstage and it seems like the whole world is watching her."

"That's amazing."

"You have no idea." He shook his head, with a rueful smile now, as if unable to stop his stream of happiness. "When she's up there, and I see her speaking, and I see the whole audience captivated, it's . . . 'pride' isn't even the right word. It's like there's something inside me that was never there before, you know? Like a certainty that one day she's going to go out into this crazy world and just blow them all away. You know what I'm talking about?"

"Of course." I nodded, shifting a little uncomfortably. My voice was quiet as I spoke into my coffee. I felt a bubbling need to add more. "Santi's really good at art. His teachers are impressed by him. They say he's got a real talent for it."

And as I was speaking, as I was lying on behalf of my child for reasons that I myself didn't fully understand, I had a sudden sense that Santi and I inhabited different worlds. I had found my way to exist in this world, to sip coffee with hospital chiefs and talk about our kids, but there was a deep ravine that separated me from him. And in that moment, it felt utterly impassable.

The guilt of the lie stayed with me for most of the day. I was unable to get any work done. All I could think was that I was not doing enough for him, that I had not done enough for him, and that giving him the opportunities that other kids had was my responsibility. I'd tried to tell myself he was just developing slowly, and that he would get there in his own time. But just as I noticed my own growth and my own development, I was struck with this sense that I was somehow leaving him behind.

I felt like a failure, and I promised myself that I would fix that, whatever it took.

Because of Naoko's shifts at the hospital, I picked him up from school three times a week, but this time all those thoughts were running through my head.

When he got in the back of the car, I didn't drive straight away. Something was wrong, I could tell. He sat sullenly, staring at his feet.

"What's up?"

Wordlessly, he took a piece of paper out of his pocket and handed it to me. I plucked it out of his hands and read it. It was a note from the deputy headmistress, to be signed and returned the next day. Santi had PE at the end of the day, and they were starting swimming practice. He had refused to take part, refused to even get changed, without any explanation. "Deliberately defiant" were the words she used.

I sighed. This sort of thing was happening more and more often.

"I'm sorry, Dad." The words came out in a whisper. He put his thin arms round his chest and hugged himself with them, looking away from me.

"It's okay, Santi," I said, trying to sound supportive. "I understand. But we need to work on these things together, okay? You and me and Mum. You can't just shut down like that. I'll speak to the teachers and we can all help you when you encounter these difficult situations. Does that sound good?"

He nodded dispassionately.

"You know what?" I said, grinning at him through the rearview mirror. "I've got an idea."

"What?"

I smiled. "You'll see. We're just not going to go directly home, okay?"

His little face perked up, and beneath the sullenness, I could detect a hint of a smile. Leaning forward and putting on the radio, I took the next left turn and cut down the fifteen-minute drive through the Thursley National Nature Reserve.

As the road trundled off the main carriageway, we carried on into the wide spread of peatlands and bogs, spotted with tall, spindly trees like living Giacometti statues. I had taken Santi for walks around here when we first arrived, and he fell in love with the sparseness of the nature, the loneliness of the landscape. The sun was out in full force, and the sky was clear and blue, and as I saw the grin grow on his face, I knew that this afternoon would turn out all right.

After another five minutes, I parked up alongside Frensham Little Pond—the freshwater swimming lake that sits in the middle of the park. It was a weekday, and not quite warm enough for many other people to be out. We'd passed a few hikers in the park, but the beach was still empty.

"What are we doing here?" Santi asked as he got out of the car.

I got down to his level and gave him a reassuring pat on the shoulder. "I'm going to teach you to swim, buddy."

He blinked, taking a step back. "What?"

I seized on his surprise and pressed on before he could form a resistance. "It's time you learned. It's an important life skill. I know you had trouble today, but you're with me now. I'm going to be with you every step of the way."

He shook his head. "I don't want to."

"You *think* you don't want to," I said, "but you've never really been in the water, have you? How can you know if you don't try new things? That's how we grow, Santi."

He looked over at the lake, the water lightly lapping against the little beach. It was still and quiet. A few birds swooped overhead, wheeling and crying.

"But I don't want to."

"Well, sometimes we have to do things we don't want to do," I snapped. "That's just life."

He looked down at the ground, closely analyzing his shoes. I sighed and took his hand.

"Look, I'm sorry. But honestly, you're really going to love it once you give it a try."

"Okay." His voice was very small.

"Are you sure?" I asked.

He didn't really move. "Okay," he said again.

"Come on." I stood up and, with his hand in mine, walked down to the shore.

After stripping down to our boxers—I had not brought any swimwear, of course—I stepped a few paces into the water. Santi stood at the shore and watched me tentatively, his toes fidgeting in the sand.

I made sure I only went about knee deep before turning back.

"You can stand here," I called. "There's no current and the water's perfect."

He eyed me suspiciously.

"Come on," I said. "Do it for me."

Slowly, inch by inch, he approached the water. It lapped up onto his feet and he shivered at the feel of it. He dipped a toe in further, then his whole foot. And, like a child learning to walk with his arms out in front of him, he made his way to me.

"It's cold," he said, as his hands clasped onto mine.

"No, it isn't. Don't be silly." I splashed water on him and he squealed, shivering. The edges of a smile started to spread across his face.

"See?" I splashed him again, but he dodged me. "It's not so bad!"

After a couple of minutes of playing around, where I gradually moved us out a little further until the waterline was above Santi's waist, I decided to try the next step.

"I'm going to hold you the whole way," I said. "I won't let go. All you have to do is straighten yourself out and paddle your arms and legs. You'll be great, I promise."

Cautiously, he nodded and lowered himself into the water. I let him stretch out into my arms and I held him up, still so light and gangly. He looked at me—timid, hesitant—and shakily moved his hands.

"That's it," I said, moving him forward a little. "Now try your whole arms, and your legs, too."

As he paddled, I carried him forward in the water, getting out to the depth of my chest and then spinning him around again and bringing him back.

"You're doing it! See! You're a natural!"

He looked up and, seeing the joy on my face, he laughed, paddling harder with his arms and legs. "I'm swimming!"

"You are! I knew you would be amazing!"

The moment seemed to last forever: the two of us, him in my arms, laughing and paddling and twisting around, with the warm sun beating on our necks and backs. When we stopped, his face was flushed red. He was up to his waist in water and his hands were still splashing about in it.

"I want to do that again."

"Sure," I said, with a big grin on my face. "But hold on two seconds. Just stay here where you can stand. I want to get my camera from the car. I want to remember this moment forever."

"But—"

"Don't worry. I'll be back in less than a minute. Just move a little and enjoy the water, okay?"

I remember feeling a need to document this: my boy swimming, smiling and splashing in the water like he belonged there. It seemed like the most important thing in the world. *He's twelve*, I told myself. *He'll be fine.*

I fumbled in the glove compartment for my camera. It had been a gift from your dad, Ben, a few Christmases before. He'd posted it to me in the mail because I hadn't had the time to join him for the day. I remember thinking: *We'll go to Ben's next Christmas. Then he'll meet Naoko, and Santi—the little suns that the solar system of my life now revolves around.*

Grasping the camera, I turned around to get some shots of him from a distance.

He wasn't there.

I frowned, walking forward as I scanned the shore. Had he got out? Where had he gone?

With each step that I took, a sense of unease spread across my whole body like a cancer, making my hairs stand on end and my arms shiver.

Then I saw him: in the water, facedown, not moving.

My stomach heaved, and I scrambled forward, stumbling over the sand and rocks. Time slowed down—my body wasn't moving fast enough, *wouldn't* move fast enough—and as my feet and ankles plunged into the water, they tripped me and I fell flat, splashing frantically.

He was still too far away.

I pushed on, a mixture of swimming and running against the lakebed. I was dimly aware that I was shouting, screaming his name, screaming for help, screaming for anything.

When I reached him, he was so cold. His body was floppy, floating flat on the surface with his face down. Drowning. Or drowned. I didn't know.

I tugged him up into my arms and pushed back to the shore. The water felt like treacle, and my legs wouldn't move fast enough. His limbs sprawled on either side of me, lifeless and cold.

He had tried to swim. He had wanted to swim some more, but he couldn't. He wasn't strong enough. *I* had made him try to swim.

As soon as my feet hit dry land, I laid him on the beach. Three or four hikers had started to arrive, approaching us. They must have heard my cries.

"*Call an ambulance!*" I screamed. "*Now!*"

Putting my fingers against his neck, I held my breath, desperately hoping to feel some kind of a pulse. I could have sworn there was something there, but it was faint—so faint!—like the echo of a whisper.

Pushing his nose back, I started mouth-to-mouth. My training took over, burying the rest of me, howling, deep into my mind.

Seconds stretched to eons, until, eventually, he coughed.

Water dribbled out of his mouth and down the side of his cheek. Not enough, I remember thinking. Not enough. It must be mostly in his stomach, not his lungs. I leaned in and held my ear to his face—it was still so cold—and I felt little puffs of breath against my skin. Relief flooded through my whole body, shaking me to my core. I almost screamed. My eyes were wet with tears. He was alive.

He was breathing and he was *alive.*

But I knew he wasn't out of the woods yet. I'd seen enough drownings to know that the next few hours were crucial. He needed care and he needed it now.

"Where's the ambulance?" I spun around. Four or five people were around us now, wringing hands and looking worried. "Did someone call?"

"They're on their way," one man said. "They said to stay put. They'll be about ten minutes."

"*Ten minutes?*"

I knew that meant fifteen, at best, and every lost minute was making the possible danger worse. My mind was dancing, panicked, fevered. I picked Santi up again. He was so light, like a feather. I rushed over to my car.

"They said to stay where you are!" the man shouted after me. "They told me you shouldn't move him."

I didn't bother telling him I was a doctor, that I knew what I was doing. I just ignored them. *They don't know what they're talking about. Waiting's just standard procedure that they tell the public, but not* my son. *Not me.* He needed to get to a hospital immediately, and Surrey County was only twenty minutes away. Less than fifteen, if I ignored the speed limit.

He'd be in a hospital bed before the ambulance even got here.

There were more shouts of protest behind me, but I barely heard them. Laying him flat in the backseat and tying a quick seat belt around his legs and arms, I turned on the car and sped away.

I don't know how long I drove for. It felt like hours.

When I skidded up in front of the hospital, I dashed him into A&E.

"He's unconscious," I said. "Drowning. He's breathing, but only just."

The nurses started jostling around me. A gurney was produced, and I placed him on it.

"He definitely didn't spit up all the water. He needs gastric decompression immediately."

"We've got this," one of the nurses said. "You need to leave this with us."

"Like hell I do," I shouted. "I'm coming into the ICU."

"You're not allowed—"

"Do you know who I am? Do you want me to get Dr. Idris in here? Do you want to lose your *fucking job*? I'm going in."

They didn't argue. We ran down the corridor, wheeling him into a room with a crash cart.

"I need a syringe and tube for gastric decompression," I said.

"We need to give him arterial oxygen first," the nurse replied. "We don't know how hypoxic he is. We should really wait for a doctor to—"

"I *am* a doctor. I'm the best doctor you've got. He's got water in his gastric system. I'm sure of it. He's breathing. He's getting oxygen, but we *need* to do a decompression."

"I really don't think—"

"*NOW!*"

She backed away, nodding. Gesturing to another nurse, she handed over the syringe and the tube and I started to perform the procedure. It was one I'd done a million times. I knew what I was doing. I kept repeating that to myself.

It's just a patient. It's not Santi. It's not my little boy.

I know what I'm doing.

The syringe went into his stomach, and I pulled back.

There wasn't much water, just a few drops. I frowned, confused. But he must have swallowed more than that. He must have.

"Harold." I looked up to see Paul Idris standing at the door. "I'm going to need you to leave right now."

"Paul, I'm glad you're here. I was just—"

"Harold." His voice was firm. Hard. "Please. Don't make me call security."

I looked down at Santi—he was still breathing, but not much. His body looked so fragile. He was just in his boxers. So was I.

I looked back at Paul and realized how wrong this must look. But I was just doing the best for him. I was just trying to save him.

"Please just make sure he's okay," I begged, more to God than to anyone. "Please, Paul. Please."

"We'll let you know as soon as we can," he said. "But you need to step outside."

I sat in the corridor, on a bench, with my head in my hands. Shaking.

I don't know how long I was there. I asked the nurses to call Naoko, to send for her in the hospital. I can't even remember what I said. Everything was a blur, like I was underwater. All I remember is that it felt like I was also drowning, that I couldn't breathe.

I paced up and down. I tried to drink something, but I couldn't get it down. I felt sick. I went into the bathroom and vomited into the toilet.

When I came out, Paul was waiting for me.

I knew that face. I had seen that face so many times before. I had worn that face for other patients, for other children.

"He's on a ventilator." His voice was gravelly.

"Is he awake?"

Paul shook his head.

I moaned, putting my hand to my head. "So he's in a coma. That's okay. As long as there isn't any brain damage. We can manage that. He'll be—"

"Harold." The word cut through me like butter. "He's not in a coma. I'm afraid he went without oxygen for too long. He no longer has any brain-stem functions that we can detect."

I was drowning. I was underwater and I couldn't breathe.

"What are you saying? That he's brain-dead?"

Paul's lips came together tightly. "I'm afraid so. I'm so sorry."

"But how? He was breathing. He was breathing!"

"I don't know if you need to hear—"

"*How?*" I grabbed him by the collar.

He took my hands and pulled them off. "It was a ventilation-perfusion mismatch. The fresh water destroyed the surfactant in the alveoli. The lungs were getting oxygen, but the blood in the lungs wasn't able to absorb it. It's not uncommon in freshwater drowning victims."

I fell to the floor. It happened in one swift movement, like a building collapsing. My brain went blank. Paul helped me up, asked me if I wanted to see Santi. But I couldn't reply. I was just numb, from head to toe.

Crumbling onto a bench, I curled up, inside and out, until I was so tiny I didn't have to think.

At some point, I looked up and Paul wasn't there anymore.

I'd been left alone.

"—wouldn't have happened if he'd just waited."

I blinked the tears out of my eyes, lifting my head slightly. That was the nurse I'd shouted at earlier. She'd just arrived behind the station and hadn't seen me.

"It's so horrible," one of the other nurses replied. "Going like that."

"The ambulance would have given him oxygenated blood. It was only a couple minutes after he left that it arrived. Freshwater? They would have suspected hypoxemia immediately."

"Didn't you try to put him on an IV as well?"

"Oh, sure. Seemed obvious to me. But the dad was screaming in my face. He knows Dr. Idris. Threatening my job. What was I meant to do? If he hadn't been so bloody arrogant, his kid would be fine."

It hit me like a tidal wave.

I had done this.

I had made him go into the water when he was too scared to, when he knew it was dangerous, because I knew better.

I had left him all alone to get a fucking photo, because I wanted to prove it. To prove I was right.

I hadn't waited for the ambulance.

I hadn't listened to the nurses.

I had assumed that I knew better, that I *was* better. That God had given me this family and this child so that I could show the universe that I was good enough to be his father.

And I was *wrong*.

Because I was wrong, I had killed my son.

I had murdered him.

When Naoko appeared, I couldn't talk to her. I couldn't even look at her. And I knew, deep down, that I wouldn't ever be able to again. I found out later, from Paul, that she had pulled the plug. I didn't even go in to see him.

Brain-dead just meant dead. I knew that. Santi wasn't in there anymore. Just the scene of the crime I had committed.

I left. I ran. I got my stuff and I got on a plane and, like the coward I am, I disappeared as fast as I possibly could.

I've been running ever since.

I NO LONGER KNOW WHEN IT IS.
THE CAVE, THE MOUNTAIN.*

Dear Harriet,

The storm still rages. The Warden hasn't come back.

We are still waiting.

It is so high up here that we are beginning to need oxygen to keep us conscious. We've each worked through a canister and have had to move on to another one. There are only a few left. I don't know how much longer we'll be able to sustain waiting.

I'm searching through the Polaroids with my flashlight, trying to find us a way out—backtracking through where I think we must have gone. Safe from the wind, the cave feels a little warmer, and I'm able to think without the howling cold in my ears. I think I can pinpoint us on the map, but the next step is not so easy. Going back through that nearest fold takes us straight into the caves. That's not an option I want to entertain.

After emptying myself into my last letter to you, Hattie, I felt hollow. I wanted to cry, but I couldn't. I wanted to bawl my eyes out, to

---

* EDITOR'S NOTE: This is the third letter of the three sent to Harriet in 1991.

feel the cathartic pain that comes from confronting the darkest parts of yourself, because then, at least, I would feel human.

But instead, I just sat there inside the cave, wordless.

Naoko sat down beside me, looking off into the same middle distance that I was staring at. In the dim light, I could barely make her out at first—just a shifting mass of clothes and gear. Her arm twitched a little, as it still does now and again. For all we have been through, she is still not fully healthy, not fully herself.

For the longest time, she didn't say a word. She didn't have to. The weight of my shame and guilt, dredged up after all these long years, must have emanated off me in waves.

Eventually, after a lifetime of waiting, I spoke.

"I loved him more than anything I've ever known."

Beside me, I saw her head nod slowly. "I know."

"I thought I could forget about him. That I could forget about you. That I could run away from everything and keep running. But I can't."

"I know."

"I've tried to move on," I said. "To start things anew. I've tried everything to keep him out. I keep locking it all up, hiding it away inside of me, but nothing keeps it shut anymore! Not even guilt. Not even hate. I've hated myself for so long, Naoko. I'm worn down by it. I'm *tired* of it!"

I turned to look at her. Her eyes were wet. Her skin flushed red under her layers. She didn't say anything. She just reached out to take my hand—my broken half hand—in hers.

"What can I do?" I pleaded. "I'm sick of this guilt. Of this shame. Tell me what to do."

"Do you remember the netsuke I used to make for my mother?" she asked, her voice quiet.

"Of course." I frowned, unsure what she was saying. "The turtle."

"Even though I missed her every day, and it brought me pain, I remembered her every day. You can't just pretend the past doesn't exist and move on. There are no new beginnings, Harry. They carry all the old ones with them. The only way to live in the present is to embrace the past, to use it as a seed to grow the future."

I bowed my head down low. I didn't want to hear this. I didn't want to do this.

"You need to be able to talk about him," she pressed. "To remember him. *We* need to be able to talk about him."

My whole body shivered. I shook my head.

"Yes," she pressed. "Yes, you can. You can do it, Harry. Do it for me. This mountain, it . . ." She put a hand to her forehead. "Please. It will help me feel like myself again. Just tell me some of your favorite memories, the very best ones, and I'll tell you mine."

And—slowly, stutteringly—I did: I told her about the Giacometti exhibition we went to in London. I told her about the stories we would make up before bed, endless lists of tales and journeys. I told her about the way he would hold my hand when he was scared.

She told me about the paintings they would make together when I was at work, about the way he would steal vegetables from the kitchen while she was cooking and run around the flat with them.

And somehow, despite the opening of the box and the baring of my soul that I had been so certain would tear me apart, the fact that Naoko and I were talking made everything okay.

It was going to be okay.

"You did so much good for him," she said. "So much good. I'm not telling you to forget what you did. What you blame yourself for. But when you remember him, can you remember all of that, too?"

I took in a deep breath. "I don't know. All these years I've told myself that either God doesn't exist, and this is all my fault . . . or God does exist, and He's punishing me somehow. Thomas thought we were all part of God's big plan. Does that mean He planned to make what happened to us happen?" I shook my head. "Thomas was probably crazy. Maybe we all are. Maybe God is real, but He's stupid, or He's evil, and none of this is meant to make any sense. I don't care. I *really* don't care. I don't give a shit about any of that anymore, Naoko. I just know that I want us to live. That's all I want: for us to get through this, together. We've lost so much time, so much time we could have . . ."

I trailed off, staring in her eyes. I could lose myself in them for a lifetime and still go back for more.

"I just miss him so much," I said.

She reached over and put her arms around me. "I know," she said. "Me too."

And I cried. Not a hysterical, bawling madness, but a soft lament that comes from years and years of sadness. I buried my head into her shoulder, and I slowly let it out, bit by bit.

When I was done, I took both her hands in mine.

"When we get through this," I said. "Not *if*. When. We'll start over. No, not start over. We won't forget the past. We will continue. We will take the next step. I love you."

She smiled.

"I've always loved you, Harry. I always will."

She leaned into me, and I held her close: the weight of her body pressed against me almost made me feel weightless. Free.

I sighed and glanced around the cave. The light was very dim and Palmer and Bettan were getting out their flashlights. Neil was sitting about five meters away from us, staring intently at Naoko and me, as though he were watching a film. I couldn't help but feel he'd been watching us for quite some time.

* * *

It had been dark for a few hours. The storm still raged on and the Warden still hadn't returned. Palmer was getting anxious, pacing back and forth. Her hands were tightly clenched at her sides. From time to time, she would stop and look outside the cave. Muttering to herself, she would shake her head and resume pacing.

Naoko and I were curled up together in a corner, pressed against each other for warmth. She was nestled into my chest and her eyes were closed. We'd been sharing an oxygen tank and trying to spend as little energy as possible to get us through the night. Bettan had sat down and was staring fixedly at a cave wall, silent for what felt like the first time. Neil was lying back on the ground, looking relaxed.

As Palmer crossed by us for the umpteenth time, she stopped.

"I'm going to go out there."

"You can't," Bettan said, looking up. "This is the one refuge we have at the moment. Against the storm. Against those things. And while I can shoot a gun, you're the only one I trust to defend us if they show up. At least while the Warden's gone."

"I can't just ignore him."

"We need to be ready to move as soon as he comes back. We're running out of oxygen and time. We need to get to the summit. Harold—where do we go from here?"

I leaned back, my arm around Naoko. "I don't know yet. I've tried looking at the map again, but things have been so . . ." I shook my head. "I need more time."

"Then you'd better fucking get back to it, don't you think?"

I wanted to snap at him, tell him to back off. But he was right: when the opportunity arose to get out of here, we needed to be ready to take it. That meant having a route.

Lifting my arm, I tried to gently extricate myself from Naoko. She roused, lifting her head up with a sleepy smile.

"I've got to go back to work."

She nodded, standing up and stretching, pacing back and forth a little. I pulled the Polaroids out of my backpack, organized and labeled from before, and shone a light on them.

Palmer hadn't moved. She was standing still, rigid. "We can't leave him out there."

"What choice do we have?"

"Someone needs to go out, at least nearby. He could have fallen. He could be stuck. If they take a flashlight and stay close—"

"Who?" Bettan asked. He was the one pacing now—his footsteps on the rocky ground echoing around the small cave. "If you go, we've got no defense. If Harold goes, we've got no map. If I go, and I don't come back, you're fucked when the time comes."

"I could go," Naoko said. My head jerked right to where she was standing, swinging my light toward her. "I could take a flashlight, stay close."

"On your own?" I blurted. "That's crazy."

"What if I went with her?" Neil said, and everyone jumped. He was standing straight up, tall and gangly as ever, looking down at me. "We would take care of each other."

I frowned. "That's not—"

"Think about it," he said, smiling at us. His voice was warm, soothing like honey. "We all have our parts to play. If you stay here, you can work out our way to the top. If Palmer stays here, she can protect you. If Bettan stays here, he can make the necessary preparations for us to leave immediately. Where does that leave me and Naoko? Surely we must be the scouts. It makes the most sense."

Bettan nodded. "He's right."

I squirmed a little. The idea did *sound* right. It sounded logical to me, on some basic intuitive level. But underneath that, on a more primal, emotive level, I didn't really want Naoko going out into the snow.

Did I?

"With me, she'll be fine. There's nothing to worry about."

"It makes the most sense," Palmer said, echoing Neil's words. They sounded more sensible the second time. More obvious.

"I suppose, if you both stayed close, then . . ." I trailed off, looking down at the photographs beneath me.

"There's nothing to worry about," Neil said again. I smiled a little, feeling the creases in my forehead smooth out. He was right. There really wasn't anything to worry about.

I would stay here, work out where we were, and map a route. Neil and Naoko would find the Warden and bring him back, and we could all go to the summit together.

Yes. I ran through it again in my mind, as I saw Naoko take Neil's hand and step out into the dark.

Yes.

It makes the most sense.

Hattie—

We have to go out into the snow. Now. Everything has changed. I'm itching to go, but have to wait for the others to be ready. I shouldn't go alone—they are right—even though I am desperate to. I feel so stupid. I can't believe I missed it, Hattie.

It's been staring me in the face for so long.

Shortly after Naoko and Neil left, the Warden returned.

He stumbled in from the night, shaking and jittering. His whole body was covered in a white sheen of snow.

Palmer ran to him, and for a moment looked as though she was about to throw her arms around him. But as she got close, she slowed down. They stopped awkwardly in front of one another.

"You okay?" Palmer asked, her voice a little gruff.

"He's not there," the Warden said, a pained look in his eyes. "I looked and I looked, and I kept seeing a glimpse of him. But he'd just disappear. Like a ghost. He's . . ." He looked around at us. "Wait. Where is everyone else?"

"Naoko and Neil just left," Palmer said. "They went to look for you."

He put his hand to his head. "And you let them go? It's a nightmare out there. They'll be lost in minutes. Naoko and *Neil*? Why did you send them?"

We looked at each other, feeling a little strange. No one seemed quite able to articulate it.

"It seemed like the right idea at the time," Palmer said.

"What?"

"Well," I added. "He sort of . . ." I frowned. Why had they gone out into the snow?

"Fuck." The Warden shook his head, putting his hand to his forehead. "I'm going to have to go get them. Those two! I get why we've got a doctor here, but Neil? I still don't know why they had you sign an anthropologist up for this expedition, Grace, but—"

"What?" She straightened up, her whole body tense. "What did you just say?"

"I mean, I'm sure he's great in his field, but this—"

"You oversaw his recruitment."

He stared at her. "No, I didn't."

"Yes, you must have. Because I didn't. He was one of your recruits."

"Wait," I said, a strange thought percolating down through my brain. The way he had looked when he walked away. The strange effect his words had on my thoughts. "Wait, wait. Stop for a second."

"What is it?"

I had missed something. Something very obvious.

"What's his name? Say his name again."

"Neil?"

"His full name."

Palmer frowned. "Neil Amai?"

"Spelled A-M-A-I?" I asked.

"Yes."

I burst into laughter. I couldn't help it. It wasn't humor—it was a mad, crazed expression of desperation.

Sometimes all you need is for someone to turn it on its head, Neil had told me. *Like turning a picture upside down, or spelling a word backward, and suddenly there's a whole new meaning.*

"They've been fucking with us this whole time," I said, my head in my hands. "From the beginning. How did we not see it? Oh, shit. They've been watching us since the start."

"Who?"

I breathed, trying to gather my words, knowing how manic I must have looked. "Don't you see? Don't you get it? It's all a big joke to them. It's a huge fucking game. I need to get out there, *now*. Naoko is not safe."

"Harold?" Palmer put a hand on my chest. "What are you talking about?"

"Neil Amai," I repeated. *"Neil Amai*. Spell it backward."

I watched as the look of realization spread across their faces.

I am alien.

My dearest Harriet*

This is likely the last letter I will write to you about this experience. It may well be the last letter I ever write.

We ventured out of the cave together, just as the light was beginning to strengthen. The edges of the horizon glimmered in palettes of soft whites and blues. The wind was dying, and with it came a crisp freshness—a cold bite to the nose and throat. Snow drifted lazily down from the clouds. We were down to our last six oxygen canisters—maybe ten to twelve hours each of supplemental oxygen, and that wasn't including Naoko. The only food we had left was protein bars.

The Warden had emptied his pack of anything but weaponry and ammunition. His eyes glared, mouth turned down—furious that he had missed an intruder in our ranks all this time. Palmer's face was also set, but in comparison she seemed softer, more weary. Less aflame with the righteous anger that the Warden and I shared. They both had shotguns over their shoulders, pistols holstered at their waists,

---

*EDITOR'S NOTE: While much effort has been made to organize these letters chronologically, Harold's dating ceases to be recorded here. Despite appearing nonsequential, the following pages were collated and numbered together in the original documents, and so will be presented as such.

and Palmer had taken a string of grenades, hanging them from her jacket.

He had been in our camp. He had climbed with us, slept with us, taunted us. All this right in front of our noses, like he was mocking us. I use the word "he," but I realize that I have no idea what he even is. The more I picture his strange gait, his funny turns of phrase, and the odd way he would seem to sneak up on you—as if you had forgotten he was there, until he appeared behind you—the more I kick myself for not having noticed sooner.

Is he like Jet? Or like John was? A man driven mad by the mountain and the creatures that inhabit it? Somehow, I don't think so. Something else is going on here. In my head, images of the cave walls keep reoccurring: the deities that were painted in there and the worship that I saw.

And he had Naoko. That scared me most of all. He had spirited her away from underneath our noses, and now she was alone with him. I had no idea what his intentions were.

I had to find them. I had to save her. I *could not* lose her, too. Not now.

My rudimentary examination of the map was fettered by anger and loss and confusion, and I had not had enough time. I knew two things for certain: that the fold we'd exited when we were running before was close, and that entering it would take us deep into the caves.

There was another fold nearby, perhaps, if we could find it. It would take us somewhere, maybe closer to the summit, but it would be without Naoko. None of this mattered without her.

Bettan took the lead as we pushed out into the snow, hoping to find some kind of sign. But after just a few steps, I realized how futile that would be. The storm had died, but the snow still fell, covering any tracks that might have been made. Visibility was much better, but I couldn't think of any way that we could find them.

It didn't matter. I had to try. I had no choice.

Bettan stopped just ahead of me.

"This is fucking ridiculous," he shouted, waving his hands at the storm.

"Do you have any better suggestions?"

"Find another fold. Continue the ascent. Get to the summit. The fold we came through is just up ahead. I think we go back through it and then work forward from there."

I stared at him. "And leave her behind? With *him*?"

He shrugged. "Whoever the fuck he is, he managed to hide in plain sight from the very start of this expedition. He managed to convince us all to let him take her. Even if there was a snowball's chance in hell of us finding them, which there *isn't*, what are we going to do?"

"Kill him," the Warden said, his voice bristling. "Find out what he knows. Then kill him."

"Stupid," Bettan replied, pointing an accusatory finger at him. "Idiotic. You don't even know what he is. You don't even know if you can kill him. We know one thing, and one thing only: that the summit is there waiting for us. Maybe they'll be there, too. Maybe the answers that you're looking for are—"

I pushed Bettan hard.

He took a few staggering steps backward and straightened, a glint of laughter in his eyes.

"What the fuck was that?"

I clenched my throbbing fists, the right searing in pain from the wound. I could no longer ignore him: his arrogance, his ego, his insolence.

Everything that I had hated about myself for so many years. All the things that led to Santi's death. Everything that I have tried so hard to crush. It was right in front of me, like a distorted mirror.

"We're not going anywhere until we've found them," I said.

"You are not the leader of this expedition. Losing your girlfriend isn't a qualification."

A thunderous shake ran through the ground. The tremor sent us stumbling. I fell forward, my hands darting out to catch myself. My wounded stumps hit the rock, and I screamed. Pain jolted up my arm like lightning, like fire shooting through my nerves.

The sound of scuttling whispered through the air.

I scrambled back, looking from the Warden to Palmer to Bettan. All their faces told me exactly what I feared.

We were not alone.

The Warden pulled his shotgun up to his chest. Palmer did the same, and as Bettan pulled out his pistol, Palmer pressed a pistol into my hand.

"I've never used a—"

"Point it at the thing you want to kill and squeeze the trigger." Her words were fast but clear. "Don't point it at us."

She pulled me toward them. Bettan and I fell back-to-back in the middle, and the Warden and Palmer circled around us with their shotguns raised high. There was another scuttling sound, and more slithering. The wind rose, blowing freezing snow across our faces. Off in the distance, just at the very edge of my vision, I caught a glimpse of a dark tendril wisping through the air.

And then another.

"They're scared of our weapons," I said. "Jet said they were."

"If there are enough of them out there," the Warden replied, "I don't think it matters."

The slithering and scuttling rose from all around us, encircling us in a perimeter of fear. I couldn't see a damn thing—only the occasional swipe of movement, a dark tentacle slipping through the snow. The dreadful sounds grew and grew, cacophonous, until it felt like the very mountain would collapse under their weight.

Then it stopped. Silence.

Only the susurrus of light wind remained, whistling through the rocks.

A figure stepped out of the snow and into sight.

"'To see a world in a grain of sand,'" Jet said, his eyes wild. "'And a heaven in a wild flower. Hold infinity in the palm of your hand and eternity in an hour.'"

Bettan lifted his pistol and fired. The crack of the gunshot rang across the mountain, and Jet staggered backward, his hands going to his chest. He looked down at his body, and it seemed to glitter, as though it were made of metal. How long had he been down in those caves now? How much of him was still human?

He started to laugh.

It was a cackle that burst out of him like a wave.

"Oh, excellent. So very decisive," he said between breaths. "The usurper acts, but he does not *see*! This achieves nothing. I am no longer like you. I am the leviathans' conduit. I am the path through which you discover your destruction."

His laugh receded into a little smile, and he cocked his head sideways.

Darting forward with impossible speed, Jet closed the twenty meters between us like lightning. Palmer swung her shotgun round and fired, missing as he barreled at us. His arm knocked me aside and I went tumbling. The bulk of him went straight into Bettan and they fell into the snow, scrambling and clawing at one another.

Palmer tracked them with her shotgun, but didn't fire again. Couldn't. They were too close together.

A tentacle slithered out of the storm and slammed into her chest.

Her shotgun flew out of her hands and went sliding across the snow. She crashed onto the ground, rolling onto her side. With a scream of fury, the Warden lifted his gun and started firing at the beast.

Deafening booms thumped as he fired and fired again. Inhuman rattling and squealing as the response; splatters of blue exploded into the air.

Anger and madness seethed through me, but I recognized it, and I pushed it down. That was *not* who I was. Naoko was still out there, and she still needed me.

As the Warden reloaded, another leviathan galloped toward him, risen high on its tentacles as they pounded against the ground. I lifted my pistol, pointing vaguely in its direction, and fired. My hand jerked backward, unfamiliar with the recoil. I gasped, regulator falling off of my face and the freezing air biting the insides of my cheeks.

Nothing had happened. My bullet missed, flying off into the distance.

My arm ached, my body protesting against the exertion. We were so high up.

Another boom exploded. Palmer was on her knees, shotgun back in her hands, firing. The leviathan reeled, spilling blue blood onto the snow, and tumbled over sideways. She got up and took a few steps forward, firing again point-blank between its eyes.

The Warden clicked his gun back in place and joined her, back to back.

I turned to see Jet on top of Bettan, hands around his neck. Bettan slapped at him, trying to knock him away, but the hits were weak and flailing.

"Shit," I muttered, looking at my gun again. "Shit, shit, shit."

Raising it, not knowing who or what I would hit, I pulled the trigger. Jet jerked, the bullet hitting him right in the side. The impact knocked him over, sending him rolling onto the ice.

Bettan scrambled to his feet and ran.

Toward me.

"The fold!" he shouted, pointing ahead.

"But—"

"*GO!*" the Warden shouted, firing again at the leviathans. We ran, Bettan and I taking the lead. Palmer and the Warden took turns reloading and firing, holding the back line. I looked over my shoulder, scanning for Jet, but couldn't see him.

But that leads to the caves, I wanted to say. But we now had no choice. We were surrounded and there was only one way out. I did not know what horrors waited for us on the other side, but I *did* know what horrors surrounded us here. I could already hear more creatures scuttling out of the ice. It was the caves or death.

Clambering over the rocks, we reached that strange hole of black emptiness. The Warden and Palmer grabbed me and Bettan by the arms, and holding on to one another, we leaped straight into it.

* * *

As we stumbled out into the caves, the full force of the hum rose in my brain again. This was the epicenter of the leviathans' rage. There were flashes of memory and emotion—thoughts that I could recognize, if only I chose to let them in—but they were not my own. I knew that.

I knew who I was.

My body felt immediately lighter—as if I'd lost a hundred pounds—and I realized we were at a much lower altitude now, deep inside the mountain. I took a deep breath, letting real air fill my lungs.

Not for long.

The fold behind us shifted, pulsating a bluish light. A tentacle slid out of it, swooping forward, reaching out toward us.

"*Run!*" the Warden shouted.

We sprinted. Down the corridor, through the tunnels. Torches flickered on either side, shadows dancing across the alien murals on the walls.

The creatures thundered after us, slithering, scuttling—an oncoming wave of death and destruction.

Down and down we ran, turning left and right, cutting further into the caves.

Deeper.

We had no sense of direction.

We were just trying to stay alive.

And the deeper we got, the more I hoped that we might stumble across another fold, something to get us out of there and back onto the mountain, even if we didn't know where that would be.

As we reached the end of one of the tunnels, it opened out into a giant cavern. The ceiling was hundreds of meters above us, receding into the dark. In the center was a phenomenon unlike anything I had ever seen before in my life.

Suspended a foot or two up in the air, there was what I can only describe as a huge tear in the fabric of our reality. A pulsating, swirling hole of madness—flickering through a thousand different colors: shades of purple and red and blue and green.

It had *weight*, tangible weight that pressed down on me even at a distance. It was a struggle to look at, impossible to look away. It dominated the cavern, the mountain, our entire plane of existence.

"What the *hell* is that?" Palmer whispered, unable to keep the wonder out of her voice.

We had stopped, the danger closing in behind us all but forgotten.

It consumed our entire minds. There was nothing else we could think about. No space for fear or panic.

Only awe.

"It's the edge," I said. It was right in front of us. I wanted to reach out, to touch it. "It's the crossover between our dimension and theirs. It's the heart of the tesseract."

She glanced at me. "I have no idea what that means."

"This must end," Jet said behind us. We tore our eyes away from the mountain's heart. We had waited too long. He was there, and an army of leviathans writhed behind him. "They will not simply be *cast aside*. You *will not* take this away from them. You will die. There is nowhere left to go."

"That's not exactly true."

I glanced at the hole in space-time behind us.

The realization of what I was suggesting passed through him, and his whole face twitched, twisting in fury. *"You can't."*

I glanced over at Palmer, at the Warden, and then at Bettan. The reactions were different—a deep sigh, a resigned nod, a shrug—but the meaning was all the same: *What have we got to lose?*

"Watch us."

As one, we ran and threw ourselves into the tesseract.

A depthless kaleidoscope of black and color consumed me, and I was tugged upward, lifted out of my body and into infinity.

[1]*

Hattie, my dear. It has been ten years since I set foot on that mountain. I know this by the movement of the calendar, and the ticking of the clock, marks made against walls, and letters penned. But I do not *feel* time pass anymore. All moments are locked in place, forever.

I know that I am waiting for your father to come to me, and to release me from this prison, but without a sense of what waiting means, I feel I shall be here eternally.

---

* **EDITOR'S NOTE**: Despite its content, the type of paper and ink indicate that this section of the letter was not written later in St. Brigid's, but was indeed written alongside the earlier letters.

I wonder sometimes why I addressed those letters to you, Hattie: what this experience has to do with you, and why I have made you a part of it. The truth is I'm not sure that I was ever certain. At first, I told myself the letters were little more than a record, a journal of events that might allow me to process them on some deeper, subconscious level. But a journal is a letter to yourself, and every time I sat down to write in one, it felt false. I'd devoted my life to hiding from myself, to denying my past, to burying my identity under new challenges and new mysteries. Any honest conversation with myself was impossible. The words wouldn't come. They stuck on the page like tar.

When I abandoned Naoko in that hospital room—when I did everything I could to remove the memory of Santi from my life and cover up the festering guilt—some part of me remained. It's impossible to erase yourself completely. The past doesn't work that way. Perhaps, for some reason, that small unspoken part of me clung to you, as a surrogate for a love that I had left in the dust.

You will be quite old now. I am an old man, if I can even be called that anymore. The truth is I died at the top of that mountain, all those years ago. Life clings to me pointlessly now.

Now I just wait for my time.

The wait feels longer with every passing moment.

[2]

Where am I?

I am in the present, Hattie, *a* present, but it is far in the past. Deep in the recesses of time: it is the past of all living things. I have no body that I can discern. I wonder for a moment if this should bother me, but it doesn't. The thought passes—fleeting, like all things. The earth is red and bubbling: it spits anger and fury and lava. Rivers of molten core twist and swirl across its surface.

It is night, but it is bright. A huge moon sits above, though I have no real sense of physical space. I am here, but I am also there, as I am everywhere. It is exceedingly close, only having just broken away from its rocky home and taken up orbit. Closer now than it will ever be, like another planet, it swallows most of the sky.

Tidal forces rock the Earth—gravity battles against gravity—the planets push and pull against each other, a cosmic tug-of-war, an ancient dance. Waves of lava the height of skyscrapers sweep across the surface, crashing and exploding against newly born mountains, rendering them to ash and rebuilding them again.

There is no life here. At least, not as I recognize it. But there is something. Something older than life. Something deep in the earth that emanates outward. It is neither good nor evil. Neither benevolent nor malevolent. It simply *exists*.

I blink and I am on the surface. I do not have eyes with which to blink. Nor eyelids. Nor face. Yet I register the sensation of blinking: of light going out and light coming back in a flutter of movement.

Why am I here?

This is deliberate. I am being shown something.

The surface I am on is rocky. That's all there is on the Earth at this time: rock and lava; solid and fluid. There is no ice yet. There is barely water. The rock is black and porous, volcanic remnants of a million years of eruptions, like boils upon the planet's face.

In front of me there is a man. I do not recognize him, but I recognize him to be human. He is naked—like Adam. I see him in full, from his head downwards: his shoulders, his stomach, his genitals, and his feet. He stands with his legs slightly apart, his arms open like the Vitruvian Man.

He is no mere painting, though. He is real. There is emotion in his eyes: a soft pleading. I recognize instantly that he is like me, with hopes and dreams and fears and passions.

The skies above him shudder. The moon creaks in its canopy, pulling and pushing. The stars flicker.

I watch in horror as he is lifted slightly into the air by some unknown power and he is torn apart. Limbs are pulled from body: arms ripped out of their sockets, legs torn from their hips. Blood gushes everywhere. His face twists in agony. Hands are removed from wrists. Feet. Then further, the body is broken down into pieces: five, then ten, then twenty. The head remains intact, hovering at the center, and the pieces of this man arrange around him in the air, geometric.

He is being unmade, and his pieces are being twisted into new forms, new shapes. They circle one another now, like a swirling fractal. They search for new rhythms, guided by some invisible hand. His body is a tool to be perfected, like blacksmith's tempered steel, like a musician's perfect scale.

Blood is everywhere. It infects the earth and is infected by it. It is the giver of life and it spills over everything, and still it keeps gushing until the ground is covered with it. I am covered with it. It smothers me and I want to breathe, but I have no mouth. I want to close my eyes but I have no eyes. I must experience this horror in full, unadulterate

And as I see it happen now, I see it happen always and forever. eternal making and remaking. Constantly tinkering, like an inv in a shed.

But there is so much blood. There is so much blood.

[3]

I tumbled out of the swirling portal and back onto the
was dark, and I had lost all sense of time. The air seen
I didn't feel like I was struggling to breathe. *I can't*
thought first of all. *Wherever I am, I am nowhere near tl*
around, looking for anyone else. The others had ju

me, I was sure of it, but there was no one around me now: only stretches of rock and ice, lit by a dim canopy of stars.

I couldn't find any kind of fold that I had come through. It was as though I had merely been dumped here unceremoniously—dropped on the way to something else.

There was a shuffling behind me. I looked over my shoulder to see a figure wandering up the rise.

"Harold?" he asked.

"Thomas?"

His eyes were sunken and gaunt. He lugged his body as if it weighed a hundred tons. He wasn't wearing his hat, or a balaclava. His black hair rustled in the wind. "What are you doing here?"

"You're dead," I said. "I saw you die."

He nodded. "Yes. Yes, I think that's right."

I looked around me. There was nothing but wind and snow. The only light was from the stars above. "Where are we? *When* are we?"

Thomas smiled, giving me a knowing nod. "You always were an insightful one, Harold."

"Am I dead?" I asked. "Is this the afterlife? Heaven? Hell?"

"I'm not sure there's an easy answer to that question. Maybe some cultures thought this was heaven, once. Maybe this is where the idea of heaven came from. But no, you're not dead. Not yet." He frowned. "You really shouldn't be here."

"So *you're* dead?"

"Is my body dead? Yes, I think so. I don't think that this version of me you're seeing is the same one as the one you knew. This place . . ." He put his arms up, indicating the mountain around him. It seemed to stretch on forever, empty and lifeless. "It doesn't exist just in your time. It exists in all times simultaneously. It's like looking at a line and seeing the whole thing at once: there are points on it where I'm dead, and there are points on it where I'm alive. They're all here. One is no more real than the others."

The wind rose, lifting the snow from our feet and swirling it lightly in the air.

"I saw you out in the storm. Why were you out there?"

He knelt, picking up some snow and letting the wind blow it out of his hand. He wasn't even wearing gloves. "I'm a part of this place. As are all of those who aren't alive in your time anymore. They are still alive in time somewhere. And so they remain here: a place that exists at all times."

I took a deep breath, the implications of his words burning hot inside of me. "They're all here? If I stay, will I be able to see them? Will I be able to see *him*?"

He frowned, then shook his head. "No, no. You don't want to do that. If you stay too long, you won't be able to leave, just as I can't leave this mountain anymore. This is not for you. Not yet."

I heard the wind whistling, but could feel nothing. I pulled off my balaclava, and it somehow felt neither cold nor warm. There was a nothingness to this place: a lack of any movement but the wind.

"Do you know why Sisyphus keeps climbing," Thomas asked, looking up at me, "even though he knows he'll always end up back at the start?"

John's last words—echoing back at me across space and time. "Why?"

He smiled and stood up. "Because that's what life is. A constant climb. Eternal growth. The continual battle against entropy. It doesn't matter what the destination is, or what's at the top; all that matters is that you keep climbing. That's what it means to be alive, Harold. That's what it means to be human." He turned away from me, walking off into the night.

"Wait!" I shouted. "What's the point? If everything's all set out for us, what's the point in doing anything?"

He stopped. The stars above started blinking out, one by one. "Whatever is going to happen, it's going to happen. It's already happened. It's happening right now. It's up to you to decide how you make that count. How beautiful you let that be."

He was just a silhouette, a shadow of a frame, darkening as the sky above us dimmed.

"Good-bye, Harold," he said, and the last few stars flickered out.

[4]

I'm knocking on Ben's front door, a little nervous. It's 1983—almost eight years since the last time I saw him. When his daughter was born six years ago, he sent me a letter, begged me to come to the christening. I ignored it. I was too lost in building my own new life, in learning what that meant. But that's in the past. I don't think about that anymore.

And then—*after*—there had been other engagements: other places to be and things to do. Surely he understood.

I knock again. A little girl opens the door, sporting a sparkly red jumper and a head of blond curls.

"Hello," she says, looking up at me. "Who are you?"

"I'm Harold."

"Oh, yes." She gives me a knowing nod. "Daddy told me about you. He didn't think you would come."

I respond with a little shrug. "To be honest, nor did I."

When I enter, Ben is gracious as ever. Apologetic, even, that he's not been able to host me before, as if it weren't me but he who had prevented this from happening.

We sit around the living room table, having a glass of wine, and a silence falls over us. We are so different, my brother and me. He's a lovely man, but once we get past the initial pleasantries, we soon both find we have very little to say to one another. Ben's wife is in the kitchen preparing the turkey. Hattie is playing with a doll in the corner. I stare off into space, and can't help but wonder why I decided to come this year. Poppy couldn't even make it. Surely there are other things I could be doing.

"Can I show Harold my room?" Hattie says.

"Oh, sweetie. I don't think Harry wants to—"

"Sure," I say, looking for a reason to actually *do* something. "I'll check it out."

She nods, as if she's known all along, and puts her hand out so I can take it. I'm led down the corridor. She opens the door and pulls me in.

It's a cute room: toys and stuffed animals are dotted around, propped in a variety of positions. Next to her bed is a little toy kitchen, and in the middle of the room there is a small table, all set for dinner.

I feel a little pang in my heart that I don't want to think about.

I put it away.

"Are you having your own Christmas dinner in here, Hattie?"

"Oh, no," she says, plopping herself on her bed. "We're having a celebration."

"Oh, really?"

"Yes, but there's only a few seats at the table. Esther laid it out for us." She points at the stuffed elephant wearing an apron, propped up by her kitchen. "But she really hasn't laid enough spots for everyone. I am having trouble with the guest list."

"Will Esther the elephant get an invite?" I ask.

She ponders that for a moment, scrunching up her face. "No. She's been very silly."

"Has she now?"

"Yes. She's not in my good books."

I laugh. "And who is in your good books?"

"Well, obviously I will be there, and Prince Hector." She picks up a little dog with a crown on his head and places him in her lap. She gives me a mischievous grin, like she's hiding a scandalous secret. "We're getting married today."

"Oh!" I give her a little bow. "Well, congratulations."

"Yes, and obviously you will have to be there as well. You're the guest of honor."

"Am I?" I sit next to her on the bed. "And why is that?"

She cocks her head at me. "Do you have any children?"

I gulp, my heart suddenly in my throat. I take a deep breath. "No."

"Perfect!" She hops up and puts Prince Hector by the table. "Because Daddy is always far too busy, but I thought you could pretend you were my daddy and you could give me away."

"I don't know if that's—"

She grabs my hand and pulls me down to the table. "Please. It's very important."

And despite my trying so desperately to avoid it, a little stream of love trickles into me in that moment. A feeling that I have not felt in some time. It has nothing to do with my past, or my guilt, or anything that has happened, but for a moment, it allows me to pretend.

[5]

I am inside the tesseract.

All around me there is nothing but void. Not even black—just sightless, soundless, scentless nothingness. The only sensations I have are the taste of my own saliva, the thump of my own blood pumping, and a deep, unshakable certainty: I am at the heart of the mountain.

Not the physical core, down in the caves of our third-dimensional world, but the middle of its grand superstructure, at the intersection between multiple layers of dimensions, overlapping one another and twisting around me.

My breathing ticks like a metronome. My organs gurgle and my pulse thumps loudly in my ears.

In time, light comes to me, like holes being cut in the fabric of the void. It trickles out: a few pinpricks of white, then more, until hundreds open themselves up all around me.

Like doors.

They are doors to moments in time. All moments in time—right from the very beginning of all things to the end. The alpha and the omega, and everything in between. They multiply and multiply and I am slowly spinning, staring into the raw fabric of infinity.

The focus shifts and I see myself. Flickers of images from my youth, as a young boy, and then as an old man. The one-dimensional line of my entire life stretches out before me and I see all the moments of it happening at once.

There is no question of possibility, or chance, or change. There is no question of if or when they take place. They have to happen. They are *already* happening, simultaneously, at all times.

As I continue to turn, they clarify, like segments from an old film:

Poppy, Ben, and me—young, so young—climbing onto a canal boat in the South of France. All I wanted to do was stay home and read, but Poppy pushed me, urged me, and there we were, clambering onto the wooden deck and trying not to fall into the water.

Chasing Santi around St. James's Park—oh, Santi—how you laugh when I leap for you and miss, rolling into the grass. You run back to me and fall into my arms. You fill me with your joy.

I'm in a hospital bed. No—a care home. The monitors are bleeping. I am a very old man, struggling to breathe. Ben is standing over me, holding my hand. How did I get there? The moment feels very important: a defining one in my life. A sense of urgency beats inside me. My heartbeat races. My body shakes with adrenaline. These letters are in my briefcase. I see it and I know that it must happen. It has already happened. I'm just not there yet.

But Naoko—in this grand tapestry of my life, where is Naoko?

I turn and turn, frantically looking for her, and soon I see her again and again and again.

I'm holding her as she cries. She lost two patients today at the hospital and it overwhelms her. I have no words for her, but she doesn't need words, just to be held. Just to feel.

She takes me to the cinema to see a movie. I've never been before. I'd never seen the point. We hold hands as we watch the technicolor explosions of light and sound and she leans her head into my shoulder.

We make love for the first time and I am so shy, so awkward, but she doesn't care. She leads me through every beat and moment. My breath quickens and my muscles squeeze and contract. She opens me up to a world I never knew or cared to understand.

But that is all in my past. I can't get lost in it, as much as I want to.

I need to know where she is now, in this moment.

She is with Neil, and she is in danger, and I have to save her.

I *must* save her.

I spin furiously—tearing through my life, trying so hard to focus, so hard to find her.

My heart drops.

I see Neil taking her hand and stepping out into the snow. I latch onto the moment and I follow it, chasing it across eternity. I watch him lead her through a fold, and then through another, and another.

I follow.

Somehow, at the center of this tesseract, I follow. I barrel through the folds of dimensions and I chase them through the moments that have already happened. I think about Bettan—about his force of will— and I urge myself to manifest that. To will myself forward. To make my certainty into truth.

I see them in the now. In my current *now*. She is huddled up in the snow. He is standing over her, leaning, reaching for her. I scream and all the lights flare up around me. They explode into a supernova of space and time and for a moment—for a brief moment—I am everywhere. I am everything.

It flashes. It burns. It disappears.

I land in the snow, falling to my knees.

Several meters ahead, Naoko is lying on the ground, her body curled into a fetal ball.

Neil is nowhere to be seen.

* * *

Whatever power brought me through the tesseract and to this place, it dragged the others along with me, too. They were standing behind me in the snow—baffled, shell-shocked, staring—and I briefly wondered if they had seen the same sights that I had: their lives laid out before them like a painting.

We were on a flat snowy plain. The sun sat above in a cloudless blue sky, and the light was clear. I found myself capable of breathing easily—we can't have been that high. To the right, the plain ended in a sudden drop: a rocky ridge dipping down into snowy depths below. On the other side, jagged rocks pushed upward like teeth, each one two or three meters tall.

In between, on her own in the snow, was Naoko.

I dashed forward. Running as fast as my legs would take me, I scrambled over rock and ice to get to her.

"Naoko!" I shouted, falling down beside her. "Oh God, are you okay?"

She glanced up at me. "Harry," she whispered. "I . . . I don't know where . . . Neil was just—"

I jerked up. "Is he here? What did he do to you?"

"Nothing," she said, sitting up. "I think. I just can't quite remember what happened."

And as I looked around for Neil, who was nowhere to be found, I saw it.

Over the ridge and down to the next plateau, about a hundred meters ahead of us, a stone archway rose out of the snow. Its black center pulsed with cosmic energy. It was identical to the one I had seen at the summit.

The others arrived behind me.

"Where are we?" Palmer asked. "What the hell just happened?"

Bettan pointed at the archway. "What is *that*?"

I looked up at them. "I think that's it—the final gateway. It's the way to the top."

Naoko screamed.

We all spun around to see what she was looking at. The fold in space-time that I had exited, that I had ripped open to escape the tesseract, still pulsated. It had started to grow, the blackness expanding like a cancer, and tentacles slithered out of its heart.

Jet stepped out of the very center, and on either side of him came one, then two, then four giant leviathans.

"Enough!" he screamed. His face was twisted, his jacket torn and fluttering in the wind. His whole body glimmered in a strange patchwork of metal and skin and blood. "We will tolerate your existence no more!"

The Warden pulled up his shotgun to load it, before realizing he was out of ammunition. The leviathans scuttled forward, a high-pitched rattling screeching through the air.

"Fuck," the Warden said, dropping his weapon to the ground. Whipping out his pistol, he started firing.

The bullets ripped through the creatures, blue ooze spurting out of them, but they didn't slow. Whatever fear they had once had was smothered by their anger.

I pulled Naoko up from the snow and dragged her off to the right, hopping over to the jagged rocks as fast as we could scramble. Bettan dived left, his pistol also out, firing.

Palmer held her own shotgun in place. Just as one of the leviathans got close enough, she fired twice. Blue splattered all over her as the thing fell, skidding into the snow.

One down.

But another was right behind it, leaping over its fallen kin. It threw itself at Palmer, tentacles swirling, and she flattened herself to the ground. The creature flew over her, rolling in the snow and tumbling to the other side.

She pushed up to her knees, leaving her shotgun in the snow and rising with her pistol. Just as the creature straightened up, she fired point-blank right between its eyes. Once. Twice. Three times. A shriek, a shudder, and it collapsed, blue oozing into the snow.

In the distance, I saw Bettan backing away from a third creature. Behind him was a ridge, with a cliff drop of some ten meters. He glanced back, grimacing. He lifted his gun, but a tentacle swung forward and knocked it out of his hand. It tumbled into the snow.

"Roger!" Palmer pulled one of the grenades from her belt. "Jump!"

My mouth dropped open: it was too high. He'd never make it—not without breaking a leg, or worse.

Throwing her a crazed glance, he grinned. She chucked a grenade directly between him and the creature, and just as it rolled through the snow, he dived.

The explosion thundered through the landscape. Bits of severed tentacle and blue splatter rained down on the snow.

Bettan made an almighty twist in the air, tucking his arms in and bending his legs. But I didn't have a chance to see how he landed. The fourth creature—the largest—cut right and thundered straight at me and Naoko. I grabbed her arm and pushed her behind a rock, darting in the other direction to try to distract it.

My foot caught in the ice and I tumbled. My face hit snow. Rolling, I collapsed on my back. I looked up.

The creature was meters away.

The Warden roared, running full tilt toward me. He emptied a full clip into its back, but it barely slowed. I shuffled backward frantically, the distance between us shrinking, the creature bearing down on me just as the Warden bore down on it from behind.

Tentacles whipped out ahead of it and slashed into my side and chest, cutting open my jacket.

Searing pain sliced up my torso. Hot blood froze against my skin.

Barely a meter away from me, it raised its tentacles up high to strike again. The Warden threw his pistol to one side and, pulling a knife from his belt as he ran, he leaped on top of it.

The beast twisted. Tentacles grabbed him, slicing gashes in his arms and legs. But he clung on, stabbing furiously at the creature's body and its eyes. I lay on the snow, clutching my burning side, unable to move, unable to do anything.

A tentacle got hold, circling round the Warden's waist and tightening. He bellowed in fury.

"*Steve!*" Palmer screamed, sprinting in our direction. The creature threw the Warden to the ground and he rebounded, the crack of his bones ringing through the air. Palmer leveled her pistol and fired three times, the creature recoiling in sudden jerks.

It shuddered, turning as it let out a rattling shriek, and then, lifting its mighty tentacles back up in the air, it darted at her.

She leaped sideways, rolling in the snow and coming to her feet, running hard. The giant creature scuttled after her, a whirlwind of tentacles and fury.

With the leviathan only seconds behind her, she turned back. And as she took in the scene—me lying bloody on the ground; the Warden, his body twisted, the white snow underneath him stained with red; Naoko, still alive but helpless, weaponless, unprotected; and only one creature left, the other three dead—grim determination resolved on her face.

She turned to look at the Warden, giving him a single pointed nod.

"*Grace!*" The Warden moaned, his voice weak. He tried to push himself up, but crumpled back into the snow. "*No.*"

She pulled a grenade from her belt and ripped out the pin, spreading her arms wide.

"Come get me, you motherfucker."

The creature barreled into her with a sickening crunch, and they exploded.

The blast thundered through us. I squeezed my eyes shut, not wanting to see the pieces of Palmer spread across the ground like shrapnel. I looked at Naoko and saw she was staring at the devastation, her hands held up to her face. The Warden was sobbing, curled up on the snow, broken body unable to move.

He needed my help.

I didn't know what I could do. I didn't know what any of us could do. All I could think about was Palmer, dead, and a deep hopelessness washed through me.

And yet still, somehow, I dragged myself to my feet. Because despite the ache of my body and the screaming pain of my wounds, Palmer had died to save us: to save the Warden, and me, and Naoko. She'd sacrificed herself for us—so we could survive, so we could make it to the top.

And we would.

We would honor her choice.

I took a few arduous steps toward the Warden, hoping that by some power I would be able to save him.

Frowning, I stopped. I realized that I had forgotten something. Four leviathans had attacked us, and now they were all dead. But they had not come alone.

I spun around.

The realization hit me just in time to see Jet walk up behind Naoko and shove a knife right into her back.

"*No!*"

Her eyes went wide, a dribble of blood sputtering out of her mouth. He pulled the knife out with a grin, letting her go as she slumped to the ground at his feet.

No.

The world stopped turning.

Everything froze—time, space, eternity.

I ran, no thought for my own safety or for the insane man in front of me. I just needed to get to her. To stop this. To save her.

It was futile: as soon as I got close, Jet's arm shot out and grabbed me by the neck, biting into my windpipe. I tried to fight him off, but he batted my hands away. He was *so strong*. Squeezing, he lifted me into the air.

"This is right, Harold. This is good." His voice was laced with melancholy. "This is providence."

I choked, spluttering, my legs kicking the air.

He gave me one last grin, his eyes intently fixed on mine, before Bettan's gun appeared at the side of his head.

"Fuck off," Bettan said, and pulled the trigger.

His head exploded.

I fell, crumpling to the ground. Clambering desperately toward Naoko, I lay beside her.

"Go to the Warden!" I shouted at Bettan. "He's down."

He disappeared behind me.

Naoko was still alive, still breathing. I lifted her to a sitting position against the rock and put my arms around her. There was a hole in her back. A sucking chest wound that pulled the fabric of her jacket inward. The knife had pierced her lung, and she was drowning in her own blood. I covered it with my hand, pressing tightly, if pointlessly. I held her hard against me, close enough that I could feel her heart.

"Harry," she whispered. "It's okay. This isn't your fault."

"You're not going to leave me." My voice was thick. "I'm not losing you. Not now. Not again. Please, don't do this to me."

She shivered, shaking her head. Her voice was soft. Her eyes fluttered.

I pulled her close, hugging her tight, willing all the warmth in my body to go into hers. She softened into me, her body so thin, so frail.

"This is it," she whispered. "This is it. Don't do what you did after Santi. Don't forget about me."

"No," I said, shaking my head. I tried to be strong for her. The last thing she needed was my sobbing. "No."

"You have to tell others about this place. You have to make it to the top so you can . . . discover the truth. People need to know what's . . ." she stammered, coughing blood onto my coat. She gazed up at me, tears trickling from her eyes. "I can't die for nothing."

Whatever is going to happen, it's going to happen, Thomas said in my head. *It's up to you to decide how you make that count.*

"I'll do it," I said. "I'll do it. And then I'll come for you. I promise. Whatever comes next, wherever it is that you go after this world, I will follow you there."

She took a few short, sharp breaths, her eyes widening in fear. "What if there's nothing?"

"Then I'll follow you there, too."

She coughed again, shivering, hacking blood onto the snow, onto me.

"What can I do?" I said. "I don't know what to do. Just tell me what to do."

"I'm so cold, Harry," she whispered. "I just want to stop being cold."

I squeezed her tight. "When I come for you, I will come in a blaze of fire and heat. I will burn my way through the heavens searching for you and I will find you. I promise you that, Naoko."

She stopped shivering, falling slack against me. Her head fell forward into my chest, and I felt her breath stop.

"I promise you that," I repeated, to the mountain and the wind and the snow. "I promise you."

* * *

The Warden is dead. Bettan says he was barely alive by the time he got to him. With Palmer gone, he had nothing left to ward. He just gave up.

We are still at the scene of the devastation. Bettan is collecting oxygen canisters and supplies, whatever he can salvage from the packs of the dead. I am writing. And grieving.

There are only two of us left now, and there is only one path.

The archway waits for us, and beyond it, the summit.

Nothing is keeping us here anymore. Everything is lost.

There is only the pull, the hunger.

And beyond that?

I suppose it's time to find out.

Hattie—*

I don't know why I'm writing this. I think years have passed, but I am never sure anymore. I do not know where I am: an asylum, a prison? There are people here—real people—but they no longer seem that way to me. How long have I been gone for? Does any of it matter?

They scurry around me, like ants about to be stepped on; like lab rats discarded from their cages, useless. When they ask me questions, I can't understand any of them anymore. The words are words I know: they have the shape and sound of words that I learned when I was a child, that I used and shared as I lived my life, but they mean nothing to me now. Each word sounds like a car on a track. Every sentence scripted.

I wave them away. They seem scared of me, gabbling their nonsense, like I'm different, like something is broken.

Nothing makes sense. Nothing is okay. And as I sit here in this warm room—warmth that I never thought I would feel again—I have never felt so lost.

---

* EDITOR'S NOTE: Evidence suggests that this final letter was written in St. Brigid's, some time after his arrival there. The paper is of a different quality and the weathering is not the same.

How do I make sense of the world now, Hattie? That was always my job, wasn't it? My stated purpose. I feel that I must finally try to explain to you what happened on top of that dreaded mountain, if only to try to process the madness that now lives inside of me. I desperately hope that you will never read this. That nobody will.

I do not pretend to offer you answers. I do not have them. I do not have anything anymore.

Only a deep distance; a profound, unsettling alienation; and a burning certainty that nothing will ever be the same again.

* * *

When we stepped through the archway, we were equipped with an oxygen canister each and as little gear as we could get away with. I knew the altitude would weigh on our bodies, but Bettan argued that the faster we could climb, the easier it would be.

In the absence of any other information, I couldn't really disagree.

I think we had both resigned ourselves to the fact that whatever we found at the top, we would not be making it back down. We didn't have enough supplies. We didn't have enough men. And, if I'm honest, only the climb seemed to matter. Down was not a concept that existed in my mind anymore.

We exited the archway together, taking a few tentative steps into the snow. We were on a short plateau, no more than twenty meters wide, and in front of us was a small cliff. It would be a short climb—a clamber over rocks and ice for just a minute or two—and we would reach the top. I could see it from where we were: the point where the mountain stopped rising.

I shivered, my skin prickling from head to toes. Was that it?

It looked like nothing, like a piece of painted scenery. And yet still, somehow, the pull was all-consuming: a deep burning hunger to climb the last few steps. There was nothing stopping us anymore. But what if the hunger was still there when we got to the top?

What would we do next?

Around us, there was only down. The cliffs fell away from our plateau sharply, dropping and dropping, vertiginous, until the clouds and ice below melded into a sea of white. The only sounds were the mountain winds: there was no movement up here, no life. Just the elements. And us.

With the mask against my face and fresh oxygen flowing through me, I wasn't as overcome as last time.

In fact, glancing around me at the striations of clouds some thousands of feet below us, I couldn't help but feel a deep sadness. Here we were: the roof of the world. If Thomas was right, we stood on Mount Meru, Mount Sinai, Mount Olympus itself.

I wanted to feel awe. To be astonished. All I felt was empty.

Bettan didn't say anything to me. He just started hiking, leaving me to trail behind. Once again, I found myself scrambling after him, trying to stay close.

What if there was nothing?

As I pulled myself over a rock and up onto a ridge above me, the thought lodged itself irremovably in my mind. *What if there's nothing there at all? Just a peak. The top of the mountain, utterly nondescript.* As this thought wormed its way into me, I blanched.

The ultimate kick in the teeth. That everything we had done here, everything we had lost, was for nothing. We would die up here: a mausoleum to humanity's curiosity and ego.

I thought these things logically. They registered in my brain. But they did nothing to stop the need, the primal urge in my arms and legs and body to keep climbing.

We'd made it more than halfway when it started to become clear that the peak was not a peak. It didn't rise to a single point, as one might expect from a merging of tectonic plates, but rather seemed to flatten. From that angle, it looked as though there was another plateau at the top: a flat surface, circular in shape, like a carved pedestal.

Images of Aztec sacrificial altars flashed through my mind, and Andean mummies frozen at the top of peaks; of Egyptian pyramids, built like mountains, filled with their dead.

Childhood scripture returned to me—*They sacrifice on the mountaintops*, Hosea wrote, *where the shade is pleasant.*

Dread filled me, consumed me with each succeeding step, and yet I did not stop. I could not. When we reached the top of the bluff, the lip of the plateau was just above us. We gripped it together, looking each other in the eyes. An understanding passed through us: Whatever differences we had, or unresolved issues, they didn't matter now. Whatever waited for us above, we would face it together.

We lugged ourselves up, rolling over onto the ground and pushing to our feet. With my maimed hand and sliced chest, I needed Bettan to pull me all the way up. There was no ice, no snow. Barely a breeze. Nothing but an abnormally flat, round stone surface.

Neil was standing in the very center of it.

"So, you've made the climb. Well done!" His voice had changed— lower, darker, it vibrated as though two or three voices spoke at once. His body glimmered, reflecting the light. "I really didn't expect there to be two of you."

What?

I stared at him. My whole body shook at the sight of him—this man that had taken my wife, that had led her to her death—and the bafflement of finding him here, at the top, as if he had been here all along.

What the hell was going on?

"How the fuck did you get here?" Bettan growled, pulling his oxygen mask off his face. He clenched his gloved hands into fists. His chest was heaving, his shoulders rising and falling.

Neil cocked his head a little to the side, amused, like he was watching an animal in a zoo. "You've made it to the summit. You are the first to hit a milestone like this in over two hundred thousand years. You are the best of your species."

"The best of—" I started, mumbling into my oxygen mask. I pulled it back and found that I could breathe. Somehow, impossibly, I could breathe. The air felt full and clean, like a light summer's day.

I took a step back, tentatively peering over the edge. We were still at the roof of the world; the mountain still plunged treacherously down beneath us. But my legs no longer ached. My chest felt unshackled, open, free.

Neil's mouth curled slowly into a grin, lips creasing unnaturally at the edges. "You're at the top now. There's really no need to make things more difficult than they need to be."

I gaped at him. "What *are* you?"

"I've never lied to you, Harold. I've never lied to any of you. I'm an anthropologist. I study humans: their biological, physiological, and societal development. You could say it's a bit of a hobby of mine."

"*A hobby?*" I repeated. In my mind, images of everything we had encountered flashed: Of Jet slicing through Polya's neck. Of Thomas tumbling down the mountain. Of Palmer, grenade in hand. Of Naoko's body in my arms.

I can't die for nothing.

Bettan pulled his gun out of his pocket and leveled it at Neil. "You're going to explain what's going on here, and you're going to do it right now."

"Oh, please." Neil smiled, as if Bettan's gun were a toy. He took a single step toward us, and I had to fight the urge to take a step back, to turn and run. "There's no need for that. I will tell you all there is to know. You've earned it, in the end."

"You're one of them, aren't you?" I asked, my voice shaking. "The gods that the leviathans worship."

He sighed, shaking his head dramatically. Slowly, he started to remove his layers—hat, scarf, jacket—until he wore nothing but trousers and an undershirt. He was completely bald, his light brown skin shimmering in the sun. "Poor things. They were an early experiment. A test in forms of consciousness that didn't go quite right. Turns out we had too much involvement, you see. These things need to grow organically. We keep some of them around as a reminder. But they get so jealous of others that we have turned our attention to. It's really quite endearing."

Bettan took an angry step forward, his gun still raised. This clearly wasn't what he wanted to find. "What do you mean, 'experiment'?"

"I suppose you'd call it life, Roger." He rubbed his bald head with a large hand. "The grand idea has always been to create something that we might be able to communicate with, and perhaps even one day interact with."

A warm breeze pushed past my face, and I removed my own hat and scarf. I had forgotten that wind could be warm. I had forgotten what warm felt like at all. "Like we're doing now?"

He lowered his head gravely. "I'm afraid not. This," he said, pointing at his body, "is a very recent development. A little test in communication. It's not like we've been hiding—for millennia we've been trying to communicate with you, to show you that we're here, but you're just not ready to see." He walked to the edge of the precipice and looked down, as if assessing the impossible climb we had just made. "So I worked on this form: I'm barely even here, really. A fraction of my real state, like an echo of an echo. It does *seem* to work, but I wouldn't call it a real interaction. I did enjoy myself, though—really, this whole experience has been very enlightening."

I blinked, trying to process his words. It occurred to me that all my memories of Neil were patchy and unclear, as though he was never fully there, not until the end. He never showed up in any of our fights, or struggled in any of our climbs. He never appeared in our arguments. It was as though whenever he wasn't in the room, everyone simply forgot he existed.

How had I not noticed before? How had I not known?

"Wait," I said, putting my palm up. This was impossible. This was madness. "So you . . . created life. Created us. And then what? What is all this? You started setting *challenges*?"

He shrugged, still looking down at the mountain beneath. "Life's a tricky process," he said. "We tried setting up the initial conditions and leaving it entirely alone, but you end up with stagnation." He shook his head gravely. "And before that, we tried speeding everything up, pushing and developing new traits. The leviathans were a bit of a disaster, as you have seen. But you—" He turned back to us both. "You were the golden ticket. Turns out you can't just make life do whatever you want. It has to be prepared. It has to be ready."

"No." Bettan shook his head beside me, his eyes fierce. "No, I don't believe it. You're telling me I'm, what? A fucking lab experiment?" The hand holding his gun was shaking. He started pacing back and forth. "No. *No.* That's bullshit. That is *not* what I am."

I wrung my hands together: confused, furious, overwhelmed. "But *why*? Why take Naoko? Why . . . join us on this whole climb?"

He clicked in annoyance. "You were getting a little slow. I felt you needed some impetus to hurry you up. And I joined you to see how you dealt with the mountain. To see if you were ready."

"Ready?"

"At the right *stage*," he explained, carefully emphasizing each word. "It has happened before. Some hundreds of thousands of years ago, there was another challenge. I wasn't in charge of that one. When you passed it, we deemed you ready for the next stage of evolution."

Bettan was still pacing, bristling with more energy than either of us had been able to show in days, muttering to himself. "I don't accept this. I refuse to accept this."

I ignored him, too focused on what Neil was telling me. "'Next stage of evolution'? What does that mean?"

He held up his arms, as if to embrace me from a distance. "Language, consciousness, introspection. The ability to reason. Everything that separates you from all the other living beings on this planet. Oh, there were a whole host of new developments that we gifted you with. It worked like a treat—propelled you to such new heights. It's been fascinating to watch. But we needed to wait for you to be ready for the next one—technologically, intellectually, psychologically. The mountain is the perfect test. Every few hundred years we set the challenge again. You're the first to have made it."

I looked over at Bettan. He stood at the edge of the plateau, staring down, shaking his head. He was still wrapped in all his layers, as if refusing to accept that any of this was actually happening. The gun in his right hand trembled. His left fist clenched and unclenched.

I turned back to Neil. "What . . . what happens now?"

"The same as last time. One of you comes to me as representative of your species and I elevate you to a higher form of consciousness. You become the alpha of an entire new species: *Homo altior*—higher man. You become the spark that starts the fire."

I frowned. "Why only one?"

He took two steps forward, closing the gap between us to a couple of meters. Without his layers, his body looked bizarre—hairless and smooth, as though made of wax. Lifting his hand, he opened it up in front of me. In it, a small blue gem glowed. "There is just a single seed: perfectly designed for your evolutionary stage and physiology. We have worked on it for millennia. There will not be another like it. It will enter you, rewrite your biology, augment it, and you will breed, passing it on to others."

"What if we say no?" Bettan demanded, spinning around. "What if we choose not to?"

"No?" He laughed, like one would at a child. "You can't say no. This is the moment. It always has been. You have passed the test and now is the time you are elevated. If you walk away, then others will come. You have achieved it now. It will not be long before others are behind. It is your destiny. The destiny of your species."

"You can't just . . ." Bettan's whole body vibrated with anger as he waved his gun at Neil. "You can't just write people's destinies! You can't just wave your fucking hand and define what we are—*what I am*!"

He fired, and the shot rang through the air. Neil didn't move an inch. He looked down curiously at his chest, where the bullet had hit. There was no blood. No wound.

"This must happen, Roger," Neil said, his voice growing severe, his words clipped. "If it doesn't, the human race stagnates forever. You will never progress beyond what you are now. You will be ignored, forgotten, stuck on this pitiful little plane of existence, on this tiny little planet, and you will never amount to anything."

"But it will have been *our* choice," Bettan insisted.

Neil rolled his eyes. "Choice is such a silly human concept. You carve out your small world for yourself, created by powers far greater than you can begin to comprehend, and you call what you have choice. It's ridiculous. No—once you are elevated, you will not be able to say no, just as you had no choice but to climb to this summit." He took another step toward us, and as he did it felt like he was growing. He towered over us. "This will happen. This must happen."

Bettan stared at him, his mouth open. He looked like he wanted to argue more—to shout, to scream—but nothing came out. He looked at the gun in his hand, and his hand dropped to his side. He put the pistol back in his trouser pocket. He bit his lip, shook his head, and turned away from Neil.

I, too, looked away from him. I had to. I stared off into the glittering blue sky, the great canopy above us like a dome, stretching out to the horizon. And all of a sudden, it was abundantly clear. As I stood there at the top of the world, staring into the heavens, I felt the entirety of my existence shrink down to the size of a rat cage, and everything that I have done, or not done, or tried to do, was no different than choosing one path in the maze to another.

Thou shalt be free as mountain winds, Thomas whispered to me from beyond the grave. *But then exactly do all points of my command.*

Nobody spoke. Neil waited.

Turning back, I looked at the small blue gem in his hand—a tiny seed, filled with the potential for so much. *Like a netsuke*, I thought, *carrying the past inside it.*

Except this had nothing to do with the past.

This was about the future.

Eventually, looking out at the horizon, Bettan started to laugh. It came out as a low chuckle, then built into a hysteria. It rolled through him, and he bent over, putting his hand to his belly as he roared.

I took a tentative step toward him, worried that he had gone mad, thinking also that maybe madness was the only appropriate response. Slowly, he caught his breath, settling and straightening up.

He took off his hat, turned back around, and walked a few steps toward Neil.

"It'll be me, then," he said.

I frowned at him. "Sorry?"

"It's obviously me." There was a strange smile on his handsome face.

He unzipped his jacket and took it off. As he straightened up, his muscles bulged beneath his top. "I suppose it makes sense. You're looking for the best humanity has to offer—the apotheosis of the human race—and it's me. Of course it's me."

Disgust rose up in my stomach. My whole body bristled at the idea of Bettan being the model on which all future humans would be based. But then what was the other choice?

Me?

Still, I said, "I don't think it should be you."

Bettan snorted.

"You both made it," Neil said, his tone neutral. "It could be either of you. I have been watching you. You are both qualified, though for quite different reasons."

"Bullshit," Bettan snarled, not at Neil, but at me. "*You* didn't make it up this mountain. I dragged your sorry ass up here. I saved your life, again and again. This is mine. There is no discussion."

"That's completely—" I started, but then stopped short. I was exhausted; I was broken; I was *done.* I didn't have the strength to fight. If he wanted to be the future, he could be. I had no interest in it. There was no future for me. Not anymore. I shrugged. "Fine."

He grinned and approached Neil, who patiently waited.

"This is the only chance, right?" he demanded. "No one else can take my place?"

"There is only one seed. It is the crux of the entire experiment. It cannot be made again."

"Good," he said. "That's good." I shook my head. Even in the midst of *this*, he was still concerned about his ego. "So tell me: what do I do?"

"Stand before me," Neil said. "And open yourself to the future."

Bettan spread his arms wide.

Neil lifted the gem, holding it between his thumb and forefinger, and lowered it toward Bettan's chest. All on its own, his top peeled away at the front, as did all his under layers. They fell to the ground at his feet, leaving only his bare skin.

When the gem touched his chest, a pulse of blue expanded.

Bettan gasped, his legs buckling slightly as he struggled to stand upright. The gem fused into his chest with a crackle, tiny lightning bolts of blue spreading outward across his body. They flickered up his neck and over his face.

Soon the gem had disappeared, and Bettan's whole body began to glow: first a deep, ocean-like blue, then yellow like the sun. The color seeped out of him, through his arms and out his fingers.

His mouth was wide open, gasping for air, as he was lifted upward. He levitated off the ground an inch or two, his arms stretched wide and back arched as the light burst out of him.

A pulse of energy exploded out of him like a thunderclap.

I staggered backward, almost falling to my knees.

When I looked up again, he was standing tall.

Like something superhuman.

Like a god.

"It is done," Neil said, and I thought I heard a tinge of relief. "The seed is finally planted. Welcome, *Homo altior*, to the new era of humanity."

Bettan turned to look at me. His eyes were wide, glowing with a furious energy. He took a few steps toward me, seeming a little uneasy in his approach, like he was just getting used to his new body.

He took his gun back out of his pocket and looked at it curiously, turning it over in his hands. His face was strained, as if he was fighting some deep pain inside of him, warring against a primeval instinct.

"I am the master of my fate," he said, his voice thick. "I am the captain of my soul."

Lifting the gun to his head, he put the muzzle in his mouth and fired.

His head erupted, blood spraying through the air, and his body collapsed to the ground.

Neil gaped, staring at the scene.

"What have you done?" he whispered. For a moment, there was a flash of anger. Then his whole body drooped, collapsing downwards.

Neil let out a great sigh, and then, in the blink of an eye, he disappeared.

The mountain underneath me rumbled, shook, and then shifted out of existence. Beneath my feet, it simply vanished. I fell, suddenly tumbling down and down, tens of thousands of feet through the sky, twisting and spinning too fast. My eyes burned. My body convulsed.

I tried to take a breath, but there was nothing to catch hold of.

The world around me turned black, with streaks of light, as I passed once again through the center of the disappearing tesseract. Glimpses of space and time fired by too quickly.

I tried to grasp on to something real. Something that still existed. If all time and space was here inside this swirling blackness, then there must be something I could hold on to, something left.

I thought of Thomas, of Naoko, of anything, but all I could see was the long line of humanity, an abandoned experiment, disappearing into a black hole of entropy and nothingness.

Still I fell, spinning and twisting and burning through cloud and wind.

Squeezing my eyes shut, I focused with everything I could on the one memory I never wanted to forget again.

Santi.

The look in his eyes when he spoke his first words.

The smile on his face when he drew.

Take me back there, I thought. *I'll do anything, just take me back.*

My mind went blank.

* * *

I woke in the country somewhere, in the remnants of my climbing gear. I dumped the heavy clothes but kept my pack. It was England, though I do not know how or why. Perhaps I was deposited there. Perhaps it was where I was meant to be.

Reasons don't seem to matter anymore.

Causality doesn't matter.

People came and took me away. They took me here. They believe I am acting strangely. Inhuman, even. Fortunate for them that they do not know what being human really means.

What am I to do now, Hattie?

Where am I to go?

I sit here on this chair. I stare out the window and the emptiness stares right back.

There is nothing for me in the world anymore, yet still I feel the urge to move. Is this what Sisyphus feels, when he wakes up each morning at the base of the mountain?

He knows that the climb is futile, that it means nothing, yet still he climbs, because that is the path that is laid out for him.

Because the destination is not important, only that you keep moving.

Only the next step.

Time to get up, Harold. To take the next step.

And wherever I end up next, God help the fool who finds me.

AFTERWORD

Printed in the second edition of *Ascension*

My brother died in 2020. Since the first publication of his letters, there has been much clamoring for proof, for some evidence to support his claims. They became somewhat of a pop culture sensation, inspiring internet message boards and meet-ups dedicated to uncovering the truth behind Harold's mountain and the stories he tells.

There is no doubt that many of these people existed: a Jet Towles did work for MIT in the eighties. There is a record of a geologist named Thomas Fung living in London at the same time. Both men disappeared without a trace.

Sir Roger Bettan and Dr. Polya Volikova are, of course, the most recognizable names. Both were assumed to have died prior to the publication of the letters. When Bettan disappeared, the media reported that he died on a climb, his body never found. The Volikov family insists that Polya passed away peacefully in her sleep in Moscow in 1995. Despite this being hotly contested by skeptics, the family remains closed off and highly private, with no desire to discuss her with anyone.

There is no evidence that anyone named Grace Palmer or Steve Bautista (let alone "the Warden") ever existed. They do not appear to have been enlisted in the armed forces or ever lived in the United States at any time. Similarly, there is no hard evidence whatsoever of a worldwide corporation called Apollo.

Many online conspiracy theorists will tell you that this should come as no surprise.

Though most mainstream critics doubt the veracity of my brother's letters, much has been written about Harold himself. Indeed, in the interim between when the letters were first released and the publication of this second edition, the large number of personal investigations brought many aspects of his life to light.

There is no doubt that he lived and worked in London with Naoko, and that they adopted a young boy called Santi. Paul Idris retells the tragic story of his passing with many of the same details as Harold himself—though he insists that Harold is not quite as much to blame as he makes himself out to be. Whether this is truth or kindness, I do not know.

What has hit me the hardest is that my brother lived an entire life that I did not know about. We were never close, even from the time we were children. But to discover that he had a wife, a child, and experienced a horrible tragedy, none of which he ever saw fit to share with me—it is a mystery that will stay with me for the rest of my life.

It is clear to me that my daughter loved him, and that he loved her, and that he found in her some release from the pain of losing his own child. I can only be glad that our family was able to provide him that, if little else.

He was found in Surrey in 1991. Hikers came across him, camped out on the beach by Frensham Little Pond—the lake where his son drowned—less than an hour away from St. Brigid's Hospital, which would eventually become his home. They found him dirty and malnourished, suffering from a range of bodily wounds, unable to say how long he had been there.

He was completely nonsensical, shouting and even violent. When the police were called, they could find out no information whatsoever about his identity and were forced to commit him. He apparently left the site of that lake kicking and screaming, begging not to go.

A couple of the older staff swear that he was actually found in 1990, a year before he claims to have boarded that flight to the mountain, but any corroborating records from that time were lost during a flooding incident in the early 2000s.

A year after *Ascension*'s first release, psychiatrist Thaddeus Shaltman wrote a paper entitled "Trauma Through Fantasy: The Tunmore Letters," in which he posits that the entire experience is representative of a psychotic break over the guilt of his son dying, where Harold "imagined a sort of purgatory for himself. He fantasized a hell that he believed he deserved—one where he was powerless, one where he was being punished—and he lost himself in it."[*]

Whatever happened to my brother, whoever you choose to believe, there is no doubting it was a tragedy. But if you are a believer in these letters, as I have come to be, perhaps there is reason to be optimistic.

I know for a fact Harold did not forget his family. For all that he lost his grip on the material world in his later years, there was one ritual that he did occasionally repeat. When given the chance, a plastic knife and a bar of soap, he would carve a small sculpture

---

[*] Shaltman, T. (2020) "Trauma Through Fantasy: The Tunmore Letters." *International Journal of Psychology* 55, no. 5, 46–74.

of a woman and a child. A netsuke to always keep their memories by his side. I choose to believe that when he set himself alight, he fulfilled his final promise to Naoko: to come to find her in a blaze of fire and heat.

And if what Thomas said was true, then some part of Harold is still alive on that mountain, existing outside of the strictures of space and time. And huddled there together in some frozen moment of eternity, Naoko and Santi are with him, too.

One must, I feel, imagine them happy.

ACKNOWLEDGMENTS

This book would not exist without the support of the fantastic people who have climbed this mountain with me.

Thanks to Alex Cochran, my agent, who saw the potential in an early version of this and has unwaveringly supported me every step of the way.

Thanks to my editors, Vicky Leech and Delia Taylor, who helped me reach into the heart of this book and make it shine. Thanks also to the teams at both Harper Voyager and Riverhead Books, including Elizabeth Vaziri, Jynne Dilling Martin, Ashley Garland, and too many more to name.

Thanks to my dearest fellow writers and "Novel Nerds"—Lia Holland, Eleanor Imbody, Talia Rothschild, Lee Sandwina, and, most recently, Dave Goodman. Together, you are my rock. Without you, nothing I write would be worth reading.

Thanks to all the team at C&W that have worked hard for me and my book at every stage of this process, including Luke Speed, Anna Weguelin, Matilda Ayris, Kate Burton, Jake Smith-Bosanquet, Tracy England, and Dorcas Rogers, as well as to Alexandra Machinist and all the team at ICM.

Thanks to Tom Kitwood for correcting my bad science, and Duncan Carnegie for fixing my incorrect Latin. Thanks to Laura Cherkas for fixing my incorrect *everything else*. Thank you to all the amazing friends and early readers who supported me along the way: Danny Nason, Linda Lee, Karin Samuel, Mike Wheelhouse, Andrew Quailes, Audrey Greathouse, Ross Furmedge, Kristi Wong, Emma Wong, Jade Fok.

Thanks to my parents for your steadfast and unconditional support in everything that I pursue. It means more than you could possibly know.

And most importantly, thanks to my wonderful wife, Allys, and my amazing family. This book and everything it represents is for you. You are my everything, always and forever.